TO CAPTURE an Empath

The Captured, Imprisoned and Stolen Trilogy

BY C. READER

Copyrights

Contents

To those who want to give up, who don't think they are good enough, to those who are worried about what people may think, just do the damn thing, you got this.

Note From Author

Lovely Readers, before you read this book, please see the below content warnings. If for any reason you are triggered by the below, please know you have chosen to read at your own discretion and it's not recommended to read if you believe you would be triggered at all. Though this book is fiction

it does elude and have on-page representation of real life concerns. Trigger warnings include : Torture, Sexual Assault (No idolisation), Unaliving, Kidnapping, Physical and mental abuse, Mental health issues, Death of family members, and sex.

All good to go?

Strap in, pour yourself your drink of choice and escape to another world. Happy Reading!

Kingdom of Anam
The Weather Court
Aimsir
The Court of Light
Aotrom
The Court of Wisdom
Gliocas
The Healing Court
Slanachad
The Court of Nature
Nadur
The Court of Elements
Eileamaids
The Court of Poisen
Puinnscan
The Great Queens Kingdom
Banrigh Mhor
THE GREAT KING'S KINGDOM
Rioghacd Mor
The Court of Strength
Neart
The town of Black Forest

The Tale of Three Kingdoms

There once were three Kingdoms: one wreathed in the ethereal light of boundless empathy— The Kingdom of Anam. One aglow with the harmony of justice and peace— The Great Queen's Kingdom, Banrigh Mhòr. And one cloaked in the cold, unyielding shadows of greed— The Great King's Kingdom, Rìoghachd Mòr.

The Kingdom of Anam shimmered at the edge of dreams, a sanctuary for a rare and wondrous kind of magical being: the Empaths. Their gifts were like threads spun from starlight— delicate and radiant, yet perilously fragile.

To feel the emotions of others, to brush against the soul itself, was a power as luminous as it was treacherous. Fearful of the corruption that could seep into their gifts, the Empaths wove their lives in quiet isolation, their realm safeguarded by the ancient alliance with Banrigh Mhòr, where witches of profound and varied talents swore themselves to a sacred covenant of harmony.

This bond between kingdoms was not merely an alliance of convenience but a symphony of purpose. The witches of Anam served as guardians of balance, delivering trials to cleanse those whose hearts had soured. In turn, The witches of Banrigh Mhòr warded their sacred lands, shielding the Empaths from the clamor and chaos of the outer realms.

Yet, Rìoghachd Mòr beheld this luminous union with envious malice. To the Great King, power was not a gift to be shared but a dominion to be seized. While the Great Queen's Kingdom flourished in shared wisdom and equilibrium, the King's dominion was one of harsh singularity. He hoarded the strengths of his many Courts, wielding their magic as his own. But there was one power he could neither claim nor comprehend: the power of the Empaths— a force that could touch the very essence of the soul. To the Great King, this defiance of his absolute rule was intolerable.

And so began a dark and sorrowful era. The first war, a war of division, forbade the intermingling of the Courts. The King's decree shattered bonds of love and unity, sowing mistrust and despair. Those who dared defy him paid with their lives, and the land was left fractured, its people adrift. The second war, a crusade of annihilation, sought to erase the Empaths and all who stood in their defense. The rarest light in all the realms, was nearly extinguished.

But even within the iron grip of his tyranny, dissent stirred. The Courts of Rìoghachd Mòr faltered, their people torn between loyalty to the crown and the quiet murmur of their own conscience. Whispers of rebellion drifted through the air like ash, and trust withered beneath the weight of suspicion. The kingdom fractured further, its once-mighty unity unraveling into chaos.

And yet, deep within the shadowed embrace of the Darkest Forest, something ancient stirred. Beneath its canopy of whispering leaves and roots entwined with the bones of forgotten ages, a secret slumbered. Not merely a weapon, but a force beyond reckoning, a being of boundless power, waiting for the moment when the world would call upon it. The question loomed not just of who would uncover this secret, but who among them would dare claim it.

And who would have the courage to capture it?

Prologue

OLIVIA - 10 YEARS AGO

I couldn't tell if I heard the screams or felt the sharp, bitter sting of pain first. A scream bursts out of me— raw and strange, like it was coming from someone else entirely. The world slammed into me, thick and heavy, like I was underwater. Every sound, every movement felt slow, dragged through invisible waves that weighed me down.

Each step I took down the old, creaking staircase synced with the ticking of the grandfather clock. *Tick. Tick.* Each second stretches into an eternity. The thud of my footsteps rattled the pictures along the wall. They swayed, like even they were recoiling from what waits below. My chest ached, the pressure mounting, building, like my ribs were going to crack open. I stopped on the bottom step, frozen. Fear twisting through me, locking my body in place. I wanted to clap my hands over my ears, but I couldn't move. My hand stayed pressed against my chest, as if it could keep the pain from spilling out.

Every sound blurred together into one endless, high-pitched ringing. The cries. The ticking clock. *That clock.* It was still ticking. That goddamned noise was the only thing grounding me to this... to this reality.

Because this wasn't a nightmare. The woman sprawled on the doorstep with red hair tangled and wild wasn't some figment of a bad dream. She was my mother.

Her face twisted in agony, almost unrecognizable. The blood... *Gods, there was so much blood.* The metallic scent crashes into me, flooding my senses. She groans, rolling to her side, and that's when I saw it. The wound beneath her ribs. Blood gushing out, dark and unrelenting.

I don't remember moving. I don't remember stepping off the stairs. All I know is I was suddenly there, kneeling beside her, my knees soaking in her blood. My hands trembling, shaking so hard almost useless, but I press them against the wound anyway. Her blood was hot, seeping through my fingers. I couldn't stop staring at it, the way it flowed like a river I couldn't dam.

The pain in my chest rose to my throat, tearing out of me in rough, broken sobs. I couldn't breathe. I couldn't think. Her life was slipping through my fingers, and there was nothing I could do to hold it back.

Tick. Tick. Tick.

"M-Mumma," I choked out.

Her green eyes found mine. They were pale, almost silver at the edges, but somehow still soft. She looked at me like she always did.

"My love," she whispered, her voice shaky but still gentle. "Shh, don't cry. Stop crying. I don't feel anything. Please, let me go without your tears. Remember, don't show your emotions. Promise me. Don't show anyone how you feel."

Her words carved into me, but I nod. I had to. I didn't know how, but I did. My throat burned, and tears threatened to spill over, but I fought them back. I squeezed my eyes shut and breathed through my nose. Slowly. *In. Out.* I imagined the lump in my throat sinking down into a dark pit inside me. I push it all there— the tears, the pain, the smell of blood. *All of it.*

"That's my girl," she murmured, a fragile smile ghosting across her lips. "Obscure it. Hide the truth of who you are, what you are."

Obscure it. Hide the truth of who you are, what you are.

Her last breath left her like a whisper, and a coldness spread through me, sharper and deeper than anything I had ever felt. I stood on shaking legs, taking a step back. My eyes squeezed shut, like if I closed them hard enough, this would all vanish. I don't know who grabbed my shoulders. I don't know who pulled me away.

All I knew was the clock kept ticking, and I told myself to feel *nothing.*

Olivia

THE WEIGHT OF SILENT PROMISES

Bitterness threatens to surface as I read the letter from my father. My eyes skim the words—the notice, the threat. I don't know why I let myself hope he'll actually write to me. By writing, I mean the pretty little words a daughter wants to hear from her father. It *is* my twenty-first birthday, after all. Foolish, I suppose, to think that would change anything.

Instead, I get a notice. The art merchant will arrive before the winter solstice. Along with that, the threat. I choose to ignore that part. Denial has been my steadfast companion for most of my life, and so far, it's worked. That's the thing about written words—they're slippery, open to interpretation. I decide this is an empty threat. Because he wouldn't... would he? The acidic taste of resentment tightens my throat. My initial excitement for the case of moonshine paint from the Aotrom Kingdom fades, tarnished by the tea-stained note, its angrily scrawled writing bringing nothing good.

I slam the paper onto the desk with a guttural groan. My gaze flits between the list of expenses and the world outside the stone window. Spring greens have given way to autumn's golden hues. Anxiety settles on my chest like a heavy stone. The years keep getting colder, supplies thinner, and my thoughts spiral down the slippery slope of foreboding. Last year's roof leaks let the cold seep into our bones, just as frost takes over the deltas in the Aimsir Kingdom.

My mind whirs, calculating yields, tallying how much hunting I'll need to do to stock our stores. It isn't just me I have to worry about. I squeeze my eyes shut against the thought of those little eyes—so full of need. My breath shudders out in a sigh.

The only way to fix our cash flow is my art, my paintings. A sharp pang twists in my chest; I'm starting to hate what I once loved. The art merchant grows more particular with each order, his demands pressing down on me like a thumb flattening soft clay. If I don't comply, he threatens to take my mother's rare, unique artwork instead—the last thing I have of her.

When you're this world's best-kept secret, inspiration is hard to come by. I'm a ghost, a dirty little secret who only sees the outside world cloaked in darkness.

We live on the outskirts of the King's Kingdom, in a small mortal village just outside the Black Forest. Isolation defines us—unknown to man, Fae, or whatever lies beyond the forest walls. The Black Forest, the link between every court under the King's rule, acts as the border between the Grand Dukes' kingdoms and territories. The nine ruling Courts—Aimsir of Weather, Slanachad of Healing, Aotrom of Light, Gliocas of Wisdom, Neart of Strength, Eileamaids of Elements, Nadur of Nature, and Puinnsean of Poison—all revolve around the Great Kingdom, Rioghachd Mor. But here? Here, mortals are nothing. We live in no man's land.

"He got you new paint! That's nice." A warm voice calls from the doorway, sweet and nurturing.

I look up to see Mary standing there. She's small but radiant, like sunshine and sweet tea bottled into a person.

"It is," I reply, careful to keep resentment out of my voice. Paint doesn't make up for ten years of neglect. It doesn't make up for being used as his money grab.

"Don't let him get to you, sweetheart. He's just a fool who missed out on raising you." Mary steps into the room and squeezes my shoulder. The smell of apricots drifts from her touch, lightening the churning waves inside me. Our eyes meet, and my heart clenches. I don't deserve her kindness.

"You're too good, Mary." I take her hand, squeezing it briefly before leaning in to kiss her cheek. As I rise, the chair groans against the slate floor. I pause in the doorway, looking back at her. Her brows knit in worry as she studies the ledgers I left on the desk. The wrinkles around her lips deepen.

"I'll make it work, Mary."

She forces a smile.

"I know, my love. You always do."

Olivia

WHISPERS IN THE DARK

The town square is shrouded in a quiet gloom, the cobblestones slick with the remnants of the evening rain. Hooded and shadowed, I creep through the narrow alleyways, keeping to the darkest corners. Every nerve in my body hums with tension. The whispers from the docks grow louder with every cautious step I take—too many rumors, too many secrets. The hood of my cloak hides my face, but I know the eyes of the night watch are ever-present.

My boots make barely a sound against the wet stone, but my breathing betrays me. Shallow, rapid. I force it to steady. The air carries the faint scent of salt from the sea, mingled with smoke and damp earth. Somewhere nearby, a low murmur of voices catches my attention. I freeze, straining to hear. My heart thuds heavily in my chest, each beat loud in the tense silence.

Then, it happens.

A shout pierces the quiet, sharp and guttural. Before I can react, a heavy force barrels into me, knocking the air from my lungs. The world spins as I crash to the ground, my head colliding with the unforgiving stone. Pain explodes behind my eyes, and stars burst across my vision.

When the haze clears, I am pinned beneath a massive wolf. Its golden eyes bore into mine, gleaming with an almost human intensity.

A low growl rumbles from its throat, the sound vibrating through my entire body. I try to move, but its claws dig into the ground on either side of me, holding me in place.

Panic grips me, and I struggle to suck in air, my head throbbing from the impact.

"Kyzan! Heel!"

The voice is commanding, sharp, and filled with exasperation. The wolf's ears twitch, but it doesn't back down. Instead, its growl deepens, a warning that sends chills down my spine.

Boots scrape against the cobblestones, and then he appears. A stranger cloaked in darkness strides toward us. His presence is commanding, his movements deliberate. He snaps his fingers, and the wolf—Kyzan, apparently—reluctantly steps back, allowing me to sit up. My head swims, and I press a hand to my temple, wincing at the sharp pain radiating through my skull.

The man kneels beside me, his movements quick but not unkind. His hands hover for a moment before gently tilting my chin to examine the damage.

"You've got a nasty bump," he mutters, his voice softer now. "Hold still."

I don't have the strength to protest as his hand presses lightly against my forehead. A faint warmth spreads from his touch, soothing the ache and dulling the throbbing pain. My breath catches as a soft, golden light pulses from his palm. It is gentle, like the glow of the moon reflecting on still water. The light seeps into my skin, and the pain ebbs away, leaving only a dull memory of it behind.

"That's a lot better. Give your heart time to calm down—it's hammering like a hummingbird."

His tone seems to cast a golden light that warms my vision. I feel the breaths leaving my lips slow and even out. I wriggle my fingers in an attempt to wake my nervous system. When that works, I cautiously try my toes, hoping they will move despite the ache in my legs. They flinch in reaction. Thank the Gods. I do one more scan, and all ten fingers and all ten toes seem to be in working order. Sore, but functioning. I attempt to move, hoping I can stand.

"There we go... No, no, don't try to get up. Please, Hummingbird, stay down. Otherwise, you'll let the blood rush, and I..."

I pause. What would he do? But I relent and relax for a moment, letting my brain attempt to process the quick turn of events. This person—he has saved me, healed me with his touch.

This is bad. This is very bad.

"There you go, keep breathing. Look up at me, let me see those eyes, let me see their color."

I'm not sure if it's the way his thumb lightly sweeps my cheekbone, the accent, or my new nickname that sends flutters all the way to my core... Desperate to know if he looks as good as he sounds, my eyes track up his form to his face, and gods—he is better.

My eyes meet a sea of deep blue, visible even in the dim light that leaks through the narrow alley from the full moon above, surrounded by a rim of dark navy. The colors swirl like a storm, their vibrancy enhanced by the moonlight, streaked with lightning strikes of aqua. His eyes flare wide and sparkle as he meets my gaze. My skin buzzes. The tingle runs from my heart to my left wrist, then my fingertips. My fingers lift of their own accord and touch the side of his broad, angular cheekbone before brushing over those luscious lips. I feel the ridge of his jawbone, the muscles twitching beneath my touch as he whispers to me.

"Beautiful, your eyes are... beautiful. They are like evergreen forests. I don't know what I expected, but this outshines my expectations."

My mind wants to say the same for him, but with the look he is giving me, I don't think I can get the words out. I'm stuck in my reverie as his fingers outline my heart-shaped face, playing with the messy curls that frame it. My mind is stuck in rapture, waiting to come back down to earth.

"Let me escort you home," he offers, his tone gentle yet firm.

Panic shoots through me. I know what he is. The memory rushes back, vivid and sharp:

"Outside this cottage is a dangerous place, Olivia. The Fae from this land are conniving, powerful, and most of all, greedy. They'll use you as a weapon. Their charm is simply an illusion. For every one good Fae, there are a thousand bad, ready to trick you and take away everything that you are."

I find my footing, pushing myself to stand. The height difference is startling—I have to tilt my head back to meet his gaze. He towers over me, his mouth quirking into a small, amused smile as his eyes assess me. For a fleeting moment, his expression softens, until I say the words,

"As nice as that is, no. I have to go," I say.

I watch as his features falter. His smile fades, and his eyes darken, the playful glint replaced with something more guarded. His features school themselves into a mask of composure, but I can see the tension in the tight set of his jaw, as if he is about to protest.

I turn and bolt before he can respond. My heart pounds as I weave through the narrow alleys, the damp air stinging my lungs. Behind me, I hear him call out, his footsteps following. I push harder, my knowledge of the town guiding me through hidden paths and tight corners. My cloak catches on a crate, slowing me, but I wrench it free, inwardly cursing at the sound of fabric tearing, and dive into a shadowed alcove.

The sound of his boots slows. My breath catches in my throat as I hear him pass by, the wolf padding beside him. For a brief moment, Kyzan pauses, his golden eyes scanning the darkness. Our gazes lock, and my heart stops. This is it. He's found me.

But then, as if pulled by some unseen command, the wolf turns and trots after his master. I stay frozen, the tension in my body unrelenting until their footsteps fade into the distance.

Only then do I allow myself to exhale. My legs feel like jelly as I slip through the last alley and make my way home. My thoughts linger on the stranger, his piercing gaze, his touch—things I should not be thinking about. Things I should never have experienced.

Olivia

THE HUNTER AND THE HUNTED

The dull ache in my head is the first thing I notice as I wake. My fingers brush against the sore spot on my temple, and the events of the previous night come rushing back—the wolf, the Fae, and his piercing blue eyes that seem to hold secrets I shouldn't want to uncover. *Why was he near the docks?* The question gnaws at me as I sit up, my quilt pooling around my waist. It isn't uncommon for my powers to draw me toward souls in need, but last night was different. I recall the call was faint at first, tugging at the edges of my awareness as I left the orphanage. My mind drifts back to the moment it hit me like a physical blow, stealing my breath and freezing me in place. I remember the laughter ringing out from the docks—low, cruel—and the fragments of conversation that reached me, laced with vile promises about the new slaves they'd boarded. I should have turned away. I never meddled with the Kingdom's ships; that was a line I couldn't afford to cross.

But the cries from the ship's hull... I still feel them, like blades slicing through the night. Their despair called to me. I'd been just seconds away from doing something reckless, something that might've gotten me caught—might've ended everything.

And then, the wolf. It tackled me to the ground, knocking the breath from my lungs.

And the Fae. Gods, the Fae. What was he doing there? It's rare enough for their kind to set foot in Black Forest Town—this was a mortal town, and Fae didn't mix with "peasants." Yet there he was, cloaked, lingering in the shadows. Was he connected to the boardings?

I shake the thought away, standing on shaky legs. The creaking stairs beneath me groan in protest as I make my way down. Each step feels heavier, as if the weight of my thoughts takes a physical form. By the time I reach the dining room, I'm no closer to answers. The low hum of conversation stops as soon as I walk in. Mary, Cooper, and Hecate turn to look at me, their expressions ranging from concern to mild reproach. "You have been extraordinarily busy," Mary says, her steel-blue eyes twinkling in the morning light. "We have hardly seen you. Shame you haven't caught anything on your hunting trips. I know Hecate was saying we're a bit low. And the chickens are slowing down their egg-laying, so Cooper is going into town to see if we can get a few new ones. I sold some of my quilts yesterday to pay for them." "Which quilts?" I ask, suspicion creeping into my voice. "Last I saw, you were still in the middle of making some."

The air in the room seems to still. Mary's smile falters, replaced by a flicker of apprehension. "I sold our spare ones. I can always make more. We need a few other supplies, too. We're out of tea, unless you want peppermint. That seems to be the only one growing at the moment. Our honey has also run low—the bees have moved to a different hive. The only bonus is that Ness helped Cooper push a tree down for some firewood, and your harvest of grapes has been fruitful this year. Hecate has been working on wine, so Cooper will have some to sell to the local merchant."

I clench my fists, then force my hands to relax. Stress bounces around in my mind, a chaotic mess of worry and responsibility. I know I'll have to venture further into the Black Forest to catch something. The risk of encountering the great beasts that roam the forest looms in my mind, but we can't afford to starve. So far, I've been lucky that the beasts haven't traveled south. My thoughts drift to the book I favored growing up—the one that tells tales of Caorthannach, Questing Beasts, Oilliphéist, and Sluaghs. Creatures of fear and death. Maybe Lady Luck is only on my side because I never venture past the mortal border. But now... "Maybe I could see if the Kingdom needs a violinist for Samhain this year," I offer, though the idea sits uneasily with me. "I'm not sure if the money will be good enough this year from my paintings."

Mary's expression tightens, her usual warmth replaced by a rare seriousness. "No, that's okay, love. We'll manage. The celebrations in the city can be quite dangerous. I'd feel a lot better if you stayed home." Her smile doesn't reach her eyes, and her words carry a weight I can't ignore. If only she knew.

I furrow my brows but lack the energy to argue. Instead, I make myself a plate and eat in silence, the weight of Mary and Cooper's unspoken worries pressing down on me. Their shoulders sag as I absorb their tension, but it leaves me drained. By the time I leave the dining room, my body feels heavy, and my thoughts are no clearer. They may have relaxed, but I can't. My mind is still tangled with images of the Fae and the dark secrets that linger near the docks.

Ness gives me a low rumble of greeting, her breath brushing against my cheek as though sensing my unease. The sound tugs at something inside me, pulling me from the tangled mess of thoughts that have been circling since I woke. She towers above all other horses, her golden bay coat shimmering even in the dim candlelight of the stable. Each strand of her fur seems spun from sunlight, a sharp contrast to the ink-black mane that pours down her neck like a dark river.

Drawn toward her as if by some magnetic force, I reach out to touch the white blaze on her forehead. The moment my hand meets her warm skin, calm floods through me. It isn't a gentle wave but a fierce rush, as if she knows I need more than comfort—I need an anchor. "Good morning," I murmur, resting my forehead against hers. Her golden eyes meet mine, brimming with unspoken understanding. She doesn't judge the weariness I carry, the questions that haunt me. Instead, she simply is—a presence that asks for nothing but trust.

Unlatching the stable door, I step back as she moves into the crisp morning air. Her hooves clatter softly against the stone floor before transitioning to the muted thuds of the paddock's black sand. I secure her harness with practiced ease, the metallic clicks of the buckles blending into the rhythm of her breaths. Clipping my bag of supplies to her side and strapping my bow and quiver to my chest, I vault onto her broad back.

Riding tack-free isn't just practical for us—it's a connection, one that doesn't need reins to guide it.

As we ride along the fence line, the morning begins to unfurl around us. Moss the color of emeralds clings to the wooden posts, while bright hummingbirds dart between violet salvias. Their delicate movements bring a brief smile to my lips, but the moment is fleeting. A voice echoes in my mind—deep, teasing. "Hummingbird."

My heart flutters, much like the tiny bird's wings. His voice lingers like a song I can't forget, one that doesn't belong here. I shake my head, urging Ness toward the Black

Forest. The dense pines swallow us whole, their shadows casting the world into a twilight hush. The scent of pine needles and damp earth wraps around me, grounding me as my powers extend outward, searching for life hidden in the underbrush.

The salty tang of the ocean grows stronger, mingling with the earthy undertones of the forest. When we reach the dunes, I dismount, letting the golden grass cradle my weight as I sink into its embrace. Ness lies behind me, her warmth a steady presence. I draw my violin from its case, the smooth wood cool against my skin as I rest it beneath my chin.

The first note pierces the air, soft and melancholic. The melody flows from me like water, weaving itself into the rhythm of the crashing waves. My bow dances across the strings, and the music seems to carry my thoughts away, spilling them into the golden horizon. Images of piercing blue eyes and a cloaked figure haunt the edges of my mind. He is danger personified, a forbidden melody that shouldn't exist in my world. Yet, he is there, near the docks, his presence lingering like a shadow.

Hours pass, the sun sinking lower as I let the violin fall silent. Music never fails to soothe the storm inside me, but tonight, its effects feel fleeting. Mounting Ness, I ride back into the forest, the thick canopy above swallowing the last light of day. My senses prickle, a warning crawling along my skin. I dismount near an alcove, securing Ness before stepping into the shadows with my bow drawn and an arrow nocked.

The forest is alive with tension. My powers reach out, brushing against a presence nearby. The emotions are cautious, hesitant—prey. A glint of silver catches my eye, and I draw back the bowstring. But something makes me hesitate. A low rumble from Ness confirms what I already know. This isn't ordinary prey.

He steps into the clearing. Tall, broad-shouldered, and confident. There isn't a shred of fear in him, only a quiet challenge that radiates from his stance. My heart skips a beat as his name comes to me, unbidden. "Kyzan?"

The wolf kneels before me, his golden eyes watching mine with an intensity that is neither hostile nor submissive. I lower my weapon cautiously, my gaze darting around the clearing for the man who calls his name. But we are alone. Ness paws the ground behind me, her head lowered in warning. Kyzan seems to take note, his massive frame bowing lower as he creeps forward.

When he reaches me, his head comes to rest against my hip, his golden eyes searching mine. The air between us shifts, no longer heavy with tension but something softer, quieter.

My hand moves instinctively to his pelt, fingers sinking into the thick silver fur. He leans into my touch, a low rumble of pleasure vibrating through him. I can't help but laugh. "Some big scary beast you are. Have you come to apologize?"

His head tilts, curiosity flickering across his features. But before I can say more, my attention is pulled away by the faint presence of two small souls. I straighten, scanning the forest as Kyzan follows my gaze. Lowering to the ground, I creep toward the clearing, careful not to disturb the pine needles beneath my feet. Kyzan moves beside me, his every movement deliberate and watchful.

The clearing opens to reveal a lagoon, its still waters reflecting the twilight sky. The hares appear moments later, their movements skittish and quick. My first arrow strikes true, the hare's emotions flickering from panic to nothingness in an instant. The second follows, and then a third. As I move to collect my quarry, Kyzan's growl stills me. His body presses against mine, a barrier between me and the forest.

The air shifts, thickening as a massive form slithers from the grass. Iridescent scales glimmer in the fading light, shifting into the dappled pelt of a predator. A Questing Beast. My heart seizes as the creature's forked tongue flicks toward me, its tail whipping through the air with deadly precision. Kyzan's snarls fill the clearing, his hackles raised as he stands protectively before me.

Adrenaline surges, pushing me into action. My first arrow strikes its eye, the screech of pain tearing through the forest. The second arrow follows, blinding the beast entirely. But it isn't enough. Its tail lashes toward us, and Kyzan presses close, urging me to run.

My lungs burn as I sprint through the trees, the sound of the beast's pursuit deafening. Kyzan stays at my side, his eyes flicking between me and the danger at our heels. The forest blurs, every step a fight against exhaustion.

A figure appears ahead, tall and cloaked in shadow. "Quick, get behind me!" he orders, his voice cutting through the chaos. His strong hands push me behind him as he steps forward, his presence radiating authority. "Close your eyes," he commands.

Preservation takes over—I close them. Even with my eyes shut, the light that comes next is blinding. The pain of the beast's death hits me straight in the chest and leaves me weak. Kyzan supports me as I bury my head in his pelt and press my hands over my ears. The silence after passes in rapid heartbeats.

A soothing voice comes close. "It's gone." There is a pause, and a soft hand rests on my shoulder. "You have quite a remarkable aim, young huntress." The deep baritone of his voice sends soothing caresses over my ears.

I look up and see the large male crouched before me, one muscular arm resting against his knee, the other petting Kyzan in familiar strokes. I blink away the darkness, noticing the faint glow emanating from his form. *Light Fae.* His eyes swirl with technicolor. His jaw is wide and strong, cheekbones soft yet prominent. I feel the wave of concern and curiosity that filters into me, though I sense something in him I know all too well. A numb sort of darkness lays heavy in his chest. He gives me a small smile as he looks down at me. He stands and offers his hand. Tentatively, I take it. I nearly gasp when I'm hit with deep sorrow and loneliness. Its dry tartness makes my mouth parched.

In reflex, my mind flutters with familiar memories: the smiles from home, the feeling of the warm sun on my skin—every little bit of peace I have ever felt. Dark swirls of color flash and stars dance in his eyes. His mouth gapes. I instantly regret what I've just done. I force my features to remain blank, trying to hide it. I can hear my mother cursing me from her grave. *Stupid, stupid girl.*

"Thank you." I pull my hand away, brushing the pine needles off my britches. "You are welcome. Though, you seemed to have it under control, little huntress." There is something in his smooth baritone voice that changes. A lilt, a twinge of curiosity that flickers between the words. *What is it with Fae males and their nicknames?* I most certainly don't feel like I have anything under control. I somehow manage to keep my fear at bay, but I feel my heart still hammering in my chest.

"I would advise a mortal like yourself to not travel so far into the Black Forest. The beasts from the north have been traveling farther south. It's not safe, even for a good huntress like yourself."

My slip-up must not be enough for him to know I'm not mortal. Luckily my appearance is simply a mask for what lays beneath. "Thank you, Sir, I will keep that in mind. I best be off," I give a polite smile, wanting to escape from his intense gaze. I try to hide my inner panic about encountering two Fae males in such a short span of time. It isn't good. This mortal land is normally free from them, with only the occasional one passing through the Black Forest before heading to the Queen's lands. I need to find some answers, and soon.

"Goodbye, little huntress." Before I can turn, he disappears into thin air. *Yep, this is very bad.*

Olivia

THE WOLF'S SILENT OATH

I ignore the slight quiver in my knees from the fading adrenaline and let my focus settle on the wolf leaning against me. His steady presence is a balm to the whirlwind of new occurrences that seem to flood my life. A low noise vibrates through my leg, and I glance down to meet his golden eyes. For a moment, I could swear he is reading my thoughts. Maybe that's just wishful thinking. Doesn't every animal lover dream of a connection that deep? Perhaps it's just me.

A sharp gasp pulls my attention away from Kyzan. Mary stands frozen, her wide eyes darting between the two of us. I feel her fear like a sharp, smoky tang in the air, a hot wave brushing against my senses. Her small, weathered hand flies to her chest, clutching her apron dusted with flour. Her fingers quiver. Cooper appears at her side almost immediately, his hand steady on her back while his other curls into a fist, ready to defend her. His steely eyes mirror her shock. Kyzan tenses beneath my hand, then eases, and I feel a small ripple of relief in their emotions as I instinctively reach out, blanketing the room with calm. It is second nature to me—an automatic act of protection. I've always thought my powers are safe to use here, but after my recent slip-up in the forest, I realize how untrained I truly am.

"We have a new pet?" Cooper asks, his voice carefully calm as he raises a skeptical brow. I feel his emotions battle against the calm I've cast, fear pressing at the edges like a persistent tide. But I am stronger, and the room remains steady. The faintest trace of fear lingers in his mind, and I work to soothe it further, my hand resting on Kyzan. Kyzan seems to understand his role in anchoring me to the emotions I hold at bay. He lets out a low rumble, a vibration of approval, though the narrowing of his eyes makes it clear he doesn't appreciate being referred to as a "pet."

"He doesn't seem to appreciate being called a pet," I say, my voice distant. To test myself, I carefully draw back the blanket of calm I've placed over the room, allowing Mary and Cooper's emotions to surface naturally. The fear hangs heavy, sharp and tangible, pressing into my chest like a foreign weight. I close my eyes briefly, breathing through the discomfort as I work to filter the feeling out of myself. I remember my mother's words, a bittersweet echo in my mind. *"Now you know, you can learn to control your emotions. You can choose what you feel from others, and what you want others to feel."* I try to follow her advice, building a barrier against the fear. It isn't strong enough, and traces of it seep through, but I don't stop trying. My training ended the day my mother dies, leaving me to practice on my own, fumbling through the art like a student without a teacher.

Cooper breaks the silence first. "A new companion, then," he says, his sharp gaze moving between Kyzan and me, assessing us both. With a subtle nod, I will the tension to fade from the room. Taking a step toward the kitchen, I adjust the three hares slung over my shoulder. Though Mary and Cooper say nothing, their eyes follow me, their unease lingering like smoke in the air.

The situation is diffused, but their emotions weigh on me. A single question echoes in my mind: Do they feel as exhausted as I do?

I sit by my small desk, waiting for the darkness of night to settle. My paintbrush spins idly between my fingers, its worn wooden handle splintering against my skin. At my feet, Kyzan watches me with an intensity that borders on admiration. I find inspiration in his steady gaze. With a deep breath, I let the brush guide my hand, each stroke tethered to the emotions he silently feeds me. It feels as if an invisible thread connects us, pulling colors and shapes from my heart and laying them bare on the canvas.

Time blurs as I work, the world around me fading until a deep, husky voice breaks through the quiet. "I heard we had a new family member."

Hecate stands in the doorway, her maroon eyes glinting with a sharpness that always leaves me a little on edge. Her gaze flicks to Kyzan, who responds with a low snarl. Hecate's eyes flare red in warning, and I watch in amusement as Kyzan lowers his head, submitting to her dominance. No one messes with Hecate.

"Well, with another mouth to feed, those rabbits won't last long," she says, her tone brisk. "We'll need more meat for the winter." "I'll handle it, Cate," I reply, my smile tight.

The reminder stings, though I know it isn't meant to. As much as I love bread, cheese, and wine, it won't be enough.

Hecate nods and leaves the room, the candlelight flickering in her wake. I sink back into my chair, closing my eyes against the weight pressing down on me. "Think happy thoughts, Olivia. Life could be worse." But even as I repeat the mantra, I know the truth. I need to move. I need to act before the darkness creeping at the edges of my mind swallows me whole.

Though I am an adult, sneaking out of the house still feels like second nature. It's better this way. I don't need them worrying about me getting captured. Being a half-breed and the last of my kind paints a target on my back—a prize any Fae would kill to claim.

This time, though, sneaking out comes with a new complication. Kyzan pads silently beside me, refusing to leave my side. I can't help but watch him out of the corner of my eye as he tilts his head with each carefully placed paw, his movements almost comical in their exaggerated caution. His wide eyes scan the kitchen, his concern palpable. I bite down on my lip to stifle the laugh threatening to bubble up.

We slip through the kitchen like whispers on the wind, careful not to wake Hecate. Her room is far too close for comfort. Once outside, the gravel path crunches faintly beneath our feet until we reach the safety of the open road. I pull my hood up and adjust the satchel across my shoulder, silently cursing the way Kyzan's silver coat gleams under the moonlight.

"Don't you have any magical powers to conceal yourself?" I mutter. He turns his head toward me, his expression a clear rebuke, as though I'm the crazy one. So, no magic. Great.

"Must you follow me? Can't you stay back?" I try again, more out of hope than anything else. Kyzan shakes his head and continues forward, unbothered by my frustration. "Perfect. Just spiffing," I mutter under my breath.

Sticking to the shadows, I duck into dark alleyways, avoiding the dim glow of the streetlamps. I don't need to see to find my way; my senses guide me with a precision born from years of practice. I follow the pull of pain—the gnawing ache of hunger, the sting of cold on bare skin. But there's something else, a pain more profound, more elusive. It seeps into me like a whisper, unformed but insistent.

"Cecil? Maggie?" I hiss into the darkness. "Livy! You came!" Maggie's small voice trembles, her relief cutting through the night like a warm beacon.

I kneel in front of them, my eyes adjusting to the moonlight illuminating their frail forms. Their teeth chatter in a rhythm like the ticking of a clock, counting down the moments before the cold claims them completely. The stench hits me next—a foul, putrid odor of decay. My scarf becomes a necessary barrier, the only thing keeping my stomach from lurching.

Gently, I press a hand to each of their foreheads. Maggie's skin is cool, but Cecil burns with fever. The infection is bad. Worse than I imagined.

"Cecil..." I begin, my voice softer now. "It's nothing, Liv," he says quickly, his pride a shield against my concern. "Show me," I say firmly.

Reluctantly, Cecil lifts his pant leg, revealing an angry, festering gash. My breath catches, but I don't let my alarm show. "Cecil, you need to come to the cottage. Let me treat this properly." "No," he says, shaking his head stubbornly. "You do enough for us. Besides, it's a long walk back to town. I've got work lined up—we'll be fine."

Such a proud young man. Too proud. I bite back my argument, knowing it will only push him further into his stubborn resolve. Instead, I pull out the bread and cheese I've brought, handing it to them as they scramble to eat. From my satchel, I retrieve the flask of pure spirits Hecate made, dampening a cloth with the liquid.

Drawing on my power, I let ribbons of warmth and comfort flow into the cloth as I press it to Cecil's wound. He doesn't flinch as the alcohol cleanses the infection, but I feel his body relax under the flood of love and calm I send through him. The process is slow, meticulous. As I scrub away the pus and dirt, I find myself wishing my powers extended beyond emotions. It feels so small, so inadequate—just enough to distract from the pain but never enough to truly heal.

"Thank you, Livy," Cecil murmurs. "You have magic hands. They always take away the pain."

Before I can respond, a ripple of unease prickles across my senses. Three waves of emotion wash over me, each distinct but overlapping, their complexity a familiar chaos. Kyzan stirs in the shadows, his nose lifting to the air. Maggie whimpers, her eyes wide as they land on the wolf's gleaming coat. "W-what is that?" "That's Kyzan, my watchdog," I say, my voice calm and steady. Kyzan radiates familiarity, his emotions clear. He is weary, but not afraid. Whatever lingers in the darkness, he recognizes it.

I turn back to the children. "I have to go. Please, keep that wound clean, Cecil. If it gets worse, come to the cottage. We'll care for you, and we'll find work for you both. At least think about it. If not for yourself, then for Maggie."

Cecil's guilt weighs heavily in the air, his pride warring with his love for his sister. It's admirable—and foolish. With a sigh, I rise, adjusting my satchel as I step into the shadows. Kyzan falls into step beside me, his gaze flicking between me and the unseen figures in the distance. The pull of my next destination looms ahead, heavy and insistent, and I walk toward it, bracing for what is to come.

Jeyr

LOST MUTT

A cacophony of murmurs surrounds me as I step into the Black Forest Inn, my presence barely acknowledged by the mortals milling about. Their whispers weave around me like an irritating tune, out of sync and endlessly grating. The tightness in my chest, however, is more familiar—yearning. Damn that mutt. Nearly half a century together, and he just leaves me. I spent the better part of the day scouring every corner of that damned forest, and yet he was nowhere to be found.

The earthy growl from the booth at the back pulls me from my thoughts. "Where is Kyzan?" Caomh's voice is sharp and biting, cutting through the noise like a blade. He leans casually against the velvet booth, but his posture betrays his irritation. His white shirt hangs open at the collar, his vest unbuttoned and his sleeves rolled up to his elbows, revealing golden skin. Those golden amber eyes lock onto mine, their intensity drilling straight into me. His fists clench and unclench at his sides, his irritation a living thing that ripples through the room.

Jethro appears in a flash, his suddenness as natural to him as breathing. "The traitor decided a little huntress is to be his new charge," he says, sliding into the booth across from Caomh. A faint smirk tugs at the corners of his lips, his tone laced with venomous amusement. "What?" Caomh growls, his voice dipping into something almost feral as he leans closer to Jethro. "I followed him," Jethro says with maddening amusement. "Saw him slip out. Naturally, I was curious. He made his way to the Black Forest and approached a huntress. And then..." Jethro pauses, his grin widening as though savoring the tension. "He bowed to her."

Caomh's expression mirrors my own, though I am certain the storm in my chest is worse. "Sorry, what?" he bites out, his voice barely above a whisper. Jethro's smirk grows. "Not just that. She's got a Svadilfari who doesn't leave her side. There was a questing beast, and she blinded it. Seems Kyzan has decided she's worth his loyalty."

The words hang heavy in the air. My body tenses as something sharp pierces my chest—a pang of panic, fleeting but undeniable. "Was this female a petite redhead, by chance?" Caomh's voice is quiet now, but it carries the weight of impending wrath. Jethro's raised brow is all the confirmation I need, though his expression seems to tease, *How did you know?* Caomh's molten gaze turns to me, fury simmering in its depths. "Jeyr," he begins, his tone as sharp as the edge of a blade. "How is it that the woman you save and somehow manage to lose is now a huntress, slaying questing beasts and claiming our guard wolf?" "She didn't steal him," Jethro interrupts, his amusement softening. "He swore himself to her."

I sit silently, my mind racing as I try to piece together the fragments of what I've heard. Questions pile up faster than I can answer them. Caomh rubs his hand over his face, his frustration palpable. "Jethro," he says finally, his tone low but commanding. "You have a new assignment: find the girl and follow her. It's unheard of for a mortal female to have two rare creatures determined to guard her."

Jethro's eyes flicker with something unusual—excitement. It's subtle, but to those who know him, it's as obvious as a flare in the dark. Both Caomh and I exchange a glance, our shared curiosity over Jethro's reaction breaking through the tension.

It's been half a century since we've seen even a flicker of emotion cross Jethro's face. His heart is tied to another Court, a bond that leaves him suspended in a limbo of longing. But now... now there is something different. Something lighter.

A pang of jealousy twists in my chest, unwelcome and jarring. My mind drifts back to her—the huntress. I picture her face, her eyes, the quiet strength that clings to her like a second skin. Each memory sends a rush of heat through my veins, a dangerous mix of curiosity and something else I dare not name.

Caomh's voice cuts through my reverie. "Change of plans. We go tonight. Let's see what this little huntress is up to." "Did you follow her after this whole huntress performance?" Caomh's sharp voice adds, the tension cutting through the air like a whip.

Jethro rolls his eyes, leaning against the wall with a casualness that belies the weight of the room. "Is my job to be your spy?" he asks, sarcasm dripping from every word. "Jet, straight answer," Caomh growls, his tone brooking no defiance. Jethro sighs, his usual mask of indifference slipping. "Yes, I followed her," he admits sharply. "She went back to a hidden cottage in the Black Forest." Caomh's lips press into a thin line. "Well, why are we not there already?" He hesitates, his eyes narrowing slightly.

As for me, I can't deny it any longer—I want to see her again. And this time, I won't lose her.

"She isn't here." I stand in the small bedroom, my eyes drawn to the paintings scattered across the walls. Each one seems to pulse with something alive, something more than color and canvas. "Her horse is, though," Jethro says, his voice a dry rumble that breaks the room's fragile stillness. He leans awkwardly in the corner, his broad frame making the space feel even smaller. The room itself is no larger than a storeroom, with just enough space for a narrow path between the cot and the furniture. Yet, for its size, it's meticulously kept. The bed is perfectly made, the headboard painted with detailed depictions of the kingdom's castles.

Her art desk stands to one side, vines curling up its legs as if it's grown straight from the forest. Portraits and sketches are neatly stacked on its surface, wax paper separating each piece with care. Miniature paintings decorate her vanity like tiny windows into secret worlds. But it isn't the beauty of her work that tightens my chest.

It's the way the room itself seems alive, humming with emotions that cling to every surface. It feels like stepping into the eye of a storm, a cyclone of feelings swirling just beneath the surface. None of us dare move, too wary of unraveling whatever fragile balance keeps it contained.

"Gods, this room... Are you feeling this too?" Jet's voice breaks the silence, raw and unguarded. He reaches toward a painting but jerks his hand back as though the image has burned him. He shakes his fingers, his usual nonchalance replaced with unease. "Something's off," he mutters. "Maybe she's a witch. Everything feels... haunted. These paintings—they don't just show emotion. They're bleeding it."

The storm presses harder, dragging me under. My body fights against itself, torn between the urge to flee and the strange pull to stay rooted. My heart races, my hands turn clammy, and my lungs strain as if the room is stealing the air from me. I feel trapped, tethered to the floor by a force I can't see.

"Jet," Caomh's voice cuts through the tension, low and commanding. "I think she'll need more than a wolf and a Svadilfari horse to protect her."

He moves to a painting, his fingers hovering over it before finally tracing the edges. The canvas depicts a pair of maroon eyes staring out from shadow, piercing and unrelenting. I watch as his face pales, his golden complexion draining to ash.

"Caomh…" My voice comes out rough, taut with unspoken questions. He doesn't turn to me. His eyes stay locked on the painting as he speaks. "She isn't from here. I… I thought her kind is extinct. But if she's alive…" His voice drops, heavy with unease. "She's in great danger. Or we are."

His cryptic words send frustration clawing at me, my mind spiraling with unspoken demands. Before I can press him, Jet's grip tightens around us, and shadows sweep in, wrapping us in their cold embrace. The world shifts, twisting like smoke, until the darkness gives way. We stand on the empty streets of Black Forest town, the faint flicker of gas lamps casting jagged shadows that seem to claw at the cobblestones. The air is thick, carrying the mingling scents of frost and lingering smoke, heavy enough to sit in my chest.

"Why are we back here?" I ask, my voice sharper than intended. "I think she's here," Jet says, his smoldering eyes scanning the street. His ability to manipulate light gives him an edge, letting him see what others can't. The town feels dead, save for the occasional drunkard swaying in the shadows. Smoke rises lazily from a few chimneys, but most cottages are cold and silent.

I step away, drawing in a breath to steady myself. As I pass an alley, a glint of silver catches my eye. A figure cloaked in black moves with quiet purpose, a hood drawn low over their face. Beside them pads a massive wolf. My heart thuds loudly in my chest. *It's her.*

Before I can act, Jet wraps us in shadows again, masking our presence. Hidden in the dark, I watch her move. Her steps are cautious but deliberate. She isn't running—she is tending.

We watch in silence, hidden in the shadows as she moves with quiet purpose. Her hands work with practiced care, tending to a child's wound with an almost reverent precision. The boy's faint voice breaks the stillness, his words trembling with awe as he whispers something we can't hear. Whatever it is, her touch seems to ease his pain, leaving behind a fragile light in his tired eyes.

"So, what is she?" Jethro's voice carries a mix of curiosity and suspicion as we trail her through the alleys.

I haven't realized how many homeless souls fill the streets of Black Forest until now. She moves among them like a ghost, familiar with each face. She cleans their wounds, offers them scraps of food, and leaves something far more valuable in her wake—hope. I see it in their eyes, the way despair lifts just enough to let in a sliver of light.

"She's an Empath," Caomh says, his voice weighted with certainty.

Jet and I spin toward him, his words hitting like a thunderclap. "What? I thought they were extinct," I say, disbelief thick in my voice. "As did I," Caomh replies. "But she's here. How she survived, how she concealed herself... I don't know. If the King finds out... she's as good as dead. Or worse, he'll use her. We can't leave her unprotected—reckless, reckless woman."

I watch her crouch beside another child, her care unwavering. A warmth blooms in my chest, softening the edges of my bitterness. "Maybe she's reckless," Jet says quietly, "but at least she's helping them. In this world, that's rare." Caomh nods, his usual stern expression giving way to something more thoughtful. "What she's doing is stupid, exposing herself like this to mortals—the kind who would do anything to grasp even a sliver of power in a world consumed by poverty and desperation." Caomh mutters, "The only thing working for her—her mental shields are some of the best I've encountered. I can't get in without letting her know we're here."

Good, I think. *She's protecting herself.* Pride stirs in my chest as I watch her. She doesn't realize it yet, but men will follow her into battle. She is a beacon in a world ravaged by hate and deceit. She is hope.

"Seems Kyzan's smarter than we gave him credit for," Caomh says, a faint smile tugging at his lips. "He's aligned himself with the last living Empath."

Olivia

THE WEIGHT OF KINDNESS

I know they are still following me. I should go home. Every time I turn in the direction of home, I only see sad lonely faces. I can't leave them. I don't know when I'll get a chance to do this again.

With the winter solstice right around the corner, every street is going to be flooded with celebrations. Many travel through the town this time of year—it's peak time for trade before the weather gets too cold. It's too dangerous for me to come out; tonight is too dangerous. I have three figures watching me, following me. The only thing that keeps my nerves at bay is Kyzan's tranquility.

Yes, I am a trusting idiot, trusting a random wolf who comes into my life just today... I ignore my self-deprecating thoughts. They may be right, but something in my mind tells me he will protect me. Or maybe *I am* being too trusting. My gauge on emotions hasn't done me wrong yet. I'm at my last stop as it's nearly time for the children to wake. I would have liked to be here sooner, though it seems the lack of food affects more people this year. People's fears are heightened with each degree the temperature drops.

My gift can't help itself. It calls to touch those who are drowning in the depths of despair. If I just walk away from those helpless souls sitting there without any comfort, it's like an itch I can't scratch. If I can do any good, however little, I will.

As I climb up the fire escape, I hear the small whimper from Kyzan. I look down, and the wolf's golden eyes leer up at me. "I won't be too long. Sit guard." Those big eyes beg me to stay. Gods, for such a big beast, he's nothing but a big baby. "I'll be right back," I promise. On the top level, I push up on the old wooden window, cringing as it groans in protest. It gives way just enough to let me slide in on my stomach, wood splinters stabbing into me as I push through the frame. I land silently on the broken floorboards, welcomed by countless pairs of little eyes.

"Livy!" All the love in the room hits me in full force. I send back a wave of affection and watch as their eyes well with tears. I know that feeling—that feeling of receiving love and affection after being so on your own for so long. Unfortunately, the matrons who watch over them are to be feared. These children are in the holding grounds before going to hell. They will eventually be traded to the docks and sent to the Fae Courts as slaves.

These walls would seem like heaven compared to the treatment they'll receive as humans in the Fae Courts. That's why Cecil and Maggie hide from the child collectors at all costs. *Well, except for the cost of coming to live with me.*

I sit on the bed nearest the window. Lilly, who is sixteen but all of four-foot-nine, snuggles into me. She's the oldest but thankfully, due to her small build, she's been able to forgo being chosen for the slave trade. Each night I come here fearing that I will never see her face again. And each time I wave goodbye, I wonder if it will be the last. I touch her shoulder and think of the ocean, of the breeze on my face. I feel a happy little shiver run through her body. I hope one day I can afford to buy her, to set her free in the hope that she can feel that breeze on her face. She deserves to see the little joys this world has to offer, ones that aren't given as snippets from me. I want that for all the children. Though I'm better off than they are, I know we are only just getting by.

I pull out the food and ten pairs of hungry little hands take what they can. The children, ranging from the age of four to sixteen, huddle around the bed, using each other for warmth. Last week, there were twenty children in this room. I try not to think about the other half that are no longer here, try not to think of the emotions I once felt as my own. That's the thing about being an empath—every person you meet leaves a stain on your soul. What they feel, you feel. It tattoos itself on your memories, forever there.

"Story! Please Livy, pleaseeeee!" I look down at the youngest little boy, Maximus. At the age of four, we've begun working on his language. He's getting better with each visit, despite the occasional whine in his tone. I laugh and rest against the iron headboard, clearing my voice to begin.

Jeyr

A LIGHT IN THE DARK

I can't be certain if she notices our presence in the shadows of the musty attic. The room is cramped, suffocating under the weight of poverty. Children's cots line the space, nearly bare. There are no heavy blankets, just thin sheets that barely hold off the creeping cold. My stomach churns as I take in the sight. The snow has not yet arrived, but the southern winds carry frost—a harbinger of the harsher days to come. These children have nothing to protect them.

I let my mind wander, unbidden, to my own lands. Even those considered destitute in our society live with far more than this. Yet, the children here do not shiver or complain. They huddle close to one another, seeking warmth in shared proximity. Their faces, smudged with dirt, light up with eager smiles as the woman they call Livy begins to weave her tale.

"Once upon a time," she begins, her voice soft but steady, "there was a kingdom ruled by a Queen. This Queen was fair and just, and her lands were peaceful. She was blessed to have an alliance with another kingdom ruled by their own Queen. This alliance was a secret for years, for the second Queen lived on a small, deserted island—protected, and hidden from the world by a shield designed by the gods.

"Those with good souls could pass, but those with bad souls had to go through a trial to see if they could be healed. The Queen from the Great Lands discovered this, and the alliance was built. Any man, woman, or beast who caused a crime had to go through trials. There, they had to face their demons. Only those who were healed could return to the motherland, now a good Samaritan to society."

Her words wrap around the room like a spell, drawing the children closer. Their wide eyes reflect the faint moonlight filtering through the attic's small, grime-covered window. "What about the bad people?" a child whispers, her voice hesitant.

"Those who can't be healed," Livy continues with a solemnity that belies her youth, "must endure the trials until their soul is cured. Some never make it through. You see, the people from the island believe the world isn't born with bad people, but creates them. Their mission is to fix those who have been broken. This alliance lasts for years, until a whistleblower in the Great Queen's kingdom revealed where the criminals have been sent—her secret to peace. Then beasts from another world attack the sacred witches. They were not built to fight

, only to heal broken souls. The Queen of the Great Lands gave them refuge in her kingdom."

Little gasps ripple through the room like raindrops on a still pond. From the corner of my eye, I see Caomh's jaw tighten. *Reckless,* I can hear him think. *Reckless and exposed.*

"What happens next?" a child asks, her voice trembling with the weight of the tale.

""They stayed safe in the Great Queen's kingdom for some time," Livy says, her tone now laced with sorrow. "But then they vanished. The King's Knights found them, killing every last one. Or so he thought. But in a faraway land, one survived. And that was a secret we had to protect. For if the last of the healers was ever found, the world would lose the one soul capable of mending its broken pieces."

A hushed oath fills the room, each child pledging to keep her story secret. Their voices are small but resolute, the kind of solemn promise only the young can make with such conviction. "Good," Livy says, her lips curving into a sad smile. "Your mission in this world is to spread kindness, to bring light into the dark. You don't need powers for that. No matter how much this world tries to break you, strive to be better. Don't be the reason another soul shatters. Be the reason they see hope." "Promise, Livy," comes the soft chorus, their little voices weaving a vow into the air.

Satisfied, she moves through the room, her fingers brushing each child's forehead or cheek. They melt under her touch, their small bodies sinking into rest. Even the cold seems to retreat as a warm glow settles over the attic. Their breaths steady, their faces soften, and their eyes glitter with dreams of futures they might never see.

From our corner, we watch as she slips out through a narrow gap in the window, her slim frame disappearing into the night. The room remains aglow with the peace she leaves behind, a quiet sanctuary in the midst of squalor.

My own chest tightens as I turn away, unwilling to admit the flicker of warmth her actions stir in me. Whatever she is, she is unlike anyone I've ever encountered. She gives hope to those who have none, and yet she walks the edge of destruction with every step. Without a word, we winnow out of the room, leaving the children to their fragile, fleeting peace.

"That reckless, stupid woman. She all but discloses who she is!" Caomh spits, his voice sharp as a blade. "But do you see the joy she gives those children?" Jethro counters, his usual indifference replaced with a rare edge. "She gives them strength, hope, and a bit of light in their shitty lives." "False hope," Caomh shoots back, his words burning through the mental link.

"She's filling their heads with nonsense. One day, those children will grow bitter. They'll need money, and they'll sell her out. Not to mention what happens if someone with mind powers crosses them. She's the stupidest woman I've come across!"

I hold back, observing the fire that blazes between them. I know the Great Queen's Kingdom is a raw nerve for Caomh. My mind drifts to how my brother and commander has lost his mother, just as I have.

That war takes everything from us: his home, his heritage, and my sense of innocence. Caomh isn't just angry; he is protecting something fragile within himself, even if he won't admit it. But I can't deny my own feelings. Torn between wanting to take her by the shoulders and shake her for being so reckless and wanting to kiss those defiant lips for the kindness that defies logic. And then her voice breaks through the stillness, shattering our thoughts.

"Are you three done following me?" Each of us tenses, hands instinctively gripping the hilts of our swords. Kyzan moves in a blur, stepping protectively in front of her, his teeth bared and gleaming. "Well, obviously no love lost there, mutt," Caomh mutters, his voice carrying an unrelenting authority. "Kyzan, heel!" But the wolf doesn't budge, standing firm as her unwavering shield. She steps out from behind him, pulling back her hood and lowering her scarf, revealing those sharp, calculating green eyes. Morning light kisses the horizon, bathing her in golden hues that highlight the challenge written across her face.

I sheath my sword first, the shame of drawing on a weaponless woman weighing heavy. Jethro follows suit, though his smirk tells me he's finding this far more amusing than he should. Caomh, however, remains still, his jaw clenched as Kyzan's growls rumble low and steady.

"You didn't answer my question," she says, her tone steady, measured. "I find it curious why three Fae males are following a lone woman through the night while she simply cares for the poor." Her voice carries a strength that matches Caomh's, and yet I see the subtle way her fingers fidget against her thumbnail—a crack in her otherwise poised exterior. "We find it curious why our wolf abandons us for a mortal," Caomh finally replies, his tone clipped. "And now we see why. You've a knack for capturing rare creatures." Her eyebrow arches in challenge, her gaze locked on him. She doesn't spare me or Jethro so much as a glance. "Maybe my soul is kinder than yours, and the beast simply prefers me," she quips.

Caomh laughs, the sound sharp and humorless. "Your soul? Kind? You're an Empath. You hold the power to crush souls, to control armies with a single thought. And you waste that power giving false hope to children who are worth less than the meat in the market." Her eyes flicker, the golden rings around her irises brightening for a brief moment before dimming again. She inhales deeply. "You can live in whatever fantasy you've built for yourself, believing I'm an Empath because I brought a little joy to a few children," she says, her voice calm yet unyielding. "I give them five minutes of happiness in a life that will likely break them. Perhaps you should try it sometime."

I hear a strangled sound escape Jethro—a half-laugh he tries and fails to suppress. Caomh, on the other hand, is grinding his teeth so hard I think they might crack. "You know the story of the two queens," Caomh says, his tone shifting into something darker. "Explain that, young princess." Her posture straightens, a wry grin curving her lips. "Oh, have you never met an educated woman? Or are the people in your kingdoms so brainwashed they don't know the truth? Do they believe the lies written to suit political propaganda?"

Caomh's jaw clenches as Kyzan settles beside her, his sheer presence a wordless act of defiance. For the first time in years, my brother is rattled—not by strength, but by wit.

She is small but unyielding, commanding the space with an authority that leaves no room for argument. And yet, in the briefest flicker of motion—her fingers lacing together, a subtle shift of unease—I catch the smallest crack in her armor. A silent prayer to the gods, a moment of hesitation she likely thinks goes unnoticed.

Jethro, on the other hand, is thoroughly entertained. Watching a five-foot-four redhead hold her ground against one of the most formidable Fae commanders is a sight he clearly relishes. She hasn't called upon her empathic powers once, yet she stands firm, unwavering. It's unsettling. If I'm honest, a little terrifying.

I've never encountered an Empath before. The princesses of Anam have been nothing more than distant legends to me, though I've crossed paths with their guardians—forces of nature, spoken of in whispers even by the bravest warriors. And yet, watching her now, I have a sinking feeling that if I ever witness the full force of her power, it will shake the very ground beneath me.

"Well, that's some education you must have, young princess," Caomh says, his voice dripping with disdain. "I am no princess," she replies coolly, her tone unwavering. "I am a mere mortal with a will to make a small difference while I can." The words might be convincing if not for the tell.

I fight the smirk threatening to break free as I think back to the girl I met before. The one with the concussion who touched me without hesitation, her pain flowing into me like a wave. I healed her because I can't bear not to. And now, it all makes sense: I was captured by her then. Now, I'm her prisoner in a different way, and I have no illusions of escape.

"You can continue your lies, Princess," Caomh growls. "This conversation is going nowhere. We have our answer about the wolf's loyalty. His line is a gift from the gods, sworn to protect royalty. By choosing you, Kyzan has revealed exactly who you are."

I watch her face closely, searching for a crack in her facade. But there is nothing—her heartbeat remains steady, her scent free of fear.

"Fascinating knowledge," she says, her brow arching. "Yet, the Timber Wolf's oaths lie with the Great Queen's kingdom. I am but a human from Black Forest. Should I ask why three Fae males of royal courts—have a wolf from the Queen's lands? The King might find that... enlightening."

Tension coils in the air, thick and suffocating. Caomh steps forward, but Kyzan snaps, his teeth grazing the space just inches from his former commander's hand. The wolf's loyalties are clear: he is no longer bound to the half-breed prince.

"I would tread carefully, young Empath," Caomh warns, his voice low and edged with danger. "The King would not be your ally. Do not make threats you can't uphold." She flinches, the fear flashing briefly in her eyes betraying her steady voice. "If you want to kill me, Mind Master, do it. I have no weapons, no defenses. Take my life if that's your goal."

My fists clench at her words, my blood thrumming with intensity. I don't know whose honor I want to defend—my brother's or hers. The thought shakes me to my core.

"You are the weapon, Empath," Caomh presses. "You could stop our hearts, cripple our minds, leave us broken at your feet. And yet, here you stand, preaching peace."

She rolls her eyes, her patience clearly waning. "Your threats bore me. If you don't plan to kill me or drag me away, I have work to do. I haven't slept, and my farm doesn't run itself."

I exchange a glance with Jet, who mirrors my thoughts. "I mean you no harm, Princess," Caomh says finally. "I offer you an alliance—to keep you safe. I can provide knowledge, training, and sanctuary."

Her heartbeat falters, quickening to a rhythm that matches my own. I feel the hum of energy that burns beneath her composed exterior. She speaks, her voice a growl of defiance. "So, you wish to capture me." "No," Caomh replies evenly. "You may come and go as you please. But one of my men will accompany you. Tensions are rising in the Courts. War is brewing. If they find you first... I fear for both our lands." She folds her arms, her piercing green eyes studying him with cold calculation. "What is your name?" Caomh stiffens, the weight of the truth settling over him. "Caomh Conroy." Her laugh rings out, sharp and disbelieving. She shakes her head, looking skyward as if beseeching the gods. I can almost feel her weighing his words, deciding whether to call his bluff or lay her own cards down.

"Right," she says finally, her tone thick with sarcasm. "The Marquis of Gliocas wants me to go with him. The bastard-born heir, commander of an army, the half-breed prince who rivals Lord Tierney himself. Do you think I'm a fool? Trust your army's healer? Your light master, who no doubt is your spy? Tell me, am I wrong?"

The three of us stand frozen, her words cutting with precision. "Do you mind?" she snaps. "I have things to do." "This conversation isn't over," Caomh says, his hand capturing hers before she can react.

Olivia

Veins of Starlight, Chains of Fate

My insides flutter as if my veins carry wings, the nervous energy prickling through me like a thousand tiny sparks. I blink against the light filtering into the room, trying to orient myself. *Where in the gods' names am I?* Before I can take in my surroundings, my attention locks on the three Fae males standing before me. In the early morning light, they look different—sharper, more vivid than they had in the shadowed streets. My gaze falls first on Caomh. He is tall, his broad shoulders making the space seem smaller. His golden waves gleam like a lion's mane, his amber eyes glowing with veiled irritation. His lip curls in a faint snarl, revealing the edge of a fang. If predators have a hierarchy, he is the apex.

But his emotions are schooled, his aura muted and unreadable—a stark contrast to his commanding appearance. I clench my fists, resisting the pull to test my powers on him. I don't have the training, and the odds are far from in my favor.

Then, there he is: the Fae from the alley. His intense blue gaze traces me as if committing every detail to memory. He is different now, colder, harder. I can sense the walls he has built since that day, each one standing between him and the vulnerability I glimpsed before. And yet, that spark—familiar and magnetic—remains. I realize, with a sinking feeling, that he has been following me. I have been reckless, desperate for another encounter. And now, here we are. I tear my attention away, forcing myself to take in the room. It is spartan but functional, with walls of pale wood and a floor worn smooth by time.

Silence hangs heavy in the air, broken only by the faint creak of the floor beneath their weight. They aren't speaking, yet I feel the hum of unspoken words threading between them. It is a conversation I can't hear but can sense in the faint ripples of emotion that brush against me. I cross my arms, rolling my eyes to mask my unease. They watch me like a puzzle to be solved, their gazes sharp, dissecting. The third Fae—dark-haired and dressed in black—is an enigma. His presence carries a weight I can't ignore, as though he bears the burden of countless wrongs. And yet, my instincts whisper that he is not beyond redemption. His aura isn't pure, but it isn't entirely corrupt either. I wonder if my ancestors have relied on this same inner guide when determining who could be healed. The dark-haired Fae steps forward, each movement deliberate. When he extends his hand, the room seems to shift, the air thickening with his presence. His ageless skin bears no trace of time, but his eyes tell another story. They are an ever-shifting storm of greens, golds, and lilacs, dulled like flowers wilting under a heavy sun. His lips curl into a faint grin that doesn't reach those eyes.

I hesitate, then place my hand in his. The moment our skin touches, emotions pour into me. His hand is rough, the texture speaking of battles fought and scars earned. Beneath the weight of his darkness, I glimpse a flicker of light, a small, struggling flame. My powers stir instinctively, ribbons of warmth slipping from me before I can stop them. Memories of my own happiness fill him—sunlight on a winter's day, the exhilaration of running free, the lingering heat of another's gaze. His eyes snap to mine, widening slightly as the muted hues brighten. That small flame within him flares, and for a moment, the darkness that surrounds him seems to lift. His skin gains warmth, and his features soften, the colors in his eyes coming alive like an artist's palette brought to life. My stomach drops. My secret is out. My lack of control over my powers lays bare for all to see. "Jethro," he says softly, dipping his head in a bow. His voice is light, yet there is a weight behind it. I withdraw my hand, stepping back as the light in his eyes dims again. The warmth I have given him retreats, leaving only the hollow ache of what has been. My chest tightens. It isn't just his loss I feel, it is mine too. "Nice to meet your acquaintance... again," I say, trying to keep my tone steady. But the words feel thin, strained. I step further away, and as I do, the warmth my powers have given him bleeds into the room instead, a soft, invisible glow that wraps around all of us. The silence deepens, each of them watching me with varying degrees of curiosity and suspicion.

I straighten my back, meeting their gazes one by one. My mother's warnings echo in my mind, but they feel distant. These Fae are dangerous, yes, but they aren't the monsters she has described. Not yet. Jethro's smile fades, his eyes returning to the storm of shadows I have seen before. The tattoos winding up his arm seem to shift in the dim light, their stories hidden from me. My gaze flicks to the golden band on his finger. It pulses faintly, radiating warmth, a promise of love or duty I can't understand. Yet, the loneliness I feel from him lingers, mirroring my own. I clench my fists, hating my lack of control. I can't afford to let my powers slip again, can't afford to let these Fae see any more of me than I want them to. *Stupid, sentimental powers.*

Despite the frustration bubbling beneath my skin, my power buzzes in my chest as though it has taken on a life of its own. It hums with the triumphant cadence of a victory I haven't earned, a sensation as foreign as it is exhilarating. Around these Fae, my powers feel untethered, as if they no longer belong solely to me. Fear coils in the pit of my stomach, heavy and unwelcome, but it dissipates as I catch the faint glow of joy radiating from Blue Eyes. His calm, quiet delight spills out like a breeze carrying the scent of wildflowers. It softens the sharp edges of the moment, wrapping around me in fleeting, blissful warmth.

The spell is broken by the rough clearing of a throat. My gaze snaps to the golden-haired Fae, his amber eyes fixed on me with a predatory gleam. If my powers have exposed anything, he gives no indication. His expression betrays nothing but curiosity, though the amused quirk of his lips sends a ripple of unease through me. "It seems you've made your mark on my brothers, little Empath," he says, his voice deep and gruff, like stone grinding against stone. *Shit.* My chest tightens, shame curling around my ribs. There is no hiding it now—my powers have betrayed me.

His tone carries a weight that mirrors his towering stature, but beneath the sharpness of his words, I feel something faint: a flicker of brotherly affection. It emanates toward the two males standing beside him and echoes in the faint hum of the manor's walls. Despite their differences, their bond is undeniable, unshakable. It is the kind of connection I've never known—a sharp contrast to the loneliness that has defined my life.

"Forgive us for whisking you away," the golden Fae continues, his movements deliberate as he steps closer. "Three Fae males, a wolf, and an Empath in the streets of Black Forest would draw too many eyes." His tattooed hand extends toward me, his amber gaze challenging me to take it. Hesitant, I place my hand in his. The moment our skin meets, I feel the sensation of a chisel against my mind, tapping at the edges of my consciousness. The soft flutter of wings stirs in my chest, but the tapping grows insistent. My body flinches as a sharp headache stabs through my skull, and I snatch my hand back. His amber eyes glint with satisfaction, a smug grin tugging at the corners of his mouth. "Impressive," he muses, his voice a gravelly rumble. "For someone so far removed from the Fae world, you've managed to shield your mind."

I don't fully understand his words, but the tension in the room deepens as he turns back to his brothers. Their expressions have darkened, their lips curled into faint snarls. The air between them crackles with unspoken warnings. Kyzan presses against me, his teeth bared, a low growl vibrating through his chest. The Fae males don't flinch, but their stances shift subtly, as if preparing for a fight. My heart stutters in my chest, the calm facade I cling to slipping away in the face of their silent confrontation.

Then, the knock returns, gentler this time, a faint rasp against my mental wall. A voice follows, deep and deliberate, threading through my thoughts with startling clarity. "I wish you no harm, Princess. I am simply testing you. I could have pushed harder, shattered the fortress you've built. But I am kinder than most Mind Masters."

I straighten instinctively, the realization hitting me like a cold wind. *That voice isn't my own.* He is in my mind. Princess. The word twists uncomfortably in my chest, a reminder of everything I'm not. I am no princess. My mother wasn't a queen, and my life is far removed from anything resembling a courtly upbringing. My confidence, the veneer I wear so well, is built on scraps of knowledge—a fragile mosaic pieced together from the old newspapers my father used for wrapping. They've been my only window into a world that feels like it should be mine but is forever out of reach.

There is something haunting about knowing half of yourself is missing, a part of your soul untethered and incomplete. The kingdom my mother has left behind is little more than a shadow in my mind, a distant echo of something greater than I can comprehend. It leaves me with an ache that no amount of pretending can fill. For years, I've clung to what little I can glean, hoarding knowledge like a starving child collecting crumbs. And yet, faced with these Fae, I feel wholly unprepared. I clench my fists, forcing my breathing to steady as I meet the golden Fae's gaze. His smugness burns through me like a taunt, daring me to falter. But I won't. Whatever games they are playing, I have survived too much to bow now. My mother may have left me untrained, unarmed, but I have my instincts, and they haven't failed me yet. "Caomh, back off."

The sharp command breaks the tension, my eyes snapping to the Fae who steps forward. His piercing blue gaze meets mine, and for a moment, the air between us seems to *hum.* His expression softens as if he can sense the pain Caomh has attempted to inflict. My heart betrays me, its rhythm quickening with each step he takes. No amount of internal coaxing can slow it. "You okay, Hummingbird?" he asks, his voice low and steady.

The endearment sends another jolt through me, and I nod quickly, too quickly. My movements feel jerky, unconvincing. "We never got your name," he says, his tone quieter now, almost hesitant. He is close—too close. His scent is a mixture of wild pine and ocean storms, crisp yet grounding. I want to step away, *need to step away,* but my feet refuse to move. The confidence I've found with Caomh falters under the weight of his presence. It is as if those lightning-blue eyes have struck my blood, sending bolts of electricity coursing through me. "Olivia," I finally manage. My voice is steadier than I expect. "I never got yours."

His lips curve into a soft, tentative smile. Despite my efforts to contain my emotions, I know my thundering heart is betraying me. His ears will catch every erratic beat. "Jeyr," he says, his voice wrapping around the name like a melody. "Most people just call me Jey." I extend my hand, even though every nerve in my body screams against the contact. "Nice to meet you, Jeyr." I deliberately let the R roll off my tongue, savoring its weight. Shortening his name feels like a crime. "The pleasure is all mine, Olivia."

Our left hands clasp, and the moment his skin touches mine, the jolt hits us both. A sharp intake of breath escapes his lips as his composure falters. His hand recoils as if burned, and I shake mine instinctively, trying to dispel the lingering static. "One would think you hail from Aimsir," I say, attempting to lighten the moment. "You've got some serious lightning running through you." He blinks, his shock evident before a half-smile ghosts across his lips. "I'm just a simple healer, Hummingbird." But his eyes betray him, the storm behind them swirling with unspoken questions and hidden truths. My heart continues its rebellious drumming. I need a distraction, anything to ground myself again. "So," I say, my voice sharper than I intend. "What do three Fae want with me?"

Their gazes shift to one another, the faintest flickers of emotion crossing their faces. A silent conversation passes between them, one I can't hear but can feel rippling through the air like a distant drumbeat. Caomh steps forward, reclaiming his position as the leader. "We want to offer you protection," he begins, his tone unwavering. "The courts are shifting, and we're against the changes they bring. It's in our best interest—and yours—that you don't fall into the wrong hands. The courts would use you as a weapon." I cross my arms, letting his words sink in. Gliocas, the neutral court of the mind, is a name I know well. It sits on the plains between kingdoms, a court that brokers knowledge and controls the flow of information. For Caomh, one of their own, to stand before me and declare opposition to the courts? It is treason.

Whispers of unrest have already reached Black Forest—lower factions disappearing, rumors pointing to Puinnsean. Their leader, Grand Duke Bane, and his strategist, Tierney, command the King's right-hand army. Their grip on power makes them untouchable, and the last thing I need is to be dragged into their web of intrigue. "How am I to know you're on the right side of this war?" I ask, narrowing my gaze. "I've kept myself safe this far. My half-blood helps me hide in plain sight." Caomh tilts his head slightly, a faint smirk tugging at his lips. "We found you without trying. You're not as hidden as you think." My mouth gapes in an attempt to answer, but I am caught. Caomh, knowing this, relaxes his features if only just for a moment. "We won't use your powers as a weapon—that's how you know we're on the right side. We want to protect you from those who would turn your gifts against entire armies." I scoff. "You know as well as I do that my kind could never be used that way. You know what kind of weapon an Empath is. We're one-use. That's it." Jeyr and Jethro exchange glances, their expressions tightening as the weight of my words settles over them. Their gazes snap back to Caomh, seeking confirmation.

He nods solemnly, the gravity in his eyes answering their unspoken questions. "Empaths have a history," he says simply, his tone laced with regret. "It's a history the courts want to rewrite. They won't care about what you can or cannot do, they'll find a way to use you, even if it destroys you in the process." His words hit harder than I expect. For all my mother's warnings about Fae, I have never imagined this—a world where my kind can be hunted not for what we are but for the potential of what we might become.

Jeyr

Explosive Women

What does she mean by that? Jet's voice cuts through the silence, sharp and direct, yet edged with unease. I don't respond. The truth is, I don't want to know. I don't want to think about what will happen to the girl standing before us if the wrong person discovers what she is. Her power thrums faintly in the air, subtle yet undeniable. I can feel how she pulls at the emotions in the room, drawing on the tension, leaving us emptied of something intangible. And if that power can do the opposite? The idea alone makes my chest tighten.

Her people self-implode.

Caomh's voice answers through the mental link, measured but grave. *Their power is a cycle—give and take. They draw in the negative and release the good. But when that cycle is reversed, when they're forced to emit bad emotions instead... it's catastrophic. Imagine a silent bomb detonating, but instead of shrapnel, you're struck by every dark, destructive feeling they've ever absorbed. It flattens battlegrounds. Most caught in the blast don't survive. The few who do...* He hesitates, the weight of his words thickening.

They go mad. The King tried to harness that, to create weapons of despair. He failed. Not one Empath could withstand the torment. Their own power broke them. Every single one.

Jet curses, his usual composure cracking.

Exactly, Caomh replies. *And now, if you can help me convince this stubborn woman that we don't intend to harm her, I'd appreciate it.*

You do realize you're doing a terrible job of that already, right? Jet counters, his tone laced with dry amusement.

I shake my head, exhaling slowly as I step forward. "Olivia, we don't mean you any harm," keeping my voice steady. Her green eyes flick to mine, wary and unyielding. "I know trusting three strangers is difficult, especially Fae. You're right to be cautious. But Jet and I have already shown you we prefer you alive, haven't we? Your instincts are sharp, Olivia—trusting Fae isn't wise. But we aren't like the others. We operate in a faction apart, one that seeks to bring balance to the two great kingdoms. By revealing this, we've already made ourselves traitors to the crown. We're risking everything to protect the fractions that Rioghachd Mor and Eidheann Puinnsean are trying to control."

I gesture to Jethro, who remains silent but watchful. "Jethro is the captain of Aotrom. I'm his healer, and Caomh is the mind behind it all—the wealth and the strategist. He isn't on the throne, and his father would prefer he never gets there. Like you, we're hiding from a world that would rather erase us. But we want change. You use your powers to bring light to the forgotten. We use ours to slow the powers trying to dominate everything."

Her eyes flicker between us, her gaze sharp, weighing every word for truth. I watch as her heart races, its rhythm quickening like a war drum. It is as if I can see the moment she makes her decision, where her loyalties will lie. "Fine," she says at last, her voice steady despite the storm of emotions thrumming beneath it. "But only on a trial basis. You'll have to earn my trust. I will remain in my cabin with my family. In turn, you will help me with my powers. I've never had the chance to practice with the Fae. If I'm to be captured, I'd rather be prepared. I will likely regret this, and I'm certain my mother is rolling in her grave. So, do. not. cross. me." Her words carry a weight I haven't expected. Despite myself, the corners of my mouth lift. She has the bearing of a warrior who has never seen battle, a princess waiting to ascend a throne she doesn't know exists. "That was too easy," Caomh's voice filters through our link, a low chuckle rumbling with it. I don't like his tone. "Oh, and Caomh?" Olivia's voice is sweet, but it carries an edge so sharp it could cut steel.

Caomh stiffens, the shift in his posture subtle but telling. She stands before him with a grace that makes it seem as though she wears a crown. Her head held high, her shoulders squared. The weight of her gaze pins him in place. She is unshakable. *Impeccable*. For the first time, I see Caomh bristle. His eyes narrow, his jaw tightens as he regards her. I bite back a grin. My brother—commander of Gliocas's army, heir to the neutral court, and one of the most dangerous Fae I have ever known—has finally met his match. A woman of equal strength, perhaps more, who can stand in defiance of him without blinking. I can't tell if he respects her or hates her for it. "Yes, Princess?" Caomh drawls, his voice laced with mockery. But I see it—just for a moment. She has rattled him. And I don't think he knows whether to admire her for it... or to fear her.

Olivia

DANGEROUS BLUFF, A DEADLY GAME

My pulse quickens at his sly smile. He thinks my agreement to their "protection" is his victory. His poker face is impressive, but he's shown his hand without even realizing it. That sinister glimmer of emotion—the elation of thinking he's won, tinged with fear that he might lose—is unmistakable. A dangerous cocktail of confidence and uncertainty. His bluff is my tell.

"Be careful what you wish for," I say, my tone laced with quiet defiance. "All those emotions you think you can ignore? I'll make you face them. Let's see how well you handle training with me. You might regret bringing an Empath into your home."

The words are a blatant threat. I'm not proud of it, but a girl has to do what a girl has to do, especially when bluffing her way through a precarious situation. The truth is, I need the training more than I care to admit. A single morning in their presence has left me drained. The spontaneous surges of my power only make things worse.

Humans are simple. Their emotions burn hot and bright, ephemeral and fleeting. They live day by day, their limited time amplifying their feelings. Fae? They are an entirely different story. Their emotions span centuries, deep and tangled like the roots of an ancient forest. They let their traumas simmer, burying them beneath layers of time. And when those unresolved emotions fester too long? They become something far worse.

Humans who die with unresolved pain become spirits, ghosts, or poltergeists at their worst. Fae become Sluagh. Twisted creatures of power and torment, their emotions fuse with their magic, creating terrors that haunt the lands and claim lives indiscriminately.

When my kind walks the earth, we are the ones to soothe those lingering spirits.

But now, with Empaths gone, the world is plagued by the remnants of unresolved souls, left to roam in limbo.

Jethro and Jeyr both smirk at my challenge, but I don't miss the flicker of unease behind their eyes. They are wary, as they should be.

"So, where do we begin?" I ask, mimicking the arrogance Caomh exudes like it's second nature. His cocky grin widens, and I fight the urge to roll my eyes. Jeyr's polite smile follows, but it grates against my senses like sandpaper. It isn't real, there is no true joy behind it. His mask is impeccable, but my powers itch to unravel the threads, to peer behind the bland, polite facade. I clench my fists, scolding my power as it purrs with curiosity.

With Jeyr, it is different. My power flares near him, torn between fear and the overwhelming need to understand what makes him him. That electric shock we share serves as warning enough.

As if they've silently come to an agreement, Jeyr steps forward.

"We'll start simple," he says, his voice calm. "Shifting emotions in and out. Jethro and I will work with you first. Caomh has other matters to attend to, but eventually, you'll train with him as well. His mental abilities will be essential practice for defending against those like him."

I nod, keeping my expression neutral, though my stomach twists at the thought of being alone with Caomh. He has earned his arrogance, and he knows how to wield it. I can bluff confidence all I want, but facing a mind master who can sift through my weaknesses with ease? That is far less appealing.

Caomh's grin grows, as if he senses my discomfort. He inclines his head in a mock bow before warping from the room, leaving behind the faint scent of pine and fire.

Jethro steps forward, his smile warmer this time as he gestures toward a doorway. I mirror his polite smile and walk through the double doors, Kyzan pressed firmly against my side. My fingers curl into his fur, his steady presence anchoring me. Each step brings comforting vibrations through my body, grounding me in a way I haven't realized I need.

The foyer gives way to a room that is large yet somehow intimate. Navy-blue couches and armchairs are arranged around a massive stone fireplace, their plush cushions inviting and well-worn. Two walls are made entirely of glass, revealing a breathtaking view of long, coastal grass swaying in the breeze atop a cliff. Gulls dance on the wind, their cries faint as they ride the current. An open window lets in the soft scent of salt and wildflowers, mingling with the warmth of the fire.

The room has no decorations, no paintings or tapestries. Its simplicity gives it a quiet sincerity, as if this is the one place these Fae allow themselves to breathe, to be vulnerable. I feel the weight of it, the peace that permeates the space. And it strikes me how sad it is that they have brought me here. My presence, with all my uncontrolled power and emotions, will tarnish the purity of these walls.

I brush my fingers across the back of one of the chairs, drawn to the room despite myself. The textures, the colors—it all feels genuine, as if this is the heart of their home. And now, I am here, an intruder who will leave an indelible mark. For a moment, I almost feel guilty. Almost.

"Make yourself at home." Jeyr's voice is soft, almost distant, but his eyes tell a different story. The calm blue depths trace my features with the tender care one might use to soothe a fragile wren perched on their palm. A shiver prickles over my skin, unwelcome and too intimate.

I turn away from his gaze, unwilling to let my reaction show. Despite his apparent gentleness, the rest of him—his posture, his expression—remains detached, leaving a hollow ache in its wake. It reminds me too much of my parents, of the people I grew up with, who always seemed just out of reach. Sometimes, it is exhausting to want the attention of someone who won't give it to you.

I accept his invitation and curl up on the two-seater couch closest to the fire, Kyzan draping himself over me like a shield. The weight of him is grounding, a silent reminder that I am not entirely alone in this house of Fae.

The quiet breaks with a subtle clearing of a throat. My eyes flick to Jethro, seated in a winged chair, his elbows resting on his knees. His strong, chiseled features look softer in the firelight, his moonlit gaze meeting mine with a quiet warmth. For a fleeting moment, his presence seems to shrink the room until it holds only the two of us.

"All right, little huntress," he says, his tone as rich and inviting as mulled wine. "Let's start with something that comes naturally to you. Empaths of the Queen's Kingdom are healers of the soul, soothing pain and filling voids with warmth. You already have that ability—to take emotional pain and replace it with something easier to bear. So, let's work on that. Single out me and Jeyr. Take what we feel, replace it, then pull it back."

His instructions are simple, but the way his voice wraps around the words makes them seem monumental.

I nod, taking a steadying breath before dissolving the glass cage I keep around my mind.

I start with Jethro, letting the warmth he gives me flow back into him—a quiet, steady comfort. His moonlit gaze seems to brighten, encouraged by the twinkle of something resembling hope.

"Good," he says, his voice lighter now, almost teasing. "Now pull it back, little huntress."

I hesitate, feeling the weight of what I am taking from him, but I obey. As I withdraw the warmth, his chest rises and falls with a heavy sigh, a trace of longing etched in the set of his jaw.

"Now Jeyr," Jethro instructs, his tone more measured this time.

I turn to the blue-eyed Fae. He mirrors Jethro's posture, leaning forward as if bracing for what is to come. My power flickers, hesitant. I reach for him, but instead of the soft warmth I give Jethro, I send him the heat of the alley—the fire that seared through me when we first met. The raw intensity of it is something I can't forget, and I want him to feel it too.

He flinches. His eyes darken, the serene blue fracturing into stormy topaz. The connection burns between us as I pour the emotion into him, making him feel the electric current he sent through me. The giddiness, the rush, the ache—it is all his now.

And then, like a cruel child, I rip it away. Every spark, every ember vanishes, leaving behind a hollow chill. The room responds to the shift. The fire dwindles to a faint crackle, and the autumn breeze slips through the cracks, snapping cold against my skin.

Kyzan bristles, pressing closer to me, his warmth anchoring me against the chill I have unleashed. Jethro's eyes widen, flickering between me and Jeyr. The light that briefly touches Jeyr's features is gone, replaced by the shadows of his age.

I hate myself in that moment. I hate that my fear, my own insecurities, have turned a simple exercise into something personal. I have taken the warmth from someone who needs it most, even if he will never admit it.

Leaning into Kyzan's solid form, I steady my breathing and release a gentle pulse of warmth into the room. The fire swells back into a steady glow, its flames dancing evenly as the cold recedes. The ribbons of my power unfurl, weaving into Jethro and Jeyr, pulling back the lingering shadows and placing their burdens neatly within the growing book of emotions I carry in my chest.

The room settles into quiet contentment, the tension easing as my power wraps around them like a comforting blanket. I watch as their bodies relax, their muscles uncoiling as they melt into their chairs. Little sighs of relief escape their lips, and for the first time, I feel the weight of what I can give—the power of making someone feel whole, even if only for a moment.

But the cost is heavy. My own emotions churn beneath the surface, hot and cold warring within me. These Fae are not like humans. Their emotions are rich, aged, potent like a fine wine. I could drown in them if I'm not careful.

"I need to go," I say, my voice sharper than I intend. The room, the emotions, the vulnerability—it is all too much.

Jethro rises to his feet, his expression softening.

"Very good, huntress," he says. "Tomorrow, we'll work on shielding—learning how to hide your emotions and stay undetected. This was a good start."

I nod stiffly, gripping Kyzan's fur as I rise from the couch. The air in the room is lighter now, but the heaviness in my chest remains. Whatever comes next, I'm not sure I am ready for it.

Jethro walks me to the door, his towering frame exuding a quiet strength that, somehow, feels anything but threatening. As we reach the threshold, I glance up at him, offering a small smile. My hand moves instinctively, squeezing his forearm.

"Thank you," I say softly. "For your help today and yesterday. Your kindness is... appreciated."

The words feel heavy in my mouth, awkward even, but they are honest. His smile widens, genuine and warm, and before I can fully register it, he pulls me into an embrace. His arms wrap around me like a shield, his presence steady. The hug isn't fleeting; it is deliberate, intentional. For a moment, I let myself relax into it, the tension in my shoulders ebbing away.

When we part, a dull ache stirs in my chest, a longing I haven't felt in years. Tears prick at the corners of my eyes, and I blink them away quickly, refusing to let them fall. Little words whisper in the back of my mind, scratching at the hardened mask I wear.

He likes me. He hugged me. He... likes me.

"You're welcome," he says, his voice soft yet firm, carrying a sincerity that settles into my bones. I return his smile, feeling the truth in his words. For the first time in what feels like an eternity, I feel... wanted. The realization unfurls like a quiet bloom in my chest. I've never had a friend before, not really, and my heart flutters with a desperate, embarrassing giddiness at the thought of having one now.

I turn toward the door but hesitate, my gaze shifting to Jeyr. He stands apart, his stillness unnerving, his sharp blue eyes fixed on me. A small part of me hopes foolishly that perhaps he might step forward, offer to walk me home, or even reach out as Jethro has. But his feet remain rooted, his expression unreadable.

"Good work today," he says, his tone carefully neutral. There is a faint crackle of apprehension in the air around him, subtle but unmistakable.

"Jet's on guard first, so... I'll see you around."

I feel the void in his words, the deliberate space he places between us. Something in him makes me instinctively pull my powers back, shielding myself from the rejection I fear will surface if I dig deeper. I'm not ready to confront what lies behind his walls, nor am I prepared to unravel why he keeps closing himself off.

So, I offer no smile, no warmth. If he wants distance, I will give it to him.

"See you around, Jeyr," I reply, my voice flat.

The silence that follows lingers longer than it should. Without another glance, I step outside, the autumn air crisp against my skin. The door closes softly behind me, and the weight of the past few days settles heavily on my shoulders.

Three days. Three incidents. Three Fae.

My mother has always said fate is fickle, that it has let us down long ago. I've spent most of my life ignoring it, refusing to believe in its whispers. But now? Now I'm not so sure. Perhaps the fates are working in my favor, stitching together something I can't yet see. Or maybe... maybe I've made a catastrophically bad mistake. One I will come to regret. Or one that will kill me first.

Olivia

WHISPERS OF WAR AND WILDFLOWERS

As I step out the door, the manor looms behind me like a sentinel, perched on the cliff's edge. The roar of waves crashing against jagged rocks below mixes with the drumbeat of nerves coursing through my veins. The cool air kisses my cheeks as I hesitate, spinning briefly to take in the stone structure. Guilt prickles at the edges of my mind, tugging at me for keeping yet another secret from Mary and Cooper. But what would worrying them achieve? My recklessness is my own burden to bear.

A flicker of rebellion flutters in my chest, hot and sharp. Adrenaline surges through me, quickening my blood. This is my chosen poison, and I plan to drink deeply.

The manor stands resolute against the shifting horizon, large yet unpretentious, its presence warm despite its imposing structure. Its slanted roof bristles with chimneys, and light spills from its myriad windows, some clear, others adorned with intricate stained glass. A soft invitation seems to radiate from its weathered stone, a silent assurance that it belongs to a time when homes are built with purpose and care. Flowers spill from its garden beds, kissed by the wind as butterflies flit lazily among the blooms. A single hairstreak butterfly, its wings a contrast of brimstone and black, dances along the edge of the garden, oblivious to the weight of the moment. "No warping," I say, breaking the silence. My voice carries more command than I feel. "I'd like to walk." Jethro arches an eyebrow, his expression touched with amusement. "As you wish, Huntress," he replies, the words rolling off his tongue like warm whisky.

I roll my eyes, but the tug of his lips doesn't go unnoticed. There is something infectious about his understated humor, a sweetness that lingers, unspoken. He walks beside me, a quiet presence that guides without imposing. On my other side, Kyzan presses close, his fur brushing my leg as though he senses the torrent of emotions churning within me. We move through the golden grass, its soft hiss welcoming us as we climb toward the cape's edge. The coastline stretches below, the sands flat and glittering in the fading sunlight. The slope is steep, but the pull of the sea calls to me with a childlike giddiness I haven't felt in years. "You sure you don't want assistance getting down, Huntress?" Jethro asks. I turn to him, a playful spark igniting in my chest. "How about a race instead?"

Before he can answer, I drop to the soft sand and let myself slide. The rush of movement steals a laugh from my lips, giggles spilling freely as I tumble to the bottom. I hit the ground with a soft *oomph*, breathless and laughing as Kyzan bounds down after me, his exuberance infectious. He circles me, yipping and wagging his tail, his joy a reflection of my own. A shadow falls over me, and I glance up to see Jethro standing at the top of the slope, arms crossed and an eyebrow raised. His expression teeters between amusement and disapproval, though I can feel the battle within him. The childlike urge to join me fights against the stoic composure he wears like armor. "Don't know how to play, Light Master?" I tease, brushing sand from my clothes as I stand. "No," he replies curtly, turning and beginning his descent with slow, measured steps. I watch him go, my gaze tracing the strong lines of his frame. His soldier's posture speaks of discipline, but the faint curve of his shoulders betrays something deeper. He carries his burdens like an art form, balancing them delicately so they don't crush him, but I wonder how often that balance tips, how often he allows himself to falter. My chest tightens with an unbidden kinship. I know what it is to carry weight you don't want to share, to lock it away where no one can see.

I hurry to catch up, the shorter length of my legs requiring more effort. Jethro doesn't quicken his pace, but I feel him acknowledge my presence with a subtle tilt of his head. Something about him makes my power hum faintly, as if recognizing another creature that, like me, holds something powerful within. "You're trying to read me, aren't you, Huntress?" he asks, his voice a mixture of warning and intrigue. I shrug, feigning nonchalance. "I can't help it. Your emotions are... interesting. They remind me of concrete." His eyebrow arches, the gesture surprisingly endearing. "Concrete? Are you saying I'm a brick?"

I laugh, the sound surprising even me. "Outwardly, maybe. But it's more like... you've got so many emotions swirling around inside you. They've been left untouched for so long they've hardened, settling into something solid and immovable." His lips quirk into a smirk, his eyes glinting with challenge. "And you think you're going to chisel through it?" I shrug again, offering no answer. Time will tell.

We walk in companionable silence, the breeze tugging gently at my hair. The autumn sun bathes the land in golden light, its warmth a fleeting promise before the chill of night creeps in. There is something about this moment, this quiet, that feels sacred. For the first time in what feels like an eternity, I feel calm. "I don't think I've felt this at ease in a long time, Huntress," Jethro murmurs. The tightness in his shoulders has eased, his features softer, more youthful without the weight of his usual seriousness. "How old are you, Light Master?" I ask, my tone teasing but curious. He huffs a quiet laugh. "Isn't that a rude question?" I smile but say nothing, and after a moment, he relents. "A hundred and fifty suns," he says. "Too many wars, too much loss. Jeyr has been my healer for most of them. Caomh, our commander, keeps us alive on the battlefield with his mind as much as his blade. We've all seen far more destruction than peace."

My chest tightens, guilt creeping in for my own complaints. My life, with all its hardships, has been spared the horrors of war. These men carry centuries of grief, their souls weathered by battles fought in the name of power and pride. "So... you were alive when Empaths were?" I whisper, almost afraid of the answer. He nods, his expression darkening. "Aye. I wasn't in the war against your kind, but I remember it well. Our courts... we failed your people, Huntress. We failed you." The sincerity in his voice is a weight I'm not prepared for. His eyes carry a thousand unspoken words, each one laced with regret. "Your family told you?" he asks gently. I nod. "My mother made sure I feared this world, that I would never return to where she came from. That war changed her. She lost everyone. I think she feared if I knew too much, I'd follow the same path." Jethro's hand brushes mine briefly, a fleeting touch that carries an unspoken apology. It's a small gesture, but it settles something inside me. "I hope to prove that this time, I'll stand on the right side of the battlefield," he says. "This world could use something good."

"The world does have good," I say, my gaze drifting to the horizon. "It's just... we're too afraid to hold onto it. But it's there, in the music that takes us away, in the art that resonates. We're all just scared it'll be taken from us."

He watches me closely, his expression unreadable. For a moment, I wonder if I'm foolish to hope, to believe. But that small fire within me burns on, stubborn and unyielding.

I won't let it die.

Olivia

THE WEIGHT OF EXPECTATIONS, THE ECHO OF GUILT

"Goodbye, Huntress."

That was all the dark Fae said as the cottage came into view, his figure dissolving into thin air before I could form a response.

I focused on the gravel crunching under my feet, letting its rhythm distract me from the spiraling thoughts that churned in my mind. The faint light of evening painted the landscape in hues of gold and rose as I passed the stables. Cooper's steady movements caught my attention. He swept the alleyway, the last chore of his day.

Rays of light filtered through the old stone structure, catching the motes of dust stirred by his broom. They danced around him like enchanted fireflies.

Cooper paused mid-sweep, resting the broom under his chin as his sharp, bright eyes locked on me. His gaze was the same as always, scrutinizing every inch of me for injuries or signs of change. I offered a small nod, a silent reassurance, and buried my unease beneath a polite lie to shield him from worry.

"Busy day?" he asked, his voice gruff but edged with care.

"I laid some snares," I replied, the words tasting like ash on my tongue.

"Kyzan kept me company."

His eyes lingered on me, cataloging every detail. It was something he always did, as though taking a mental snapshot of me, committing it to memory as if he feared I might vanish.

Cooper was a man of few words, but I liked to think his glances carried the weight of all the affection he struggled to voice. Each blink was a quiet declaration: *I care. I love you.*

"Do you need help tomorrow, Coops?" I asked, though I already knew the answer.

His lip quirked slightly in what passed for a smile.

"Nah, kid. All good. The harvest was finished today since you left Ness at home. Mary helped me plant the winter crops in the greenhouse. Just make sure to get some meat stores this week, and we'll be set. Ness also helped pull some firewood from the forest."

I nodded, but guilt gnawed at me like a persistent shadow. Cooper wasn't disappointed, yet I couldn't shake the bitter taste of self-reproach. I owed Mary and Cooper everything. They had given me love, guidance, and purpose when I had none. The weight of my gratitude pressed heavily against my ribs.

I offered a curt goodbye and slipped into the kitchen, where I was met with the full force of Hecate's crimson glare.

"Where have you been, child?" she snapped, her nose twitching as she scented the air around me. Her sharp, fiery gaze felt like a dagger cutting through my carefully erected wall of indifference. I pushed back against the intrusion, blocking my emotions from spilling out. Hecate's flinch told me I'd succeeded.

"Rein in that power!" she hissed, her tone dripping with fury. "You snuck into the village again, didn't you? Are you trying to give Mary and Cooper a heart attack? Do you know what it would do to them if something happened to you? You selfish girl."

The word *selfish* struck me like a bolt of lightning. My throat tightened, but I remained silent. What could I say? She wasn't wrong. Using my powers to help others filled a void in me, but it came at a cost to those I loved.

"Your actions affect others, Olivia Arouz," she continued, her words sharp as talons ripping through my composure.

"Your mother taught you better. And what about me? I spend half my power warding this house to keep your presence hidden. If you attract Fae here, do you know what they'll do to us? To you?"

Her power flared with her anger, washing over me like a thick, oily tide. Hecate's wards protected our home, masking the strength of my emotions from those who might exploit them. Without them, the Fae— or worse—would find us in moments.

"I know, Hecate," I murmured, my voice dull and heavy. I shoved down the ache rising in my chest, smothering it beneath a blanket of numbness. *She was right, after all.*

"Good. Now clean the kitchen before you eat," she ordered, her tone clipped.

"Tomorrow, you are to hunt and come straight home. Do you hear me?"

"Yes, Hecate," I replied quietly, turning toward the sink. A single pot sat waiting for me, its remnants of stew clinging to its edges. Kyzan nudged my leg, his protective presence a steady anchor.

"No, Kyzan," I whispered, shaking my head. "She's right. I am selfish."

The words tasted bitter as they left my mouth, but the truth of them settled heavily in my chest. My mother had called my powers a curse, and in moments like these, I understood why.

The memory surged before I could push it away. My mother's fiery green eyes, brimming with fear and disgust, bore into me.

"Gods, Olivia! If I'd known breeding with a human would make your Empath powers uncontrollable, I would never have risked marrying your father. It was supposed to help you, to make you stronger, more capable of control. But instead…" She trailed off, her fiery green eyes narrowing as they fixed on me. "You need to switch it off! Get into the storeroom until you learn how to rein it in. You are going to ruin everything."

The venom in her words made me flinch, but it was the fear pouring off her that hollowed me out. She was terrified of me.

"Mumma, I can't!" My voice cracked as I sobbed, the words bursting from me like a flood I couldn't dam. "It won't let me! I don't know how to not feel!"

My gaze searched hers, desperate for even the smallest crumb of comfort. I needed her to hug me, to tell me I wasn't broken, that my feelings weren't some fatal flaw. But there was no comfort in her eyes, only fear. She was afraid to touch me, afraid of what I had become.

I turned to Hecate, hoping for salvation, but her expression mirrored my mother's. Fear. Sorrow. A deep, aching sadness that cut deeper than my mother's anger. They didn't see me, they saw a threat, a liability.

"You have to learn," my mother said, her voice colder now, sharp as shattered glass. "Or you will be the death of us both. I was wrong. I was all wrong. Now I am stuck with an emotional man who makes reckless decisions, and a daughter who is just the same. Emotions steer you wrong. Get into that storeroom until you can control it!"

I choked back another sob, my legs trembling as I stepped past the threshold.

"Yes, Mother," I whispered. My voice sounded hollow, a brittle echo of itself.

The door clicked shut, and her green eyes, so much like mine, held my gaze until the darkness swallowed me. Tears streamed down my face, falling in relentless sheets, but they couldn't wash away the jagged shards of her words.

Through the thin walls, I heard her voice— low, strained, cracking under the weight of her frustration.

"Cate, what am I to do with her? She's a liability. Amery... this was what she wanted. This was her idea. Every day, I'm reminded of her. And every day, I fail her— fail both of them. She's too powerful, Cate. Uncontrollable. She'll be the reason for another war!"

Hecate's response was softer, but no less heavy.

"Clarity, she's young. She'll learn. She's overwhelmed, but she'll grow into it. Amery wouldn't want you to give up."

"I need her, Cate. I need Amery back. This is killing me. This child is killing me. She's untrainable."

"She's not untrainable," Hecate said firmly. "She's the weapon we need. If she can learn to harness her power, she's the answer to saving our Queendom. To saving Amery and my sisters. That power alone could destroy our enemies."

"What kind of mother am I?" My mother's voice cracked, raw with anguish.

"I'd willingly hand her over to them— to be their weapon, their sacrifice. She'd kill them, kill herself, just to save..."

Her voice trailed off, the silence that followed heavy with realization. I froze, my tears stilling midstream. My chest tightened, the air around me pressing in like a vice.

For the first time, I didn't cry myself dry. Normally, the tears would fall until exhaustion stole me, but now... now I felt nothing. Not sadness. Not despair. Not bitterness. Nothing. Her words had carved me out, hollowing the part of me that still clung to the hope that I could be more than this. More than that child.

The door opened slowly. Her green eyes assessed me with cold precision, scanning for what I wasn't sure. My emotions were gone, obscured by the emptiness I'd built in their place. Her gaze softened— brightened, even.

"That's it, my girl," she murmured. Her voice was low, approving, almost reverent. "You've got it. Obscure it. Don't feel it."

For the first time in my eight years, I saw pride in her eyes. Pride, and something dangerously close to hope. Hope that her daughter was becoming the nothing she needed me to be.

I sat in the darkness long after she left, the sound of my own breathing the only anchor to reality. I closed my eyes, letting the weight of her expectations settle over me like a shroud. If I was to be nothing, so be it. If I was to be their weapon, so be it.

I wasn't Olivia anymore. I was what they needed me to be.

I blinked back to the present, the screech of the scourer against the pot grounding me in its harsh simplicity. The task, mundane as it was, silenced the voices in my head. But the memories lingered, their weight unshakable.

I scrubbed harder, wishing I could erase not just the grime but the echo of my mother's disappointment, Hecate's anger, and my own unyielding sense of inadequacy.

But no amount of scrubbing could make me clean.

Jeyr

GOBLINS AND DISAPPOINTMENT

The mental clang of the bell, the groan of the heavy door, and the suffocating stench of mildew clinging to the stone walls are my reluctant invitation into the orphanage. It isn't my first time in a place like this, and the memories it stirs threaten to choke me. Warmth and cruelty, tenderness and despair—those recollections come as a mixture of fire and ice, burning and freezing in equal measure.

There is always something about certain women—rare, remarkable women—that pulls me out of my darkness, forcing me to feel something other than hate. Yet as I am often reminded: kindness invites killing. This world seems to loathe those who are too good for it. The fates strip them from us, leaving nothing but the void of their absence.

The clang summons a figure from behind an iron door, her frayed hood slipping back to reveal her face. I force my expression to remain neutral even as disgust coils in my stomach. A goblin. Of course. She wears a human's form, but her stench gives her away—a rank odor of rot that sticks in the back of my throat. Her tangled black hair is wild, sticking out in uneven clumps, and her beady eyes glitter like damp obsidian. Thin lips, tinged with silver, press together before curving into a sneer. Her mangled yellow teeth are impossible to ignore.

"My lord," she rasps, her voice like gravel dragged over broken glass.

I straighten despite the disgust threatening to choke me. "Are you the operator of this facility?" *Facility.* The word feels like bile on my tongue.

This is no orphanage. It is a child farm. The muffled scream of a woman giving birth in the chambers below sends a jolt through my power, as if it can sense the pain in the air. I clench my jaw and shove it down. Does Olivia know what kind of place this is?

"Yes, my lord," the goblin replies, her tone oozing false deference.

"I'm here to purchase some children," I say, the words tasting like ash. Her thin brow arches, suspicion flickering in her dark eyes.

"And what are they for, my lord?" she asks, her lips curving into something resembling a smirk. "I'll make sure you get the best of the lot."

I don't need my powers to feel the mistrust radiating from her. I don't trust goblins either, particularly not one running a farm that sells children like livestock.

"I want to see all of them. I'll decide for myself. I'll pay extra for your discretion, but if I find you've spoken of this, I'll send my mind master to you personally."

Her beady eyes narrow, her lips tightening as if weighing the cost of defiance. Call my bluff, I think darkly. And I'll make sure Caomh pays you a visit.

"Come, my lord," she says at last, her tone wary. "I have ten children in my care. If you're not satisfied, you'll be the first to know when more arrive."

She leads me through the dank corridor, its walls stained and crumbling with age. The air thickens with the smell of decay as we ascend a narrow staircase. My ears catch the scuffle of small feet above us. The iron door groans open, revealing the attic where Olivia has snuck in to read to the children.

The faces before me are nothing like they were the night before. Gone are the wide eyes of curiosity and tentative hope. In their place are hollow stares, haunted and wary. Ten pairs of eyes, dull and lifeless, regard me like I am the devil come to claim their souls.

Something twists deep inside me, flashes of memory surfacing unbidden. Children in war, wielding weapons they are too young to hold, fighting for Fae who see them as nothing more than expendable pawns. Women, bound and violated in breeding camps, forced to birth half-breeds destined for the king's armies. The pure Fae are too valuable to waste on war; their mixed offspring fight and die instead.

My gaze lands on the eldest girl, a fragile beauty with more flesh than the others—a detail that makes my stomach churn. I know what fate awaits her, and for a brief moment, I see my sisters in her place. My fists clench at my sides.

"I'll take all of them," I say abruptly. The goblin's eyes widen as I withdraw two blocks of gold, more than double what she would earn from selling them elsewhere. She doesn't deserve a single ounce of it, but the children do. The thought of leaving them here, only to encounter them later as broken servants, is unbearable. Olivia's despair would be too much to witness.

The goblin bows low, greed lighting her eyes.

"Thank you, my lord. I'll have them loaded immediately. Would you like me to notify you if more arrive?"

"Yes," I reply coldly. "And remember, your discretion is bought, not earned. Test me, and you'll regret it."

The flicker of fear in her eyes is satisfying. I watch as the children are herded into the wagons, their small forms huddled together under the weight of their silence. I send the unmarked carts toward the manor, my jaw tightening as I turn back toward the alleyways. There are two more children I need to find.

"WHY ARE THERE A DOZEN CHILDREN IN HERE?"

The roar of Caomh's voice echoes through the halls, followed by the muffled whimpers of the children upstairs. I stand in the doorway of his office, bracing myself against the inevitable storm. His golden eyes blaze as they lock onto me, his fists pressing hard into the desk.

"Because they were in a fucking child farm," I snap. "I couldn't just take one! I wasn't about to let them end up in the slave trade!"

"We are not a charity, Jey!" he growls, his voice sharp enough to cut stone.

"No, we aren't. But they'll earn their keep," I say evenly, refusing to rise to his anger.

Caomh's jaw tightens further.

"One of them is four years old. What the fuck am I supposed to do with a four-year-old? This isn't a place for children, and you damn well know it."

I hesitate, guilt biting into my resolve.

"I couldn't leave him there," I say quietly. "You know what would've happened to the eldest girl. And the solstice is coming. You know what that means."

Caomh runs a hand through his hair, his frustration palpable.

"If you did this to please the Empath—"

"I didn't," I interrupt. But the image of Olivia reading to the children, her light touching their hollow souls, flickers through my mind.

"I couldn't leave them there."

Caomh's glare softens, just enough to show he understands. But his final words freeze the blood in my veins.

"Your father has sent a summons."

Olivia

FRIENDS IN SHADOWY PLACES

I feel him before I see him, the subtle interplay of shadows and light that radiates from his presence. It isn't oppressive, but it isn't comforting either. It simply is. Jethro. My eyes flutter open to find him standing near the fireplace, his dark form outlined in the glow of the smoldering embers. His gaze is fixed on the painting I finished the night before—the Questing Beast, captured in strokes of fierce detail and muted dread.

The room is still cloaked in darkness, the faint whisper of dawn nowhere to be found. I stretch, a rare moment of calm filling me. For the first time in as long as I can remember, I've had a dreamless sleep. "Do you make a habit of standing in women's bedrooms while they're sleeping?" I ask, sitting up and quirking an eyebrow at him.

He turns, his lips curving into a faint smirk, a glimmer of mischief playing in his sharp blue eyes. "It's not my first time," he says, his tone light. "Comes with the job. Do you often go nights without sleep?"

I frown, the weight of his question more personal than I care to admit. "No..." The lie tastes bitter on my tongue.

He scoffs, turning to lean casually against the mantle. His presence dominates the room, filling the quiet like a storm waiting to break. "You were in the kitchen until four this morning," he begins, his voice calm, matter-of-fact. "Cleaning, reorganizing stores, preparing breakfast. After that, you came up here and painted until you passed out at the desk."

I blink, confusion cutting through the fog in my mind. Wait... what?

He continues as if I haven't reacted, his tone maddeningly nonchalant. "I may have carried you to bed. You got six hours of sleep, which is probably the most you've had in weeks. It's midday now. You promised your family you'd hunt, and you promised us you'd train. So, get changed. I'll meet you at the border."

I look toward the window, expecting the pale light of morning to greet me. Instead, the room remains cloaked in shadow, and the unease of my restless nights creeps back in. "But it's dark," I mutter, glancing back at him.

Jethro's smirk deepens, a flicker of amusement dancing across his face. With a wave of his hand, the room floods with golden autumn light. It washes over the walls, soft and warm, like the sun itself has been commanded to rise. "You needed the sleep," he says simply, before disappearing as swiftly as he came.

For a long moment, I stare at the space where he stood, the quiet hum of his presence still lingering in the air. My thoughts churn, torn between irritation and the faintest twinge of gratitude.

Get up. Move, I scold myself, pushing the warmth of the bed aside. There's no time to dwell on the strangeness of it all. Rising quickly, I make my way to the mirror. My reflection stares back, startling in its unfamiliarity. My skin is fresh, the hollows beneath my eyes gone, the shadows that clung to me lighter. I blink, struggling to remember the last time I've felt this... alive.

The thought of my mother flickers across my mind, a fleeting shadow in the light. Not even then, I realize. Shaking the thought away, I brush through my tangled hair and dress swiftly, my hands moving on instinct as my mind tries to piece together the puzzle of Jethro's presence.

I bound down the stairs, the familiar creaks grounding me. The hum of morning activity fills the house, warm and bustling. "Off to hunt!" I call before anyone can stop me, the words rushing out as though they can keep the lingering questions at bay.

A chorus of acknowledgements follows, punctuated by Mary's gentle, "Okay, dear."

Outside, the world feels too still, too bright. Ness greets me with a soft nicker, her large, steady frame a reminder of the simple comforts in my life. I work quickly, readying her for the ride. I don't pause to listen to the wind or watch the butterflies dance among the flowers. The golden grasses sway in welcome as we ride past, but I ignore them too. My focus is singular.

We gallop toward the manor, the rhythm of Ness's hooves pounding against the earth in a steady cadence. The air is sharp and bracing, the kind that seeps into your lungs and reminds you that you're alive.

Jethro is waiting for me on the beach, his silhouette dark against the shimmering horizon. His posture is relaxed, but the weight of his gaze is anything but. I glance at him as I ride past, my pulse quickening at the quiet intensity of his presence. When I turn to look again, he's gone.

Jeyr

CASTLE TARNISHED BY TIME

Guards snap to attention as I enter the castle grounds, their polished armor reflecting the midday sun like fractured mirrors. Soldiers halt mid-strike in the training yard, and the ever-present hum of staff moving through their routines falls to silence as I pass through the kingdom gates.

Thanos lands with a heavy thud, his talons scraping against the stone courtyard. He lets out a piercing screech that echoes across the grounds, his voice rolling over the palace like thunder. The wyverns stabled nearby answer with their guttural cries, a cacophony of sound that sets the hairs on my neck bristling. Commander Caves steps forward, his expression unreadable but his stance rigid. He bows deeply, first to me and then to Thanos, his deference practiced but sincere. "Your Highness, back so soon from aiding the Aotrom army?"

I give a short nod. "The Grand Duke summons me."

His eyes flicker with something I can only describe as unease before he masks it. He's right to dread my father. Raiden's reputation is well-earned, a ruler who wields storms and fear in equal measure. Once, his power is a force for balance, but grief hardens him into something unyielding, sharp-edged, and merciless. Caves, like the rest of us, has learned to tread carefully. "Kelton!" Caves calls sharply, his voice cutting through the murmurs that begin to rise around us. "Take Thanos to the wyvern stables."

A young stablehand emerges from the shadows of the granite outbuildings, barely out of his adolescence but moving with the confidence of someone used to handling creatures far larger than himself. I shake my head. "Caves, I'll take Thanos myself," I say, my voice firm. Any excuse to delay this meeting is one I'm willing to take. "Your father wouldn't be pleased if we kept you waiting, Your Highness," Caves counters, his tone respectful but resolute.

I sigh heavily, the weight of inevitability pressing down on my shoulders. Reluctantly, I dismount. Thanos rumbles low in his throat, his massive head lowering in expectation. I pull a sugar cube from my pocket, and his molten gold eyes light with a flicker of eagerness. Despite myself, a small chuckle escapes me as I stroke the rough scales beneath his chin. For all his size and ferocity, the big bastard is putty in my hands. "Make sure he's fed well," I say, my voice harder now as I step away. "We travelled hard." Kelton nods, gripping the reins with steady hands. "Yes, Your Highness. He'll be given the royal treatment."

I linger a moment longer, watching as Thanos is led toward the stables. His massive wings fold neatly against his back, and his tail flicks lazily as he follows. For all his power, there's a peace in his movements that I envy. But there's no delaying the inevitable. Straightening my shoulders, I turn toward the palace and begin the climb to the atrium. The marble stairs stretch before me, their pristine white surface gleaming like frost under the faint light filtering through the high glass ceilings. Portraits line the walls, the faces of ancestors staring down with expressions that seem more judgmental than reverent. I ignore their gazes, letting my focus drift instead to the echo of my boots against the stone and the faint hum of activity in the halls. From somewhere deeper within the palace, I hear the faint laughter of my sisters, light and carefree. It grates against the tension coiling in my chest. This place isn't a home, it's a cage. And I'm walking willingly into its heart. The heavy marble doors loom ahead, their polished surface reflecting the faint glow of the glass palace behind me.

As I approach, the footman, Max, straightens and smiles faintly. His weathered face betrays a flicker of sympathy. "Good to see you, Prince Jeyr," he says quietly, his tone as familiar as the crackle of a hearthfire. I place a hand lightly on his shoulder. "Good to see you, Max. Any idea what this is about?" His hesitation speaks louder than words. Whatever waits beyond those doors isn't in my favor. "You'll see soon enough," he says, opening the doors with a slow, deliberate movement. "Your Highness, Grand Duke Raiden, Marquis Niall, Prince Jeyr has arrived," Max announces, his voice steady but distant.

I catch the faintest edge of disapproval in his tone, and it strikes a sour note in my chest. Even he seems resigned to whatever is about to unfold. I step inside, the weight of the room pressing down immediately. My father sits at his desk, his face carved into an expression of stone. He hasn't smiled in a hundred years—not since my mother died. She took more than his happiness with her when she passed; she took the part of him that makes this kingdom more than a machine.

Niall stands beside him, his posture stiff, his face schooled into the perfect mask of a politician. Gone is the older brother I once knew, the one who carried me on his shoulders and laughed like the world isn't falling apart. His warmth is swallowed whole by duty, leaving behind a hollow shell. "You summon me." My voice carries the weight of stone, cold and deliberate. I wish, not for the first time, that I could borrow Olivia's power to see what they are feeling instead of Caomh's intrusive ability to know what they are thinking. The latter feels like a curse, especially in this room. "Straight to it, then, brother?" Niall's voice has a hint of mockery, though it's softened by a veneer of civility. "No hello? We haven't seen you in ten years."

Ten years. A breath in the span of our lives. *A blink. A heartbeat.* For me, it isn't long enough. This castle, this gilded prison, is haunted by ghosts—some dead, others very much alive. Its walls whisper her voice, my mother's voice, weaving memories of love and agony. I learned here not to trust anyone, not to hope for anything beyond survival. The family turned into a business, cold and calculated. I left when I could, fleeing a cage that still manages to hold me by the thinnest of chains.

And now, I stand in its heart, staring into the eyes of a wolf who has lost his matriarch. My father, the Grand Duke, grows cruel without her touch, his leadership sharp and unyielding, stripped of warmth. "Why am I here?" I demand, my fingers brushing the titanium hilt of my sword. Its presence anchors me, a symbol of the life I choose. "I have duties on the battlefield."

Niall's voice softens, the ghost of the brother he once is flickering briefly, "Jeyr..."

"Niall, don't bother," I snap. I don't have the patience for his false sympathy.

My father rises from his desk, his presence towering and oppressive. Time hasn't been kind to him, nor has it dulled his ability to command a room. He looks older than his years, his face a reflection of my own but lined with anger and grief. A neatly trimmed gray beard frames his mouth, perpetually fixed in a scowl. His dark hair, streaked with silver, is swept back, though I see the telltale signs of his frustration—the way his fingers rake through it habitually.

"Jeyr," he begins, his voice measured, clipped. "Your time as a healer for the Aotrom Army comes to an end. They have thanked us for your many years of service and understand that I have recalled you to the kingdom." His words stop my heart. My life, my purpose, my brothers-in-arms—it isn't his to take. "You can't pull me from the army!" I roar, my voice echoing through the atrium. "That army, my brothers—they are my life. The life *I chose*."

He leans forward, his hands clasped tightly on the desk until his knuckles turn white. The storm brewing outside answers his fury, the white clouds darkening into a roiling gray. Thunder rumbles ominously, a warning to the kingdom of their ruler's wrath. "I can and I will," he thunders. "You are a Prince of Aimsir. Wars are brewing, Jeyr, far worse than the skirmishes and trade disputes you've been mired in. A world war is on the horizon. I will not have my son serving under another kingdom's banner while our own hangs by a thread. You've served your time, as all royal blood must. Now, it's time for alliances—alliances that will strengthen our family, our kingdom."

"*Alliances?*" My voice is low, guttural. The word carries the weight of history, of mistakes that can't be undone. "What do you mean by alliances?" My heart was still in the momentary silence.

"You are to marry the Princess of the Kingdom of Puinnsean."

The world stops. The breath in my lungs stills, replaced by a searing, bubbling rage. I may not wield the power of storms like my father, but there's a tempest building inside me, raw and uncontainable. "I would rather renounce my title, my position, my very name, than marry anyone from that cursed kingdom," I snarl, venom dripping from every word. Lightning flashes, illuminating the room in harsh, white light. My father's eyes glow with raw power, the white-hot intensity of a brewing storm.

Niall turns pale, pity etched across his features. I want him to see the hate in my eyes, to feel the disdain I hold for both of them. At that moment, every ounce of love I once have for them turns rancid, curdling into something sharp and unrelenting. "You will do as I command, boy!" my father bellows, his voice a thunderclap that rattles the glass walls of the atrium.

"This alliance will ensure the safety of our kingdom! Do you think I have a choice? Puinnsean will wage war if we refuse, and you know this. It's that, or your sister Althea marries his son when he comes of age. The war will likely hit before then." My blood boils. "Mother would be ashamed of you!" I shout, my voice cracking with rage. "Did you learn nothing from what happened to Aella? Are the scars on her face not enough of a reminder of what your decisions have done to your children? If you force Althea into a marriage like that, you may as well put her in the grave yourself. I will not stand by while another of my sisters suffers for your ambition. I will give them the protection you cannot." I turn to Niall, my tone no less scathing. "And you—don't even get me started. You're the eldest. It's your duty to protect us, but you've done nothing. You've both failed us. You can both go to hell."

"Jeyr Raiden Aimsir!" my father roars, his voice shaking the walls. "Get back here before I sentence you to treason against the crown!" I turn, my sneer cutting. "Do it, Father. Execute your own son and see how this kingdom remembers you. I've served in their ranks. I know their names, their faces. They respect you, but they love me. Go ahead. Try me."

Thunder rolls as I stride from the room, leaving my father's fury and Niall's silence behind. At the doorway, my steps falter. Althea and Aella stand there, hand in hand, tears brimming in their eyes. My strong, beautiful sisters. Aella's scarred face holds steady, though her clenched jaw betrays the emotion she tries to hide. "Jey, you can't leave," Aella says, her voice steady, resolute. A queen in all but title.

I cup her cheek, tracing the scars I haven't been able to heal. "I have to," I whisper. "But promise me this: marry only for love. Never for duty. Never for him." They nod, their tears falling freely now. "I love you both," I say, my voice breaking. I kiss their foreheads, savoring the moment as if it might be my last. Then I turn and leave, leaving behind my kingdom, my family, and the ghosts that will never stop haunting me.

Olivia

THE SMILE OF A CHILD-HEALING JUST FOR A LITTLE WHILE

"The stables are over there, connected to the house," Jethro says, his voice even, though a glint in his eye suggests he knows more than he lets on. I nod, guiding Ness toward the light stone attachment that mirrors the manor's elegant simplicity. The large wooden doors groan as I push them open, banishing the sharp coastal wind behind me. My breath catches in my throat as the scene before me unfolds.

Four familiar faces turn to greet me, each holding brooms, buckets, and pitchforks, their expressions lit with joy. "Livy!" A chorus of young voices rings out, bright and melodic as bells on a clear morning. I press a hand to my mouth, overwhelmed. The boys—clean, dressed, and glowing with life—stand as though plucked from a dream. Cecil, his infection now a faint scar peeking above his polished boots, wears a neat woolen jacket and matching cap. His navy-blue eyes sparkle with the same crooked grin I know so well.

For a moment, I almost don't recognize him, but the spirit behind that smile is unmistakable. "Thank you! Thank you for getting me this job!" Cecil's words tumble out as he dashes toward me, throwing his arms around me with the unguarded enthusiasm of a child who has known too much hardship. I freeze, speechless, as his embrace anchors me in the moment. A stable door creaks open behind him, and Maggie appears, her face wreathed in a smile as she skips toward us. "The ponies here are so pretty, Miss Livy!" she exclaims, wrapping herself around my other side. Her small frame presses against me, her curls bouncing with every movement. I stroke her hair, clean and soft now, and feel tears prick my eyes.

I glance back at the stable entrance, where Jethro leans casually against the frame, arms crossed and a faint smirk playing on his lips. "Did you do this?" I manage to choke out, my voice trembling as I stroke the children's hair, my fingers memorizing every strand as if it will prove this isn't a dream. "Nope," Jethro says lightly, though his tone betrays a hint of pride. "Jeyr's the one with the soft spot. Just don't bring it up with Caomh, it's a touchy subject."

A huff of laughter escapes me, mingling with the tears that slip down my cheeks. It's too much—this kindness, this joy. I glance down at Maggie and Cecil, their faces scrubbed clean, their clothes warm and whole. Cecil's infection is healed; Maggie's freckles glow on her sun-kissed skin. They smell of fresh air and salt instead of the rancid sludge of the streets. For the first time in what feels like forever, they look like children. "Master Jeyr gave us the stable residence," Cecil says proudly, standing a little straighter. "So Maggie and I can stay together. I'm teaching Milton, Tycho, and Billy how to work here, and Master Jeyr said he and Master Jethro will teach us hand-to-hand combat!" I bite my lip, fighting the tremor that threatens to break my composure. Their happiness fills me to bursting, bright and effervescent like champagne. I'm drunk on it, lightheaded with their joy. "Thank you, Miss Livy," Maggie says, her voice soft but steady, full of wonder. "We're so grateful to be outside, working with such fine horses." I nod, unable to find my voice. Behind me, Ness snorts, her impatience an almost theatrical interruption to the moment. The children turn to her, their eyes widening at her sheer size. "Cecil, Milton," Jethro's voice cuts through the stable, commanding but calm. "Ness will take the back hay shed, it's the only one she can fit in. There are step ladders in the back; make sure you towel her down properly." The two eldest boys straighten, saluting as if they've been soldiers all their lives.

I turn to Ness, placing a hand on her massive neck. "Be good," I murmur, narrowing my eyes at her. "Let the children care for you. No funny business, you hear me?" Ness snorts and tosses her head, as though to say, When do I ever misbehave? With a flick of her tail that narrowly misses me, she lumbers toward the hay shed. The younger children follow behind her, their awe palpable. "I trust Ness will behave?" Jethro murmurs, his voice brushing against my ear. I glance up at him, his brow arched in mild amusement. "She has a soft spot for children," I say with a small smile, though my nerves flare briefly. "She came to me when I was ten, I like to think she remembers what it was like to care for someone small."

Jethro nods, though his gaze lingers on the children for a moment longer, a shadow of concern crossing his features. His expression is fleeting, but I catch it—a reminder that these Fae are more than their stoic exteriors. My instincts about them have been right. "Shall we?" he says, motioning toward the manor. Kyzan pads to my side, his silver fur catching the golden afternoon light. As I follow Jethro out of the stables, I can't help the small, quiet swell of hope rising in my chest.

"So, all of them... are here?" My voice wavers slightly as I take in the magnitude of what Jethro is saying. "Yep. Caomh has already sorted the ranks in Jeyr's absence," he replies, his tone as nonchalant as if we are discussing the weather. "Lily's been made head girl. We moved the rooms around, so they're on the opposite end of the manor from us. The youngest, Maximus, won't have to brave the stairs every day. I even brought in an old friend to help—Claudia, from my kingdom. She's a fantastic cook and a taskmaster when it comes to organization. She's already teaching them how to work in the kitchen, while also crafting an education plan to teach them language, math, geography, and a host of other skills they'll need in the future."

I blink, processing the enormity of it all. "You did all this?" Jethro shrugs as if it's nothing, but I can feel the quiet pride radiating from him. His nonchalance belies a deep care, one I hadn't expected but can't help admiring.

Stepping into the foyer, I am immediately bombarded by a chorus of voices calling my name. The sound ricochets off the high ceilings, echoing through the grand space. I barely have a moment to register what's happening before I'm enveloped in hugs and grins, a whirlwind of excited faces and eager chatter.

"We get to learn!"

"Look at these clothes!"

"Olivia, my bed is as soft as the clouds!"

"Claudia said she's going to teach us how to bake a cake, and we'll get to eat it!"

Laughter bubbles from me, unbidden and bright. I catch snippets of their joy, each word like a spark catching fire. My chest feels full, my emotions on the brink of spilling over.

"Girls!" A lilting northern accent rings out, cutting through the chaos. The children quiet almost instantly, their wide eyes turning toward the hall.

A petite woman emerges, her mousy brown hair framing a face alight with warmth. Her golden eyes glow faintly, a telltale sign of her Fae heritage. "We have hungry men waiting!"

"Good day, Lady Olivia," she says, dipping her head politely. Her smile radiates kindness, and her presence carries the same steady comfort as Mary's. I like her instantly. "Good day, Lady Claudia," I reply, my voice soft with gratitude. "Thank you so much for watching over the children. If you need anything, please let me know."

Claudia waves off my thanks with a casual flick of her wrist, already turning to shepherd the girls toward the kitchen. Only Lily lingers behind, her steps hesitant as she approaches me. Tears shimmer in her eyes, though her face is set in a determined mask.

"Livy..." Her voice breaks, and I understand without her needing to say more. I know what this means to her. She had been destined for the ships, her beauty and youth marking her for a fate too dark to dwell on. Now, standing before me in clean clothes and with hope flickering in her eyes, she is a different girl entirely. "Don't thank me," I say quickly, brushing her tears away. "It's the Lords of the manor you should thank."

But she shakes her head, her tears spilling over. "You played a part, Olivia. I didn't want to tell you—I didn't know how to say goodbye. But you saved me. You encouraged them. You saved me."

She throws herself into my arms, her body trembling with relief. I hold her tightly, her sobs soaking into my shirt. The weight of her gratitude presses against me, bittersweet and overwhelming. This isn't just relief, it's release. She is shedding the burden of a life she had narrowly escaped.

With one final squeeze, Lily pulls away and walks toward the kitchen, her head held high. She doesn't look back.

Once the foyer quiets, I turn to find Jethro still watching me, his expression unreadable. "You said Jeyr was absent?" I ask, searching his face for any hint of what he isn't saying. He nods, his features tightening for just a moment before smoothing back into their usual calm. That flicker is enough. He is worried. The emotion tugs at something in me, as if his concern is a thread tied to my own chest. "Family matters," he says shortly. "He'll be back soon."

I nod, feigning indifference, though a strange bubbling sensation stirs beneath my skin. It isn't mine—not entirely. The feeling sits on the surface of my consciousness, foreign yet familiar. "All good, Huntress?" Jethro's voice brings me back to the present.

I shake my head, trying to make sense of the strange emotion. "I don't know. It's not yours or mine. It's this... weird bubbling. It tastes like resentment, but it's not quite that. It's different."

Jethro frowns. "Could you be picking up on someone else in the house?"

I close my eyes, letting the ribbons of my power stretch outward. The golden tendrils spread across the floor like roots searching for soil, veining toward the emotions that cling to the people within the manor.

"No," I say finally. "It's not anchored to anyone. It's... external but internal, like it's etched into my skin rather than coursing through my blood. A tattoo rather than a scar." I open my eyes, meeting Jethro's curious gaze.

"That's pretty amazing—and also my worst nightmare," he mutters, a wry smile tugging at his lips.

I laugh softly, though the feeling still lingers, shadowing my thoughts. "It's both," I admit. "A gift and a curse. It connects me to everyone around me, but sometimes it's enough to drown me."

I force the sensation aside, focusing on the present. "So, training?" I ask, eager to distract myself.

Jethro's grin turns wicked. "Think you can wield a sword as well as you can shoot a bow?"

I raise a brow, my lips quirking. "Careful, Light Master. You might regret challenging me."

His chuckle is low, his amusement palpable. "Don't get cocky, Little Huntress. You've yet to face a Fae in combat—let alone a Light Fae."

Challenge accepted.

Regret. Gods, I regret everything. Jethro's tall, infuriatingly perfect form exudes pure smugness, and I hate him for it. Fuck him. He reads my irritation as easily as if I've scrawled it across my forehead. "Come on, Huntress. You're quick, but not quick enough. You don't even use your powers, I can't feel anything," he says, his tone calm but biting.

"Good," I grumble, though I know I'm only feeding his smugness. "How?" he presses, his voice gaining that irritating edge of a tutor who knows their student is failing. "You could slow me down in an instant if you felt like it. A thread of unease would throw me off balance, make me hesitate. But instead, you let yourself stumble. You're getting more insecure with every strike. Hold your ground, Huntress."

Each word strikes me harder than the blows he's landed during our sparring. His finger jabs my forehead, a gesture that feels more invasive than any mind control power could have been. He doesn't need magic to get under my skin—he's doing just fine without it.

The training has stretched for an hour, and despite the unbroken night of sleep Jethro granted me, my body is already flagging. My legs tremble from holding defensive stances, my arms burn with the effort of blocking his strikes, and my mind spins from the constant critique. "Enough for today," he says, stepping back and lowering his blade. "At least now I know what we need to work on. Next time, try using what's already in your arsenal. Don't make me guess." He studies me for a moment, then adds, "It doesn't take an Empath to see you're exhausted. And you promised you'd hunt this afternoon."

The way he says it makes me pause. There's no mockery, no irritation, only a quiet acknowledgment of the promise I made. He cares about that—about promises. I like that about him. Despite his irritating confidence, he has a moral code, one he upholds even in small things. I nod, and together we head back toward the manor. The cliffside wind tugs at my ponytail, snapping it across my face like a whip. I barely notice. Unease has begun to creep up my spine, sharp and insistent. That same acid resentment I felt earlier bubbles beneath my skin, but now it's sharper, like a thousand tiny needles piercing my mind and stealing my focus. The sensation isn't just unpleasant—it's invasive. My power stirs restlessly in response, thrumming against the door I keep tightly locked.

It isn't asking this time. It's demanding. This is no soft pull toward soothing someone's pain. This is primal, urgent, a force pounding against me like waves against stone. Whatever is causing this disturbance needs to be fixed. Now.

By the time Jethro and I reach the manor's back door, my unease has grown into a storm. The wind whipping around us seems a mere whisper compared to the words I hear inside. I'm not gifted with Fae hearing, but I don't need it. The hot, spitting venom of an argument hits me like sandblasting in a coastal gale. Each word scrapes against my skin, raw and abrasive, demanding my attention. My power surges, a fierce beast clawing to be let loose. I tighten my grip on it, teeth gritted, knowing I'm walking into something far more dangerous than a sparring session. And yet, I can't stop myself from stepping inside.

Jeyr

A Storm on the Horizon, A Fire in the Heart

Thanos lands on the roof without a sound. Not even a whisper from his wings, as if he's mocking the chaos twisting through me. My chest feels tight, like a coiled spring about to snap.

"Back so soon?" Caomh's voice ripples into my mind, smooth and uninvited. I don't respond. Instead, I slam my mental walls into place, shutting him out. Let him guess at the turmoil I carry.

My boots strike the stone stairs as I descend, the sound sharp and deliberate. Around me, life carries on—swords clash in the training grounds, children's laughter rings faintly from the lower levels, and the earthy scent of roasted vegetables wafts through the halls. These small, ordinary things claw at the edges of my control, but I shove them aside. Today, nothing breaches my defenses.

The boots I wear click sharply against the stone floor, but I don't care to soften my steps. Each one thunders, an unspoken declaration that my anger will not be caged. By the time I reach the office doors, my pulse is a drumbeat in my ears. I shove them open with a force that sends them crashing against the walls before they swing shut with an echoing thud.

Caomh looks up from his desk, surprise flickering across his sharp features before his usual calm settles over him like armor.

The black-paned window behind him frames the turbulent sea, and the room is shadowed by the dark clouds gathering on the horizon. He leans back slightly, golden eyes cool as they study me.

"Brother?" His voice is cautious, probing. I feel the faintest brush of his presence against my mind—a gentle knock, asking for entry.

"Don't," I growl, my tone sharper than steel. "Stay out of my head." He nods, his hands folding neatly on the desk. The golden waves of his hair fall over one eye, and for once, he doesn't push. He knows when to bide his time.

"What's happened?" he asks after a moment, his voice quieter. "Your sisters—are they all right?"

Are they? I'm not sure. I've left them to fend for themselves, walking away from Althea and Aella without a plan. Guilt gnaws at me. I've told myself I was protecting them by refusing our father's commands, but have I only made things worse?

"No, I am not fucking okay!" The words explode from me, filling the room like a clap of thunder. Caomh rises from his chair and leans against the edge of the desk, his posture relaxed but his eyes sharp, watching every flicker of emotion on my face. He doesn't speak, doesn't try to calm me, just waits.

"He promised me to Princess Ameliana," I spit, pacing the room like a restless predator. "He's tying our kingdom to Puinnsean. To *them*."

"And you're mad?" His tone is maddeningly even, as if we're discussing a strategy map instead of my life.

"Mad?" My voice rises. "He promised me to the kingdom that killed her! The ones who blinded Aella! How can I not be mad?" Caomh's shoulders rise and fall in a slow, deliberate sigh.

"Yes. But this is war."

"It's not war yet!" I snarl, slamming my hands onto the back of a chair. The impact reverberates through my arms. "He's allying with devils! What does that mean for the rest of the kingdoms? They won't trust us. They'll abandon us when we need them most." He sighs, his shoulders slumping slightly.

"What was the alternative, Jeyr? It was you or Althea, wasn't it? You can't tell me you'd sacrifice her happiness for your own." The air leaves my lungs as if he's struck me. No, I wouldn't. I couldn't. Althea is the light of our family, the only thing untouched by the shadows that have consumed it. I can't let her bear the burden that's meant for me.

"It's a bluff," I mutter, raking a hand through my hair. "He wouldn't do that to her."

"Maybe," Caomh says carefully. "But you know her. If she thought it would save the kingdom, she'd do it. She wouldn't hesitate." I clench my jaw, his words cutting deeper than I want to admit. He's right. I hate that he's right. My mind wars with itself, caught between rage and guilt.

The door creaks open behind me, and I turn sharply, ready to unleash my fury. Olivia stands in the doorway, her face pale but determined. Her tangled curls frame her face, her coat draped over her arm. Her chest rises and falls as if she's just run a mile. Despite her disheveled state, there's a calm authority in the way she stands. Her presence is magnetic, and the anger roaring in my chest falters for just a moment, quieted by her strange, soothing energy.

"The emotions in this room are not for you to control, Olivia," I snarl, my voice low and dangerous.

She flinches but holds her ground, her spine straight.

"Maybe not," she says evenly, her tone calm but firm. "But you have a house full of children, and it doesn't take an Empath to feel what's coming off you right now. You're scaring them." Her words hit like a dagger to the chest, sharp and precise. I hate how right she is. The anger simmering inside me ebbs slightly, though I refuse to let her see it.

"She's right," Caomh says, his voice steady. "Take her home. Get some air. You've taken responsibility for those children, Jeyr. Let's not terrify them on their first day here."

"I will go ride Thanos. Olivia knows how to care for herself," I spit, turning to head out the door.

My heart protests against my tone, but I can't be with her when I'm like this. When this undeniable attraction between us can go nowhere because there's a high chance I'm going to marry another woman in three months.

"Give me another command, Caomh. Send me somewhere else. I can't be here any longer," I say, my voice tight.

He shakes his head, pinching the bridge of his nose.

"I can't. I would, considering the circumstances, brother. But your father would find you. This is not something you can run from. I command you to stay here and protect the Empath. Three months, and then we will have to find another station. But for now, for your safety, you must remain here. Three months, okay?"

"She can look after herself. But yes, Commander, I will stay." Olivia's voice cuts through, sharp and cool.

"She is right here. I can protect myself. Don't bother commanding him with my company, Caomh." She doesn't use her powers to make me feel the stab of pain that comes with her words. She doesn't need to. I feel it under my skin. I grit my teeth, running a hand over my face as if to wipe this entire nightmare away. There's nowhere my heart will be safe—not here, not anywhere.

Olivia stands in the stables, her hands floating like whispers around the children's as they fumble with buckles and straps. She never intervenes, never rushes them, only catches the leather when it slips from their grasp. Her patience is maddening. It seeps into the air, soothing even the most restless of hearts. Mine, however, resists. It gnaws at the edge of my control, testing the frayed limits of my composure.

Three months. That's all I have. Three months to watch over a woman who has lodged herself too deeply into my thoughts. Three months to decide whether I will sacrifice myself by marrying a woman bred of poison or die trying not to. Her gaze flicks to mine, and I feel it under my skin—soft, probing, yet restrained. She doesn't take anything, nor does she give anything. She leaves me to stew in my own misery. The stable gates groan open, and Cecil leads Ness and Leannan onto the slate floor. Ness, with her towering frame and unbridled power, makes Leannan look like a pony. My grey mare nickers, her dappled coat catching the light as she trots toward me. Aella has given her to me as protection—her words, not mine. She is swift, sure-footed, and as stubborn as her previous rider. Aella, now tied to the skies, has abandoned the earthbound steed when she lost most of her vision.

Olivia circles around me, Ness and Kyzan her ever-present shadows. Before I can ponder how she manages to mount such a beast, Ness bows, her massive frame lowering with reverence. In one fluid motion, Olivia vaults onto her back, as though it is second nature. She turns, her face impassive but one brow quirked in question: Are you going to follow orders, Jeyr? I nod, mounting Leannan with less grace than I'd care to admit. I feel like a troll beside her. Olivia moves like the wind—subtle, commanding, and unyielding. Though she looks human, her essence carries the weight of something otherworldly.

Her head bobs, silent but firm, as she leads the way toward the cliff edge. The air is crisp, biting through the thick fabric of my coat. Olivia's scuffed leather jacket isn't nearly enough against the coastal winds, and I watch as she shivers under its chill.

Our horses descend the sandbank with cautious precision, their hooves crunching against the loose grains. When we reach the flat expanse of the coast, Olivia tilts her head back, letting the sun warm her face. She is a terracotta sunflower, her golden-red hair catching the light like a beacon. When she turns to me, there is mischief in her expression, a spark of defiance that sets her apart from anyone I've ever met. "Catch me if you can," she challenges, her grin sharp and reckless. I only have a second to process her words before she launches Ness into a gallop. She is a storm on the horizon, wild and untamed, clinging to the beast's thick mane with one hand. Her body moves with Ness as though she is born to ride her. She isn't just riding; she is flying. Leannan tosses her head, eager to chase. "Go on, then," I murmur, loosening the reins. My mare surges forward, her stride a rhythmic drumbeat against the sand. She is smaller, lighter, built for speed, but Ness's powerful legs devour the ground with unnerving ease.

Olivia glances back, her laughter caught by the wind. She stretches her arms wide, surrendering herself to the freedom of the moment. Her head tilts back, eyes closed, a picture of unrestrained joy. I can't look away. Her presence is magnetic, pulling me toward something I can't name. For a moment, the weight I carry slips away, replaced by the warmth she radiates. I don't realize how empty I've felt until she fills the void. Her voice breaks through my reverie. "What?" she asks, her laugh soft and melodic. "How do you do it?" My words feel heavy, out of place. "How do you feel everything—your own emotions, everyone else's—and still manage this? Still find a way to lift your head and... smile?" She shrugs, her answer maddeningly simple. "The heaviness never leaves. It clings like shadows. But there are moments—brief, fleeting—where the sun breaks through. You have to seize them, savor them before they're gone. Happiness is rare, freedom even rarer. You can't let them slip by unnoticed."

Her words are a balm and a wound. She believes them wholeheartedly, lives them as though they are scripture. "So wise despite your age, Hummingbird," I say, the nickname slipping out before I can stop it. She smiles, but it doesn't feel like victory. It feels... like truth. "Maybe. When you live through others' pain, you learn quickly. It's like reading a thousand lives, each one teaching you something new. Time doesn't matter when the lessons never stop."

"Maybe that's it," I murmur, more to myself than to her. I can't fathom what it's like to be her. The things she carries, the pain she absorbs—it's incomprehensible.

By the time we reach the dunes, the sun is dipping below the horizon. Olivia slides off Ness, her feet sinking into the sand. She wanders to a patch of grass nestled between the rolling hills, her gaze fixed on the horizon. I dismount, following her at a distance.

Something about her presence draws me in, but I don't dare get too close. She is a storm I can't weather, a fire I can't touch without burning. She stiffens, as though sensing my thoughts. Her head turns slightly, her eyes meeting mine, and for a moment, I feel laid bare. The emptiness I think I carry alone now feels shared. And in that shared silence, I wonder who is truly carrying whom.

Olivia

A Friendship Forged in Fractures

J eyr is giving me whiplash. In the short time I've known him, it's a constant push and pull, sweet and sour. *"The emotions in this room are not for you to control, Olivia."*

"Let me see those eyes."

"She can look after herself."

"Beautiful. Your eyes are like evergreen forests... outshining my expectations."

It's maddening the way he opens and closes himself to me like a clam in the ocean, yearning for my waves one moment and retreating the next. He makes me feel unsteady, my footing unsure. I pride myself on my ability to understand emotions, but with him, I'm adrift. His emotions are an unfinished sentence, a pen hovering over paper but never writing.

I can't do it anymore. This limbo of hot and cold is unbearable, a constant war of closeness and distance. Without a word, I rise, brushing the sand from my pants and turning toward the dunes. Even if the time between knowing and unknowing is short, it feels like I'm tethered, yearning to an unknown ending and a possible beginning.

"Where are you going?" His voice calls out behind me, sharp with confusion. "Why does it matter?" I say, glancing back at him. "You don't care, Jeyr. And you shouldn't. It's clear you don't even like me."

"What?" He's on his feet now, his boots crunching against the sand as he steps closer. His brow furrows, his mouth opening and closing like he can't decide what to say.

"I'm not stupid," I continue, crossing my arms over my chest. "One moment you're kind, saying things that make me think... I don't know what. Then the next, you act like I'm just an inconvenience, something you've been forced to endure. It's exhausting, Jeyr, and I don't have the energy to keep wondering what I did wrong."

"You didn't do anything wrong." His voice is soft, almost a whisper.

I shake my head, bitterness lacing my words. "Then why do you act like you hate being here? Like protecting me is some punishment you're trying to escape?"

"I don't hate being here," he says, stepping closer. "It's just..." He sighs, running a hand through his hair. "My life isn't here, Olivia. My life is on the battlefield, with my brothers. This—" He gestures to the coastline, the waves crashing behind me. "This isn't me."

"That's not an answer," I say, my voice trembling.

He takes another step closer, his fingers brushing against my wrist. "It's the only one I have," he admits.

"Don't touch me," I whisper, though I don't move away.

His hand drops instantly, guilt flashing across his face. "Olivia, I do like you."

"Don't," I snap, cutting him off. "Don't say that if you don't mean it."

"I do mean it," he says firmly, his eyes searching mine. "But I can't... This can't... I can't be what you might need me to be."

I laugh bitterly, the sound sharp and hollow. "Don't flatter yourself, Jeyr. I don't need anything from you."

His hand reaches out again, this time cupping my cheek with a gentleness that makes my heart ache. "You're wrong," he says softly. "I see you, Olivia. I see how much you feel, how much you carry. And I admire you for it."

I blink, unsure if it's the wind or his words that have stolen my breath.

"I want to be here for you," he continues, his forehead nearly touching mine. "But I can only give you friendship. That's all I can offer."

His words slice through me, sharp and deliberate. *Friendship.* Of course.

"Fine," I say, stepping back, breaking the delicate web of tension that has woven itself around us. "Friends, then."

He frowns, his hand dropping to his side. "Olivia..."

"No," I interrupt, my voice steadier than I feel. "I get it. You're doing your duty. And I appreciate it. But don't act like this is more than it is."

He nods, a muscle in his jaw tightening as if he wants to say more but can't.

Without another word, I turn and walk toward Ness, the cool wind biting at my cheeks. My chest feels heavy, like a storm cloud threatening to burst. But I won't let it. Not here.

Not now.

Jeyr stays where he is, his figure silhouetted against the setting sun, his emotions as closed off as ever.

Olivia

SHADOWS AT DUSK, LIGHT AT DAWN

I enter the Black Forest alone, the cool wind brushing against my cheeks as I try to focus on the task at hand. Jeyr's lingering presence still gnaws at my thoughts—his whispered words, his fleeting touches, his indecipherable emotions. Friends. The word sits bitterly in my chest, but I shake it off, urging Ness forward. A hunt will clear my mind, ground me. Ness hums beneath me, the low vibration of her movements soothing the chaotic energy swirling inside me.

As we approach the forest's dense edge, I halt her. Taking a deep breath, I loosen the threads of my power, sending them out like fishing lines, hoping one will catch. My mental walls snap into place as I shield myself from detection. The ribbons of my energy drift through the shadowy trees, searching. There—a taut line. I feel it: the calm, alert emotion of a creature nearby. Sliding off Ness, I follow the string with silent, practiced steps. Behind me, I feel Kyzan and Ness waiting, their presence steady and watchful.

The elk comes into view, its antlers a crown of bone against the elderberry tree it grazes upon. I slow my breath, nock an arrow, and take aim. The threads of its emotion tether me, guiding the arrow's path. The twang of the string breaks the silence, and I feel the elk's panic bloom, sharp and overwhelming. I reel back, throwing up my shield to block out the wave of pain that follows. By the time I reach the fallen creature, the panic has dulled to resignation. I kneel beside it, pressing my hand against its side. My power reaches out, carrying the elk's fading spirit to a place of tranquility. I conjure the sound of gentle waves and the golden light of the morning sun, letting peace settle over its final moments.

Its last breath escapes in a soft whisper, and I sigh, the weight of its passing leaving my chest. Kyzan nuzzles my cheek, his soft coat brushing against me like a warm blanket. He sits beside me, his golden eyes locked on the elk with thinly veiled hunger. "Help me get it onto Ness's back, and I'll make sure you get your share," I murmur. With a happy rumble, Kyzan leaps to his feet, gripping the elk's thick neck in his powerful jaws. Together, we heave the creature onto Ness, who waits patiently on the ground. Once secured, I swing onto Ness's back, adjusting my seat as she rises with fluid grace. With a nudge of my thighs, we move deeper into the forest.

I let my power stretch out again, a silent sentry. The ribbons weave between the trees, brushing against the emotions of the forest's inhabitants. Suddenly, a line snaps taut, sharp and jarring. A sinister energy simmers in the darkness, its presence suffocating. My heart stutters as I yank the ribbons back, reinforcing the walls around my mind. Ness responds to my silent command, her stride quickening as Kyzan keeps pace beside her. I don't look back. Whatever lurks in the shadows of the forest isn't something I'm ready to face.

The picket gates of the cottage come into view, and I exhale in relief. Cooper, Mary, and Hecate stand waiting, their faces lighting up as they see the elk slung across Ness's back. "Well done, Kid," Cooper says, squeezing my shoulder and planting a kiss on my cheek. His rare smile is enough to make my own lips twitch upward. His joy is palpable, warming me in a way no fire ever could. Together, we unload the elk. Ness lays down with practiced ease, and each of us takes a portion, carrying it to the storeroom. Hecate wastes no time, setting to work with her sharp knives and deft hands. "You've outdone yourself this time," she says, handing me a slice of fresh bread and butter as she works. "This will nearly see us through winter... though I suppose we have one more mouth to feed."

Her maroon eyes flick to Kyzan, who has stationed himself by my side, his head resting on my knee. His golden eyes look up at me with pure devotion, and I can't help but laugh. "He's worth it," I say, scratching behind his ears. "He's waiting for you to eat first," Hecate says, a wry smile tugging at her lips. I frown. "What?"

"He sees you as his Alpha. He won't eat until you do." Amused, I take a steak from the butcher's block and sear its edges over the stove. Once it's cooked, I bite into the tender meat, humming in satisfaction. "Eat, Kyzan," I command.

With a joyful yip, he devours his portion in seconds, then returns to his spot at my side, resting his head on my lap. Hecate chuckles as she continues her work, her hands steady and precise. Every cut is deliberate, every piece of the elk utilized. The pelt is already with Cooper, the bones are being prepared for broth, and the meat is either preserved or readied for drying. As I clean the kitchen, Hecate claims a stool and begins carving the elk's horns into daggers. The maroon glow in her eyes as she works is mesmerizing. These quiet moments with her are my favorite—unspoken appreciation lingering between us like a soft hum. There's something sacred about days like this, when life feels steady and simple. The chaos of the outside world fades, leaving only the rhythm of work, the warmth of family, and the quiet hum of contentment. For now, it's enough.

Every fiber of my being aches—physically, mentally, emotionally. The weight of the day presses down on me as I sink into the small mattress, its lumps and creaks an afterthought against the overwhelming tide of exhaustion pulling me under. My eyes flutter closed, surrendering to the veil of sleep. The emotions from the day swirl like shadows at twilight, heavy and consuming, before they dissolve into the quiet void beneath me.

The darkness comes swiftly. It chases me, relentless and cold, pressing in from all sides. My steps quicken as my breath turns shallow, each gasp laced with rising panic. I turn frantically, my voice breaking in a desperate plea. "Kyzan?" Silence. "Ness?" The name slips from my lips as a whimper, barely audible against the sinister chuckling that fills the air. It surrounds me, oppressive and vile. The shadows creep closer. My legs move faster, stumbling over unseen roots and jagged rocks. The chuckling grows louder, a mocking serenade to my desperation. I reach back instinctively, fingers brushing my quiver—only to find it empty. My chest constricts. No weapon. No defense. The malevolence clings to me, a suffocating weight. Hands—cold and unyielding—grab at my arms, my shoulders, my waist. I scream, raw and primal, the sound tearing through the void as I thrash against their grip.

"Hummingbird, wake up." Jeyr's voice cuts through the chaos like sunlight breaking through dense fog. It's rich and steady, velvet-wrapped steel, pulling me back from the brink. "It's a dream. It's not real." My eyes shoot open, wild and wet with tears. The room comes into focus: the wooden beams of my ceiling, the soft glow of moonlight spilling through the curtains.

Kyzan's golden eyes glint with concern, his body pressed protectively against my side.

Jeyr's face hovers above mine, his brow furrowed with worry. His hand brushes away the tears staining my cheeks, but the fear lingers. It's not just a dream. It's real—or at least, it feels real. The darkness from the forest, the weight of its sinister presence, has been there. I've felt it. I've ignored it.

I shake my head, trying to dislodge the gnawing terror. More tears spill, warm and unwelcome against the coolness of his palm. "Hey," he murmurs, his voice softer now, a balm against my frayed nerves. "It's okay. You're safe." Before I can protest, he shifts onto the narrow cot, his larger frame making it creak in protest. He guides me gently against his chest, his arms wrapping around me with an ease that feels both foreign and comforting. His hand begins tracing slow, soothing patterns along my back. Each stroke seems to unravel the tension in my muscles, grounding me. His heartbeat thrums against my ear, steady and sure, anchoring me to the present. "Sleep, Hummingbird," he whispers, his breath warm against my temple. "I'll keep the bad dreams away."

His words settle over me like a shield, a promise I somehow believe. As his hand continues its rhythmic motion, I feel the darkness ebb, retreating into the far corners of my mind. The torrent of emotions stills, leaving only the gentle cadence of his touch and the soft rumble of his breath. My body melts into his, the terror slipping away like shadows at dawn. In his embrace, I find quiet. Peace. And as his warmth wraps around me, I drift back into sleep—this time dreamless. This time safe.

THREADS OF LOYALTY, SHADOWS OF DOUBT

I left before the first rays of sunlight could catch on the freckled curve of her cheek, before the pull of her presence could snare me further. I let my guard down, something I couldn't afford to do. Not then, not ever. Jet was already at her side, his calm energy a balm to her restless sleep. He didn't need my interference. And yet, I stayed long enough to feel the tremors of her dream—her panic pulling me in like a riptide. I hadn't planned on holding her, hadn't planned on falling asleep with her in my arms. But Empaths don't just feel; they radiate. She surrounded me in a cocoon of peace, and for the first time in what felt like centuries, I rested.

Now, as I stride through the manor, the chill of the early morning air settles into the hollows she leaves behind. Her warmth is gone, leaving me hollowed out in a way I hate to admit. Dangerous, I remind myself. Her power is dangerous. She strips away my defenses without even trying. The weight of that realization lingers with every step I take toward Caomh's study.

The sunlight streaming through the tall glass windows does little to warm the chill clinging to my skin. Caomh stands by the window, his back to me, his stance as unyielding as the cliffs outside. I step into the room, letting the heavy door close behind me with a quiet thud. The study is familiar, its shelves lined with volumes that hold the secrets of our kind, of our Courts, of betrayals and truths too dangerous for most to know. I sink into the leather chair opposite his desk, watching as he rolls his sleeves up, movements slow and deliberate. "I've lost contact with Gwynn," he says, his voice low and measured, but there's no mistaking the gravity of his words.

The air in the room seems to still, pressing in on my chest. My pulse quickens. "Does Jet know?"

Caomh shakes his head, his golden features shadowed by something deeper than fatigue. "Not yet. His wedding band is still intact. She's alive, but... she's missing."

A bitter curse slips from my lips. My hands grip the armrests of the chair as the implications settle over me. Gwynn is more than Jet's wife; she's one of us, a cornerstone of our brotherhood. She fights alongside us, bleeds alongside us. Losing her isn't an option. "This hasn't happened before," Caomh continues, his words strained. "I've always been able to reach her. Always. But now? Nothing. Just silence. Jet hasn't said anything yet, but he'll know soon enough."

I lean forward, elbows on my knees, head bowed. My thoughts race, but one thing is clear: I can't sit idly by. "I'll go," I say, the words heavy with resolve. "I'll send word to Bane, requesting to meet his daughter before the marriage. While I'm there, I'll find her."

Caomh's gaze snaps to mine, sharp and assessing. "You're playing with fire, Jeyr."

I let out a bitter laugh. "When aren't we, brother?"

His silence is an agreement of sorts. We both know the risks. My heart rebels at the thought of allying with Puinnsean, at tying myself to their kingdom through marriage. But Gwynn's life is worth it. My sister's safety is worth it. I'll do what needs to be done, even if it means tearing myself apart in the process. "There's no need for that yet," Caomh says, his voice quieter now, though the weight of his words remains. "But if we can't make contact soon, we might need to consider it. And we need to be prepared for the possibility that she's turned."

My head snaps up, anger flaring in my chest. "Gwynn would never. She's risked everything for us, given up her life for this mission. She's loyal to us—to Jet."

Caomh doesn't flinch, but his expression hardens. "Fifty years, Jeyr. A lot can change in fifty years. And you know it."

I stand abruptly, pacing the room as I try to shake off the unease clawing at me. The image of Olivia comes unbidden to my mind—her soft, steady breathing, the way her presence smooths the jagged edges of my thoughts. I clench my fists, banishing the memory. "Don't get distracted," Caomh says, his tone sharp. "There's no room for weakness here. We both know how this ends. None of us get out clean. None of us get a happily ever after."

I scoff, the bitterness in his words echoing the truth I hate to admit. "I know. Trust me,

I know."

He doesn't press further. He doesn't need to. We both carry the weight of too many choices, too many sacrifices. And as I leave the study, his words follow me, heavier than the silence that fills the halls of the manor. I don't look back. I can't.

Olivia

ECHOES OF COMFORT, SHADOWS OF LONGING

I wake to find the room empty, the warmth from the previous night gone, replaced by a chill that settles in my bones. The faint light of dawn creeps through the narrow window, casting pale streaks on the uneven walls. Rain lashes against the glass, its rhythm somehow amplifying the quiet ache in my chest. I rub at my arms, trying to chase away the lingering cold, both inside and out. The fire in the hearth has long since died. I kneel to relight it, the spark catching with ease. As the flames grow, the shadows they cast dance along the walls, flickering like the emotions still tumbling through me.

I set a blank canvas by the window, the rain outside whispering for me to join in its sadness. With trembling hands, I lift the brush. The strokes come slowly at first, the weight of my thoughts bleeding into each line, each color. I paint the heavy press of loneliness, the faint glow of fleeting joy. The canvas bears my truths, truths I'm not ready to speak aloud.

The day passes in a haze of quiet moments. Dinner with Mary, Cooper, and Hecate is a welcome distraction, their laughter like threads weaving the frayed edges of my emotions back together. Cooper's jokes are as terrible as ever, but the way he laughs at himself makes it impossible not to join in. "Like that one, Ky?" I ask, glancing down at Kyzan, whose unimpressed grumble sends us all into fits of laughter.

Mary shares her stories from the village, her voice lighting up as she speaks of the blankets she's given to those in need. Hecate chimes in with her runaway chicken tale, her rare laughter filling the space like sunlight breaking through clouds.

For a while, it feels like the world outside our little home doesn't exist. There's no lurking darkness, no heavy weight of what lies beyond the Black Forest. After dinner, we play music by the fire, the melodies weaving through the room like magic. Mary's hands dance over the old piano keys while I follow with my violin, the improvised harmony soothing every corner of my soul. The music holds us, suspended in a moment that feels like it belongs to another life, a simpler one.

When the night grows late, I retreat to my room, feeling lighter than I have in days. But as I step into the doorway, I freeze. Someone is there.

My eyes flick to Kyzan. He is calm, his golden gaze steady on mine. His lack of reaction tells me all I need to know. Whoever is here isn't a threat. "It's just me."

The voice, rich and warm, melts the tension in my shoulders. Jethro sits on the small wooden stool by the window, his broad frame somehow making the space feel even smaller. His mismatched eyes catch the faint glow of the fire, their depths revealing more than his guarded expression. I step fully into the room, closing the door behind me. "What are you doing here?"

He stands, closing the space between us with measured steps. The weight of his presence presses against my senses, but there's no malice, only a gentle concern. "You didn't show up for training. I was worried. But then I heard you with your family, laughing, playing music. I knew you were fine. Still, I wanted to make sure."

I tilt my head, a small smile tugging at my lips despite myself. His worry bleeds into the room like indigo ribbons, soft and quiet but unmistakable. "I just needed time to recharge," I admit, my voice soft. "When the emotions build up, I need space to sort through them. I don't want to burden anyone."

A tear slips free, unbidden and unwelcome. Before I can brush it away, his hand is there, catching it with a tenderness that leaves me breathless. His palm cups my cheek, warm and steady as his thumb strokes gently along my skin. "You don't burden me, Little Huntress," he murmurs, his voice a quiet promise.

I shake my head, pulling back from his touch, even as a part of me screams to stay. "You should go," I whisper, my words a shield I don't want to hold.

His brow furrows, his expression a mixture of confusion and hurt. "Do you want me to leave?"

Do I? My body says no, every part of me longing for the comfort he offers. But my mind is louder, reminding me of the fleeting nature of moments like this, of the walls he'll likely rebuild as soon as he steps away. "I don't know," I admit, the vulnerability in my voice making me wince.

Jethro hesitates, then sits on the edge of the bed. His presence fills the space, his long legs folding awkwardly over the side. "I don't want to leave if you don't want me to."

I sit beside him, our shoulders brushing. The contact sends a shiver down my spine, but I force myself to focus on the warmth it brings. "Did Jeyr send you?" I ask, hating the way my voice wavers.

He shakes his head. "No. He's dealing with other matters."

His words feel like a small blade, sharp and precise. Of course, it isn't Jeyr. My foolish hope withers, leaving behind the bitter sting of disappointment. I force a smile, hiding the ache behind practiced ease. "Thank you for checking on me, Jethro," I say, leaning my head against his shoulder. His warmth is a comfort I don't want to lose, even if it isn't the one I long for.

"Call me Jet, Little Huntress," he says with a soft chuckle, his voice brushing against the edges of my soul.

I close my eyes, letting the sound of his laughter settle the unrest within me. Maybe this is enough—having a friend who cares, who listens. Maybe, for now, it has to be.

THE WEIGHT OF LAUGHTER, THE STING OF DESIRE

I lean against the doorway, arms crossed, watching Olivia and Caomh spar with words and laughter. My teeth grind together as jealousy curdles in my chest. They're lost in their own world, as if no one else exists. It's like watching two actors rehearsing for the stage, their movements fluid, their expressions shifting. Caomh's face displays more emotions than I ever thought him capable of.

"So, what does this training involve?" I cut in, my voice sharper than I intend. Caomh glances at me, his lips twitching as if fighting back a grin.

"I'm teaching her to manipulate my emotions," he says breezily. "Jethro's been wanting her to use her powers in combat to gain an upper hand, but she's been... reluctant. So, I'm encouraging her, using my own gifts to resist."

My brow arches, the bite of his words lingering. I don't trust Caomh's idea of encouragement, not where Olivia is concerned.

"Don't talk about me like I'm not here," Olivia interrupts, her tone sharp, though her lips curl into a faint smile. "For the record, I'm making him feel giddy."

Caomh's shoulders shake, his composure slipping. "*Giddy*" is an understatement. He chokes on a laugh, his face a picture of barely restrained mirth.

"Cao, you look like the cat that ate the cream," I say dryly, though amusement tugs at my own lips.

Whatever Olivia does next snaps his restraint entirely. Caomh doubles over, clutching his stomach as he lets out a string of uncontrollable laughter. His gasps for air fill the room, his pleas fragmented between hysterical chuckles.

"S-stop! Please!"

I straighten, alarm flaring as he crumples to the floor. But then Olivia's giggles join his, light and melodic, wrapping around the room like sunlight breaking through clouds. I don't want to laugh, but gods, I can't help it. Her laughter is contagious, pulling me under until my chest burns and tears stream down my face. My ribs ache, my lungs feel like they might burst, but I don't care. It's chaos—blissful, torturous chaos.

"Liv! Gods, make it stop!" Caomh wheezes, his tear-streaked face flushed crimson.

His wide, helpless grin only makes me laugh harder. I can't remember the last time we laughed like this. Perhaps we never have, not like this—so free, so alive—even if it's a lie by the powers of an Empath.

"Okay, okay," Olivia gasps, clutching her side as she tries to steady her breath.

"Let me... focus."

With a soft exhale, the madness dissipates. A wave of calm washes over us, leaving the three of us sprawled on the floor like battle-worn soldiers. We wipe at the stray tears, lingering chuckles bubbling up as we catch each other's disheveled appearances.

"Well," Caomh finally says, his voice hoarse, "that's one way to disarm an opponent. I couldn't even think to get into your mind. We'll have to keep testing that... see if I can overpower you next time."

Olivia's smile is sharp, triumphant. "Call me anytime you need another dose of laughter medicine."

She tilts her head, a wicked glint in her eye. "And I told you, Commander, I could overpower you." Pride radiates from her like a beacon. Caomh smirks, leaning back on his elbows as he catches his breath.

"For now, Princess. You caught me off guard. Next time, I'll be ready."

She leans back, gazing at the ceiling with a dreamy smile. My eyes trace the soft curve of her lips, the gentle rise and fall of her chest. She glows, utterly radiant. My mind betrays me, conjuring an image of her like this after a round in the bedroom, her body alight with satisfaction. The thought hits me like a punch to the gut. I clench my jaw and close my eyes, trying to force it away.

When I open them again, I find her watching me. Just one green eye, piercing and knowing, meets mine. I feel her power tug at me, a warm thread weaving through the chill that settles in my chest. She doesn't speak, but her gaze says everything. I glance at Caomh, half expecting his usual teasing smirk. Instead, he's watching me with an expression I never thought I'd see: sadness. "I wish it could be different, Jeyr. You know that, right?" Caomh's voice fills my mind. But it's not. Is all I can reply.

Olivia

SHATTERING THE SHIELD, BREAKING THE SILENCE

The golden leaves of autumn cascade to the earth like a slow sigh, marking the rhythm of my days as they fall. Training becomes routine, though "routine" feels like the wrong word for it. Each day is a new dance, a new challenge, with Caomh and Jet leading me through drills that test every facet of my strength and control. And Jeyr—always watching, always hovering on the edges like a shadow. His polite smiles haunt me, the half-hearted tug of his lips both infuriating and magnetic. They stir something in me that is maddeningly undefined—a cocktail of longing, frustration, and something deeper I can't name.

The children join us often, their laughter ringing across the manor's grounds as they clutch wooden swords and stumble through the motions. The girls are particularly tenacious, and watching them reminds me of the strength hidden in small bodies.

One warm afternoon, the golden light filters through the bare branches, casting dappled patterns on the grassy field where we train. Jet stands at the front of the ranks, commanding the children with the authority of a seasoned general. "Cecil, arm up! Strong, now none of that noodle nonsense!" he barks. His voice carries easily, drawing a reluctant chuckle from me as Cecil stiffens, lifting his sword like it weighs a thousand pounds. "Next stance!" Jet bellows, his tone softer but no less firm.

I walk the line of children, weaving between them as they shift into position. Jeyr moves alongside me, his quiet presence making the air hum in that strange way it always does when he is near. He stops at Maisy, who is wobbling precariously, her feet misaligned.

Jeyr crouches to her level, his voice low and gentle as he turns her foot into the correct position. "Keep your weight even, sweetheart. That's it, balance is key. You'll be ready to move wherever you need to." Maisy nods, her focus sharpening. When Jet calls the next move, she lunges with her wooden sword, her stance steady, her eyes blazing with determination. "There you go!" Jeyr says, grinning at her like she's just conquered the world. "Watch out, everyone—Maisy's ready to take on an army."

Her radiant smile is contagious, and for a moment, I forget myself. My stomach twists into a knot, warmth spreading across my face as I quickly turn away. The flush on my cheeks betrays me, and I hope Jeyr doesn't notice. Walking the line again, I let my powers unfurl, a soft ripple of confidence spreading through the children. Their movements steady, their bodies growing sure with every strike. Jet demonstrates the stances, and they mirror him with precision that belies their youth.

The air buzzes with focus, their determination sparking like embers in the autumn sunlight. But I can feel their energy beginning to wane, the weight of practice tugging at their small limbs. I catch Jeyr's eye and give a small nod. He relays the signal to Jet, who claps his hands together, his voice a booming announcement. "Break time! Inside, everyone!" The children cheer, their weapons clattering as they rush toward the house. Jet follows, herding them like an overworked shepherd, but not before shooting me a look of quiet amazement. "You're an asset to any army," Jet says, shaking his head with disbelief as he herds the children inside. His words linger like a soft warmth in my chest, but my thoughts are already elsewhere. My eyes drift to Jeyr, who stands still, his tall form casting a long shadow on the golden autumn grass. For a fleeting moment, he looks like he might speak, his lips parting slightly, but then his mask falls back into place. That polite, carefully neutral expression I have grown to hate. With a small nod, he motions for me to follow.

"Caomh has asked me to work with you today," he says, his tone clipped. "Jethro has other tasks." The words strike me as strange—almost apologetic. Jeyr rarely engages me unless prompted, his distance as much a defense as it is a rejection. Yet here he is, volunteering to train me. I don't know whether to feel wary or grateful.

We climb the stairs to the attic training room in silence, each creak of the wooden steps echoing louder than it should. The thick walls of this room hold memories of frustration and breakthroughs. It is my sanctuary and my battlefield. I need the insulation here to stop my powers from leaking into the rest of the manor. We learned our lesson after an incident last week. Caomh was trying to teach me to wield a physical weapon along with disarming my opponent emotionally. I grew frustrated with myself for not being able to do as Caomh instructed, and that projected to the children in the stables. Our training session was halted by the sound of the boys fighting.

"How about we work on anger? I have yet to feel you angry," Jeyr queries, an eyebrow raised at me.

My gut twists into a knot. Jeyr's face tightens, eyes dimming in concern. I admire his black and silver fighting leathers as his feet close the distance between us. His large, six-foot-plus figure looms over me. A feather-light touch lifts my gaze to his. His features search my own.

"What triggered you just then?" His voice holds a protective tone I've grown to love.

I want to look away from the apprehension in his gaze, but the emotion is unavoidable. It flows through his fingers to my core, shooting through my veins like ice. My eyes burn with tears threatening to surface. Pictures flash through my mind, memories of my mother and that dark cage. Reminders of how I felt so alone and out of control.

"Liv," Jeyr whispers in encouragement. The slight lift of an eyebrow on his strong features has the unspoken words written all over his face: "You know you can talk to me."

I sigh in resignation. I know I can. He isn't the problem, I am. I feel unable to talk about what happened to me all those years ago. Like my feelings, the words have been pushed so deep inside. I fear what will happen if I let them out.

"I was never allowed to feel anger. My mother made that very clear—never feel anger. It always had to be channeled elsewhere." Memories flood my thoughts, the musty smell of preserved meats swallowing the clean air, the heaviness of the room, the darkness. My heart begins to flutter, my stomach clenching at the threat of that room.

"How? How can you never get angry? It's a normal emotion for any being, whether human, Fae, animal, or monster." Jeyr's voice is soft, coaxing. His eyes draw the words out from my chest.

"She would lock me in the storeroom until I calmed down. I do know what anger feels like. But being locked in that room, sometimes for hours on end, anger became... numb. I suppose I was punished for feeling. I was never taught shielding, never taught how to control myself. I was punished for how my emotions pooled over others. Every time I became too much, I got locked up. So, the thought of getting angry... I can't..." My voice comes out hollow, as if those walls are closing in on me once more. I crave the ocean, I crave to get on Ness and run away from this conversation.

Jeyr stiffens. A low growl rumbles from deep in his chest, the primal sound awakening my nerves. Jeyr composes himself as I begin to shake. My power grapples with me as I put up a shield around myself, blocking the fear that threatens to radiate from me. It is becoming a muscle, tired from constant training, but I feel that muscle growing in strength each day.

"I can handle it, Liv. I can handle your anger. You need to feel it in order to know how to shield yourself from it. Come." Jeyr angles his head in a gesture to follow. We walk to the side of the room, and he tosses me a pair of leather gloves. As I put them on, he dons protective pads for his own hands. He holds them up, bracing himself for the impact.

"Hit left-right-left. With each hit, I want you to think about what annoys you. And punch at it. It's okay, I won't tell Caomh that he may be one of those things." Jeyr winks playfully before nudging my shoulder with the pad in encouragement.

I take in the tall male in front of me. He is built like a god, every muscle making his fighting leathers stretch taut across his frame. The softness in his face always makes my heart constrict. I nod, tunneling my focus on each hit. My focus is on the movement of my arm, to hit with the right amount of force or to angle my hand a certain way to keep it protected. I continue the left, right, left pattern over and over.

Not a single shred of anger leaves me.

Jeyr nudges me back, turning on his feet to make me keep up with him. I play along until I see the smirk. He quickens his pace, his Fae agility much quicker than the human half of me can keep up with

He appears behind me, nudging me from behind. I stumble forward but quickly regain enough equilibrium to spin and face him once more. As I prepare to throw my next punch, he moves again, quick as a flash.

"Come on, Liv. Come play." He winks, white fangs showing as his smile turns devilish—he is asking for trouble.

I let out a slow breath, forcing the numbness to take over. I move toward him, throwing punches to the pads that wait for them. Jeyr continues to shift, making me chase him around the room. I feel like an absolute idiot. I'm unsure how much time has passed; all I know is that I'm tired. Sweat pools down my brow, my cheeks flush red. I'm burning inside and out. Frustration wants to leak from my pores. My heavy breathing pushes air through my gritted teeth. Contain it.

"There has to be something that annoys you," Jeyr's taunts poke at my flushed skin.

"Right now, it would be you," I huff. Pleased with my reaction, Jeyr darts around me. He taps my shoulder before moving out of reach once more. I'm going to punch the smug smile right off that pretty face in a minute. We'll see who's angry then.

"What about Caomh's arrogance? Hmm?" His deep mocking voice dodges around me, motioning for me to throw another punch.

"That doesn't bother me." My flat voice battles against the momentum of my body as I throw hard, heavy punches at Jeyr, my feet shifting in an attempt to keep up.

"Then what makes you mad? What makes you mad, and then sad and then mad again. But you have never been able to fight it. Tell me, Liv!" Jeyr's taunting elevates, poking the dormant animal I've locked in a cage a long time ago. Turns out he hits the right nerve. I hit harder, breathing through the tightness in my throat. Anger builds like a chemical reaction from my stomach, bubbling and fizzing in my throat, just waiting for a little more reactant before it causes an explosion.

"What about your father? Where is he? Why isn't he here for you?" My blows increase, but Jeyr easily keeps up. I watch him as he keeps a keen eye on my features. The world seems to pause as I let the pads feel my pain. I use my emotions to power my strength, but I keep that wall up.

I let the smack of leather on leather distract me. Jeyr ducks and dives out of the way, making me chase him. I let out a small growl of frustration. I feel the rumble through fangs that grow with the storm inside me. My powers make the room's air taut. I can no longer channel the frustration into my fists—I am losing control. I slam the door, dissociating myself and letting a blanket of cold, suffocating numbness blanket the heat of my anger.

"Tell me about him. Why did he leave?" he presses, taking in shallow breaths to steady himself.

"No!" I punch harder, quicker. I don't miss how his muscles jolt as I gain strength.

"Why not? Was it because of you?" Jeyr's dance pushes me off the ledge. A hiss tears through my lips, like a volcano releasing the buildup of tension.

"I don't know! Maybe he couldn't handle a life without my mother once she passed. Maybe a mortal man couldn't handle having an Empath for a daughter. He packed his bags the day after she died, and I haven't seen him since. He sends money, but I haven't had a letter—only demands. That's the only way I know he's alive. That's all. I have written, and I have sent him artwork. At first, I sent him a letter every week. Then every two. Now once a month. I have sent him hundreds of letters, and not once has he said anything in reply!"

I let powerful punches fly with my words to the beat of a young girl's heart, a young girl I have pushed aside a long time ago.

"That's got to be upsetting," Jeyr prods. He moves again, watching my lip curl. My fangs are on display, and frustration pools over my features. I am fucking over this.

"It is what it is," I grunt. My braided hair whips against my skin as my punches become relentless.

"No, Olivia. You can be upset. He has missed out," Jeyr's harsh voice tries to fight my frustrations.

"He missed nothing," I hiss.

"Olivia," he repeats in a tone I can no longer ignore.

I pause; he rarely uses my name. I stop punching long enough to look at him. He is tense, he is angry. His throat bobs as he swallows his own rising emotions. I squeeze my eyes shut. I want to leave. I can't face this. I can see him struggling against my powers as they grapple with the emotions in the room. As if they can sense the tension, my ribbons of power bounce between the two of us, feeling the need to keep him safe while also needing to let me release. *This is impossible. There is no training me.*

"It's NOTHING Jeyr! Nothing! I am nothing to him! I am nothing!" I growl. The tension cuts, the wave of numb flows into a wave of anger and sadness, the air splitting like an old tap spurting hot and cold water.

Jeyr puts his mitts up, encouraging another punch. He isn't letting me go without a fight. He grits his teeth against the tethers of my powers, his glowing eyes the only other sign of my effect on him.

"Why? Why are you nothing, Olivia? Why do you feel like nothing to him, to yourself? Why?" His voice has grown soft, tender. It threatens to push between the hot and cold flashes that take over my body. Everything I am, the chemical reaction fizzles out. The volcano calms, the fire and flames and the storms all give up the fight. I punch, letting the rawness of my words hit him.

"Because my own goddamn father doesn't want to know me. My own mother would lock me in a stone room the moment I felt anything other than that gaping hole of nothing. They made me a person who is nothing. Am I undetected? Yes. Safe? Yes, but I am nothing. I have no friends. I have guardians but they don't know me, the real me, because I have had to hide my true self for so long. They get this watered-down side where I have to be a perfect emotionless woman." With each "nothing," I hit Jeyr with a force that could push over any man.

His leg muscles jolt at each hit. Each word burns my throat, their bitterness ripe from years of being preserved in the deep pits of my gut.

"They were wrong, Olivia. What they did to you was wrong. You don't deserve it. You didn't then and you don't deserve it now."

My punches halt.

I snatch the gloves off. Turning to face the window, I rear my arm back and let the gloves fly at my reflection. I watch as the window shakes, watch the girl in the image looking back at me fall to her knees through the trembling reflection. Sweat glistens on my skin, soaking through my burgundy singlet. My hair sticks to my face, putting wet whips across my skin. I am a mess.

I don't have to look to know that Jeyr is approaching me. His slow, tentative movements are like he is approaching a crazed circus animal. He simply sits beside me and lets me sob into my hands. I can feel that he is fighting the urge to reach out, to hold me. He can feel there is more that I need to bring to the surface before he can.

"I do deserve it. I am a dangerous person, Jeyr. When I was young, I didn't understand. You know those tantrums that all children have? Imagine if that child was an Empath. The house had to evacuate until my mother could lock me up. Even she couldn't settle me. I am a weapon. I was bred to be a weapon. Every time I feel anger that my father abandoned me, I remember that. My mother regretted having me the moment I was born. She thought having a baby with a human would water down the bloodline, make it easier to control me. She thought that I wouldn't have to live by the same rules as a pureblood. But something about having human blood made me feel emotions much stronger than a pure Empath would. And because of that, my own mother, a pure Empath, feared me because she couldn't control me. I deserve how I was treated. I deserve my father leaving me. So I cannot be mad, I will not be mad. I will not be the person my parents fear. Because don't you see, Jeyr? I am a burden. I am to be feared."

The words pool out of my chest, leaving me bare, raw. My final words come out as heavy sobs. Jeyr's arms envelop me. His head rests in the crook of my neck, his slow even breath soothing me. His hands work my sore muscles, his own power healing them. I close my eyes, letting his comfort pool over me.

"You are not a burden. You will never be one. I have felt nothing but bitterness for fifty years. The moment you crashed into my life, I felt like I'd seen the first light in what seemed to be an endless tunnel. It doesn't take Empath powers to know how you make others feel. Those children, the homeless people on the street, their worries gone for at least a night because of you. Then there is Jet. I have seen Jet smile for the first time in years, and don't get me started on how you made that control freak Caomh laugh hysterically."

Jeyr tightens his grip. I am silent, letting the words sink into my soul. He lets me melt into his embrace until I am ready to part. He leaves a kiss on my forehead and watches me leave the room, wolf in tow. With each step, I wonder how I could possibly be happy with just being friends with that male.

Jeyr

BOUND BY DUTY, TORN BY FATE

I feel her quiet desuetude as she leaves me, each step pulling her further away and leaving a void I can't name. The hollowness spreads, sinking deep into my chest as if it is my own burden. I can't help but wonder how many times her mother had deemed it necessary to lock her away, a small child left to fend off the shadows of her emotions. How many times has she been forced to self-soothe, shaping herself into this fragile yet unyielding woman? The thought churns my gut.

Even now, I can feel her heightened stress flooding through me like an unspoken cry for help. It is a buzz, an incessant hum that draws me to her. Watching her crumble twists something inside me, but I don't stop it. Not yet. I need to see what lies behind her walls, need to understand the full weight of what she carries. But as much as I want to pull her back, to keep her safe, I fear getting too close. If I do, she'll swallow me whole, and I'm not sure I'll ever find my way back.

Closing my eyes, I lean into the whirlwind of emotions that batter me. The pull to be at her center is suffocating. I tell myself I stay back for her, to give her the space she needs. But the truth is I'm a coward. The moment I let her in, the moment I let myself feel everything that ties us together, I know I'll never be able to let her go.

"You know eavesdropping is frowned upon, Brother." Caomh's voice cuts through the silence, his usual bite tugging at my focus. My eyes snap open, and I find him standing in the doorway, arms crossed over his bare chest. His golden eyes dance with mischief as if he's been waiting for the right moment to interject.

Jet emerges from the shadows, his frame tall and imposing, arms folded like a fortress. "Says the mind reader," he drawls, his tone laced with a challenge. "Touché," Caomh smirks, shrugging off the jab. He steps into the room and begins shadowboxing the air, his movements fluid and calculated. The arrogant tilt of his smile dares either of us to comment. This space is ours, a room that bears witness to years of pent-up frustrations, of words left unsaid. Here, we don't need our powers. It is fists and brute strength, a raw and honest way to bleed out whatever weighs us down.

"You look like you could use a round," Caomh says, his grin widening as he turns to me. "Unless you're too distracted by a certain someone?" I clench my fists, already knowing where this is headed. "Don't," I warn, my voice low and sharp. Jet's brow arches.

"Don't like sharing your female, Jeyr?" His words are like a needle, poking at the bruise I try to ignore.

"She isn't my female," I snap, the bitterness in my tone betraying me. The words taste wrong even as I say them. I hate how easily they come, how final they sound.

The ache in my stomach twists tighter, a reminder of everything I can't have. "Because you haven't made a move. Why?" Jet's voice cuts through the space like a blade, sharp and unrelenting. His tall frame angles toward me, arms crossed over his chest in defiance. His brows furrow, his expression filled with discontent and something deeper—a frustration born from understanding. I feel their eyes on me, both of them, assessing, weighing. Caomh, as usual, knows more than he lets on, his golden gaze flickering with unspoken truths. He understands most of what tethers me to this damned situation. But Jet? We haven't told Jet. We can't. Not when Puinnsean is involved. The very mention of that kingdom stirs a fire in him, a wrath that burns hotter than most. Jet may be a fighter by nature, but at his core, he is a lover. His soul has been tied to Puinnsean in ways even he can't handle, not anymore.

"You know damn well why, Jet." The lie rolls off my tongue, bitter and jagged. I don't give him the chance to respond. My fist flies before the words fully leave my lips, but Jet, ever quick, effortlessly ducks out of the way, his arms remaining crossed as though I'm not worth uncurling them for.

Caomh doesn't hesitate. He swings at my ribs, the force of his punch reverberating through me. The pain is grounding, sharp and welcoming in its clarity. But I recover too quickly, the ache barely lingering as I retaliate, my knuckles connecting with Caomh's cheek. His smirk twists slightly, but it doesn't fade. "You're a fool, Jeyr," Jet snaps, his voice laced with exasperation. "You know what she is to you, we all know it. Why ignore it? Why not make a move?"

His words hit harder than any punch. But Jet isn't done. I see the telltale shift in his stance before he swings, his frustration fueling his movements. I anticipate the blow, sidestepping with ease and landing a fist to his chin. His head snaps to the side, but when he turns back, his eyes flare with something primal.

Caomh stays quiet, but there's a flicker in his expression, a momentary crack in his usual calm. Then he strikes, two quick blows to my sides that leave me winded. My ribs crack under the force, and for a brief moment, the room tilts.

I welcome it, revel in the sharpness of the pain. It's a distraction, a reprieve from the swell inside me.

I spin on my heel, fist colliding with Jet's face. He staggers but recovers quickly, his hand instinctively moving up to guard against the next strike. I take advantage, landing another blow to his ribs. Jet chuckles, a low, humorless sound, and for a fleeting moment, I almost laugh with him. But what's the point? Jet has speed on me, and Caomh has the precision of a predator. I'm outmatched, and I don't care.

I want the pain. I need it. The coppery tang of blood fills my mouth, sharp and metallic. I need to forget. Forget the weight of the solstice looming over me, the ticking clock that seems to echo in every corner of my mind. My fate is a letter away, waiting for my decision.

My father's voice echoes in my mind, a low, demanding rumble. He wants power, wants Aimsir to rise above Puinnsean, to crush their alliance with the Great Kingdom without toppling the fragile balance of our world. And somehow, the answer to all of it is me.

I swing again, my knuckles grazing Jet's jaw as my mother's face flashes in my mind. Her lifeless body, the blood that stained the earth. I want vengeance just as much as my father. I want to see Puinnsean burn for what they've done. But wanting vengeance comes at a cost, and I know exactly what that cost is.

Olivia.

She can never be part of this picture. She can never be mine.

"My family would never allow it," I snarl, my voice low and biting. I swing, but Jet's hand catches my fist mid-air. His grip is firm, his larger hand completely encasing mine. His towering frame leans closer, his fiery gaze boring into me.

"You're full of it if you think that," Jet growls, his voice like gravel. "Your father would celebrate the fact you've found your Companach. He knows better than anyone what it means to deny it. Especially if he found out what she is. So don't you dare use that as your excuse, Jey. You don't see what you're doing to that girl!"

"All the more reason not to pursue this!" I snap back, wrenching my hand free. My chest tightens with every word. "She'd be a target with me at her side! I'm doing everything I can to keep her safe from this, Jet. I'm hiding what this is doing to me, too. Not everyone gets to fall in love and marry who they want!"

"Jeyr," Caomh warns, his voice sharp with authority.

But Jet ignores him, his fury rising to meet my own.

"Oh, you think being in love is a dream? I worry every goddamn day. I'm terrified to wake up and find this band blackened—the sign she's gone, that she died in the arms of the enemy I thought I saved her from! But would I change my decision? Would I wish I didn't get those six months with her before she left me? No! They're still the best six months of my life. And every time I see her, it all comes rushing back, like no time has passed. You two..." He points at me and Caomh, his voice breaking. "You two close your fucking minds off to any shred of joy. Your mothers would be ashamed of you."

He throws my arm back, forcing me to stumble and regain my footing. I clench my fists, but my chest heaves with the weight of his words. Jet rakes a hand through his hair, turning away from me to glare at the coastline, his back a fortress I can't breach. My eyes shut tightly, trying to suppress the tide rising inside me. Memories of our youth crash into me—two reckless boys with stars in our eyes, dreaming of finding the kind of love our parents had.

I watched Jet find his love. I stood by him as he grinned wider than I'd ever seen, saying "I do" with Gwynn's hand in his. He was right—he'd never been happier than he was in that first year with her. And he'd tried, gods he'd tried, to push me toward my own happiness. If I'd met Olivia then, maybe it would've been different. But that isn't our reality.

"I'm promised to another, Jet," I sigh, the words heavy and hollow.

"JEYR!" Caomh's voice cuts through the air like a whip. He'd warned me not to tell Jet. We'd argued about it endlessly, but he'd finally conceded. Gwynn is still missing, and none of our spies have seen her in months. She isn't a traitor, but something is wrong. And the letter sitting on Caomh's desk spells out my fate.

Jet's head snaps toward me, his tan skin pale, his eyes blazing.

"What do you mean, promised to another?" His growl reverberates through the room. In a flash, he's in front of me, his breath fizzling against my skin. His eyes search mine, flickering with fury and desperation.

"My father gave me an ultimatum, Jet."

Jet's gaze darts to Caomh, who runs a hand over his face in defeat. He turns back to me, his frown deepening, his shoulders rising with each shallow breath. "Explain," he demands.

I exhale sharply. "I have to marry the princess of Puinnsean, or I'll be sentenced for treason. And if I refuse, Althea will have to marry their prince instead. I meet with the princess next month to finalize the contracts. Puinnsean will ally with Aimsir, and the people will be spared. Our kingdom will become a no-touch zone if—when—the war breaks."

The blood drains from Jet's face. He shakes his head, staring at the sky as though searching for an answer. "No. No, there has to be another way. I'm not losing someone else to that kingdom."

My heart clenches. "Jet... there's more."

"Jeyr!" Caomh's voice is pleading now, but I ignore him.

Jet's eyes dart between us, confusion giving way to dread. "What more? Jeyr? Caomh?"

I take a deep breath, steadying myself. "Gwynn is missing. It's been months since she last sent word. This marriage gives me a way in. I think I can get her out, for good."

Jet's knees buckle slightly, his fists trembling. Tears well in his eyes, his breath shallow. "No," he whispers, shaking his head. "She wouldn't want this. I knew something was wrong. I've been intercepting the messages. I know you've been trying to find her, but don't do this for me. Don't."

I open my mouth to argue, but he cuts me off. "And Olivia? You're going to put her through this? She won't understand, Jeyr. She doesn't know what a Companach is, but she knows something's there. Do you want her to find out after you've tied yourself to someone else? When she feels her soul scream at losing her mate to another?"

But Caomh steps forward, his voice low and steady.

"Olivia would become a target. She can't fight with her powers—not like her ancestors. She's strong, but she's not ready. Marrying her would put her in more danger than you can imagine."

Jet turns on him, his fists trembling.

"When will you realize we don't sacrifice our own?"

I squeeze my eyes shut, Jet's words ringing in my ears. But when I speak, my voice is hollow.

"Then love her for me, Jet. Protect her for me. Because I can't."

My knees threaten to buckle under the weight of Jet's words, my chest constricting as though the very air has turned against me. I want to hurl. Every fiber of my being screams for release, but I stay rooted, held captive by the unbearable truths hanging between us.

"It's that, or she feels him die, Jet," Caomh's voice cuts through, sharp and resolute. "They haven't secured the bond. There's no mark on their skin to stake a claim on each other. Jeyr is doing this for his kingdom, for Althea, who would have to marry the prince in his place. We've tried every scenario possible. There is no way around this."

Jet's growl reverberates through the room, his frustration pouring from him in waves. His knuckles whiten, his fists trembling with barely contained fury.

"There's always another way," he snarls, his voice shaking with conviction. "I refuse to believe the gods would grant you two such a bond, a once-in-a-lifetime connection, only for it to go to waste. Most of us never get that chance, Jeyr. Your father's the only man I've ever known to experience it. She feels you, Jeyr. Did you know that?"

I freeze, the weight of his words settling heavily on my shoulders.

"When you aren't even in the same place, she feels your emotions," Jet continues, his voice dropping to a pained whisper. "The day you met your father, she told me about an emotion that wasn't her own, lying beneath her surface. She couldn't place it. But I could. It was yours. Are you going to let her live with that for the rest of her life, unable to soothe it? Do you know what you're doing to her? To me? I'm going to lose not only you but her too."

I clench my teeth, fighting the inferno burning within me. Jet's words stab into me like shards of glass. He doesn't know I feel her too. Every damn day, her emotions mix with mine, a tether that only grows stronger the more I try to sever it. And when she wants me—gods, I know. The pull is unbearable.

"What do you suggest, then?" I grind out through clenched teeth. "It's marriage or death for me."

"Marriage to Olivia," Jet says without hesitation. "Show your father you already have someone—a Companach, an Empath who could protect your kingdom."

Caomh steps forward, his voice cool and level.

"Jet, that would put Olivia in danger. She can't even fight with her powers, not yet. She's strong, but making an attacker laugh themselves into submission won't work in a war. She's improving, but she's nothing like her ancestors. Whether it's her human blood or the trauma from her mother's upbringing, she can't stop a war. If anything, she'd paint a target on Aimsir's back. It's Jeyr's sacrifice, or hers."

Jet's jaw tightens, and his fist flies before I can stop him. His knuckles connect with Caomh's face with a sickening crack, sending him stumbling back. Caomh shakes it off, rubbing his jaw, but his golden eyes flare with restrained anger.

"When will you realize we don't sacrifice our own, Commander?" Jet spits, his voice trembling with rage.

"I'd sacrifice myself if I could!" Caomh shouts, his composure slipping. "You think I want to see my brother in this pain? I'm not making him do this, but do I think it's his only option? Yes. Because just like you, that Empath has made a mark on me, and I fucking hate it. This wasn't the plan. My plan was for her and Jeyr to bond, for them to become a powerful couple, to train her while we protected her. She was supposed to be the key to ending this war. But his father had other plans."

Caomh's words are a gut punch, but before I can react, Jet turns on me, his fury unrelenting.

"And you're just going to let this happen? You're going to leave her? To let her live like this, never understanding what's happening to her?"

I can't meet his eyes.

"When I go, I need you to protect her," I say quietly, my voice breaking. "Love her for me. Make her laugh that contagious laugh of hers. Don't let her sacrifice her emotions, her health, for everyone else. Please, Jet."

Jet unravels before me, his head shaking as he fights back tears. He walks to the window, his broad shoulders slumping under the weight of what I've just asked of him.

"I'm going to have to watch my friend go through what I do," he says, his voice barely above a whisper. "Every day, she's going to yearn for you, Jeyr, but in a way even I can't comprehend. She's an Empath and you're her soulmate. Once she's chosen her mate, whether you have her or not, she'll stay loyal to you until death. She doesn't understand now, but she will. And when she does, it'll destroy her."

He turns back to me, his black eyes blazing with anger and pain.

"Tell her, Jeyr. Tell her the truth. She deserves that much."

Olivia

A BED OF SOMEONE ELSE'S FEELINGS

I lay looking at my painted ceiling, tears streaming down my face for seemingly no reason. I'm in pain, the ache in my chest unforgiving. I don't know what triggered it. The session today was hard, but I walked home feeling lighter. Yet, in the darkness of my room, the tears won't stop falling. I feel like I've lost something, but I don't know what. I'm grieving, but over what? I want to dig at my skin where that emotion lies. It isn't my emotion. It isn't anyone in my home, but somehow, I can't block myself from it. I can't put it away in its locked box. It's there, tugging, pulling, searching for its home. A loud sob finally breaks from me.

I crave him. I crave that serenity he settles over me. The realization only makes me cry more.

I bury my head into my pillow to muffle my sobs. It's too much to bear.

"Shh, Hummingbird."

I freeze, taking in his scent, his voice, his touch... He takes me in his arms and cradles me against his chest. His hand cups the back of my neck, fingers threading through my hair as if he's scared I'll fade away.

"I'm sorry," he croaks.

"I don't know what's happening to me," I gasp between sobs. I turn into his warmth. His arms tighten around me, holding me together. His strong fingers massage me, distracting me from my tears.

"I'm here. I'm sorry." He says he's sorry like it's his fault, like he broke me. I shake my head against his chest, unable to form the words I want to say. I'm just a mess.

"Rest, Hummingbird. I'm not going anywhere tonight, I've got you."

Tonight? The word feels weighted, but so do I. I feel heavy, tired, weighed down by something I can't put into words. Jeyr holds me close to his chest, his lips in my hair, kissing it long and hard. I feel wetness touch my head. I look up to see tears falling. I reach up to wipe one away that escapes down his cheek. His emotions mirror mine, and I want to know what's running through his mind. But the word *tonight* rings through my head, and selfishness takes over.

If I only have one night, I'm going to take it. So instead, I tip my head back, brushing my lips over his. I watch as he closes his eyes, kissing me back with the same need for comfort. My thumbs wipe away his tears, and he mirrors the motion on my own cheeks. We sit in misery together. We're sad, heartbroken, but we aren't alone. Kissing him feels so natural. It isn't how I thought our first kiss would go, but somehow this is more than I could have imagined. Maybe that's why I'm heartbroken, for something tells me we can never be.

His hands search me with the same fervor. He has electricity on his fingertips as they come to my hips, lifting me so my chest is flush with his, my knees straddling his thighs. His calloused thumbs circle on the inside of my hip bones, riding up to hold the bare skin of my ribs, barely grazing the bottoms of my breasts. He groans, sending shivers through my body. Instinctively, my hips roll to feel the hard length below me. My hands pull at his top, wanting to feel his skin, needing to feel something else. One of his arms reaches behind his back to help me.

"May I?" He whispers against my lips, his voice thick with desire. I want that silent goodbye to be gone. I nod, and my shirt is lifted off. I'm immersed in how he takes in a hissing breath as he admires my naked breasts. His large hands reach up to cup them, lips finding my jaw, then my neck. Pleasure shoots through me, and I send it right back to him.

"Gods, Hummingbird, I feel it without your powers."

I look into his eyes. They're dark, haunted. I don't know how he feels it, but my skin buzzes in recognition, absorbing his words like how my bloodstream absorbs alcohol.

I roll my hips once again, craving more. His rumble of pleasure rattles me as he continues kissing me, worshipping every freckle, every inch of skin all the way to my breasts. His mouth claims one, his hand supporting its heaviness. I gasp, heat zapping through my veins. My body takes over, riding an invisible wave of pleasure.

His tongue flicks my nipple. I arch toward his mouth as the roughness of his britches rubs just the right spot between my thighs. The combination of the two sensations makes me forget all about the misery I felt before.

One hand holds the heaviness of my breast, while the other encourages the movement of my hips. His mouth worships me, each and every inch of me. The hand working my hip lowers so his thumb rotates in circles between my legs, causing electricity to run through me. I feel him everywhere, and the pure need for wanting more makes my inner walls pulsate, sending me crashing over an edge I never knew existed. My head falls into the crook of his neck as I muffle my cry of pleasure. My walls are wide open, and Jeyr feels everything as I do. His cry matches mine. Our heavy breathing fills the quiet room. He moves a hand to my back, holding me to him, naked chest to naked chest as our breaths synchronize.

I memorize the way his hand traces the bumps in my spine, the sides of my breasts as they rest on his chest, the ends of my hair.

"Beautiful. So gods-damn beautiful, Hummingbird," he groans, his body pulsating under me. He kisses the side of my forehead, wrapping his arms tight around me as he lays his head into the pillow. We stay completely wrapped around each other as he pulls the blanket over us.

I begin to slip into sleep, knowing I'll never be the same. I'll never love another, never be able to be touched by another. Heaviness claims me, but not until I hear his muffled cry into my hair.

"I am so sorry, my Hummingbird. I am so sorry."

I don't know why he's apologizing, nor do I want to. His emotions alone threaten to kill a part of me.

"Don't apologize. I wanted that, Jeyr. I wanted you, even if it was just for the night." The words are true, but it doesn't stop the pain. Jeyr holds me tighter, and I fall asleep holding onto that one moment, knowing it'll soon be gone forever.

I feel him leave at dawn. His lingering kiss is a manuscript of emotions pressed to my lips. Each word, each whispered breath, carries a truth I want to keep. But with the soft sound of the door closing behind him, I know it's over. The story we've written in the quiet hours of the night has come to an end.

I can't bring myself to train that day. Facing the empty space where he should've been feels like admitting it was real, that it happened and is already slipping away. Instead, I spend the day at the cottage, helping Hecate. She moves with her usual precision, but her glances toward me betray her concern. She feels my fractured emotions and holds back her questions, giving me the space I so desperately need. I'm grateful for it, even as the silence between us feels heavy.

By the next day, the weight in my chest hasn't lessened, but duty calls. It's Caomh's turn to train me, and I can't put it off any longer. Anxiety buzzes through me as I approach the manor. The great wooden door opens as I near, welcoming me into its vibrant walls. The sound of laughter and the patter of small feet fills the air, and I pause, taking it in. The manor feels alive, humming with the kind of energy it hadn't had when I first arrived.

I follow the laughter to the kitchen, where the girls are dancing and singing as they work. They knead bread and mix batter, their joy spilling out in giggles. Claudia and Lilly stand at the counter, peeling and cutting vegetables, their smiles as radiant as the morning sun.

"Lady Olivia, to what do we owe this pleasure?" Claudia calls over the lively noise, her tone teasing.

I smile, letting their happiness wash over me.

"Just checking in before I see Cao," I say lightly, though the truth is I'm procrastinating. Caomh's sessions are always a battle of my mind, and I'm not sure I'm ready for him to see how broken I feel.

"We're great, Liv!" Lilly chimes in. I look at her and marvel at the transformation. She no longer looks like the malnourished girl I knew from the orphanage. Her cheeks are full, her hair glows golden in the light, and she carries herself with a confidence that hadn't been there before.

"We trained with Jet yesterday!" Bethany chimes in, her face alight with excitement. "He showed us how to ride and use a bow! He said we'll be huntresses like you, Liv!"

Their enthusiasm is contagious, and I can't help but laugh softly.

"That's wonderful," I say, my chest warming at the sight of their joy. "Maybe tomorrow I'll come and help with the archery lessons."

Their squeals of excitement fill the room, and for a brief moment, the heaviness in my heart lifts. I soak up their happiness, holding onto it as a balm for the darker days I know lie ahead. With a final wave, I leave the kitchen, my heart a little lighter than before.

As I walk to the foyer, the butterflies in my stomach return. I know what's coming. Caomh's training isn't like Jet's or Jeyr's. His power isn't about physical combat; it's about unraveling the mind. He works to break down my mental walls, to teach me how to manipulate the shields I barely understand. He's impressed by my natural inclination for it, and I've often wondered if my mother's lessons planted the seed. But those are questions I'll never have answers to. They're lost, like her ashes scattered to the wind.

From the study, I feel his presence before I see him. His sharp, assessing gaze locks on me, and I feel the familiar scratch of his claws at the edges of my mind, seeking entry. Over time, our dynamic has shifted. Our verbal sparring softened into something more playful, more familiar. I no longer feel the constant need to guard myself around him, though his power always reminds me how easily he can dismantle me.

Caomh leans casually against the doorframe, his golden hair falling into his eyes as he studies me. "Don't keep me waiting, Princess," he drawls, a hint of a smirk tugging at his lips.

I sigh, bracing myself as I step into the room. Caomh's expression shifts as I enter, the smirk fading into something more thoughtful. His face often betrays little, a master at maintaining his mask of indifference. But I've learned to read the cracks in his facade. The small twitch of his lips, the way his eyes soften when he isn't on guard—those are the moments when the real Caomh slips through.

"Let's begin," he says, his tone firm but not unkind.

Caomh leans against his desk, arms crossed over his broad chest, his golden eyes sharp and amused as they settle on me. The unbuttoned top of his shirt and rolled sleeves reveal the hard lines of his muscled torso. He looks every bit the predator at play, the snide grin tugging at his lips, a weapon he wields far too well. His gaze slides over me—not leering, but assessing—like he's deciding whether to tease or taunt. For reasons I can't quite pin down, his scrutiny makes my cheeks warm.

I hear his voice in my mind, that smooth, sensual timbre threading through the part of me I always leave open for him. Despite the anxiety his powers bring me, there's an odd comfort in hearing him speak to me this way. Most of the time, at least.

There's one emotion I'm particularly intrigued by today, Princess.

A ripple of images flashes in the back of my mind—muscled torsos, carved from stone, glistening with sweat. My pulse quickens against my will. My cheeks burn. I swallow, trying to keep my composure, but the corner of Caomh's mouth curls higher as he carefully frames the images in my mind, like an artist perfecting a portrait.

Which one do you find most attractive? His voice is a hum, velvet and teasing.

I throw up my mental shields, slamming the door on the thought, but I know too late something slipped past my defenses. My attraction leaks out like smoke, a flickering sensation dancing over my skin, leaving gooseflesh in its wake. His laugh rolls through me, low and rich, and I curse under my breath. Gods help anyone who hears that sound in a bedroom. It's the kind of laugh that can make even the most guarded person weak.

Good shielding, Princess. But now I'm even more curious. Who is it?

The pressure of his presence presses down on me, testing the strength of my mental shields. It's a grueling exercise, like being strapped to a lie detector while trying to keep my heart from betraying me. My thoughts drift to last night, to the feel of Jeyr's chest beneath my hands. The memory flares, vivid and raw, before I shove it down and lock it away.

"I'm surprised you can shield so well, considering how little control you have over your powers," Caomh says aloud, his voice light but knowing. I grit my teeth, refusing to let him see how his words make me squirm.

Hold yourself together, Olivia.

"Use your feelings to your advantage if you can't shield and suppress them at the same time," he continues, his tone laced with amusement. He's enjoying this far too much.

The challenge sparks something in me. I smile, slow and deliberate. If he wants a show, I'll give him one.

The images in my mind shift. Instead of still figures, they move—working out in the attic, their muscles flexing and glistening with sweat. I let myself feel every ripple of desire, every flicker of heat, and then, when the tension reaches its peak, I push it outward. I send a wave of intense arousal into the room, wrapping it around Caomh like a silken noose.

His reaction is immediate. His golden eyes darken, his chest rising and falling with heavy breaths. A sheen of sweat breaks across his skin, and he grips the back of a winged chair for support. His arrogant grin falters, replaced by something raw and unguarded. I watch, fascinated, as hunger burns in his gaze.

"You're a quick study," he says finally, his voice rough. He clears his throat, trying to reclaim his composure, but the twitch in his jaw betrays him.

From the doorway, a low chuckle breaks the tension. I turn to find Jet and Jeyr leaning against the frame, their arms crossed. Jet's midnight eyes sparkle with mischief, while Jeyr's stormy blue gaze pins me in place. His stare is so intense, so consuming, it feels like his hands are trailing over my skin, mapping every inch of me.

The same emotion I used on Caomh stirs again, unbidden, and I let it slip. I watch as Jeyr's pupils dilate, his jaw tightening as he clenches his fists. His breath hitches, and for a moment, I think he might cross the room and drag me into his arms. Instead, he tears his gaze from mine, his fists tightening at his sides.

Jet laughs.

"Cheeky minx. You better be careful with that trick, Liv. You'll have men falling at your feet."

Caomh groans, running a hand through his disheveled hair.

"I need a drink," he mutters, turning toward his desk. "And I'm going into town tonight. I need a release."

I can't stop the laugh that bubbles up. The golden Fae shoots me a wry smile, his mask slipping for just a moment. In that brief flicker, I see the man behind the commander—the one who decided to go easy on me today, to give me this victory.

"Thank you, Caomh," I say sincerely. "For today."

His gaze softens, the weight of his knowledge pressing between us.

"Don't mention it, Princess," he says, his arrogance flickering back as he pours himself a drink.

As I turn to leave, my heart twists painfully. Jeyr hasn't said a word. He hasn't offered to walk me home. The ache in my chest deepens, but I swallow it down, forcing myself to move. Once again, the blue-eyed Fae has left me adrift, with no anchor in sight.

Olivia

DRAGGED DOWN BY NIGHTMARES

The air in the manor feels heavier as I enter the next day, the echoes of voices and footsteps muffled by the looming tension. Caomh is waiting for me just inside the foyer, his golden eyes sharp and unyielding as they flick toward me, assessing my every move.

Behind him, Jeyr's presence looms, a quiet shadow that seems to fill every inch of space. I don't look at him. Bitterness curls in my chest, sharp and unwelcome. I hate how much he affects me, how even his silence wraps around me like a chain.

Caomh inclines his head toward the study in invitation. His movement is casual, but his gaze holds weight—a quiet demand I can't ignore. Without a word, I follow, ignoring the heat of Jeyr's gaze boring into my back. I can feel him watching, can almost hear the soft scrape of his breath as he stays just far enough away to be untouchable. My chest tightens as I resist the urge to turn, to look for something in his expression that will only leave me more confused.

The study door clicks shut behind us, muffling the distant hum of activity in the manor. Caomh strides to his desk, leaning casually against its edge, his shirt unbuttoned at the collar and sleeves rolled up to reveal the strength in his forearms. His smirk is a blade, sharp and cutting as his golden eyes rake over me. It isn't predatory—it never is—but it's assessing, as if he's weighing my worth with every glance.

"Take a seat," he says, his tone as casual as his posture. But there's an edge beneath it, a coiled tension that mirrors the unease thrumming in my veins.

I sit, the chair's leather cool against my palms. Caomh studies me for a moment longer before he speaks, his voice slipping into my mind as easily as a whisper carried on the wind.

Today, I want you to lower your shields completely. Let me in as far as you're able. We're going to see how well you can resist when your own memories are used against you.

His words settle like stones in my stomach. I straighten my spine, masking my discomfort with a small smirk.

Kind of you to warn me, I reply, the teasing note in my voice deliberate. I need to keep him off-balance, even if only a little.

His lips curve into something sharper.

I'm far kinder than you think, Princess. Trust me—the things I don't do prove as much.

The venom in his words pricks at me, and I feel my smirk falter. I nod, pushing away the unease curling in my chest.

Fine. Go ahead.

Closing my eyes, I let my shields fall, opening the labyrinth of my mind to him. The space is vast, filled with doors of every shape and size, each one holding pieces of me I'm not sure I want him to see. His presence brushes against the edges of my consciousness, golden tendrils swirling as they explore the pathways. He pauses at a dark wooden door, his light knocking against its surface, asking permission.

I hesitate, then sigh and open it. Pine floods my senses, sharp and earthy, and the room around me seems to dissolve as the memory unfolds. I'm small again, standing over my first kill, then my second. Images flicker like turning pages of an art journal, each one more vivid than the last. The fear, the blood, the weight of life ending in my hands—it all comes rushing back.

Murderer.

The word echoes through my mind, Caomh's voice cutting through the memory like a blade.

Murderer.

The images speed up, the reel spinning faster and faster. Each kill replays in excruciating detail, each emotion sharpened to a painful edge. My chest tightens, my breaths shallow and uneven.

Murderer. You killed them all. Their blood is on your hands.

I look down, and red coats my hands, dripping onto the floor. The scent of blood fills my nose, thick and metallic. My knees buckle, and I wrap my arms around myself, desperate to hold the pain inside, to stop it from consuming me. But the images keep coming, faster and faster, until the weight of it all threatens to crush me.

Kyzan's growl breaks through the fog, low and steady, but it isn't enough to pull me back. The arrows of guilt and pain keep striking, each one sharper than the last. I can't stop the cycle. Fear, pain, death—it's a loop I can't escape.

Then, warmth. A hand cradles my face, grounding me. A voice, steady and familiar, cuts through the chaos.

"Liv, listen to my voice," Jeyr says, his breath warm against my skin. His thumb brushes away the tears I hadn't realized are falling. "It's not your pain, Liv. Whatever you're feeling—it's not yours."

The calm in his voice wraps around me, anchoring me. I focus on him, letting his presence pull me out of the swells of my nightmare. His hands guide me, steady and strong, as he whispers,

"Push it out. Make the walls feel it. Let it go."

I do as he says, pushing the voice from my mind and letting his warmth seep into the hollow spaces. The pain ebbs, replaced by a calm so complete it leaves me breathless.

When I open my eyes, Jeyr is there, his stormy gaze locked on mine. His hands frame my face, his thumbs brushing away the last remnants of my tears. He doesn't speak, doesn't look away, just holds me as if I might shatter if he lets go.

Behind me, Caomh slumps into his chair, his golden eyes dark and unreadable. His chest heaves with uneven breaths, sweat dampening his brow. Jethro, standing nearby, shifts closer, his large hand settling gently on my shoulder, grounding me further with his touch. His black eyes bore into me, steady and watchful, offering a quiet reassurance that I'm not alone.

"I vote she takes a break from working with you, Cao. I don't ever want to feel that again." Jethro's voice is rough, edged with protective anger, but his hand on my shoulder is gentle. He gives it a reassuring squeeze before stepping back, his quiet strength lingering in the space between us. Without another word, he moves to the chair across from Caomh, sinking into it with a heavy exhale.

"Hummingbird?" Jeyr's voice is close. Too close. The warmth of his breath skims my skin, sending an involuntary shiver through me. His hands cup my cheeks, his forehead pressing lightly to mine. I force my gaze to meet his, those stormy blue eyes searching my face, pulling at the rawness that still lingers in my chest. I want to collapse into him, to let him hold me together, but the weight of his proximity steals the air from my lungs.

"I'm here," I whisper, the words barely audible over the pounding in my ears. My throat feels raw, parched as though I've screamed myself hoarse. I want to speak more, but the words catch, tangled in the mess of emotions swirling inside me.

"Good girl. You did well to fight that. You're here, and that's what matters. I'm proud of you." His voice is soft, his tone coaxing, but guilt claws at me. I don't believe him—not when I know I didn't fight. Caomh took hold of my mind, and I was helpless. If it weren't for Jeyr, I'd still be trapped in the labyrinth of my own pain.

"Hummingbird," he murmurs again, his lips so close to mine they could brush against them if I move. "Let me see those eyes of yours."

I hesitate but let my eyes flutter open. His gaze softens, and a small, almost imperceptible smile curves his lips. It's that smile—the one from the alley, the one that makes my heart twist in ways I didn't know it could. I try to hold back the ache it stirs, but my traitorous body reacts anyway. That yearning unfurls in my chest, a bittersweet mixture of longing and sadness, because I know. I know this is all he will give me: fleeting touches, words spoken in the safety of the moment. And yet, I can't stop myself from soaking it in.

His thumb brushes against my cheekbone before he steps back. The absence of his touch is immediate and devastating, leaving me hollow and raw. Jeyr turns and walks toward the drink stand, his movements measured, deliberate. I stand frozen in the center of the room, my arms wrapping around my waist as if to hold myself together. The void left by his warmth threatens to consume me, but before it can, Jet moves.

From his chair, he opens his arms in silent invitation. Relief surges through me, and without hesitation, I cross the room. I sink onto his lap, curling against his chest like a child seeking solace. His strong arms wrap around me, and I tuck my head into the crook of his neck, breathing in his comforting scent of pine and smoke.

Jet's hand strokes slow circles on my back, each movement radiating calm and reassurance. But even as I lean into his comfort, I feel it: the sharp sting of disappointment. I risk a glance toward Jeyr, hoping foolishly that he might react, that he might show something, anything.

Nothing. He doesn't flinch, doesn't look at me, doesn't let any emotion slip past the mask he wears so well.

My chest tightens, the invisible dagger twisting deeper, but I force my eyes shut, willing the tears to stay hidden. Instead, I let Jet's steady presence ground me, his touch a soft balm over the raw edges of my soul.

For now, I let myself rest. In Jet's arms, I can pretend, if only for a moment, that the ache isn't there, that the weight of unspoken emotions doesn't pull me under. For now, I let myself forget.

Jeyr

The wine swirls in my glass, catching the dim light as if it's hoarding it. I bring the rim to my lips, letting the liquid drown my thoughts, my guilt, my shame. The memory of her frailty haunts me. That pale face, lips blue with the cold of despair—how close have I come to losing her? My fingers tighten around the glass, the smooth surface digging into my palm as I relive the echo of her pain reverberating through me.

She has been slipping away, her body betraying her, convincing itself it's under siege. And I feel it. Each imagined blow strikes me like a storm of blades, unrelenting, unbearable. Her suffering isn't hers alone. It consumes me too, clawing into the corners of my mind, my chest, until I can hardly breathe.

I should knock Caomh out. I should have stopped him the second her shields began to falter, the moment her lips turned blue. My jaw clenches at the thought. Caomh is a brother to me, but even brothers aren't immune to a well-placed fist when it comes to crossing lines.

Yet, in that moment, Olivia is my only focus. Bringing her back, anchoring her to reality—that's all that matters.

I watch her now, her cheeks finally regaining that soft, rose-colored hue as she sits across from me. The firelight dances over her face, painting her in golden hues that rival the sun. I hate how beautiful she is, how easily she pulls the air from my lungs just by existing. Jethro has replenished her light, flowing his calming power into her, filling the cracks her pain left behind. I should be grateful—no, I am grateful—but the bitterness in my chest won't relent.

She has him, a friend. And I? I can't be that for her. I don't know how to be just her friend when every glance, every moment near her, ignites something primal inside me. That single green-eyed look from across the table makes my heart stutter, my blood quicken. Her gaze can unmake me in a heartbeat.

Kyzan trots over, his golden eyes locking onto mine with an almost human understanding. He lays his head on my knee, the weight grounding me in a way I don't want to admit. His gaze flicks between me and Olivia, his quiet judgment pressing down like a physical force. "Don't you start, dog."

He huffs in response, a sound that carries far too much opinion for a wolf. As if he's saying, *And why isn't it you?*

I let out a slow breath, trying to drown the heat rising in my chest. But the sound of Kyzan's exhale already shifts something in Olivia. She straightens, the movement drawing my eyes back to her. She sculls the rest of her wine, her lips a soft pink from the drink. Then she leans over and places a kiss on Jethro's cheek.

I hate that I notice the way his smile brightens, hate how effortless their bond seems. But it's the way her eyes lock onto mine afterward that makes my chest tighten. Green, deep, and piercing—they catch me in a snare I never want to escape. "Want to walk me home?" she asks, her voice soft but steady. It's an offer, not a demand. Yet it feels like a lifeline thrown in my direction.

My chest tightens further, the protest of my heart drowning out the rational voice in my head, the one that urges me to come up with an excuse. But I can't. The words won't come. Instead, I nod and rise from the table, my chair scraping lightly against the floor.

Olivia

THE SHORE BETWEEN US

The walk is silent, yet his presence beside me thunders louder than any words could. I feel his gaze, sharp and unrelenting, like the burn of firelight on bare skin. Each step forward is a battle not to let the weight of his concern crush me. Kyzan trots ahead, a shadow in the pale moonlight, his golden eyes glowing as he leads the way home.

"I'm okay," I whisper, my voice barely more than a breath. I slip my hand into Jeyr's, seeking to convey the truth—or what I want to be the truth. He doesn't answer, but his response comes in the warmth of his lips brushing the back of my hand.

My feet halt before my thoughts can catch up. The world seems to shrink to the abandoned stretch of beach we now stand upon, the gentle rhythm of the waves the only sound between us. I stare at the hand he kissed, the faint, lingering warmth of his lips sending a jolt of electricity up my arm. When I look up, the haunted expression on his face steals the air from my lungs. The light I once saw in him—the spark that drew me in—is buried under a shroud of shadows.

"It's okay if you're not..." His voice is soft, hesitant. His hand brushes against my cheek, and I melt into the warmth of his touch, hating myself for how easily I crave it. The scent of him—summer storms and pine—wraps around me, pulling me further into the haze of him.

"Have I done something wrong?" The words spill out before I can stop them, a whisper tinged with vulnerability. My chest burns with the unspoken questions that have clawed at me for weeks. I hate the power he holds over me, the way my thoughts circle him endlessly. I hate how the memory of his smile haunts me and how I find myself hoping to see it every time I approach the manor. Most of all, I hate how much I long for him to see me the way I see him.

His hand begins to pull away, and panic surges through me. I catch it, pressing it back against my cheek, needing the connection like air. My other hand reaches out, brushing over the stubble that shadows his jaw, tracing the path of a dimple I haven't seen in too long.

"Jeyr," I murmur, my voice trembling. I search his eyes, desperate for the light I know is there.

"You haven't done anything wrong," he says, his voice barely audible. "You are... perfect." The sigh that follows his words feels heavier than the ocean beside us, and with it comes a flood of emotions that wash over my open heart.

I want to chide myself for how easily his words unravel me, but I can't. Not when his face leans closer, his forehead resting against mine, his hands cupping my face like I'm something precious.

"You are... everything," he continues, his voice breaking slightly. "I've been distant because I'm terrified. Terrified of what you mean to me. Terrified that something might happen to you. Every moment I spend near you, I find myself... feeling things I shouldn't. My life, Liv—it's complicated. And you... you deserve more than I can give."

The ache in his voice mirrors the ache in my chest.

"Isn't it my choice?" I ask, my voice trembling. "Whether the risks are worth it or not? Jeyr, I don't know what this is between us, but I want to find out. I'd rather take the risk than live with regret. Danger will always be part of my life, but I don't want to live locked away. I want to live. With you."

He turns his face away, and for a moment, I think I've lost him. But then, his hands guide my face back to his, and his lips capture mine. The kiss is everything I imagine and more. It's soft and passionate, a confession without words. My knees threaten to buckle, but his arms hold me steady, lifting me so I can wrap my legs around his waist.

My fingers weave into his hair, pulling him closer as our breaths mingle, uneven and hungry. The world around us dissolves into nothingness, leaving only the taste of him, the feel of him, and the overwhelming rightness of being in his arms.

When we finally pull apart, gasping for air, his eyes search mine. In their depths, I see a tenderness that takes my breath away, a vulnerability that mirrors my own. His hand reaches up to brush a stray strand of hair from my face, and his lips curve into a smile—the smile I've been yearning to see for weeks.

"You are..." he begins, his voice thick with emotion. "Gods, Liv, I don't have the words. I wish I did, but..." He trails off, his forehead pressing against mine.

"You don't need words," I whisper, my thumb tracing the line of his dimple. "Just stay. That's all I need."

His lips find mine again, and this time, the kiss is slower, deeper, a promise written in the nerves that run through my skin, stained like a tattoo I can't erase even if I wanted to. As the waves lap at the shore and the stars bear witness to our stolen moment, I know that whatever the future holds, this is worth every risk.

Jeyr

Already Lost

Olivia is unraveling me, thread by thread, and I'm letting her. Maybe I can't stop her. Maybe I don't want to. Ignoring her has been the greatest torment, a quiet, slow undoing that I carry in every step, every breath. The simplest touch of her hand on my face, her thumb brushing over the groove of my dimple like it's the softest secret only she is meant to know—it undoes me completely. I feel myself leaning into her, drawn by a pull I can't name but can't deny. When my lips meet hers, it's soft, hesitant. I haven't planned for this, but the moment they touch, I'm lost.

Her body responds instantly, lighting up in my arms as her hands tighten around my neck. Her warmth bleeds into me, and a groan escapes before I can stop it. She melts against me, molding herself to me like water meeting the shore, unstoppable and perfect. My control slips. I tilt my head and deepen the kiss, letting myself drown in the tide of her. The pleasure is unlike anything I've ever known, a flow that drags me under, consuming and relentless. I lift her into my arms, her strong legs wrapping instinctively around my waist. My hands roam her back, memorizing the lines of her, the curve of her spine, the feel of her silk-like ponytail brushing against my knuckles. I wrap the strands in my fist, as though holding her tighter will keep her closer, keep her mine.

Gods, I want her—all of her, every inch of skin, every freckle, every breath that leaves her lips. But I can't. Not here. Not like this. *Stop before you can't.* The thought whispers like a warning, distant and unwelcome. My hesitation breaks through the haze, and she feels it. Her lips leave mine with a featherlight softness, her forehead pressing gently against mine. That touch, so simple, has become our unspoken tether. It anchors me when nothing else can. Her voice, soft but steady, breaks the quiet.

"What is this between us?" Her words cut through me like a blade, sharper than I want to admit. I don't know what to say because my soul has already answered her in ways my words can't. I kiss her again, unable to stop myself, as though the answer she seeks can be found in the way my lips move over hers. It's not enough—not for her, not for me—but it's all I have.

"Can I see you tomorrow?" she whispers, her lips brushing against mine as the words hang in the air between us. I hesitate, the war raging inside me. I want to say yes. Gods, I want to say yes. But I know better. This can't work. This thing between us—it isn't fair to her. She deserves more than the wreckage of my life, more than the chaos I carry like a curse.

"Only if you want to give this a go, to explore this—us," she adds, her voice trembling with the smallest flicker of fear. I feel it through the bond between us, bitter and raw, and it makes me want to kiss her all over again. She's braver than I am, stronger than I will ever be. She's willing to take the risk. I'm not.

But my body betrays me before my mind can catch up. I nod, the word slipping from my lips before I can stop it.

"Okay." It's not just an answer; it's a surrender. My arms tighten around her as I begin the slow walk back to her cottage, knowing I'm sealing my own fate. I ignore the weight of the future pressing down on me, ignore the gnawing dread that whispers of heartbreak and disaster. At that moment, none of it matters. All that matters is her. As if she senses my turmoil, Olivia begins trailing kisses along my jaw, soft and sweet, each one unraveling me further. Her scent—lavender and ocean breeze—wraps around me, pulling me deeper under her spell. A growl rumbles from my chest, primal and pleased, and I let her continue, meeting her kisses with my own, letting her desire pour into me until it consumes every corner of my being.

When we reach the stables, I lower her gently to the ground, watching as she sways on unsteady legs. A chuckle escapes me, low and warm, as I steady her with one hand on her waist. I press a soft kiss to her forehead, lingering just long enough to savor the moment.

Kyzan pads over, his golden eyes meeting mine before he turns his attention to Olivia. He moves to her side, pressing against her in quiet support, as though he too can sense how fragile this moment is. I brush a hand over his head in silent thanks before finally forcing myself to step back.

"Ten a.m.? At the beach?" My voice is calm, measured, but inside, I'm a storm. I don't know if I'm asking or begging. Maybe both. She gives me a dazed nod, her face flushed, and I turn before I can lose my nerve, before I can convince myself to stay. The walk back to the manor stretches endlessly before me, but I welcome the distance. I need it to cool the fire still burning in my veins. I need it to remember why this can never be. But as I walk, her scent lingers, her touch burns, and I know—I'm already lost.

Darkness surrounds me as I walk home. The cool, autumn air calms the fire in my veins, but by the time I reach home, I'm chilled to the bone. I miss her. I miss her warmth, the variegated feeling of pure lust for her and hatred toward myself for getting entranced by her flames in the first place.

The house welcomes me back, the warmth radiating from the living room thawing and inviting. I pause just inside the doorway. On my right, the study radiates pure agony. Olivia's pain has somehow filled the walls. My eyes shut tight, willing the memory to escape through the gutters. I turn my back to the room as my feet follow the call to the thawing warmth of a fire.

"Must have been a good walk. Your scent is strong, brother." Jethro's chuckle breaks the fog of my thoughts, his laughter light. I watch as he brings the amber liquid to his smirking lips. Gods, I need a drink. I pass Jet's relaxed frame heading toward the drink tray, listening to the soothing sound of whisky hitting the glass tumbler. I take a sip and let the burn disperse my jumbling thoughts.

"Keep your senses to yourself."

"I would if it wasn't so strong," Jet teases. Then the lightness of his tone pauses. "Is she okay?" Jet sits up bracing his forearms on his knees, searching my face for an answer, his body stiff with solicitousness.

"Yes, I think so. But on that note," I turn to Caomh, who sits in front of the fire, staring into its depths. He's as still as a statue.

"What the fuck was that? That was just cruel. Not only that, but you also pushed her. You felt something that haunted her, and you poked and poked until she couldn't fight it anymore. You put her in danger, Caomh! I felt her pain! Her body thought she was under attack, her lips were blue, Caomh, blue! You did nothing to stop. You let her get lost in the nightmare and you put us in danger by doing so."

My face feels hot as instinctive predatory anger pools from me. The walk has only fueled the fire; in an attempt to not dwell on the fervor Olivia has put into my nerves, I focus on my anger. Anger for someone who threatened her safety.

"Well?" I hiss through my canines. He doesn't move, not even a flicker of a muscle. He might as well be frozen in time. He sits there, bare-chested, drink in hand, resting on the arm of the chair. Caomh doesn't so much as blink at me.

"I am... I am truly sorry." A weak whisper comes out of a mouth that doesn't know the meaning of "weak." I flinch at my brother's tenor. That's a haunting sound I have never heard come from Caomh's mouth.

His giant frame moves, slow controlled movements. He faces me, arms limp at his side, shoulders curved under the weight of his heavy emotions. I take in his face; taut, rigid. Tears fleck his eyes, his voice matching the haunted features on his face. I feel Jethro freeze. My own body language mirrors his as the shockwave of his devastation hits me.

"I am sorry. I searched for what made her feel fearful. I wanted to know what it was so she could learn to fight it, to stop herself from fearing it. The dream caught me off guard. I found the feeling and tested the string, and she reacted. I tested again, hoping she would fight like we had been practicing. But I lost her. I have fought battles, and I have never felt the pain she feels. It made me think of every bloody person I had killed and if they had felt that exact pain. She felt my own emotions. I felt her draw on them, and the house shook in its agony. She left me locked in her mind, feeling that very pain. I was trapped. It wasn't until you touched her with your bond that it simmered down, that I could get out of it... I wish... I wish I'd never felt that. I wish I could turn back time to never feel that. The thought that that's what she feels every day... I only felt it once and it could have killed me, but it taunts her..."

My chest constricts. My eyes squeeze shut, and I rake my hand over my face, trying to wipe the memory away.

"It won't happen again. I never intended to hurt her. I thought she was strong enough to fight me off..." Caomh stops.

"She isn't ready. She is strong, but she doesn't realize how strong she is yet. How the hell is she supposed to fight you off, when she doesn't even believe in herself?"

Caomh cringes.

"I'm sorry, I fucked up. I'll take it easy on her."

I nod in agreement, but I don't like the unease that settles over me. She has such a long way to go. There are Fae stronger than Caomh. If she is to get captured by them... I don't want to think about what will happen.

Olivia

THE DAWN BETWEEN US

All through the night, his glorious eyes are dazing down at me. I feel at peace as I drink in those beams; they feel like life. I revel in my changeful dreams, thoughts following themselves as one star follows the other. I revel in the sweetness of his touch, the warmth of his body against mine, his olive skin, and his strong embrace. One sweet thought thrills me to the next. I will the night to never end. I curse as to why the morning sun has to rise.

The great pure spell that is upon me breaks with each scorching fire upon my cheek. The cool radiance of my dream begins to fall. Fierce beams strike my brow. The sound of the autumn birds singing the song of a new day only makes my own song sing sad and low. I squeeze my eyes shut, willing the veil of sleep to come back. In the distance, I still see him bathing in a blaze of gold, fading into the light as the morning rays shine brighter through the window. I turn into my pillow, calling back the night. The pillow begins to glow as the room fills with morning light from the roof to the floor. I yearn for the stars and the dreams, the gentle night to return; yearn to hide from the morning hostile light. But I know I don't really yearn for the night itself, but for the man that appears in my dreams.

My internal groan strikes me when it becomes verbal. I pull my pillow over my face and let it take the brunt of that insatiable feeling. The burn on my lower abdomen hasn't left since he walked away from me.

Kyzan's warm huff makes me pull the pillow away from my burning face. His golden all-knowing eyes glare back at me.

"Morning, Kyzan," I mutter, my voice scratchy with sleep as I feel the warmth of his breath huff against my face. He nudges me gently, his nose cool against my cheek before he places a soft, deliberate lick there as if to remind me I'm not alone. A faint laugh escapes me, the sound dry and half-hearted. I reach out, scratching the soft fur of his ears, taking comfort in his steady presence.

Slipping from my small bed, I stretch, shaking off the remnants of a restless night. My body feels heavy, as if the emotions lingering from yesterday have seeped into my bones. I pull on my worn brown britches, tucking my white button-down shirt into the equally battered leather belt around my waist. Catching my reflection in the cracked mirror across the room, I sigh. Shadows darken my eyes, exhaustion tracing lines across my face. I work my hair up into a loose, messy bun, leaving a few curls to frame my cheeks, wild and untamed as always. There is no controlling those. "That'll have to do," I murmur, more to myself than Kyzan, who watches me with a knowing look. His golden eyes hold judgment I don't want to face.

After lacing up my knee-high leather boots—old things that groan in protest with every tug—I detour through the kitchen. There, on the countertop, is the picnic basket I had carefully packed the night before. My hands brush over it, double-checking that everything is in place. I'm about to pick it up when I notice Hecate, her sharp gaze lingering on me from the corner of the room. She doesn't say a word, but her expression says plenty. She's seen how much I've packed, seen how meticulous I have been. She knows it isn't just for me.

A faint, tight-lipped smile tugs at her face. It isn't one of disapproval—more a quiet acceptance, edged with a softness that puzzles me. I nod at her, basket in hand, and turn to leave.

I don't make it far. As I descend the stairs, a voice calls out from the living room, stopping me in my tracks. "You've been spending a lot of time out and about lately. Something you're not telling us?" Mary's tone is light, playful even, but the weight of her question makes my heart skip. She sits in her favorite chair by the fireplace, though the hearth is unlit. Her silver eyes meet mine as I turn toward her, their warmth undeniable. That warmth seeps into me, pooling in the part of my heart I have carved out just for her.

"I like my time alone," I reply carefully, my voice steady. "It gives me a chance to work on more art for the merchant."

"Alone, huh?" Her voice lilts with doubt, though her expression betrays nothing. Her hands work on the blanket she's knitting, each movement precise and rhythmic, as if the act itself is a soothing ritual. A pile of finished blankets sits to one side, and to the other, a heap of soft, vibrant yarn waiting to be transformed. Mary has made it her mission to prepare as many blankets as possible for the less fortunate before winter's chill arrives. That kindness of hers—it warms me even as I feel my cheeks heat under her scrutiny.

"I'm not sure what you mean by that," I say, keeping my voice as neutral as possible, though I can feel the flush creeping up my neck. My heartbeat quickens. I'm not ready to tell her. Not yet. Not when I don't even know what this... thing is between Jeyr and me.

She simply nods, her lips curving into a knowing smirk that makes me feel as though she can see right through me. Mary always has that way about her—a motherly wisdom that often sees more than I want her to. I hope one day I can confide in her, but for now, silence is safer.

"The art merchant sent word," she says after a pause, her tone softening. "He'll be here in a couple of weeks."

I stiffen. Of course, he will be. Winter is approaching, and with it comes the flurry of trade and commerce before the season locks the kingdoms in its icy grip. My stomach churns at the thought of Vernan, the slimy little man who comes every season. His charm is as fake as the gold jewelry he wears, and his presence curdles my stomach like spoiled milk.

"I know," I say, my voice flat. "I've been up late every night finishing pieces for him. I've also decided to sell one of Mother's paintings. He offered a large sum for it last time, and it'll leave us in a good position for the year."

Mary's head snaps up, her mouth parting in shock. "Liv... you can't..."

Her voice is so small, like a kitten mewling in protest. The guilt that twists in my chest is sharp, but I force myself to hold firm.

"It's not up for discussion," I say, my voice colder than I intend. "Father isn't here, and I'm of age. They're mine to sell, and I love this family too much to see another year of struggling. This is what's best, Mary. Please, let it rest."

Her lips press into a thin line, and she nods stiffly. The look in her eyes, though, is heartbreaking. I hate leaving her like that, so I cross the room and kiss her cool cheek. Her scent—apricots and sweet tea—is a balm against my frayed nerves. My hand squeezes her shoulder, and I let my emotions flow through the touch, a silent reminder of how much I love her.

Her expression softens, and she gives me a warm, albeit strained, smile. "Have a good picnic, my love."

The weight of her words, coupled with the strain of my own choices, hangs heavy in the air as I turn to leave. The emotional pull of it all makes me hesitate, regret tugging at the edges of my resolve. But I shake it off. Today isn't the day to dwell on what I can't change. Not yet.

Jeyr

Even If Only for Now

I fight the urge to close the distance too quickly, each step deliberate as I approach her. She looks like a painting come to life, sitting there on the dunes, framed by the muted colors of the sea and sky. The wind carries strands of her fiery hair, tangling them around her face like a crown of flame. Her delicate form leans into the massive weight of Ness, the beast curled protectively around her, while Kyzan's massive head rests in her lap. She moves her fingers in gentle strokes through his fur, her gaze fixed on the horizon.

But there is something in her stillness that freezes me mid-step. The look in her eyes—it isn't peace. It's absence. The emptiness there feels like an invisible wall, and it stops me in my tracks. My chest tightens, the need to reach her warring with the voice in my head that tells me to hold back, to let her find her way out of whatever storm brews inside her. *What happened?*

She looks up at me then, a small, polite smile gracing her lips. But it doesn't touch her eyes. It doesn't reach the Olivia I know. My feet carry me forward before I can stop myself. I kneel beside her, my lips brushing the curve of her cheek in greeting. The faint contact sends a ripple through me, her warmth sparking against my skin, but it isn't enough to banish the shadow clinging to her.

I settle beside her, my body tense, hands resting on my knees as I study her. The ocean breeze carries her scent—soft lavender and the salt of the sea—stirring something raw in my chest. She doesn't look at me immediately, her fingers still lost in Kyzan's fur.

"What happened, Liv?" My voice is low, quiet.

I don't want to push her, but the need to know gnaws at me. The thought of her carrying something heavy on her own—it's unbearable.

Her eyes flick to mine, and I feel it—her power pulling the air clean of emotion. It's sudden and deliberate, leaving me with nothing but my own feelings. I swallow against the sudden void, the emptiness her shield leaves behind. "I'm sorry," she says softly, her voice tinged with guilt. "I let myself get caught up in my own thoughts."

She sighs, the sound heavy and raw, and I move closer without thinking. Her head finds my shoulder, the weight of it grounding me in a way I can't explain. My pulse quickens, every part of me hyper-aware of her. The softness of her hair brushes against my jaw, her presence washing over me like the tide. "Tell me what's on your mind," I murmur, angling toward her, hoping she'll let me in.

"It's nothing, really," she replies, her voice distant yet warm. "I just want to enjoy this—being with you."

I want to believe her, want to take her words at face value, but the faint crack in her tone tells me otherwise. Something lingers behind her quiet smile, a weight she isn't ready to share. And who am I to press her, with all the secrets I keep buried in my own chest? If she wants to keep this moment unmarred, I will let her. For now.

I nod, resting my cheek lightly against her hair.

"Alright."

My arms move around her, pulling her closer, as if by holding her I can keep the shadows at bay. I close my eyes, letting her presence fill the cracks in my walls. She is soft, warm, and so achingly real in my arms. I inhale deeply, memorizing the scent of her, the way her body molds to mine, the weight of her head against my chest.

Because soon, I will have to let her go. Soon, I will have to walk away. But here, in this moment, I let myself be selfish. I hold her like she is mine, even if only for now.

Olivia

ANCHORED IN YOU

I can't pin down the feeling that spreads through me like a wildfire. My chest feels buoyant, my cheeks ache from smiling, and a warmth I can't name courses through my veins. It has been so long since I've felt this light.

Our afternoon together blurs into a dream of stolen laughs and playful banter as we feed each other bits of cured meats and cheese. Every now and then, I sneak a piece to Kyzan, whose adoration is evident in the doting way he gazes at me.

Jeyr rolls his eyes, his tone laced with mock jealousy. "Is it bad that I'm jealous? Kyzan has never once looked at me like that."

I laugh, the sound surprising me with its lightness. "You're just not as pretty," I tease, earning a rich laugh from him that sends a ripple of pleasure through my body.

Gods, I wish I could bottle that sound, store it away for the days when my heart feels heavier. "Mm, you're right about that," he admits with a smirk before leaning in to press a soft kiss to my cheek.

My breath hitches, and I swat at him playfully, trying to disguise the way my heart hammers in my chest. "Don't start, Jeyr. The whole point of this was for me to get to know you, not for you to flirt your way out of it."

A groan rumbles in his chest as his arm tightens around my waist, pulling me closer. The sound ignites something deep inside me, and my mind betrays me, wandering to thoughts of our kiss—of his lips on mine, the heat that pulses between us, and the way his body feels pressed against mine. I swallow hard, willing my thoughts back to the moment.

"Alright," he says softly, his breath tickling my ear. "What do you want to know?"

"Family?" I ask, my voice tentative.

I feel his body stiffen beneath me, the tension in his frame shifting the air between us. My brows furrow in concern, but I give him the space to respond in his own time.

"I'm the second eldest of four," he begins, his voice steady but guarded. "I have an older brother and two younger sisters. I'm close with my siblings... mostly. My older brother, Niall, and I are... estranged. He acts as a buffer between me and my father, but over time, he's become more like our father than I care to admit. Then there's Aella. She's strong—stronger than most men I know. She hasn't had it easy, but she could run any kingdom, any army, if she set her mind to it. And Althea... She's the youngest, sweet and kind, somehow untouched by the bitterness that clings to the rest of us. She'll lead the healer's temple one day."

His smile brushes against my cheek as he speaks of his sisters, and I feel the love he has for them seep into my chest. It's a warm, steady pulse, grounding me in the truth of his words.

"And your mother?" I ask softly.

The air thickens at the mention of her. His breath rolls down my back, heavy with grief, and his voice roughens, each word laced with a numbness I recognize all too well. "She was caught in the crossfire of the Courts during the last war. She was a healer, like me. There was a battle between two Courts—small, insignificant, really—but she went onto the field to save a wounded man. They executed her as a statement."

The pain in his words pierces through me like thorns, sharp and unrelenting. I place my hands on his arms, tracing soothing circles into his skin as he has done for me so many times. His body softens, molding into mine, but the weight of his words remains.

"How... How did your family handle it?" I whisper, my voice trembling. The question feels like a betrayal, but I need to understand him, need to know the depth of the loss that mirrors my own.

His jaw tightens, and for a moment, I think he won't answer. But then he sighs, the sound heavy with years of unresolved anger. "My father's wrath was... unimaginable. He changed that day. I lost him as well. He shut himself off, became cold and ruthless. Not long after, he married Aella off to some bastard for political gain. I could have killed him for it."

My body goes still, my stomach twisting at the thought. "What happened to her?"

"She hid the bruises at first," he says, his voice low and ragged. "But when she came to me scared, her face permanently marked... I couldn't let her stay. Despite my father's ambitions, no alliance is worth her pain."

The raw emotion in his voice sends shivers through me. "You... you had him killed?" I ask hesitantly, my heart pounding. "Yes," he admits, his voice steady. "And I would do the same for you."

His words leave me breathless, torn between the Empath who recoils at the thought of taking a life and the woman who finds comfort in his fierce protectiveness. I'm not sure what that says about me, but in this moment, I don't care.

I shift in his lap, cupping his face in my hands, and meet his gaze. "Jeyr, thank you... for telling me." My voice wavers, but the sincerity is clear.

He leans into my touch, his lips brushing the palm of my hand in a gesture so tender it leaves me trembling. "You are mine to protect, Olivia. Always."

I snuggle closer to him, feeling the solid warmth of his body beneath mine. For the first time in what feels like forever, I feel safe. I feel like I have a home, and I pray to the gods that he won't shut me out again.

Olivia

THE WINTER GOODBYE

Autumn slips away, leaving behind a world blanketed in snow and a chill that has nothing to do with the weather. The cold settles deep in my bones, a sharp reminder of everything I can't hold onto. I stand on the rocky coastline, the sea's icy spray mixing with the biting wind. But even the ocean's untamed fury is quieter than the storm inside me.

Jeyr is leaving. "Do you have to go?" The words slip out, selfish and raw, but I can't stop them. I hate how small my voice sounds, like I'm clinging to something that's already slipping through my fingers. Jeyr's face is tight, his jaw set like he's bracing himself for a blow.

He won't look at me, but when he does, his blue eyes—usually so vibrant—are dim, clouded with something I can't name. *Guilt? Pain? Resignation?*

"I do," he says softly, almost like he's apologizing. "I promised them." His forehead falls to mine, the weight of it grounding me as much as it crushes me. He shakes his head, the movement brushing our temples together. His hands curl into the hair at the nape of my neck, his fingers gripping like he's afraid I'll vanish.

"Okay," I whisper, though nothing about this feels okay. "When will you be back?" My voice trembles, betraying the panic rising in my chest. My heart is already screaming that I know the answer.

His lips are so close to mine that I can feel the words before he speaks them. "I... I don't know, Liv. I—fuck. I may not be back for a long time." His words hit me harder than any blow, each one a sharp, jagged edge cutting deeper than the last. "My family... they've asked me to help with... some affairs."

I pull back as the truth—or the lie—sinks in, my body going rigid. "Wait," I snap, my anger slicing through the air between us. "Why haven't you mentioned this before now?"

For the first time, I let my frustration show, let the storm I've been holding back surge forward. He reels back like I've struck him. Maybe I have—maybe not with my hands, but with my words. My heart aches for him even as my anger burns.

"They, uh... they only just told me," he says, but the hesitation in his voice is a dead giveaway. He's lying.

I nod stiffly, pulling myself from his grasp. His hands twitch as though they want to reach for me but don't dare.

"Liv... please. I don't want to leave on a bad note."

It would be so easy to give in. I can feel his devastation, the way it radiates off him in waves that beg me to soothe him. My powers whisper that I can ease his pain, give him the comfort he clearly craves. But I can't. Not this time.

I take another step back. "Whose fault is that?" I spit, my words harsher than I intend but no less true.

"Hummingbird... please." His voice cracks, and I hate how it makes me want to crumble. When I glance up, his eyes are glossy with unshed tears, his expression raw. But I turn my head away, unwilling to let his pain sway me.

"Not unless you can promise me this hot and cold act is over," I say, my voice steady despite the trembling in my chest. "If you want a goodbye from me, you'll tell me the truth."

I watch as his shoulders drop, the weight of his indecision pressing down on him like the heavy winter sky. For a moment, I think he might say something—anything—but the silence stretches between us, fragile and suffocating.

"I... I can't tell you what's going on," he finally says, his voice low and defeated. "I just don't want our goodbye to be this way."

The word "goodbye" twists in my chest, a knife sinking deeper with every second that passes. My lips tighten, and my nose burns as tears threaten to fall. Why is it always like this? Why am I always the one left behind, with nothing but questions and empty promises?

"Fine," I say, my voice breaking despite my best efforts. "Goodbye, Jeyr."

I see it then—the crack in his composure, the pain flashing across his face before he steels himself. He realizes I'm not going to give him the closure he wants, the soft goodbye he thinks he can have.

"Goodbye, Hummingbird," he whispers, the words heavy with finality. I turn and walk away, my boots crunching against the frozen ground. I don't look back—I can't.

The coastline, once my favorite place, is now tainted. It's no longer a sanctuary but a graveyard for memories of what could have been. The waves crash against the shore behind me, the sound echoing in the hollow space inside my chest. Snowflakes begin to fall, melting on my cheeks as they mix with the tears I can't stop.

Goodbye, Jeyr. Goodbye to the warmth, the stolen moments, the unspoken promises. Goodbye to the hope I have foolishly clung to.

My mood is foul as I walk up the gravel driveway. I've heard of heartbreak, but that almost feels tame compared to the pain I feel in this moment. It should be heart shatter, or heart loss. My heart doesn't feel simply broken, it feels like it's ripped out of my chest and shattered to pieces. I've seen it coming, I've felt it coming, and yet, there isn't enough to prepare me for it.

I stop abruptly when I notice the man at the gate of the cottage, watching as if he's waiting for me. Kyzan assesses him, letting out a low warning growl.

"It's fine. It's just Vernon." His smarmy, seedy smile rakes over me like it always has—like I'm a full roast dinner. This time, though, he looks like I'm ready for eating.

"Olivia, darling, how you've grown." His pointed tongue slides from his mouth, licking his lips between each word. They slither between the gap in his teeth, leaving my gut churning.

"Cut the crap, Vernon. It's been a year. I'm the same as always." I walk past him and push the gate. His tongue darts out again as if he can taste the air. He is such a slimy human.

Cooper opens the door abruptly, offering our visitor a deeper scowl than usual.

"Vernon," he greets.

"Ah, Cooper. What a pleasure. I see you have aged beautifully. Has that lovely wife of yours done the same?"

I feel Cooper's anger spike.

"Don't speak of my wife, merchant. Get your paintings and leave."

"Oh, the hospitality! Of course. Miss Olivia, please show me the treasures you have painted." Vernon walks through the door, his greasy finger trailing over my shoulder as he walks to the dining room where I have the paintings ready and waiting.

I follow the man in red and gold merchant wear, his suit immaculate red velvet embellished with gold lining and stitching.

"Oh! These are beautiful, my girl! That new paint your father sent has come to good use I see. I will take them all."

"Fine, but the higher quality comes with a higher price, Vernon."

He gives me a sly smile.

"Oh, but of course. I already have a buyer dying to see your new collection."

"They are an extra hundred coins per piece. The two from my mother's collection are even more."

Vernon looks at me, that same smile unflinching with the hike of the price.

"Oh, I think my buyer will find he isn't losing money on this collection."

I don't like the inauspicious rays of emotion that flutter from him.

"Good. Cooper, could you please load the pictures into Vernon's cart?"

Cooper looks at me. I can see he doesn't want to leave me alone with the man, but I'm in no mood to muck around. I want him gone—sooner rather than later.

"Sure," he grumbles. Once he's out the door, I watch Vernon's eyes light up.

He hands me an envelope.

"Your father told me to give you this. I suspect we will be seeing each other sooner than you think." He reaches into another pocket and pulls out a small pouch. "Your coins. Have a good day, Olivia."

I quickly hide the letter in the lining of my jacket before anyone can see. His finger twirls one of my curls before he turns, raising his hand in the air and fluttering his finger in goodbye.

"Ta-ta! Till we meet again."

I hide at home for two weeks. I'm stuck in my feelings, not wanting to go to the manor without Jeyr being there. Eventually boredom and the itchiness to be productive take over. I try to muffle my smile when Caomh answers the manor door half dressed, hair thoroughly tousled. The musty sweet smell of sex and pleasure permeates the air surrounding him.

"Good night, Cao?" I muse, seeing the evidence of someone who has had a more eventful winter solstice than me.

He smiles, a genuine arrogantly happy smile that makes my heart clench. "Don't read my emotions, little Empath," he accuses, taking me under his arm and pressing me firmly into his bare chest. His smell reminds me of spring mornings and boozy nights, fresh with morning dew and the spice of malt whisky. I let myself melt into him, trying not to act surprised when he kisses the top of my head.

"He isn't here, Liv," he murmurs. A soft understanding taints his words.

I pause, looking up at him and ignore the way my stomach plummets to my toes. It isn't normal to miss someone like this. It feels like an important organ has just gotten up and walked out, leaving a gaping hole behind. "His family had some urgent matters they needed him to help with." I feel it—he's making it up. I feign ignorance to the emotions I feel running in Caomh's core: guilt. He's lying to me, and he feels guilty about it. I smile tightly, swallowing the lump in my throat.

Let's train, shall we? I say through the mind connection, too scared to speak. My voice would only betray the emotions I'm trying so hard to shield. Caomh smiles, genuine, soft. "Let's."

I train without breaks, not wanting to be left to my own thoughts. Caomh and I work tirelessly and except for the bustle of children, the house is empty without two other Fae males. Jet has gone back to Aotrom after word that Gwynn is returning.

Caomh toys with my emotions like they are pieces on a board, nudging, testing, waiting to see where I'll falter. When he sends me the sharp memory of Kyzan lunging at me, teeth bared, I shove back—hard. I let him feel the quiet pulse of warmth that curls around me every night, the unwavering presence of my wolf standing between me and the dark.

His smirk flickers, just for a second. A hesitation.

With every lesson, I catch glimpses beyond that polished arrogance—his walls aren't just defense; they're armor. But beneath them, behind the taunting grins and sharp remarks, I see something else. A softness, edged in caution. A moment of ease before he masks it again.

"Though you should focus on staying hidden, I want you to be able to use your power if you've been detected. I know it's against your nature to hurt someone, so let's just try using your powers to distract an opponent in a fight."

I nod with a smile on my face as a light bulb flashes in my mind.

Cao stands before me in the attic, shirtless as usual. He has his golden broadsword in hand, the green and gold leather reflecting off the light. My own is simple, lighter. Its silver and black leather handle is smooth under my clenched hand.

The sound of metal clanging pings throughout the room as our swords clash. Caomh attacks and I block, left-right. He lunges for my abandoned side, showing my spot of weakness, and then I push a wave of humor to him. I watch his body still, just long enough as I spin, sword to his chest. A smile quirks my lips. Game and match.

"Cheeky, Princess." His golden eyes simmer; one eyebrow raises. I stick my tongue out playfully.

"Try something else. Something that would stop a stranger in his tracks."

We lift our swords once more and begin the dance, letting our attacks be blocked and parried. I keep pace with him and make sure my sides are well protected. I know he's waiting for me to use my powers, but I feel the freeze within me and as if he knows, he amps up the pressure. His movements are fast, strong, and precise. His century-plus of fighting versus my two decades leaves me standing without a sword.

"Princess, I would hate to know that you would have failed in a real fight. You are using your powers too late in the game."

His growl echoes in my mind. Just as he winnows behind me, his sword meets my neck. Every inch of fear I could possibly feel, I give to him. The kind of fear that makes your heart stop.

The sword drops and I turn to see him clutching his chest, eyes wide. My own widen. I pull my power back, watching as Caomh's halted breathing starts once again and begins to even out.

"I'm okay. I'm okay, Livy. I am okay." His voice is croaked and soft.

I freeze. I don't even realize I'm shaking. I don't see him come to my side, but suddenly his hands are on my shoulders as he searches my eyes.

"Livy, please breathe, I am okay. You didn't hurt me. I am okay. Look at me."

I gaze into those golden eyes, but all I see is the fear I put there and the way his hand clutches his heart as if I could have killed him. Panic grips me. The haunting of a voice that once sounded in my mind threatens to surface. *Murderer.*

I can't take it. The ache in my lungs, the race in my heart, the tightening of my muscles—it's all too much. I am the reason for someone's pain: me. It's all my fault. I can't do this. My hand grasps my chest, pressing harder between my breasts as my body strangles itself in punishment.

"Hey, hey, Hummingbird. Easy, breathe in and out for me." Suddenly, those golden eyes are replaced by cool depths of blue. I feel pressure against my forehead.

"Focus on me, Hummingbird. You pulled your power back, you protected yourself. You did great. Caomh is okay. Please breathe for me." The smell of the ocean and pine swells around me, causing my body to relax. It's as if I'm conditioned to his scent. My heart forgets what it had felt to feel his loss, forgets the heartbreak as it leaps to be closer to him.

My legs buckle, but my weight is caught, preventing my knees from hitting the ground. A thick, supporting arm holds my waist, while a large hand massages my neck in comforting swells. My body, despite my mind, lets him catch me—lets him capture me. Lets him know I need him.

"Take a breath." The urgency and concern in his voice makes me suck in a deep breath. The cool air fills my chest. "That's it, my Hummingbird. Good girl. I know it's overwhelming to use your power like that." He strokes my back in soft circles as I nod in between deep, heaving breaths. My heart slows to an even rhythm with each loving stroke of my back. I look back into the depths of his eyes and fight back the urge to cry, crushed by the realization that I miss him even more than I thought. He's here.

"You are here..." I voice, his lips still so close to mine.

"I will always be here when you need me." Would he? He's there in some big moments, but something tells me I want him for the little moments too, for the moments I miss him.

"How did you know I needed you?"

"Caomh called Jet to get me."

I look around and there he stands. He's in the corner, his features dark and clouded. I pause. His half-smile swarms with a dark flurry of emotions.

I blink, fighting the urge to go to him. He nods a soft, sincere hello, then goodbye before he disappears into the darkness.

I look back to Jeyr. His face is covered in stubble, eyes bruised from exhaustion. My hand comes to his face. He closes his eyes and leans into the curve of my palm.

"I missed you, Hummingbird."

There's a harshness to his features, a change in his eyes. His large hands move to my face, brushing away tears I hadn't even noticed. His lips take mine, tender as feather strokes over my lips.

"Do you have to leave again?" I whisper as the soft touch of his lips leaves mine. Should he say yes, I need to prepare myself.

I let out a sigh of relief when his head shakes against mine.

"No, Hummingbird. I'm all yours now." His words are heavy, laced with meaning. I look back to his eyes, searching for the truth. He takes me in a tight embrace, curling my head to the crook of his neck.

Somehow, I don't feel reassured. I feel the tension in his body, his actions, his tone. His emotions feel mendacious. I pull away, anger surfacing at the reminder of how we left things.

"Caomh?" I turn to look the golden Fae in the eye, his striking angular features taut.

"I am so sorry, Princess."

"There is nothing to be sorry for. It was my fault."

"You did amazing. If you ever have someone try to take you, do that, exactly that. But if you are comfortable trying to range the severity you make someone feel pain, we can work on it tomorrow."

I'm not sure I can ever use that power again, but I don't tell him that. The fear of him seeing what a failure I really am has me holding back the truth.

"Thank you, Cao."

I leave, feeling Jeyr's presence close behind until Caomh's voice stops him.

"Jeyr, let Olivia walk home alone. I need to speak with you."

I'm not sure how to feel about missing the chance to get Jeyr alone. There are a lot of unspoken words that need to be aired out. A lot of questions that need to be answered for me to feel at ease in our relationship. Still, the side of me that needs him, craves him, deflates at the act of leaving him standing there with his commander.

Olivia

WOMEN SCORNED

The next day, the manor stands silent and still, cloaked in heavy snowfall that mutes the world around me. No one answers the door, despite the rhythmic knocking of my chilled knuckles against the aged wood. My teeth chatter with every sharp gust of icy wind, and my patience wears thin. I am done waiting.

I touch the handle, its cool metal biting against my palm. But then it shifts, warming unnaturally beneath my fingers. A faint click echoes as the magic lock gives way, allowing me entrance. As I step inside, the cold melts away, replaced by the crackling warmth of the manor's hearths. From the foyer, muffled giggles and low, primal sounds drift through the air. I glance down at Kyzan, who stands beside me with a bemused glint in his golden eyes. His tail wags slightly, betraying his amusement. I press my lips together to suppress my laughter as curiosity tugs me toward the source of the noise.

Peeking into the living room, I find a scene that stops me in my tracks. Caomh lounges shirtless on the long daybed by the fire, his golden skin illuminated by the warm light. A petite woman with ink-black hair is perched on his lap, her hands roaming his chest. Behind them, a larger man—broad-shouldered and dark-skinned—hovers, leaning over Caomh to press kisses against his neck and jaw. The woman giggles, arching into the touch as her hand slides toward the band of Caomh's pants, while his fingers tease at the edge of her corset.

My breath catches, and I clamp a hand over my mouth to stifle the snort of laughter threatening to escape. But mischief sparks in my veins. I step into the room, letting my presence ripple like a stone tossed into still water. "What do you think you're doing?" I snap, my voice ringing through the space. "Take your hands off my man!"

The room stills, the tension snapping taut like a bowstring. I let the chill of winter pour into the room, freezing the atmosphere with the sharp edge of a scorned woman's fury. My emotions, amplified by my powers, radiate through the air, wrapping around them like an icy vice. Caomh's golden eyes widen in shock. The woman leaps from his lap, hastily yanking her dress to cover her exposed skin. She casts me a wary glance before muttering an apology. The man follows suit, fumbling with his pants as his eyes dart between me and Caomh. Neither of them dares linger.

Within moments, they bolt, the front door slamming shut behind them. The silence that follows is deafening—until I giggle. The heavy tension dissolves into the warmth of my amusement, filling the space like sunlight breaking through storm clouds. "You little minx," Caomh grumbles, though a hint of a smile tugs at his lips. He stands and approaches me, his bare chest glistening faintly from the fire's glow. I glance at my reflection in the adjacent window. Snow clings to my messy bun, my shoulders dusted in frost. Jeyr's borrowed jacket hangs awkwardly on my frame, now damp and weighed down by the elements.

I stick out my tongue at myself, pulling off the coat and shaking the snow from my hair. "That was cruel," Caomh murmurs, his lips quirking upward in a half-smirk. "But I like cruel." He pecks my cheek before stalking off, his bare feet padding silently against the wooden floor. "You don't seriously flaunt your lovers around with children here, do you?" I call after him, arching a brow. Caomh turns, golden eyes gleaming with mischief. "Of course not. Claudia took them to Gliocas for the winter. It's warmer there, and they're safe. I've arranged for schooling and enrichment programs while they're away. They'll be back come spring." My eyes widen. "I didn't get to say goodbye."

"They left letters for you," he replies. "But yes, the house has been quiet without them. You've made it worse, chasing off the first entertainment I've had in months."

I laugh, the sound echoing through the room—until another laugh joins mine. I turn to find Jethro leaning casually in the doorway, his midnight eyes twinkling with mirth. Without thinking, I rush to him, throwing myself into his open arms. He spins me around, nuzzling into my hair as though he hasn't seen me in years.

"I missed you, Little Huntress," he murmurs, his voice thick with warmth. "But gods, you're freezing!"

He sets me down and cups my face, his hands glowing faintly with golden light. I shiver as the heat seeps into my skin, thawing the frost that clings to me. My breath hitches as the warmth spreads, soothing my icy bones and leaving me drowsy with comfort.

"Better?" he asks, his brow lifting.

"Much," I whisper, leaning into his touch.

A low cough breaks the moment, and I turn to find Jeyr standing beside the door. His eyes are dark, stormy with something I can't quite place. I smirk, relishing the jealousy I can feel simmering beneath his cool façade.

"Jealous, Jeyr?" I whisper as I approach him, my words teasing against his lips.

His growl is answer enough, sending a thrill through me. Without a word, he takes my hand and leads me to the living room.

Jeyr

LIES BITE

I watch Olivia and Caomh from across the room, my jaw tight as I lean back in my chair. Their shared smirks, the glint of mischief in both of their eyes as they speak mind to mind, irritate me in ways I can't explain. Caomh chokes on his drink suddenly, his golden eyes wide with surprise before he shoots Olivia a playful glare. Her laugh rings out softly, her cheeks flushed with amusement. It isn't fair how easy it is for her with them. With Caomh. With Jet. There's no tension there, no carefully constructed walls to climb over, no secrets hanging between them like a blade waiting to fall. It's effortless—so unlike us.

Whose fault is that? The thought strikes like a dagger. I know the answer. It's mine. Every strained silence, every step backward, every hurtful word spoken to create distance—it all leads us here. My gaze drifts back to her, drawn like a moth to a flame. Her crimson hair, parted to one side, spills over her shoulder and down to her hip in a cascade of fire. She sits with a quiet grace, her legs crossed, Kyzan's massive head resting possessively in her lap.

She idly strokes his fur as if the world around her isn't burning, as if she hasn't already set fire to my carefully controlled existence. As if sensing my thoughts, Olivia turns her gaze to me. Her eyes, green as the deepest forest, pierce through the thick, unspoken tension in the room.

"So," she says, her voice steady, though I catch the flicker of something deeper beneath her tone. "You were going to lay your cards on the table."

My throat tightens, the weight of her words pressing down on me. She's done waiting—and gods, so am I. I hold her gaze, refusing to let it slip away. She deserves that much, even if I can't give her more. I swallow hard, the memories of that day flashing through my mind like an arrow shot from a bow.

The day I walked away. The day my three months ran out. Every moment since has been haunted by that decision, by the sight of her standing on the coastline, staring after me with betrayal in her eyes. I told myself it was necessary, that leaving was the right thing to do. But my heart has never quite stopped screaming in protest.

"Olivia," I start, my voice rough, strained. I stand, my chair scraping against the floor, drawing Caomh's sharp glance. He knows what's coming—he always does—but he remains silent, retreating to give us space. Kyzan raises his head, golden eyes flicking between us before he stands and pads silently out of the room. I cross the distance between us, each step feeling heavier than the last. She tilts her head up to meet my eyes, unflinching. She's always been so fearless when it comes to me, even when I'm the coward in this story.

"I owe you the truth," I admit, my voice low. It feels foreign to say it aloud, the words grating against the walls I've built around myself. "You've deserved it from the beginning." Her brows furrow, her fingers stilling on her lap where they rested moments ago. "Then tell me," she says, her tone sharper than before. There's no malice in it—only a determination that makes my chest ache.

"Stop running. Stop hiding. Just tell me."

I crouch before her, leveling myself with those piercing green eyes. My hands flex at my sides, desperate to reach out, to touch her, to ground myself in the only thing that's felt real in years. But I don't deserve that—not yet.

"Olivia, Have you ever heard of a Companach?"

2 WEEKS PRIOR

The weight of the letter in my hand felt heavier than it should have, as if the ink itself carried the pressure of my entire world. My fingers crumpled the edge, frustration and sorrow roiling beneath the surface as I sat across from Caomh. The desk between us was laden with unspoken words and grim inevitabilities. My other hand raked through my hair repeatedly, a nervous gesture that betrayed the calm facade I tried to wear. Caomh's golden eyes burned holes into the paper, the tension in the room thick enough to suffocate. The words on the page played on a loop in my mind.

Dear Brother,

Three months are over in a week. Father has asked me to write to you, his threat has weight, Brother. The Grand Duke of Puinnsean is growing impatient. You denying father's promise will show weakness in our Court. It will show that Father has no control of his own children, let alone his Kingdom.

I beg of you, please just marry the girl. Father has been working on conditions that she live with us instead of you in their kingdom. If you come home, if you just try and help with the negotiations, we can try and

make

this work. I don't want to lose you, Brother. Come home. We need you.

Bane is threatening us after the death of Lord Tierney's son. He believes we owe him for the death of his own. He knows,

Jeyr

. He knows what you did to have him killed. He lost Aella, and he wants retribution. It's an eye for an eye now, Brother. Come home.

Niall

My stomach churned as I read the lines in my mind again, the pressure of past actions and future consequences twisting me into knots. The ghosts of my decisions haunted me. More than anything, I wanted to see that vile kingdom burn for what they had done— for taking my mother, for abusing my sister, for threatening my family. Yet here I was, bound to negotiate with them, tied to their demands. My heart was torn between the family I'd lived for and the woman who had become my world.

How could I tell Olivia? How could I tell her that after our stolen moments on the beach, the promises made with unspoken words, that I was leaving her for another? That I had no choice? I thought of her soft green eyes, the way her laughter had echoed through my chest like a melody I never wanted to forget. I thought of the way she had trusted me, let me in despite the walls I'd built around myself.

I threw the letter onto the desk with more force than necessary. Caomh didn't flinch, his expression mirroring the storm inside me.

"You have to go, Jeyr," he said quietly. His voice carried a weight of its own, thick with regret and unspoken goodbye. This wasn't the commander speaking, the diplomat who could unravel kingdoms with a single conversation. This was my brother. He knew, as I did, that this wasn't just a departure. It was a farewell.

The thought struck me like a blade to the chest—if I went to Puinnsean, I might not come back. Not as myself. Not as the man I was now. And if I stayed, Bane would ensure that everything I cared for burned.

Jet's voice broke through the suffocating silence like a thunderclap.

"Are you seriously going to let him go?"

I turned, meeting his imposing figure. His arms crossed over his chest, his posture rigid with anger. His dark eyes burned with a fire I hadn't seen in years.

"What am I supposed to do, Jet?" Caomh spat, standing now, his hands braced against the desk. "Let his head roll? Because that's what will happen if Bane doesn't get what he wants. We all know what he's capable of."

"He's our brother!" Jet roared, stepping forward, his fists clenching. "I'm not going to lose him. I'm going to find Gwynn. She'll have answers. I refuse to let this happen. I'm not losing him, and I won't come back here to see the loss in Olivia's eyes. I'm not watching this family fall apart." His voice cracked at the end, the anger slipping into something raw, something

broken.

"Jet—" I began, but he was already gone, vanishing before I could stop him.

The room fell into a heavy silence, the absence of Jet's presence leaving a hollow void. I raked my hands over my face, my breath uneven as his words echoed in my mind.

"We are family. I'm not coming back here to see the loss in Olivia's eyes."

"Fuck," I muttered, slamming my fist against the desk.

Caomh's voice was quieter now, but no less steady.

"Jeyr, we will always be family. Jet will come to understand. But you need to go. Save your family. Save your Kingdom." His voice softened further, the commander giving way to the brother. "I'll take care of Olivia. I'll make sure she's safe. I'll make sure she's happy, in whatever way I can."

I nodded, but the thought of leaving without seeing her one last time twisted something deep inside me. I couldn't do it. I couldn't leave without looking into her eyes, without hearing her voice, without telling her goodbye— even if I couldn't explain why.

"I need to see her," I said, my voice hoarse. "Just one more time."

Caomh didn't stop me. He didn't even argue. He simply nodded, his golden eyes heavy with understanding.

I didn't wait for anything else. I left the study, my heart racing as I stepped into the snow-covered courtyard. The thought of seeing her again sent an ache through me that was almost unbearable. I wasn't sure what I would say, or if I would even have the strength to leave once I saw her.

But I knew one thing for certain.

I couldn't leave without saying goodbye.

My kingdom had never looked so desolate. The winter storms clung to the air, wrapping the castle in muggy humidity. Lightning wove through the sky, illuminating the glass towers like beacons of forewarning, foreshadowing the storm I was about to walk into. Thanos beat his wings against the swirling winds, the electricity in the air fueling his powerful flight as he aimed for the granite landing port atop the castle.

With a sharp screech, he announced our arrival, his claws scraping the stone as he touched down with precision. He spun once, his spines rising in warning as his golden eyes scanned the surroundings. His tension mirrored my own, sharp and unrelenting. I placed a steadying hand on his neck, feeling the shiver of energy beneath his scales.

"Coast is clear. Settle," I murmured.

The command soothed him. His spines lowered, folding back against his body as he exhaled a puff of smoke from his nostrils. I slid off his back, boots striking the stone with a dull thud. My armor felt heavier than usual, each movement weighted by the gravity of what was to come. I brushed off the cold residue of our flight and handed Thanos's reins to the waiting stable master.

"Your Highness." Commander Cave's voice broke through the howling wind, his tone carrying an edge of unease that only heightened my own turmoil. I nodded curtly, giving Thanos one last pat before turning toward the glass archways leading into the castle. The storm outside followed me in spirit, thunder rolling in tandem with the echo of my boots on the polished granite floor.

I caught sight of my sisters lingering in the wings of the main hall. Aella and Althea stood stiffly, their hands clenched at their sides as if anchoring themselves. Their eyes betrayed what their bodies refused to show: a longing to run to me, to wrap me in an embrace. But fear held them back, fear of what my presence here meant. Their tension mirrored my own, and I couldn't bring myself to offer more than a brief nod of acknowledgment before continuing my march toward the office doors.

The doors loomed ahead like the gates of a battlefield I never wished to enter. The weight of the glass and steel, once a symbol of our strength, now felt suffocating. No footman stood to open them for me; this was a war I had to face alone. I paused, closing my eyes, willing the storm within me to still. But it was futile. I could still feel her— the flutter of Olivia's emotions, the echo of her pain pulsing under my skin. It clawed at me, sharp and relentless, and I hated knowing I was the cause.

I took a steadying breath and pushed the doors open.

Inside, my father and brother stood waiting, their dark navy military attire stark against the glass and stone backdrop. Their faces were carved from stone, unreadable as they assessed me, though I felt the weight of their expectations pressing against my chest like iron. The air outside seemed to quiet, leaving only the sound of my boots crossing the polished floor.

"Have you decided, Son?" My father's voice broke the silence, his tone devoid of the usual authority it carried. His sharp blue eyes searched me, and for the first time in years, his mask was gone. There was no anger, no command—just the raw vulnerability of a man who sensed

something had changed. He could see it in me, the way the fates had carved a path I could no longer escape.

I nodded, unable to form the words yet. My throat burned as I tried to swallow the scream building inside me. I saw Olivia's face in my mind, heard her sobs reverberating through my chest. It was like she was there, inside me, screaming for me to leave this place, to return to her. My nails dug into my palms, the sting grounding me as I clenched my fists tighter.

"Brother?" Niall's voice broke through my thoughts, his face mirroring our father's. His nose twitched, his sharp senses picking up what I couldn't hide. He stepped closer, his brows knitting together in concern.

"Jeyr..."

"I will do what is best for my kingdom," I croaked, the words ripping from my throat like shards of glass. The crack in my voice betrayed me, and I felt the weight of my resolve crumbling. My breath grew ragged, the tug in my chest pulling harder and harder, threatening to tear me apart. I pressed a hand to my sternum, trying to ease the ache that clawed at my very soul. Gods, I prayed she couldn't feel this, prayed she was spared the agony consuming me.

"No..." My father's voice wavered, the crack in his façade splitting wide open. His expression twisted with something I hadn't seen in years: fear.   "Son, tell me I am reading this wrong. Tell me that scent on you is just from a woman you lust after. Tell me I am not about to break something the fates have aligned."

The room grew unbearably heavy, the air thick with tension as his words hung between us. I couldn't meet his gaze, couldn't bear to see the hope in his eyes as he begged me to deny what we both knew to be true. My silence was damning.

I closed my eyes. I tried to hide her scent on me, but it was beginning to mix with mine. The more time I spent with her, the more I felt that invisible connection grow. The more I began to notice her emotions sinking into my skin, the two of us becoming one. That night in her room was a mistake, her arousal... We were so close to joining. I punished myself every day and now my betrayal to her was growing.

"Brother, answer him," Niall said, his own voice beginning to crack.

I looked to the sky, to the glass ceiling where the storm had paused, frozen in time.

"I will marry the Princess. I will do my d-duty." I couldn't fight the sob that forced its way free. I couldn't look away from the clouds above me, as if apologizing to the Gods for messing with whatever plans they had for me and Olivia. My palm pressed heavy against my chest. Gods I hope she isn't feeling this right now.

I wanted to know if this would have been easier three months ago. If I didn't have that three months to know her. But I would never wish those away, never.

"Oh, Gods," my brother cried. I tore my gaze from the sky, seeing my brother spin on the spot, hand raking through his hair.

"Take me, Father. Take me to Bane. I will call off my marriage to Sierra, and I will marry the princess."

My stomach twisted. I shook my head. Sierra was his long-time love. She was a lord's daughter with snow in her fingertips. Their powers together would be great for the Kingdom. Their love was simple: two best friends with one common goal. Together, they would be great rulers.

"No!" I protested. "You love her. This has been planned for half a century."

"I don't love her like that, Brother. She is my best friend. She will understand."

My father stood frozen, his stillness louder than the storm raging outside. A single tear slipped down his weathered face, and for the first time in years, I saw him as more than the Grand Duke— he was a man, a father caught in the crossfire of fate.

"Neither of you will marry her," he finally said, his voice hoarse and laden with grief. "We will have to buy some time. I... I have been a bad father. Did... Was the girl around when you came here last? The scent, it was fainter then, barely noticeable. You two are close to bonding, aren't you?"

I hadn't intended to nod, but my body betrayed me, the truth spilling out in silence.

"I thought so," he murmured, his shoulders slumping as though the weight of his mistakes bore down on him all at once. "The smell is there, but no band yet. Does she know?"

He leaned against his desk, his hands bracing against the polished wood as his eyes glazed over, lost in memories of another time. I knew the look well. He was back on the battlefield where he met my mother, the healer from another kingdom. The stories had been etched into my childhood like sacred texts— the way he couldn't stay away, praying for injuries just to have an excuse to visit her tent, to feel her touch, to bask in her presence. I felt that same pull every time Olivia crossed my mind, every time her voice reached me, every time I caught her scent in the air. The need to map every part of her, to know every piece of her heart— it was consuming.

I shook my head, grounding myself.

"No, she... she is different. Special. I don't think she knows about Companachs. She knows we have a connection, and she's expressed her desire to explore it, but... I've been fighting it, knowing I would have to marry another. I haven't been good to her, but she's forgiven me

more times than I deserve."

My father's lips twisted into a sad, knowing smile. His gaze softened for just a moment before it turned heavy again, clouded with regret. Niall, pacing the room like a caged animal, tugged at his hair, his frustration palpable.

"Where... where does she come from?" my father asked, his voice laced with something between curiosity and dread.

The question jolted me. A lump formed in my throat, and I had to force the words out. I'm sorry, Hummingbird, I thought silently.

"Queens' Kingdom," I said, my voice barely above a whisper.

Niall froze mid-step, his eyes wide as they locked with mine. The air in the room grew colder, thicker. I nodded, confirming what he feared, what we all feared. I didn't need to look at my father to know the storm brewing inside him mirrored the one outside. His head hung low, his hands gripping the edge of the desk like it was the only thing keeping him standing.

"The fates are fucking cruel!" My father's roar shattered the silence. He stood abruptly, sweeping his desk clear in a single angry motion. Books and papers crashed to the floor, scattering like the fragmented pieces of our family. The storm outside answered his rage, lightning streaking across the glass walls in blinding bursts.

"How do you expect me to believe in you?" he shouted, his voice rising to meet the heavens. "How? When you gave me the most perfect woman in the world, made me give her my heart, only to rip it away? You split my heart further with four perfect children, and then you took her from me. And now this! You give my son a Companach from the enemy— a girl born of the kingdom we've sworn to destroy! FUCK!"

His words echoed, vibrating through the walls, through the very marrow of my bones. I clenched my jaw, my own anger simmering beneath the surface. Perfect children. He never called us that. This was the man who had pawned off Aella, who had turned cold and unfeeling after losing my mother. But now, here he was, raw and broken, revealing the regret he'd carried all these years.

"Father," I said, my voice steady despite the turmoil within. His rage began to ebb, his breaths coming in uneven gasps as he clutched at his chest. "Father, stop."

But he wasn't finished. He turned to Aella and Althea, who had appeared silently in the doorway, their faces streaked with tears.

"Aella," he choked, his voice trembling. "I failed you. I failed your mother."

Aella's lip quivered, but she held her ground, her spine straight as steel.

"You did," she said, her voice calm but unyielding. "But like Jeyr, I would— and will— do anything for this family, for this kingdom. I never said anything because you couldn't even look me in the eye. I know you regret it every time you see me."

Her words struck like arrows, each one embedding itself into his chest. He let out a choked sob, his hand covering his face as though to hide from the truth. Althea gripped Aella's arm, her support silent but unwavering.

"Now, Father," Aella continued, her voice gaining strength, "you have a chance to do the right thing. Don't give in to Bane. Let Jeyr have his fated. Go to other kingdoms. Form alliances. Learn from this." She gestured to the scar marring her beautiful face. My hand found hers, and she gave it a soft squeeze, her strength bolstering my own.

My father nodded slowly, his shoulders sagging under the weight of his failures.

"Yes," he murmured. "But first, we need to meet her. We should welcome her into the family and protect her. Anyone from Queens' Kingdom isn't safe. We need to train her, teach her our native tongue."

I froze, my body going rigid as guilt clawed at me.

"We can't."

The room fell silent. All eyes turned to me, heavy with expectation and confusion.

"Son..." my father began, his voice tinged with caution.

"It would be a threat to our kingdom," I said, my voice hollow. "A target on our backs. It would put her in too much danger. Her powers... they're unique. If word got out..."

My voice trailed off, the storm outside going eerily quiet as if the fates themselves held their breath.

"Jeyr," my father said, his tone sharp and demanding. "What power does she possess?"

The silence stretched, heavy and suffocating. My throat tightened as I forced the words out, each one a betrayal to the girl who had unknowingly turned my world upside down.

"She... Olivia is an Empath."

Present

I straighten, the weight of my confession pressing against my ribs. "My father is the Grand Duke of Aimsir. I'm the second-born son." The words feel foreign on my tongue, too polished, too sharp. I force myself to keep my gaze steady. "Everything I told you about my family was true. I just didn't want you to know I was of royal blood. I didn't want you to see me differently—to decide I wasn't worth knowing."

Olivia's shoulders tense, her eyes narrowing. "And why wouldn't I want to associate with you?" Her voice cuts through the space between us, too precise, too sharp. It hits harder than I expect.

Caomh makes a low sound of amusement in my mind. *This has started badly.* I shoot him a warning look. He lifts a brow, lips curving into something too smug for the situation before turning away.

I exhale, steadying myself. "Because my family is always in the spotlight. Being near me puts you at risk." My fingers curl into fists at my sides before I force them to relax. "But not telling you who I was... it let me be myself around you. I didn't have to be the Grand Duke's son. I could just be—" I hesitate, searching for the right words. "I could just be a man who felt something real with you. And in turn, I got to know the real you too. No politics. No expectations. Just us."

Her expression doesn't change. A mask perfected through years of practice, no doubt. "And the reality?" Her voice is unreadable. "That you're a prince, and you could never be with an Empath, much less marry one?"

A lump forms in my throat. "Yes."

The silence that follows is unbearable. I can feel it—her retreat. The way she's already stepping back into the space where she believes herself unwanted, a burden. It's not the first time I've seen her withdraw like this, and something inside me clenches at the thought of letting it happen again.

I push forward, the words tumbling out faster than I intend. "At first, I thought my father would never allow it. Our kingdom is already under threat. A marriage to anyone from the Queens' kingdom would be seen as treason—let alone an Empath. But marriage to a Companach..." I swallow. "When he sensed the change in my scent, I saw something in him. A glimpse of the man he was before my mother passed. Olivia, your bloodline no longer matters to him."

Her eyes flicker, a shift I almost miss, the green darkening, silver edging the irises. She blinks, her expression unreadable. "Sensed me?" she whispers. "Sensed us?"

I take a slow breath, bracing myself for her reaction. "Have you ever heard of a Companach, Hummingbird?" My voice is quieter now, the truth pressing against the space between us.

Her brows pull together, lips pursing in thought, and gods help me, I want to kiss that expression right off her face. But I don't move.

I continue, voice steady. "Many philosophers, alchemists, healers, and ancient historians have tried to explain how Companachs come to be. How two Fae can be bound to one another, not for breeding, not for alliances, but because their souls are a match. The fates choose them—not for power, not for status, but because they are meant. Their strengths align, their weaknesses balance. No one else will ever fit them the same way."

She stays still, watching me, searching for something. Her gaze flickers over my face, as if she can see inside me, past flesh and bone, to whatever part of me has already tethered itself to her.

I let out a slow breath. "When a Companach pair meets, their scents become one. Their emotions begin to merge. The bond grows, and so does their connection—their ability to feel each other, even across great distances. No matter where they are, they will always be close. Always drawn back together."

Olivia doesn't move, doesn't speak. But something in the air shifts. The weight of the truth settles between us, too heavy to ignore.

And I wait—for her reaction, for her choice.

I hold her gaze, letting the truth of what we are settle between us. Letting her see the raw vulnerability I've hidden behind my walls for so long. Waiting, hoping, that she'll understand. She shakes her head.

"Explain." Her voice is steady, but her hands betray her, gesturing between us with a mix of confusion and frustration.

"When Companachs finally meet," I begin, my voice careful, as if the wrong tone could shatter the fragile air between us, "and both parties accept the bond, there is a mark. No one knows why or exactly how it happens. Some say it's so the rest of the world knows they are claimed—taken in a way that is absolute."

My thoughts drift to my parents' bands, the marks that once symbolized a love so powerful it could withstand anything. The golden wedding bands they wore pale in comparison to the luminous white bands etched into their skin. Those glowing cuffs, a testament to their bond, light up when their connection is being used, their love radiating like an unspoken language between them. And then... when my mother died, my father's band darkened. That radiant white turned into a sickly, black scar that wraps around his wrist, a cruel reminder of what had been stolen from him.

"Each bond is unique," I continue, "but it always manifests as a band on the left wrist. The designs are different—some intricate, others simple—but all are exclusive to the couple, a mark of their connection."

I watch her, the way her eyes drop to her wrist as if she's already imagining the mark, weighing the risks and rewards of accepting this fate. She doesn't look at me, not yet, but I can feel the battle raging inside her.

"That yearning you feel," I say softly, my voice breaking into the quiet that has fallen between us, "the pull that I feel—that's the bond trying to take place. If we both fully accept it, the bands will come. But once it's done, Liv... there's no going back. There's no one else for us after that—not truly."

Her gaze finally lifts to mine. Those green eyes, edged with silver when her emotions heighten, study me like I'm a puzzle she's not sure she wants to solve.

"What else don't I know?" she asks, her voice even, but her composure like a fortress. Her warmth is gone, replaced by a measured coolness that leaves my chest aching. "I can feel that you're hiding something else."

I let out a slow, steadying breath, bracing myself. "Since the war... since the loss of my mother, I stay with Caomh and Jethro. We build a team— a brotherhood— with the common goal of taking down Bane and the King for what they take from us. Along the way, I lost my father— not to death, but to grief. He changed after her death. He chose to try and ally with Puinnsean, desperate to stop the bloodshed, to bring peace to our kingdom. But in the attempt to solidify that alliance? He was forced to offer something in return—proof of his loyalty."

I swallow hard, my throat tightening as the memories claw their way to the surface. "That proof? It was giving my sister, Aella, to the son of the man who murdered our mother. And my father—he agreed to it. Like it was nothing. Like she was some coin he could toss across the table. She nearly died because of it."

Olivia's fingers twitch, her knuckles whitening as she clenches her hands in her lap. Her silence screams louder than any words.

"We killed him. Her husband. Got her out. But I never went back home after that. I still can't look my father in the eye. I don't think I ever will—not after what he did to her. And then... he called me. After I met you."

I hesitate, watching her for any flicker of emotion. She gives me nothing but a blank canvas, her face unreadable.

"He called to tell me I had to marry the Princess of Puinnsean," I continue, the words bitter on my tongue. "I refused at first. I said I would denounce myself from the throne before I would agree to it—that I would rather die than be aligned with them. But as time goes on, Bane begins putting pressure on my family. Denying his daughter means Althea— my youngest sister— would have to marry his son instead. I have only months to decide: me or my sister."

I clench my fists, the sharp sting of my nails grounding me in the present. "At Winter Solstice, I went to my father to tell him I'd do it. That I'd marry her. I couldn't risk Althea—not after what Aella went through. I wouldn't let her face that kind of fate. But when I got there... my father, he sensed you on me. Sensed the bond between us. And everything changed."

I let the silence hang between us, heavy and oppressive. I search her face for a sign, a crack in the stoic mask she wears, but her expression doesn't shift. She simply stares at me, her gaze unwavering.

"Say something," I murmur, my voice barely audible, the weight of her silence pressing down on me.

She blinks, finally. But her lips remain closed, her jaw tight. And I know, whatever she is feeling, she isn't ready to share it— not yet.

Olivia

THREADS OF TRUTH AND THE CHILL OF NIGHT

I grit my teeth, to gather enough control to leave. The room feels suffocating, thick with tension and betrayal.

Jethro and Caomh stand silently, their postures stiff, watching me as if I might shatter. For months, they have watched me follow Jeyr like a lovesick fool, all while knowing the truth they have kept hidden. Three months of hot and cold. Three months of thinking I was going insane because I couldn't get the blue-eyed Fae out of my head.

I look at them, one by one, the men I have let in. Assassins. Royalty. **Liars.** My gaze lands on Jeyr last, the weight of his deceit crushing me more than the others combined. All those moments when I let him see me, all the times he could have told me the truth... Didn't he trust me? Didn't he think I deserved to know? The disgust churns in my chest, sharp and bitter. I think of my mother, how she moved through life with a quiet, impenetrable calm, never letting anyone see how deeply she felt. I grasp at that same facade now, because if I let myself be anything but her—if I let myself be me—I will break.

"I've heard enough," I say, my voice flat, each word cutting like shards of glass. "I'm sure there are centuries of secrets you've hidden from me. But it's too late. Three months ago, I placed my trust in you—all of you. Not just that, I placed my heart in your hands. And each of you took a part of me I will never get back. I trusted you with who I am. I let you into parts of me I've kept hidden for over half my life." Caomh's golden eyes widen in shock, and then his voice is in my mind, soft but pleading. *Livy, please...*

I flinch at the intrusion, the whisper of his thoughts feeling invasive now. His apprehension is etched into his features, but I can't hear him. I close my mind to him, blocking out his pleas.

Jethro steps forward, his large frame looming, hand outstretched as if to anchor me. "Little Huntress... please..."

I shake my head sharply, silencing him before he can say more. I thought we had shared a true friendship. I thought we had opened up to each other without reservation. But he has left out the most important truths—the ones that would cut the deepest. I raise my hand to stop him, unable to summon the words to express the depth of my hurt. My feet carry me toward the door, each step weighted with anger and grief.

"Hummingbird, please stop. Please, don't end things this way."

Jeyr's voice, strangled and broken, freezes me in my tracks. His words hit me like a physical blow, his desperation clawing at my resolve.

"I need time to think," I say, my voice trembling now, unable to hold the stoic facade much longer. I turn to him, meeting his gaze. "You made me fall in love with you, Jeyr. You exposed me, encouraged me to open up... and then you decided to leave, to marry another—without telling me. Regardless of the circumstances, I had a right to know the truth. All of it. You played with my heart, Prince of Aimsir. And I don't know if I can forgive that."

His face cracks, a single tear escaping down his cheek. He doesn't wipe it away, just lets it fall to the floor between us. I turn before I can let the invisible thread—the one that ties us together in ways I still don't understand—tug me back to him.

And I leave.

The crackling fire hisses as though it wants to join the conversation, the flames swaying in a slow, hypnotic dance. Mary's voice cuts through my thoughts as I stand before the hearth, my arms crossed, trying to warm up after the biting ride home.

"I can feel your sulking, Olivia. If you're going to sulk, at least lie down and do it properly."

I turn to see her perched on the daybed, her withered hands smoothing a pillow across her lap. There is no judgment in her tone, only an invitation that's impossible to refuse.

With a sigh, I cross the room and let my head fall into the pillow. Mary's touch is light, her fingers combing through my untamed curls. It's the kind of motherly affection that strips me bare, leaving my carefully constructed defenses useless.

"Why have you been home so much lately? What happened to getting out and about?" she asks softly, her words brushing against the raw edges of my heart.

"Have I been bothering you?" My voice carries a thin thread of humor, but underneath, I worry the answer might be yes.

"No," she chuckles, her fingers weaving through the knots in my hair. "Though you've been here, your mind is not. You're a world away, daydreaming about whoever it is that's taken up so much of your time lately."

I stiffen. My thoughts slam to a halt as embarrassment heats my cheeks. Mary's chuckle deepens, her knowing smile brushing away any attempt I make to appear unaffected.

"Do you think I hadn't noticed you coming home in a loved-up haze these past few months? You think Hecate and I didn't see you riding into the stables, or legs wrapped around that tall, strapping man? Completely oblivious to us watching from the storehouse window?"

The words hit me like a blast of cold air, stealing my breath. My nerves flutter as the realization strikes: I wasn't as discreet as I thought. Mary's smile softens, her voice dipping lower.

"I have half a mind to scold you, but the love that flowed through this house afterward... well, it made it very hard to stay upset."

Her words pull at my heartstrings, conjuring memories of the warmth I once felt, the way his gaze made the rest of the world blur into insignificance. That warmth has been replaced with a cold ache.

"What happened?" Mary presses gently. "Did you fight? Does Cooper need to pay him a visit?" Her teasing tone gives way to concern, and it's that concern that unravels me.

"He was hiding things from me," I admit, my voice breaking under the weight of the truth. "He said it was to protect me, but he never gave me the choice to decide. So many lies, Mary. I'm over being lied to."

Mary hums softly, considering my words.

"I don't know the whole story, Olivia, but I know this much: that man loved you. I saw it in the way he looked at you. I may not be an Empath, but I felt it. It poured off him every time he looked at you—as though leaving you was like leaving a part of himself behind."

The burning ache in my chest rises to my throat, and I have to pinch my nose to keep the tears at bay.

"I know you felt it too," Mary continues, her voice as gentle as the touch of her hand. "I know you can sense the truth in someone's feelings. Your instincts are strong, Olivia, and they've never steered you wrong. Tell me... did he ever feel like a bad person? Even with the lies, did you ever think he would harm you?"

I shake my head slowly.

"No," I whisper. "I never felt any threat from him... or his friends. I trusted them. I confided in them, and they with me. That's why it hurt so much."

Mary's wrinkled hand brushes my tears away, her steel-grey eyes glimmering with love. "Sometimes we lie to protect the ones we love," she says softly. "It's never easy and it hurts us too. I know we haven't always been the best guardians, not with the pressure you've been under, how much you've had to hide. I appreciate you for not resenting us, Olivia. I am so sorry." Her voice cracks, and her apology strikes a chord I don't know I need to hear. Years of quiet resentment I haven't even realized I carry seem to fall away, settling like dust.

"You did as my mother wished," I say, my voice trembling. "For that, I can't be angry. But they... they knew my story, and they still chose to lie."

Mary's lips tighten into a pained smile. "I'm not saying he was right to lie to you, but maybe he needs your forgiveness. And maybe, Olivia, you need it too." Her gaze softens. "I don't know these Fae who've taken you under their wings, but I've waited my whole life to see you happy. I'll forever be grateful to whoever they are for giving me my wish." Her words make me freeze. "Are you not scared, like Mother was, that they'll take advantage of me?"

"No," Mary says simply. "They trained you, Olivia. We've noticed the difference. You control yourself better now, and you're not projecting like you used to. You've grown. Also..." She hesitates, a flicker of amusement crossing her face. "The Prince of Aimsir's mother was a dear friend of your mother's and Hecate's. Hecate has been keeping tabs on them for years—your Fae male included. She says he's a good man. His friends are good people too." My heart stills. "Why did no one tell me this?" Another voice answers from the doorway. "Because, child, we wanted you to have your freedom and make your own decisions for once."

Hecate's eyes are soft as they meet mine, but the weight of their words presses heavily on my chest. There is so much I don't know, so much that has been kept from me. I look between the two of them, my chest tightening with the sharp sting of betrayal and the ache of understanding. "I... I have to go," I murmur, my voice cracking.

Before they can stop me, I turn and run out the door, the chill of the night biting at my skin.

Olivia

SHADOWS IN THE SNOW

The snow cascades around me as I hoist myself onto Ness's back, the cold biting at every inch of exposed skin. I nudge her forward, directing her toward the Black Forest, but my mind is far from the path ahead. It churns with the weight of betrayal. Everyone has lied to me, and I am left questioning how I can ever trust anyone again. The trees blur into dark streaks, echoing my frantic thoughts as Ness gallops deeper into the forest.

I slow her as my breath becomes visible puffs of frost in the air. The wool-lined coat I wear, still faintly holding the scent of Jeyr, is a poor shield against the frigid winter. Pulling the hood over my ears, I pray for relief from the bitter wind stinging my face. Yet it isn't just the chill— it's the silence. The forest is unnaturally still. Not a single rustle of leaves or snap of branches disturbs the suffocating quiet. The air hangs heavy, pressing against my chest like an invisible weight, making it difficult to breathe.

My instincts whisper warnings I don't want to hear. The hair on the back of my neck rises as I struggle to steady myself. It's just the winter, I try to reason, just the cold swallowing the forest whole. But as Ness and Kyzan move deeper into the labyrinth of trees, the nagging unease in my gut grows louder. I close my eyes and release my power, sending it outward like invisible tendrils. It dances between the skeletal branches, searching for a spark of life. There. I feel something— a creature moving lazily, unaware of my presence.

Urging Ness forward, I follow the pull of my magic, her hooves crunching softly in the snow. My muscles tense the closer we draw. The creature's energy shifts, spiking in excitement. A deep bell rings within me, an instinctive alarm.

It's time to leave.

Kyzan's low growl shatters the silence, his hackles raised, muscles taut and ready to strike. My pulse quickens, fear flooding my veins in icy waves. Without hesitation, I yank Ness's reins and spin her around. "Let's go, now!" My frantic command sends her surging forward, Kyzan at her flank, his sharp golden eyes flicking toward the darkness behind us. I feel it too— the presence, the thrill of the hunt emanating from something unseen. This time, I'm not the hunter. I'm prey.

Pain tears through my shoulder like a lightning strike. I gasp, glancing down to see crimson blossoming across the fabric of Jeyr's coat. An arrow protrudes from my flesh, the sharp burrs digging deeper with each jolt of Ness's stride. Blood drips hot and thick against the biting cold, staining the snow in my wake.

"Kyzan, get help!" I rasp, my voice shaking with pain. "Get Jeyr. Anyone!" My wolf falters, his ears flat against his head as he glances between me and the shadows behind us. His golden eyes mirror the agony I can't voice. "Go!" I bark, forcing the command. Reluctantly, Kyzan sprints into the darkness, his figure disappearing as Ness pushes on, her breath steaming in the frigid air.

Another arrow whistles through the forest. My breath hitches as it strikes, embedding itself under my ribcage. White-hot pain explodes in my side, stealing the air from my lungs. Blood pours from the wound, soaking my shirt. "Fuck," I hiss, my trembling hands gripping Ness's reins. Darkness edges my vision, my body weakening with each second.

A third arrow buries itself in my left side. The sharp agony forces a guttural cry from my lips, but I can't stop. Ness steams forward, her body heaving with exertion. I cling to her neck, my hands slick with blood. My vision blurs as the shadows around me seem to grow darker, the forest spinning. The world tilts as Ness jolts, and I feel my body slipping. Gravity pulls me down, and I hit the frozen ground with a sickening thud.

The impact drives the arrows deeper, wringing a scream from my chest. Snow presses against my face, its icy burn offering a cruel contrast to the fire searing through my body. Through the haze of pain, I see Ness rearing at the edge of a ring of flames. Fire encircles me, trapping me. My breaths are shallow, labored, as blood pools beneath me. "Find Kyzan... Ness..." I choke on the words, blood spilling from my lips. "That's an order."

Ness's hooves thunder away, leaving me alone in the suffocating silence. The spots in my vision grow, swallowing the forest whole.

"You're not very wise, sending off both your protectors," a voice hisses, dripping with malice. A figure emerges from the darkness, his presence suffocating. I try to focus, to call on my powers, but my mind is a foggy, fractured mess. White-hot heat courses through my veins, clashing with the icy numbness creeping through my limbs.

"Ah, the viper bàis. Its toxin has settled into your blood now," he sneers, his shadow looming over me. I gurgle, choking on blood as I fight to respond, but my body betrays me. His hands are cold, invasive as they search me. My coat falls open, and the icy air slices into my wounds, amplifying the agony.

"I wonder what kind of pay I'd get for an Empath's soul," he muses, his voice laced with cruel delight. Something sharp presses against my ribs, digging deeper until a scream rips through me. Pain overtakes every sense, drowning me in a sea of agony.

"Fucking shut up," he growls, his hand covering my mouth as the instrument pierces my chest further. Tears spill down my face as the world dims, the darkness dragging me under. My screams echo in the cold, empty forest until they're swallowed whole.

THE LAST HOPE AND THE TIES THAT BIND

Something twists inside me, sharp and unrelenting. Pain surges up my arm, seizing my breath as I double over, clutching the edge of the desk. My nails scrape against the wood, my fangs bite into my lip until I taste blood. I can't focus, can't think past the searing ache that pulses with every beat of my heart. Something is wrong. Terribly wrong.

"Jeyr!" Caomh is at my side in an instant, his voice taut with alarm. He freezes mid-step, his eyes dropping to my wrist. His sharp features twist in horror, the color draining from his face. I follow his gaze, my heart stuttering at the sight. The figure-eight bands on my wrist, the mark of my bond to Olivia, glow a deep, bruised purple. The darkened color spreads, winding up my arm like creeping vines. My stomach drops. "Olivia," I whisper, her name falling from my lips like a prayer.

Caomh echoes my thoughts. Without another word, we bolt for the door. The sound of it slamming open reverberates through the hall as Jethro descends the stairs, still wrestling his arms into his shirt. "Kyzan," Jethro pants. "I can hear him. He's howling from the forest." "Where?" I bark, the word barely audible over the pounding of my pulse. "The coast!" Jethro doesn't wait for us to follow his lead. He reaches for our shoulders, and in a flash of blinding light, we land on the frozen shoreline.

The icy air bites into my skin, but it's nothing compared to the gut-wrenching sound of Kyzan's howls. The wolf tears toward us with unrelenting speed, his paws pounding against the snow as his golden eyes lock on mine. He stops short, his breath clouding in the cold air. His entire body vibrates with urgency, his gaze flicking between us and the

Black Forest.

"Kyzan," I call, my voice cracking under the weight of my fear. My chest tightens, and I look down to see the bands on my wrist darkening further, the pain spreading deeper into my core. *No.* Kyzan turns, bolting back toward the forest. Without hesitation, we follow. My legs move on instinct, propelling me forward through the dense trees. Then I hear it—her scream. The sound tears through the forest, raw and jagged, sending an ache so deep into my chest I falter mid-step. Jethro and Caomh aren't faring any better, their hands clutching their ears as they stumble forward. Kyzan's cries join hers, a desperate, guttural sound that mirrors the agony ripping through my body.

When we reach the edge of the clearing, the sight before us nearly brings me to my knees. Fire encircles Olivia, a perfect ring of flames that roars high into the sky. Ness rears at the edge, her hooves pawing at the ground in frantic protest.

Then the flames extinguish, collapsing inward as if snuffed out by the weight of her agony. My gaze snaps to the center of the circle, where a hooded figure looms over her. He turns, his face obscured by shadows, but his smile—a cruel, mocking twist of lips—is visible even in the dim light. "The last Empath is no longer a secret," he sneers, his voice low and venomous. Before any of us can move, he vanishes, leaving only the echoes of his words.

My knees buckle as I fall to her side, my hands trembling as they hover over her. She is still, too still. Her pale skin is almost translucent, her golden glow reduced to a faint flicker. Blood pools around her, staining the snow crimson. My breath hitches at the sight of her wide, unblinking eyes. They are black—empty, endless voids.

"Olivia," I whisper, my voice breaking.

"Jeyr, help her!" Caomh's voice cracks with panic, his hands gripping my shoulders. "Heal her!" I press my palms against her wounds, willing every ounce of power I have into her. But the moment my magic meets her body, it recoils, the resistance hitting me like a physical blow.

"It's not working," I choke out, my hands trembling. "Something's stopping me..."

"Poison," Caomh breathes, his realization hitting him like a blow to the chest. Jethro's face pales, his hands shaking as he hovers near her wrist. Kyzan stands guard over her, his body trembling with rage and despair. "We need to move her now," Caomh commands, his voice firm despite the anguish in his eyes.

Without hesitation, Jethro winnows us back to the manor. I cradle her lifeless body against me, her golden light flickering weakly beneath her skin. She feels so small, so fragile, and I can feel her slipping away with every passing second. I lay her on the bed, my hands brushing the blood-soaked hair from her face. Her skin is cold, her breathing shallow. I press my forehead against her hand, a sob tearing from my throat as I whisper, "Please, Hummingbird. Please fight. Don't leave me."

"Move."

The voice cuts through the room like a blade, sharp and commanding. Hecate's small frame appears before me, her eyes burning crimson as she chants under her breath. The air thickens, charged with something ancient and volatile. Jethro's instincts flare, his sword halfway from its holster before Caomh's steady hand stops him.

"Who is she, and what is she—" Jethro demands, his voice edged with mistrust. Caomh exhales sharply. "Well, I should have known..."

I barely register their exchange. *I can't.* Not when Olivia's breathing hitches—then stops. The world shatters. My limbs lock, terror splitting through me like ice fracturing over a lake. My gaze snaps to Hecate, to the blood on her hands, to the stillness in Olivia's form.

"Don't," Hecate warns, her voice iron-wrought, her palm lifting before I can come undone. "She isn't dead, so no grieving. But I need you, now." I force breath back into my lungs, though it feels like knives scraping against my ribs. Olivia is still here. I can feel her. But the moment is slipping.

Hecate's eyes, still alight with unnatural red, meet mine with the force of a storm. "I have paused her death, but we don't have much time. The venom is inside her, poisoning her body. I can hold her frozen in time, but I need the venom itself to make an antidote. Without it, she dies the moment I release my hold." I swallow past the lump in my throat, my mind battling between devastation and action. Hecate turns to Jethro and Caomh, both still as statues, their faces ashen with shock.

"You... You're one of the witches... the coven sworn—" Caomh's voice is laced with awe.

"Yes, I am from the coven sworn to protect Empaths like her. And I am the last of my kind—at least, that I know of," Hecate says, her voice unwavering. "The wolf informed me of trouble. Now shut your gaping mouth and do as I said!" I snap from my paralysis, my voice reverberating through the manor like a war cry.

"Cao, get Althea. Jethro, find Aiden—his trade connections might lead to the viper bàis or its venom. Get Lorkan. Get every healer we know. NOW!" The windows tremble at the force of my command.

Caomh and Jethro both straighten, nodding before disappearing in twin bursts of wind and light. The room falls into suffocating silence. I turn back to Olivia's still form, my vision blurring as I fight the sickness clawing its way up my throat. The golden glow in her chest flickers, weak but there. Holding on. I grit my teeth so hard my jaw aches, but I can't look away. I can't move. Hecate steps closer, kneeling at Olivia's side. She takes her cold, limp hand into hers, her voice thick with grief and fury.

"In an Empath, their power lies in the soul," she murmurs, her fingers tightening around Olivia's.

"It's the very essence of them. That's what makes them able to feel others—to care, to heal. There is no such thing as a bad Empath. To be an Empath, you must have a certain kind of soul. One open to others. To love. That is why they were hunted. In the war, the Great King and Bane didn't just kill them—they took them. If an Empath didn't die from being used as a weapon, they died when the enemy stole their soul."

Her voice wavers, but her grip on Olivia never does. "What they did with them, I don't know," she continues, her maroon eyes shimmering, nose red against the burn of fighting tears. "I have spent my life trying to figure it out. But whoever did this to Olivia... It was the same way they killed her mother." The words twist through me like a dagger. I clench my fists, my nails biting into my palms, but the pain is nothing compared to the abyss opening inside me. I've been too late. Again.

My breath comes in slow, shaking draws, my body fighting the primal need to winnow back into the forest and tear through whatever poor bastards dared to do this. I want their throats. Their hearts. Their screams. But none of that will bring her back. None of that will undo the damage already done. I force myself to focus on her. On the fragile thread of life she still clings to.

I've always known Olivia is strong. But as I look down at her now, barely breathing, her body fighting even when it's been torn apart... I realize she's stronger than I ever could have imagined. And gods, I will not lose her. Not like this. Not ever.

The sound of thundering footsteps shatters the suffocating silence, jolting me from my trance. I tear my gaze from Olivia's still form, my fingers frozen against her blood-slicked skin, as the room fills with familiar faces. Shock ripples through them, their eyes taking in the horror before them. My sisters are the first I seek out, their piercing blue gazes locking onto mine. Despair lines their faces, their expressions stricken. Althea's gaze trails over me, searching—until it lands on the dark, twisting bands that now run up my left arm. The mark of a bond half-formed. A bond that can be severed at any moment. My fingers clench.

Aiden stands rooted in place, his auburn hair slightly disheveled, his green eyes flickering between me and Olivia. "Mother above," he mutters. Then, he pulls a small glass vial from his pocket, the liquid inside darker than night. "I have the venom—" Before another word can leave his mouth, Hecate is on him. She snatches the vial from his grasp and disappears without a trace, her departure nothing but a whisper of air. "What the fuck was that?" Aiden's eyes widen as he stumbles back. His gaze darts between us, searching for an explanation.

"Olivia's last hope," I answer, my voice tight with restrained emotion. My jaw aches from the force of my teeth grinding together. Every second wasted is a second closer to losing her. "I need all of you," I say, my voice like steel, slicing through the thick air. My brothers and sisters snap to attention, their faces hardening with purpose. "Caomh, you need to hold her mind. Keep her calm—take the pain." Caomh flinches but gives a sharp nod.

"Althea, you and I will heal her as fast as we can." "I will use every ounce of my power, Brother," she vows, her voice shaking with fury. Her thick, chocolate waves tumble over her shoulders, her sharp brows drawn together as those ocean-blue eyes burn with determination. Despite the horror in front of her, she stands tall, unwavering.

"Jethro, use your red light to speed the healing process. Aiden, I need you to keep her warm. Aella, keep her heart beating." My voice is steady, but my hands tremble as my eyes flicker to her open chest. My stomach twists violently, my vision blurring. I have healed countless warriors, pulled them from the brink of death. But this... this is Olivia. *My* Olivia. And my hands have never felt so useless. "Of course, Brother," they respond in unison, their devotion unwavering.

Aiden takes a sharp breath. "I can cauterize the wounds to stop the bleeding if needed." His jaw is tight, and though he tries to mask it, I see his hesitation. I give a firm nod of appreciation. I can barely speak. If I open my mouth, I'm not sure I will be able to hold myself together. "What about me?" A soft, familiar voice calls from the doorway.

My eyes snap up, locking onto Gwynn. Her brown eyes are filled with determination, her stance sure and steady. I didn't expect to see her, but the surprise fades quickly. Of course, she is here. I should have known. "Extra hands to hold her down won't hurt," I say, offering her a weak smile that I know doesn't reach my eyes.

She gives a resolute nod. At my side, Jet's eyes burn into her, his entire body vibrating with restrained emotion. His wife, his love, is standing before him once more, and yet he is stuck in place, torn between running to her and staying here. I know he will never leave Olivia's side—not now. More footsteps pound down the hall, and the heavy presence of two more warriors enters the room. Lorkan and Michael.

"We hear you might need some support, Brother," Lorkan says, his deep voice calm yet firm. He towers over the others, his black hair tousled from the wind, his violet eyes sharp and unwavering.

Caomh tenses beside me, his shoulders locking as his gaze clashes with Lorkan's. For a moment, something unsaid passes between them before Caomh tears his eyes away, jaw clenched.

"Can you shapeshift into a healer?" I ask, desperation making my voice rough. "We may need all the help we can get."

Lorkan gives a curt nod, and in a blink, he shifts. My own face stares back at me. Althea gasps.

Hecate, who has just reappeared with the vial in hand, goes utterly still. Her lips part slightly, her red eyes locking onto him as if she's seen a ghost.

Aiden rolls his eyes. "Show-off," he mutters, crossing his arms.

"Do you need strength?" Michael asks.

I look at them all—the warriors who have fought beside me, who have been with me through war, bloodshed, loss. It has been fifty years since we've all stood in the same room together. I never want Olivia to meet them like this. I never want them to see her this way. And I never want to feel this powerless in front of them.

I rip my gaze away, unable to meet their eyes any longer. I turn back to Olivia's limp form, to the pitch-black gaze that once held the entire world in them. Then I look up, to the heavens, to the invisible fates that have woven our paths together.

If any of the gods are listening—if they have any mercy left in their immortal hearts—please, let me save her.

I sit in a chair beside the bed, my gaze fixed on the wooden floor, unable—unwilling—to look at her. The weight of the room presses down on me, thick and suffocating, wrapping around my throat like a vice. This isn't her.

The blackness in her eyes, the eerie stillness of her chest, the absence of that warm, steady hum of emotion I have come to know as uniquely hers—it's all wrong. She's wrong. My Hummingbird is gone.

The others left hours ago, lingering downstairs as they wait for Hecate to complete the anti-venom. The house is silent, the kind of silence that scrapes against my bones, sharp and hollow. Even Caomh, who never leaves my side in battle, has stepped away. Perhaps he can't bear to see me like this—cracked open, unraveling, breaking with each passing second.

The clock ticks on, relentless in its reminder that time is slipping through my fingers like grains of sand. Each movement of the hands drives the knife deeper into my chest. The ache burns, raw and all-consuming, radiating through my ribs and settling deep in my heart.

I clench my fists, fingers digging into my palms as another wave of agony shoots up my left arm. My tattoo—the mark of our bond—has darkened further, the once soft, glowing swirls now inky black. A sickness settles in my stomach as I trace the lines up my forearm, feeling the way they pulse, as if trying to pull me toward her, to tether me to her failing body.

She is dying. And I am dying with her.

I let my head drop into my hands, exhaling a shaky breath, willing whatever gods are listening to take me instead.

Twenty-four hours later, I finally move. I take slow steps down the stairs, my legs threatening to give out beneath me. The sound of my footsteps is loud to my ears. I follow the murmur of voices to the dining room, where I find my family sitting, emotionless. Utensils scrape against their ceramic plates. Caomh sits at the head of the table, Jethro to his left with Gwynn beside him and Michael on the other side of her. Facing them are Aiden, then Althea and Aella.

Every single one of them looks at me as I step into the room. Their eyes hold no lies, their worry painted clearly across their faces. Lorkan stands by the mantlepiece, watching over the group. When his eyes meet mine, he offers a tight smile.

"We don't have long. The bond has nearly gone dark." I stand at the end of the table, a numbness I've never felt before creeping over my body.

The frigid temperature of the room makes me wonder if I'll ever feel again. Can I feel anything without her here? How did I feel before her?

Every past memory feels like a scratch on the surface compared to what I've felt since we met. I watch as everyone rises, the scraping of chairs grating against the hardwood floor. I turn to find Hecate standing in the doorway, her eyes ablaze. Dark circles bloom beneath them.

"I need you all to listen quickly." Her commanding tone rings through the room. "We have one chance. I will break the time spell, administer the anti-venom, then you must all follow Jeyr's commands in healing her. We will have to be quick."

Everyone nods at her command. I don't hesitate—I shoot up from my seat and move up the stairs.

The room is suffocating with the weight of unspoken prayers, bodies pressed close, surrounding her broken form. The sheer force of our collective will, our desperation, thrums through the air, thick as the scent of blood and burnt flesh.

Outside the door, Kyzan howls, his cries low and mournful, the only sound piercing through the heavy silence before it shatters. Hecate gives us a single look—her expression unreadable but final.

The time spell will break. With a flare of red eyes, the magic snaps, releasing its hold, and Olivia's final scream rends through the room. The sound of it—of her agony—rips something vital inside me, but I don't have time to fall apart. I shove past my own terror and roar the orders, my voice carrying over her cries, each command followed without hesitation.

"Hold her down!"

"Aella, hand on her heart!"

"Aiden, burn the arrows!"

"Jet, be ready by Althea!"

"Lorkan, focus on the arrow wounds!"

The chaos is instant, and yet, within it, we move like warriors on a battlefield, each knowing their role in the fight for her life. Gwynn springs forward, pinning Olivia's shoulders as Michael secures her legs. Caomh places his hands on her head, his body rigid with effort, brow creased deep in concentration. A single bead of blood slips from his nostril, but he doesn't flinch. He's inside her mind now, trying to take her pain—to ease the war raging in her body. Lorkan—who still wears my face—watches Caomh warily before nodding, a silent promise that he is ready. Hecate wastes no time. She injects the anti-venom, stepping back as the real battle begins. Aiden moves first, turning the buried arrows to ash in quick, precise bursts of fire, clearing the wounds for Althea. My sister's hands press firmly to the gaping tear in Olivia's chest, golden bands of magic seeping into the wound, willing muscle and sinew to knit back together. Lorkan mirrors her, lending his strength where she falters.

I grind my feet into the floor, letting my own power surge through my body, pulling from the depths of my very being. Every thread of healing magic I have ever possessed—every ounce of energy—flows into my hands and into her.

Come back to me.

My love.

Come back.

I repeat the words like a prayer, a spell cast from the marrow of my bones. I can't lose her. I won't.

Althea and Lorkan soon join me, their power merging with mine as we work to piece her back together. I barely have to glance at Aiden—he knows exactly when to cauterize the worst of the wounds, the searing flesh the only thing stopping the blood from pouring too fast for us to heal. Aella's hand never leaves Olivia's heart, sending delicate yet forceful electric pulses, keeping it steady. Keeping it beating. The concept of time vanishes. There is no before. No after. Only this moment—only this fight.

Then, with a gasping sob, Althea collapses beside the bed, knees hitting the floor as she sways. Lorkan follows, shifting back into his true form, his chest heaving. Blood trickles from my nose. I barely register it. Caomh is next, his body slumping to the ground as if someone has cut the strings holding him upright.

And then Olivia convulses. The explosion of pain that shoots through the room is unlike anything I have ever felt. A force so violent it sends me crashing to my knees.

Her scream...

It isn't just sound—it's a living, breathing thing, a creature made of raw agony that sinks its claws into my chest, into my very soul.

Kyzan's howl rises in tandem, the depth of his sorrow a dagger to the gut. My vision blurs as I drag myself forward, crawling, reaching for her. My limbs shake, strength depleted, but I have nothing left to lose.

I slide onto the bed, pulling her against me, cradling her trembling, blood-soaked body as her cries soften into shuddering sobs.

The sound of it, the way her body curls into mine—it's unbearable.

And yet, it's a relief.

Because she's alive.

Barely. But alive.

I touch my fingers to her wrist, seeking out the erratic beat of her pulse. At the fragile, unsteady rhythm beneath my touch, my breath catches, the entire room pausing with me.

The relief is dizzying, but short-lived.

As if sensing me, Olivia tilts her face toward mine.

Her eyes...

Still black.

Still void.

Still lost.

I press my forehead to hers, closing my eyes, forcing back the panic clawing up my throat.

This. This simple gesture has always been our tether. The moment I first touched her forehead to mine, I knew—this is how we can reach each other.

"Hummingbird, settle your breathing," I murmur.

Her cries crack, breaking into harsh, jagged gasps for air.

"That's it, love. Listen to my voice. I am here. Breathe, my love," I coo, rocking her against me, my hand gliding up and down her back in slow, steady motions.

Her body remains taut, but little by little, her breathing steadies, the sheer weight of her sobs lessening.

Then—darkness.

Not hers.

Mine.

I'm being pulled under, drowning in the abyss of her mind.

Don't panic.

Caomh's voice settles over me like a whisper in the void.

I am connecting your mind to hers. Keep drawing her out.

I nod absently, too lost to respond.

The room fades around me. The blood. The pain. The exhaustion.

All that remains is Olivia—my fragile, trembling, broken mate in my arms.

And I cling to her as the darkness swallows us whole.

Jeyr

THE BRINK OF LIGHT AND SHADOW

I stand in the abyss, the darkness swallowing every flicker of warmth, every trace of color. Before me, a lone figure drifts within the swirling void, her slight frame enveloped by the shadows that slither and curl around her like living tendrils.

"Liv!" My voice is raw, a desperate plea that echoes into the nothingness. I push against the wall of darkness separating us, but like two opposing forces, it repels me, rejecting my presence with a violent shudder.

Please, my love. Let the darkness go, please! I cry into her mind, my power reaching for her, searching for even the faintest trace of light. She turns, and for the first time, I see them—her eyes, twin pools of black, empty and depthless. The sight of them, so void of life, steals the breath from my lungs. My hope wavers, trembles, threatens to shatter.

Liv, please, I love you. It comes out as a broken sob, my throat raw as though I have been screaming for centuries, as though I have been waiting a lifetime for her to hear these words.

A flicker. A tiny, golden ember sparks within the abyss, barely there, trembling like a candle in the wind. But it's enough. ***I love you, Liv. Don't you dare die before I can say it to you. Stay in the light!***

The ember stirs, the glow pulsing ever so slightly, fighting against the weight of the shadows. Hope surges in my chest. I reach for her, but before my fingers can brush against her skin— I'm ripped away. The darkness vanishes. The connection severs. I gasp as reality slams back into me. My senses roar to life—the scent of blood, the stifling silence, the grief pressing into the walls. I blink, disoriented, my vision adjusting to the dim candlelight of my chamber. My hands are still on her, forehead still pressed against hers. But when I look down— **Black**. Her eyes, still open, are black as death. **No.**

A strangled sound leaves my throat, but I refuse to believe it. My gaze darts around the room, as if searching for confirmation that this is some cruel illusion, some trick of my broken mind. Jethro is curled against the bed, one hand resting on Olivia's back, the other clutching the blood-soaked sheets in a death grip. Silent tears stream down his face, his body trembling with the force of his grief.

Aella's hand is pressed to her mouth, her blue eyes wide, drowning in sorrow. Aiden holds Althea close, her body shaking violently as she buries herself against his chest. His emerald gaze lifts to mine, shattered. Lorkan braces himself against the fireplace, his violet eyes locked onto Caomh's crumpled form on the floor. Blood trickles from Caomh's nose, his golden eyes wide, unseeing. And Hecate... Hecate stands frozen at the foot of the bed, her hands clasped together so tightly her knuckles have gone white. I turn back to Olivia. Her lips are blue. The room turns cold, as if death itself has reached out and wrapped its skeletal fingers around us.

No. No. No. No.

I don't realize I'm screaming until the sound rips through my own ears, raw and hollow. I turn to Caomh, his knees pulled to his chest, his head resting against them as his chest heaves in silent, broken sobs. "No, no, no, NO!" I refuse this reality. Refuse to believe in a world where my friends and family mourn her, where they weep at her bedside as if she is already gone.

I refuse to live in a world without her.

I turn back to Olivia, searching her lifeless face for any sign, any whisper of warmth. But the blackness in her eyes is still there, the coldness sinking into my own bones. I press my forehead to hers, desperate.

"Let the light in, Liv. Please, let the light in."

Nothing.

I hear the sobs of my family thicken, their grief growing heavier with each second that passes, but I refuse to let them grieve her. "No, you will live, Olivia."

I kiss her cold lips. I push all the air from my lungs into hers, willing my breath to replace the one she has lost. I give her everything—every ounce of my power, every sliver of my soul, everything I have ever been or could be. My hand slides to her chest, to the place where her soul has been torn from her, where something monstrous has tried to steal the very essence of her existence.

I will my magic into her, will my healing into the depths of her being, past the poisoned veins, past the fading pulse, past the void that threatens to consume her. "If that soul light is still beaming, please flow through her. Please, show her the light. I am here. Her Companach, her soulmate." My voice cracks between kisses, holding her tighter, refusing to let go. "I am your link to this earth. Accept our bond. Don't leave me."

Silence. Then— A single pulse. A flicker of gold beneath my palm. Faint. Weak. But there. A sob tears from my lips. My body trembles with exhaustion, but I don't let go. I press my forehead to hers again, whispering against her lips. "Come back to me, Hummingbird."

Olivia

THE LIGHT BETWEEN SHADOWS

With my last breath, I scream.

Pain convulses through my body, a vice tightening around my abdomen, crushing, consuming, drowning me in its merciless grasp. I can't breathe, can't think—only suffer. Through the obsidian mist, I feel hands clawing at me, holding me to the ground. My mind reels, flashing with grotesque images—claws digging into my flesh, a blade splitting my insides, tearing through me like I am nothing. A voice, dark and haunting, coils through my mind like a viper.

"You're not very wise." "Goodbye to all that is good." I want to fight, to push back, but the agony is relentless. It drives me further into the abyss, deeper into the shadows that whisper my name. Then— A hand covers my mouth, stifling my screams.

Shh, it's okay. Settle, Livy.

That voice. I know that voice. It curls around me like smoke, familiar, yet lost in the fog of my mind. I sob into his palm, his touch steady, grounding, sweet like honeyed liqueur.

It's okay, little Empath. I am here.

I stand in the darkness, tears streaking down my face, the tunnel in my mind stretching before me like a void. The shadows call to me, their whispers curling like tendrils around my limbs, tugging, urging me forward.

"Little Empath."

Only one person calls me that. But the knowledge is just beyond my reach, slipping through my fingers like sand. The pain sharpens, tearing through my chest, and his grip tightens, holding me to him as if anchoring me in place.

No. Stay with me, little Empath. Stay with me, Princess.

Another shock of pain lances through me, and his hand clenches harder over my mouth, silencing my cries. I collapse into the darkness, my body weightless in the void.

We will get through this together. Give me your pain, Livy.

Strong arms wrap around me, pressing my face into his chest. The warmth of him is foreign in the cold abyss, his voice a whisper of solace in the cacophony of my suffering.

Give it to me. I can handle it.

And so I do. I let my screams die against his chest, let the overwhelming agony transfer to him. He holds me tighter, the immovable force against the torment that rages within me.

That's it. Only let me feel your pain. Keep fighting. We will leave here together.

His embrace is the lifeline tethering me to reality. My gasping sobs rack through me, but he never wavers. His arms never loosen, even as a wave of frigid air passes through me. The grip around my limbs falters. I look up, and my heart clenches in horror. Blood pours from his nose, his face pale as death. The arrogance that always dances in his golden eyes flickers for just a moment, replaced by something far more raw—something fragile.

Then he smiles.

What have I done?

I reach for him, but he is already fading.

"You killed Cao. You killed him."

A voice hisses in my mind, and in his absence, the pain returns tenfold. The agony is unbearable, and I can't stop myself from crawling toward the darkness. It calls to me. Promises reprieve. I scream, and the sound echoes through my own mind, reverberating like a thousand voices at once. I am back in that dungeon, back in that wretched place where my pain has no limits, where my suffering bleeds into the souls of others. I drag my body toward the tunnel of darkness, willing the torment to end.

Then—

A warmth touches my wrist.

I freeze.

I turn, breath catching in my throat as my gaze falls upon the glowing white band wrapped around my left wrist. It pulses, swirling in intricate figure eights, weaving around my ring finger and disappearing into the space between my breasts. A warm pressure presses against my forehead, familiar, steady, safe.

Hummingbird, settle your breathing.

The voice curls around my soul, filling the hollow, aching space within me.

"Hummingbird."

My lips tremble, my breath hitches. His voice touches something deep, something sacred. It pulses in my chest, a tether I have nearly severed.

"That's it, love. Listen to my voice. I am here. Breathe, my love."

Love.

My love?

A turmoil far worse than the physical pain stirs within me. The mist twists, recoiling from his presence. My heart aches, a desperate cry echoing in my mind—

Why don't you remember him?

"Please, my love. Let the darkness go, please."

I turn toward the voice, my gaze locking onto a tall figure kneeling before me. Blue eyes. His oceanic depths stare back at me, pleading. His brown hair tumbles over his strong, angular face, the set of his jaw tight with restraint. Beautiful. Hauntingly familiar.

"Liv, please. I love you."

Jeyr.

His name explodes through my soul like a shattering star. A gasp leaves my lips, my body trembling as flickers of memory surge through my mind. A smile on the beach. A stolen kiss. His arms around me as we dance beneath the moon.

"I love you, Liv. Don't you dare die before I can say it to you. Stay in the light."

Okay...

I turn away from the darkness. The shadows recoil as I step into the light. Memories surge back, filling the void. The door to my prison unlocks, and for the first time, I am free. A tunnel stretches before me, bathed in golden light. A warmth buzzes up and down my spine, urging me forward.

Go.

I take a step, ready to leave the darkness behind.

Then—

A tug.

I turn, sensing a presence behind me.

Jeyr stands there, his hand outstretched, his blue eyes locked onto mine with an intensity that threatens to unravel me.

"I am your link to this earth. Accept our bond. Don't leave me."

He reaches for me, grabbing my wrist and pressing my palm to his heart. Then he kisses me. A bruising, desperate kiss that steals my breath and fills my lungs with fire. The golden tether between us pulls taut, binding me to him. My fingers curl into his hair, my arms wrap around his neck, clinging to the only thing that feels real.

The world erupts into color.

Not just light and dark—something more. A land in between, where technicolor spills from my soul, where our bond is forged in something deeper than fate.

"Accept our bond. Link yourself to me. Come to me!"

His plea carves itself into my chest, raw and unyielding.

There is no hesitation this time.

My soul has already decided.

Ocean blue. Will always be my favorite hue.

"Jeyr..." His name leaves my lips as nothing more than a breath, raw and unguarded. "Please, never stop saying my name." His voice is hoarse, desperate.

I drink in the sight of him—the red-rimmed eyes, the tears still slipping unchecked down his face. His lips, bitten and swollen, tremble into something between a sob and a smile, that familiar dimple teasing his cheek. Every part of him looks wrecked, utterly broken. And yet, here he is, holding me together. Our breaths mingle, and his scent—ocean and pine—wraps around me, clearing the last remnants of blood and death and burnt lilies from my senses.

"I mean it, never stop. This heart of yours, it needs to keep beating. Those lips need to keep speaking your sweet words. Those eyes need to keep shining brighter than the emeralds from the Aotrom Mountains. There isn't a world I want to live in without those things. I can't breathe—I can't be—without you."

His large hands bracket my face, thumbs sweeping across my cheeks, catching the tears before they can fall. His stormy blue eyes search mine as though memorizing every detail, terrified that if he blinks, I will disappear.

"I love you, Olivia. I need to be able to say this to you every morning and every night. Please." His voice cracks, and so does the last of my resolve. My fingers twist into the fabric of his bloodstained tunic, clutching at him, anchoring myself in the reality that I am here, alive, and in his arms. I nod, unable to find the words, unable to do anything but pull him closer.

A quiet throat clearing shatters the moment, and I become painfully aware of the room around us. I blink, tearing my gaze from Jeyr to see Caomh leaning against the wall, head tilted back, exhaustion weighing heavy on his features. A lopsided smirk graces his lips, but I can see the toll this has taken on him. His golden skin is streaked with dried blood, his nose still crusted from where it bled. A wave of concern presses against my ribs, but before I can speak, his voice brushes against my mind.

I'm okay, Princess. I still look a hell of a lot better than you.

I huff a quiet laugh, my lips quirking in the closest thing to a smile I can manage. *Maybe, but I still have the power to make any person you want to bed run for the hills.*

Caomh snorts before his expression turns serious. *I am sorry, Olivia— for everything. You are family, I mean it.*

The words settle over me, heavy and unexpected. The last thing I said to them before I left— before I bled out in the snow— seems so small now. Death has a way of making grudges feel insignificant.

A warm, steady hand lands on my shoulder. I turn to find Jet standing beside me, his dark eyes filled with unspoken sorrow. But his touch is fleeting. His attention belongs to the woman in his arms, her face buried in the curve of his neck. *Gwynn.* His grip on her is tight, as if afraid she might slip through his fingers, his lips brushing against her hair in silent worship. More unfamiliar faces linger. Across the room, green eyes watch me carefully. Their owner is a tall, red-haired Fae, his arm draped protectively around a smaller brunette with soft freckles dusting her nose. My gaze flicks to Jeyr in silent question, and he gives me a subtle nod—his sister.

Beside them, a strikingly tall woman stands with a scar running down the left side of her face, one eye clouded white, the other an icy blue. *Aella.* I know who she is without needing to ask.

Then, in the farthest corner, Hecate stands motionless, glowing eyes locked on me, grief and relief warring in their depths. A man stands behind her, impossibly large, his massive hand swallowing her shoulder as he squeezes it. She flinches, fighting the urge to move toward me. I swallow hard, overwhelmed by the weight of so many eyes, so many emotions pressing into me. But before I can react, a commanding voice cuts through the tension.

"We will give them a moment."

Aella's tone brooks no argument, her presence commanding the room as though she has been born for war. "Everyone will have time to embrace the happy couple later. Out! Everyone out of my brother's bedchamber!" She claps her hands, shooting pointed looks at each of them. A tired, grateful smile tugs at my lips. I meet her gaze, silently thanking her. She inclines her head in understanding before she ushers the others out, one by one.

Jet hesitates, his gaze bouncing between me and Gwynn, torn between his love and his loyalty. But with one final look, he guides his wife toward the door. The room empties, leaving only silence and the steady sound of our breaths. Jeyr stays exactly where he is, fingers tangled in my hair, forehead resting against mine. His chest rises and falls in slow, controlled movements, but I can feel the truth in the way his hands still tremble.

"I thought I lost you," he whispers, voice so broken it nearly shatters me. I close my eyes, my lips brushing against his in the softest of touches. "You never will."

Jeyr

BLOOD AND WATER

I don't mean to fall asleep, but exhaustion claims me, pulling me under like a heavy tide. And in sleep, I dream of obsidian eyes swallowing me whole, of tendrils of mist creeping over my skin, of golden light flickering like dying embers in the dark. But there is warmth too. Small, steady breaths ghost over my chest, little kisses of air pressing against my skin. Love whispers through each exhale, a silent hymn of relief, of survival.

I don't know how much time passes before my senses sharpen, pulling me from the tangled web of dreams. My first breath is filled with her—lavender and sea mist—but beneath it, something darker, metallic. The scent of blood. My eyes fly open.

Her red hair, normally a halo of wild fire, is stiff and matted with blood. My stomach clenches as I slowly pull away, careful not to wake her. My gaze rakes over my Companach—her delicate frame still covered in dried blood, her skin pale against the crimson stains. The sound of running water catches my attention, and I look toward the end of the room. The bathroom door stands ajar, steam curling into the air. The heat of the fire that joins both the bedroom and bath sends flickering light across the stone walls, casting golden glows over the room.

I move to rise, but something holds me down. Even in sleep, Olivia's grip on me is strong, fingers curled tightly around my waist. A sharp pang shoots through my chest—an ache I welcome. She has accepted our bond. Even in sleep, she refuses to let go.

So I don't either.

Gently, I slide my arm beneath her legs, the other around her waist, lifting her into my arms. I walk toward the bath, pausing at the doorway as Kyzan pads up beside me, his whimpers low and desperate.

I kneel down, allowing him to press his head against Olivia's. The wolf lets out a soft, huffing breath, his golden eyes filled with something so human—relief, grief, devotion. "Our soulmate is okay, Ky," I murmur, my voice a rough whisper. He pulls back, eyes locking with mine in understanding. There's no denying it now—Olivia will always belong to more than just me. She is tethered to all her four-legged beasts, and I will have to share her with them for eternity.

A small movement in the bath chamber catches my attention, and I look up to find Mary bustling around, her small frame moving with quiet efficiency as she prepares the bath. The tub, positioned beneath a wide window overlooking the cliffs and ocean beyond, gleams under the firelight. A vanity mirror and a small antique sink rest against the far wall, the gold accents catching the glow of the hearth.

Mary turns as I step inside, her light blue eyes falling to Olivia in my arms. A small, strangled noise escapes her, but she quickly straightens, pressing her lips together. Her hands tremble slightly as she reaches up, brushing the back of her fingers over Olivia's cheek. Something deep inside me twists.

This is not how I wanted to meet her guardian, her adoptive mother. I wanted to come to their door with flowers in hand, to sit across from them at dinner, to promise to cherish and protect their daughter. Not like this. Not with Caomh arriving at their doorstep, telling them their daughter had nearly died.

Mary's hand moves to my arm, grounding me. "Thank you." Her voice cracks. "Thank you for bringing her back to us."

I nod, unable to speak past the tightness in my throat. She pulls away and leaves the room, the quiet click of the door the only sound as we are left alone once more.

I turn to Olivia, pressing a kiss to the top of her head. "Come, my love. Time to clear this blood from you." She makes a small sound of protest, her fingers tightening briefly in my shirt. A chuckle rumbles in my chest. "Come on, Hummingbird. It's time to get cleaned up."

With a reluctant sigh, she loosens her grip, and I carry her to the wooden chair by the vanity, settling her down carefully. I kneel before her, fingers working at the ties of her blood-soaked tunic, pulling the ruined fabric from her body. The scent of burnt lilies still clings to her skin, a reminder of the poison that nearly stole her from me. Without hesitation, I throw the garment into the fireplace. The flames consume it instantly, crackling hungrily as they devour the remnants of her suffering.

I move to her tights, peeling them from her legs with careful hands, followed by the delicate lace of her underclothes. She remains limp against me, her head heavy on my shoulder, trusting me completely. My breath catches as my gaze rakes over her body. She is thinner than before, the venom having drained the life from her. Dark bruises mar her pale skin, ugly reminders of what she has endured.

Gods, how many times have I imagined seeing her bare before me? But never like this. Never in pain.

Swallowing hard, I strip off my own clothes, lifting her into my arms once more. Her naked form presses against mine, sending embers skittering across my skin, an undeniable current sparking between us. But I force my thoughts aside.

She is still beautiful, despite the scars, despite the blood and bruises. She is the most beautiful thing I have ever seen. I step into the bath, lowering us both into the warm water. The enchanted tub instantly adjusts to my optimal temperature, the heat sinking into my muscles, drawing away the tension that has settled deep in my bones. Olivia murmurs sweetly against my chest, her small sounds sending a low, satisfied rumble through me.

I watch her toes curl in pleasure, feel her Empathic power ripple through me, filling me with warmth, with light. My breath hitches at the sensation.

I take a steadying breath, focusing on the task at hand. Dipping a cloth into the water, I begin washing away the blood and grime, watching as the once-clear water turns crimson before magically purifying itself.

Olivia

FROM DEATH… TO YOU

Pleasure curls around me like golden threads of warmth, winding deep into my core, binding me to the present, to the man who holds me so carefully against his chest. Each gentle caress of his fingertips is a song of devotion, humming against my skin, erasing the ache of all that has been lost. I want to sink into it, into him. I want to let the feeling consume me, to dissolve in the heat of his love, the reverence of his touch.

I have been hovering in the space between dreams and wakefulness, wrapped in the cocoon of Jeyr's arms, not daring to stir, not daring to shatter the fragile peace that has settled between us. The moment I woke in his arms, I made the choice— I will never let go. My soul has already surrendered to him, and now, my body follows.

The moment my bloodstained clothes were stripped away, the moment my bare skin met his, an electric thrill runs through my body. The friction, the way my breasts press against the firm expanse of his chest, sends cinders of pleasure licking up my spine, pooling low in my belly. I feel it— his love, his longing, his unspoken vow wrapped in the way he touches me, as if I am something precious, something sacred.

The warm water filters between us, slipping into every crevice where our bodies do not yet touch. A soft, involuntary murmur of pleasure rolls from my lips, and Jeyr answers with one of his own. A deep, low rumble that vibrates against my skin, sinking into my bones, branding itself into my very essence. If the water could catch fire from the way my body responds to him, I am certain it would.

Then, he begins to cleanse me. Every fiber of my being that withered under death's grip now seeks renewal under his hands. As he washes away the remnants of blood and battle, I let myself be reborn in his touch. A sigh, pure and sweet, spills from my lips as he runs a warm cloth over my skin, erasing every dark thing that ever tainted me. I settle deeper against his chest, my breath aligning with his, our heartbeats a synchronized rhythm, pulsing together in the quiet sanctuary of the water.

It is as if I am feeling life for the very first time. The early morning sun peeks through the window, casting slivers of light over us, kissing our damp skin, a silent witness to the love that exists in every stolen breath, every gentle stroke of his hand. My body flushes, warmth spinning through my limbs, pooling in my toes, my stomach, my heart. I feel him everywhere— not just against me, but inside me, within every part of my being.

His hands move to my hair, threading through the tangled locks, massaging them clean with slow, deliberate care. I melt into him, a soft whimper of pleasure slipping from my throat. His hands travel lower, working away the tension in my neck, kneading into my shoulders, dissolving the last remnants of pain into oblivion.

I am weightless. Free.

Then, his lips brush against my throat— just a whisper of contact, the ghost of a kiss.

A shiver runs through me, awakening something deep, something primal. My breath catches, my fingers tighten where they rest over his heart. Jeyr's mouth lingers against my skin, his own breath hot and unsteady, and in that moment, I know— we are no longer simply existing.

Jeyr

LOVE AND BLINDING BEAUTY

Olivia's soft breaths are fire against my skin, igniting something deep and primal within me. My body fights the urge to take her right then and there. I can feel the pull, the spiraling force of our bond, the way it begs to be sealed— to tether her to this life, to me.

Her soft hums of pleasure send waves of heat through my body, her sighs pressing against my skin like whispered prayers. I work the soap into her hair, massaging until the golden and crimson hues turn to liquid silk between my fingers. In the morning sunlight, she glows, each freckle kissed by light, each bruise vanishing under my healing touch. I wash her as if I can erase the horrors of what happened, as if I can restore all that has been taken from her with my hands alone.

She turns her face up to the sunlight, eyes closed in quiet reverence. I am entranced, watching her bask in the warmth, her features softened by peace, by trust. Gods, how did I get so lucky?

I fight the need to see her eyes, to claim her lips. I let her revel in the simple act of my touch, let her lose herself in the moment. I lean down, brushing a kiss over the delicate spot where her pulse thrums against her throat. The way her body trembles beneath my lips sends something dark and wanting curling in my stomach. That beat. That sweet, steady rhythm against my mouth... A growl claws its way up my chest, vibrating against her skin.

I pull back, needing to take her in, to look at her once more.

I freeze.

Green eyes meet mine, full of fire, of brio, of life.

Her fingers find my damp hair, smoothing it back, slicking it against my head. That sensual, knowing smile tugs at her lips— the kind that has me forgetting how to breathe, how to function. That smile is going to be my undoing. Warmth slides down my cheek as she traces the sharp lines of my face, her fingertips feather-light, reverent. My breath is already coming too fast, too ragged, but when her lips brush over mine, I lose all sense of reason.

She shifts her weight, pressing her chest against mine as she turns fully to face me. I am helpless against her spell, moving with her as if pulled by invisible strings. I sit up, her slim legs sliding around my waist, fitting herself against me as if she has been made for this— for me.

My hands bracket her hips, grounding myself, forcing myself to catch my breath. She feels my hesitation, my restraint, and pulls back just enough to search my eyes. "I want you, Jeyr," she whispers, her voice breathless, full of need. "I need this."

Gods, help me.

I swallow thickly, my control slipping like sand through my fingers. "Hummingbird... are you sure? We—"

Before I can finish, she shifts, presses herself fully against me. My vision blurs, the wet heat of her nearly sends me over the edge right then and there. "Gods, Liv," I choke out, my grip on her hips tightening. "Are you sure? Tell me you're sure." She gasps against my mouth, her green eyes locking onto mine, dark with certainty. "Yes, Jeyr. Please."

Then she sinks down, taking me in, inch by inch. I feel the sharp clench of her body, the quick wince of pain, and I still. My hands curl into the flesh of her hips, my jaw locking, my entire body trembling with restraint.

But Olivia doesn't stop.

Her fingers tangle in my hair, her nails scrape against my scalp as she impales herself completely, taking all of me inside her in one swift motion. "Olivia," I groan, my voice breaking under the weight of sheer, blinding pleasure. Something animalistic within me awakens, something feral and desperate. My hips rock instinctively, and the pleasure is almost unbearable. She cries out in answer, her head falling back, hands tugging at my hair.

I need to see her.

I push her wild, wet hair over her shoulders, my eyes drinking in the sight of her—flushed cheeks, parted lips, full, perfect breasts rising and falling with every unsteady breath. She is beautiful. Gods, she is perfect.

My lips find her throat, trailing kisses along the elegant column of her neck, biting, sucking, leaving proof of this moment, proof that she is mine. Then the world explodes. A glow fills the room, technicolor waves pulsing around us as our bond snaps into place, permanent.

She gasps, her left hand lifting to touch her wrist. I follow her gaze, watching as an intertwining band of infinity symbols wraps around her delicate skin, bright as the aurora borealis.

Lifting my palm, I see my own mark—its white band now shifting, glowing in brilliant colors that wind their way up my arm, curling into my chest, to my heart.

My heart. Our heart.

Olivia's palm comes to my cheek, her fingers trembling slightly as she traces the mark. I mirror the movement, brushing my knuckles over her face, memorizing her, burning this moment into my soul. Our foreheads meet, our bodies moving together in a slow, intoxicating rhythm. "Gods, you are beautiful, Liv. My Hummingbird."

That smile again—that seductive, knowing smile. Then I feel it. Her shields drop completely. I feel everything.

Every pulse of pleasure. Every shudder of ecstasy. Every sweet, perfect tremor inside her as she clenches around me. Her pleasure reflects mine, amplifying, feeding, growing—"Oh Gods, Olivia," I gasp.

She clenches again at the sound of her name. My name on her lips, my name in her mind— It's too much. I'm too close. She feels it. She knows. "Forever," she breathes, her fingers tangling back in my hair.

Yes.

"Forever," I swear, sealing my promise against her lips. She moves, and I feel my impending release rise, building, crashing over me. Each nerve ignites, the pleasure shattering through us both as we tip over the edge together, our climax sending tremors through the bond, sealing it fully, forever.

"Jeyr," she breathes, her body quaking around me.

And I am gone.

Her name tears from my lips as my release claims me, pleasure rolling in thick, pulsing waves.

Mine.

She is mine.

Forever fused. Forever one.

BOUND IN FIRE AND FLESH

Jeyr moves first, stepping out of the bath, water cascading down his chiseled form in shimmering rivulets. I watch through hooded eyes, mesmerized as the morning light highlights every sculpted line of his body.

Gods, this male.

He reaches for a towel, drying himself off before turning to me, eyes dark and burning with purpose. Without a word, he bends down, lifting me from the water with effortless strength, cradling me against his chest. The towel is forgotten as his hands work over my skin, drying every inch of me with reverent slowness. Though I am perfectly capable of doing it myself, I let him. I let him care for me, let him show his love through each stroke of cloth against my damp skin, each lingering kiss pressed to the curve of my shoulder, my collarbone, my wrist.

When he reaches my hair, a bead of water trickles down, slipping between the valley of my breasts. Jeyr follows its path, his hot tongue tracing the trail before catching the droplet with his lips. I shudder. A moan slips from me as heat licks through my core. My arms find their way around his neck, my fingers tangling in his damp locks. My body knows what it wants, what it needs. My legs wrap around his waist, holding him against me, anchoring me to this reality—the reality where I am alive, whole, his.

A deep, primal noise rumbles through his chest as he presses his face into the crook of my neck. His teeth scrape over my skin before he bites, just enough to send a jolt of fire racing through my veins. A sharp gasp leaves me, but my lips are quickly claimed. His kiss is brutal, desperate, devouring. There is no hesitation, no space between us, only the heat of his mouth and the overwhelming sensation of his body against mine.

"From the moment I met you, Hummingbird," he growls between kisses, "this pretty body has been all I could think about. These beautiful breasts... made for my hands, and my hands alone." As if to emphasize his point, his palm closes around one, squeezing just hard enough to elicit a sharp gasp from me, the mix of pleasure and pain making my head spin.

"And this plump ass," he continues, his other hand sliding down, grabbing hold of me. "Gods, how you teased me. Every time you walked away, the way it swayed, the way it called for me to grab it, to have you wrapped around me just like this..." His fingers dig into the flesh of my hips, pressing me harder against him. I feel him—hard, hot, ready.

"Jeyr, please." The words are breathless, trembling from my lips. "I need you. I need to feel you."

"Gods, say please, and you will get whatever you want. You name it." His voice is thick with lust, rasping like embers in the wind. "You," I whisper. "I want you. Need you. Inside. Now." A shudder racks his body, a curse slipping from his lips. Then, with one swift motion, he thrusts into me.

A sharp cry tears from my throat as he fills me, stretching me to the brink. My head falls back, my fingers claw into his shoulders. Gods, the pressure, the pleasure.

Jeyr groans, his head dropping to my shoulder, his body tensing as he buries himself inside me. "Fuck, Liv," he drawls, his breath hot against my skin. "Jeyr, please, please." I don't know what I'm begging for—more, harder, faster. Everything.

But he knows. He feels everything I feel. With a growl, he moves, walking us backward until my back meets the cold stone of the bathroom wall. The contrast against my heated skin makes me gasp. And then he angles his hips. White-hot pleasure shoots through me, my nails dragging down his back as he hits that spot.

He feels it. Gods, he feels it. "Fuck, Jeyr!" I cry out, clenching around him. "I love when you swear when I'm inside you." His voice is a rough, sinful purr against my ear. "I love feeling this beautiful body claim me. But most of all, Hummingbird, I love you. I love you so godsdamn fucking much."

His words send me spiraling. My entire body tightens, my core pulsing around him, claiming him, branding him as mine. "I love you," I gasp, over and over, with every thrust, with every stroke of pleasure that wracks my body. His hips snap against mine, and I shatter.

A scream rips from my throat, my orgasm crashing through me in violent, consuming waves. Jeyr follows, my name a reverent prayer on his lips as he spills into me, his body trembling as he collapses against me, completely, utterly mine.

We stay like that, panting, our foreheads pressed together, our bodies still rocking in the aftershocks of our release.

His hands frame my face, his thumbs smoothing over my cheeks. He takes me in, his stormy blue eyes burning with devotion. "Thank you for coming back to me, Humming-bird," he murmurs, his voice thick with emotion. "Thank you for giving me this. Gods, I don't know what I've done to deserve you, but I am never letting you go." A tear slides down my cheek, but I smile, brushing my fingers through his damp hair.

"You do deserve me, Jeyr," I whisper. "And you better keep that promise. You better never let me go." His answer is a kiss, deep and slow, sealing the vow between us. I have never felt so complete.

It just happens—the natural flow between us.

There is no urgency, no frantic need to claim and possess. Every touch is soft, every kiss a lingering whisper against my skin. We ignore the slight fear that trembles between unsaid words, the fear of what the future may hold. Neither of us speaks of the past, of the darkness that almost swallows me whole. For the next twenty-four hours, we do nothing but love.

On the bed, tangled in silken sheets. Against the wall, where Jeyr catches me as I try to slip away to wash up, his need for me insatiable.

"I can't help it," he growls into my ear, hands gripping my hips. "Your beautiful, perky ass is asking to be touched." His low, rumbling voice sends a shiver through me, making my knees weak. I let him feel my arousal, let him feel the joy flooding my soul. His answering growl sends a happy squeal bursting from my lips.

This happiness, this ecstasy—it's all I ever want. And I'm going to soak up every second of it. It isn't until our stomachs betray us with their desperate growls that we realize we have to surface.

Mary brings clothes, and I smile at the sight of the cozy garments she crafts herself. I pull on soft britches and an oversized cardigan, the knit thick and comforting. Settling in front of the vanity, I run a brush through my sex-matted hair, wincing at the tangles.

My reflection makes me pause. I look thinner than I remember, cheekbones more pronounced, a hollowness shadowing my face. Too much has been taken from me.

Yet, something new lingers beneath the surface of my features—something untouched by pain. There's a glow to my skin, like a torch has been lit inside me. A twinkle in my green eyes, as if something brighter has taken root in my soul. I touch my face lightly, unsure whether to embrace or fear what I see.

"Making love suits you."

My favorite chuckle comes from the doorway. Jeyr.

His head rests against the wooden frame, arms crossed over his broad chest. He's changed into a deep blue button-up, the color making his ocean eyes look even more breathtaking. Dark textured trousers fit snug against his long, powerful legs.

My heart skips. He doesn't miss it either. A wide smile brightens his face, those goddamn dimples halting my entire existence. "I could say the same for you." I meet his gaze in the mirror, watching as he approaches with slow, deliberate steps. Each footfall sends electricity humming beneath my skin.

Jeyr presses a kiss to my temple. I close my eyes, humming softly as his warmth wraps around me. I try to keep my composure as I tie my hair into a high ponytail, but I feel his stare. His eyes trace my every movement, leaving ghosted kisses in their wake.

"Someone is dying to see you." Jeyr's voice is too controlled. He flinches at his own words, a flicker of dark blue shadowing his eyes before he masks it. A twinge tightens my chest, but I push it aside.

Instead, I watch as Jeyr steps toward the bedroom door and opens it. A gray blur comes flying at me. "Kyzan! Heel!" Jeyr barks, but it's useless.

The massive wolf ignores him entirely, colliding into me with the force of a storm. I let out a startled cry as we topple backward, crashing off the vanity stool. Before I can react, I'm buried under thick fur, my face assaulted by slobbery kisses. Kyzan's massive paws trap me beneath him as he whimpers and whines, his body shaking with pure, unfiltered joy.

"Kyzan— okay!" I giggle, trying in vain to shove the wolf's enormous head away. But he only licks harder, nuzzling into my neck, pressing himself against me like he's trying to absorb me back into his body.

Jeyr rushes forward, panic bleeding into his scent as he tries to pull Kyzan off me. But something makes him pause.

It takes me a moment to realize why.

The room is filling.

At first, I only hear the laughter, the hushed murmurs from beyond the doorway. But when I sit up, I see them. A crowd has gathered in the entrance to the bathroom. Some I know. Some I don't. Every single one of them has their hands on their chests, eyes glazed over, as if they're feeling something too powerful to contain.

My happiness.

I look to Jeyr, see the wonder in his expression as he kneels beside me, taking in the same scene. My laughter has filled the house, and now my joy has reached them too—seeping into the walls, radiates outward, wrapping around each of them in a way that no one can ignore.

"Okay, bud, that's enough."

The last of my giggles subsides as Kyzan finally relents, allowing me to stand. I dust myself off, righting the fallen stool before turning back toward the sea of faces watching me. My heart stutters. So many eyes. So many emotions fill the room, pressing against my skin like waves in a shifting tide.

I swallow the lump forming in my throat. They're all here. My gaze moves first to Jeyr, his soft smile grounding me. My anchor. Then to Jethro, standing beside a beautiful brunette whose delicate fingers rest gently on his shoulder—Gwynn.

A broad, well-built redhead stands near them, his arm draped protectively around the petite brunette at his side. Her eyes are so like Jeyr's that I have no doubt she's his sister.

Hecate stands off to the side, her maroon eyes swollen with unshed tears. She looks away the moment our gazes meet, and I catch the movement of a broad, tanned arm squeezing her shoulder. The towering man beside her is unlike any of the others, his features sharp and dark except for his striking violet eyes.

Another figure looms in the distance—a man with deep brown skin, his dark, buzzed hair catching the candlelight as he gives me a slow, polite nod.

And then there's Caomh.

Leaning against the doorway, arms folded, his golden eyes lock onto mine with unwavering intensity.

Everyone is just happy to hear your laughter, to feel your warmth, Little Empath.

His words slide into my mind, gentle yet weighted. *Especially after seeing you in such pain, feeling such pain.*

The nickname strikes like an arrow to my chest. Memories flood back—of the blood, of the pain, of his pale, broken face in the darkness. I thought I had killed him. A sudden choked sob tears from me, and before I can think, my feet move on their own straight to Caomh. He meets me halfway, his arms sweeping me up without hesitation, lifting me off my feet as he buries his face in my neck.

The moment his arms wrap around me, something inside him cracks—the piece of himself he always tries to control. His breathing hitches, his body trembles slightly against mine. The warmth of his soft cotton shirt registers under my fingertips, and despite my tears, a muffled laugh escapes.

"You're wearing a shirt," I tease, my voice raspy with emotion. "Are you feeling okay?" A few choked laughs echo around the room.

I missed you, cheeky minx. You gave me the fright of my life.

Thank you, Caomh. I let the words flow from my mind into his. *Thank you for weathering my pain.*

Images flicker—his pale face in the darkness, the blood that pours from his nose as he fights to keep me anchored.

Princess, I will never let you battle the pain alone.

His promise rings through my mind like a solemn vow.

Slowly, he sets me back down, but our gazes remain locked—no words needed, only understanding. I press my palm to his cheek, sending a warm current of love through my fingertips. He smiles, soft and knowing, before pressing a kiss to my palm in return.

When I turn next, Jet waits, his star-flecked eyes glistening. A single tear slips down his face. I move instinctively, catching it with my palm, letting my love flow through my fingertips. He leans into my touch. But then I feel it.

A sharp flicker of green energy—jealousy. My eyes lift, instantly understanding. I withdraw, my hand sliding away from Jet's face with a polite smile, just as the strong, golden-skinned woman beside him wraps her arms around his waist in quiet claim.

His wife.

I step back gracefully, retreating into the comfort of Jeyr's waiting arms.

He pulls me close without hesitation, wrapping his arm securely around my waist. A possessive kiss lands atop my head, and I close my eyes briefly, breathing him in.

I look up at him, meeting his gaze with the smile I know he loves. He smirks, low and dangerous, his breath whispering against my ear. "Careful, Hummingbird," he murmurs, his tone dripping with amusement. "We have company."

Then, standing straighter, his voice shifts—commanding. "Shall we have some food? I am starving."

A dressed command for everyone to clear the room.

Olivia

The Banquet of Bonds

"So, are you going to introduce me to..." I gesture toward the unfamiliar faces that fill the grand banquet hall. Jeyr's smile softens as he takes my hand, leading me toward the largest of the group. My neck strains as I look up at the beast of a man, his broad frame towering above everyone else. His sun-kissed skin stretches over corded muscles, his biceps fighting against the tight fabric of his white button-up. A sleeve of intricate tattoos weaves its way down his right arm, and as I look closer, I spot a wolf and what appears to be a black cat nestled among the swirling ink.

"This here is Lorkan." A massive hand—one that could easily swallow both of mine—extends toward me. His violet eyes glimmer beneath thick dark lashes, soft despite his ruggedness. "Your Highness, it's a pleasure to meet you." I stiffen at the title. "Oh, no, I am not royalty. Olivia is fine." Lorkan merely smiles, his voice as deep as shifting earth. "Olivia, your kind were royalty in my land. Though you had a Queen, every Empath was titled a Princess, for the bloodline was a royal one." My breath catches in my throat. "Y-your land? You... knew Empaths?"

Hope flares in my chest, quick and bright, burning away the cold ache of loneliness that has settled in my bones. "I know of them," he says, his voice edged with something ancient. "The Empaths kept to themselves. Only those who needed their services were allowed to meet them. But I am from the Queens' Kingdom. Like you, my kind was wiped out." Sorrow shadows his violet gaze. "Lorkan is a Shifter," Jeyr adds, his fingers tightening around mine. "The King eradicated their kind before he went after yours. He feared their ability to shift into any creature or Fae, even if they could only mimic weaker versions of those abilities. He saw them as too great a threat to his reign."

Sadness settles over me, wrapping around my ribs like a vice. Without thinking, I step away from Jeyr and wrap my arms around Lorkan's massive frame. "I am so sorry," I whisper, meaning it with everything in me. The rumble of his deep chuckle vibrates against my cheek. "Oh, Little Empath," he murmurs, his arms gently enclosing around me. "There is nothing to be sorry for. It is a good day to know the King has failed, for there is still one Empath and one Shifter in this world."

He pulls back, giving me a soft smile before retreating—but not before I catch the flicker of tension in Caomh's golden gaze as he tracks Lorkan's movements. Jeyr's voice is quiet, almost amused. "That's the most the man has said in years." I follow Lorkan's retreating form, then turn to Caomh, narrowing my eyes at his sudden interest. A conversation for later. We move to the next man, standing with Althea. "This is Aiden. He's from Eileamaids," Jeyr says, nodding toward the red-haired Fae. "He is our eyes on the trade ports." I take Aiden's offered hand and give it a firm shake. Before I can speak, however, a delicate hand knocks his away.

"I am Althea," the petite brunette says with a grin, her blue eyes twinkling. "Little sister, healer extraordinaire." I laugh, instantly knowing I'll like her. Jeyr chuckles as Althea wraps her arms around his waist, embracing him briefly before continuing the introductions. I meet Aella, who is more reserved but polite, and Michael, who hails from Nadur.

And then there's Gwynn, her hand entwined with Jethro's, their fingers locked as if they'll never let go again. As introductions end, we find ourselves seated at the grand banquet table, wine filling our goblets as Jeyr and Caomh war over filling my plate. I shoot Caomh a pointed look.

You have lost so much weight, I could snap you in half, his voice slides into my mind like silk. I roll my eyes. *I can serve myself. I'm not a Princess.*

*You're **our** Princess,* he quips.

I flick my gaze to Jeyr, who's still piling food onto my plate. I place a hand on his wrist, halting his movement mid-reach for another slice of meat. He sighs, guiltily setting it back down.

See?

I nudge at Caomh. *Shut it, Cao. I already have him babying me, I don't need you adding to it.*

Fair. Sorry.

A deep rumble of laughter echoes across the table. "Whatever you two are saying to each other, please say it out loud. This table is quiet enough," Lorkan grumbles, his rich baritone sending a ripple of shivers down the spines of every female in the room— and a few of the males, too. I bite my lip, hiding my smirk. Does the man even realize his effect on people?

Jeyr, sensing my amusement, grips my knee, his fingers tightening. The heat in his gaze sends fire up my spine. "I was just saying to Cao how proud I am that he is finally wearing a shirt at the dinner table," I tease. Jet snorts, choking on his food. "Well, the smell of sex is already thick in the house. I didn't need to add to the aroma," Caomh quips, a smug grin on his face.

"You obviously have an unrealistic understanding of how people react to you being shirtless," Lorkan counters. The table falls into silent laughter, heads bent down, shoulders shaking. Caomh frowns, clearly unamused. I grin, feeling emboldened— maybe it's the wine, maybe it's the high of our bond, but I tilt my head and raise a brow. "I've merely evened the score for all the times you strutted through this house with your lovers clinging off your arms."

Laughter roars through the room. Jeyr leans in, his lips grazing just behind my ear. "Love-making really does suit you, Hummingbird," he murmurs, sending sparks of pleasure straight down my spine. Gods... will this feeling ever fade?

Caomh groans, leaning back in his chair, rolling his eyes. "That doesn't give you permission to rouse her more, Jeyr." Jeyr smirks, lifting a brow. "You're just jealous, Brother." He kisses the soft spot behind my ear— deliberately. I bite back a moan. Caomh grumbles, muttering something about "mating males being unbearable." "You two are making me nauseous. Can we please eat?" Lorkan sighs. The room turns to him, surprised by the gruffness in his tone. He realizes the attention and quickly masks his expression, focusing intently on his food.

The warmth of the room wraps around me, cocooning me in a sense of belonging as the sounds of laughter and conversation hum like a song between mouthfuls of food and sips of wine. The fullness of the space—so many people, so much contentment—settles a peace in my chest that I have never known before.

I catch the sound of gratitude murmured around the table, a chorus of thanks aimed at Hecate. My eyes seek her out, and for the first time, I see her at ease. Comfortable. Relaxed. She sits among them, conversing as though she has been here all along. It has never crossed my mind that perhaps she has been just as lonely as I have been. "You have outdone yourself, Cate," I smile, my voice filled with warmth. Hecate's red eyes find mine, but there is something different in them. The way she looks at me, as if memorizing my face—like it might be the last time.

"I got help," she shrugs nonchalantly, casting a glance at Lorkan. My brows lift. "You cook, Lorkan?" He holds my gaze, something soft glinting in those intense violet eyes. "When you live alone and have a taste for fine food, you learn." His voice is deep, measured, and the timber of it sends ripples down my spine. "My mother was a talented cook, so I grew up eating only the finest."

A wave of something strange flows through me as I watch him speak. Though massive in form, rugged and imposing, there is a deliberate gentleness to him. A quiet grace beneath all the brute strength. And yet, when I glance around the table, I notice the shock on everyone else's faces. I suddenly have so many questions. How have all these men found each other? How do they go from being strangers—Fae from different kingdoms and courts—to brothers?

The conversation shifts as everyone leans back, stomachs sated, sipping their drinks, falling into comfortable chatter. Jeyr's arm curls around me, anchoring me close as if he needs to keep me there— as if anyone would dare take me away. I take the opportunity to ask what I have been wondering all night. Aiden, the Fire Prince, is next to speak. "I know you've heard of me," he smirks. I have. The Kingdom of Eileamaids is one of the most powerful trading ports and a neutral force much like Gliocas. They have strong alliances across the continent, their merchants known for their wealth and influence. He is the only son, but as I learn, his older sister is heir—because, in Eileamaids, a male heir isn't required to rule. "Why is it that every court is different? Why can't they choose who should take the throne?" I muse, sipping my wine. Michael, from Nàdur, answers. "Each court has different beliefs—different prophecies, different gods." He leans forward, his voice steady, his knowledge rich with history. "Our lands were once separated, more than just by the Black Forest and the Dark Mountains. Though we share many of the same gods, we go by different bibles, different traditions."

He glances at Jeyr before continuing. "In Aimsir, only one person has full control over the weather—Grand Duke Raiden. Everyone else has lesser aspects of it. When a Grand Duke dies, his power passes into his heir. In history, it has always been a firstborn son, so naturally, they have always inherited the title. Niall has inherited control over rain. But Jeyr... Jeyr was born with his mother's power, which changes everything. It means there is no doubt about who the next Grand Duke will be. However, if both Jeyr and Niall were to fall before an heir could be born, then Aella would be the first Grand Duchess in their history, as she too has weather-based magic."

I nod, absorbing the information. "And Eileamaids?" "In Aiden's kingdom," Michael continues, "the Grand Duke or Duchess is chosen at birth. Aiden's sister, Eden, was born with the ability to master all elements. Aiden, on the other hand, was born with only fire." Aiden grins. "Yeah, but I am the best godsdamn fire wielder in the Kingdom." His cocky smirk makes me laugh. "Gods," Caomh mutters, shaking his head, "another one of you."

"And the other courts?" I press.

Michael hums in thought. "Aotrom is unique. They have had the same Grand Duke for centuries—Lumiere. He lost his wife in the Great War, but even before that, they were never able to have children. There is no certainty as to who his power will pass to when he falls. Everyone assumes it will be Jethro, since he is his nephew, but no one knows."

My gaze flickers to Jethro, but his features remain unreadable. "Slànachad, the Healing Kingdom, is ruled by two Grand Dukes—Aison and Bliant. They don't follow tradition, never have. Their leader is chosen based on the strength of their magic. Jeyr's mother is one of their daughters, which means he or Althea could be chosen as their heir."

My lips part in surprise. Michael continues.

"The Kingdom of Nàdur is... an outlier. It's home to beasts and natives—they follow a monarch system. They once had a strong alliance with the Queens' Lands, but after the war, they have kept to themselves. Their ruler, Grand Duchess Gaia, is said to have once loved an Empath."

My breath hitches. "But since the war, they've stayed in isolation, relying on their horticulture and medicinal trade. Gaia has many partners and many children, all with different gifts. To choose a successor, they compete—only the last one standing takes the throne."

My stomach churns at the thought. "And Puinnsean?" I ask softly.

The room falls silent. Michael's jaw tightens. Jethro's muscles tense, his arm wrapping tightly around Gwynn's shoulders as he presses a firm kiss to her hair. "Puinnsean only ever has a man on the throne," Michael murmurs darkly. "Bane, like Lumiere, has ruled for centuries. His wife, Desdemona, went missing in the Great War. His daughter, Ameliana, remains a mystery to us all."

I catch the flinch in Gwynn's shoulders, the way Jethro holds her closer. The air feels heavier, thicker, filled with bitterness. My voice drops to a whisper. "My mother never really told me all of this... I was always taught that men held all the power."

Michael exhales sharply. "She wasn't wrong. The Great King holds all of us in his palm. The rulers of every kingdom bow to him. No woman speaks at his table. Even when Gaia or Eden rule their courts, they must have a male proxy to sit in their place. And the only magic the Great King does not possess..."

His chocolate eyes lock onto mine, voice weighted with meaning. "...are the ones that come from the Queens' Lands. The Witches. The Empaths. The Shifters."

I freeze. Jeyr's grip on me tightens, as if he can moor me in place, as if sheer will alone can hold me safe within his grasp. There is still so much we haven't discussed, lingering between us like stagnant air. "I would... I would appreciate it if who I am remained a secret among us," I murmur, my voice steady despite the unease curling in my gut. "Though it may already be too late. Someone knows. Someone is trying—or rather, tried—to take that power from me. Hopefully, they believe I died, but..."

I am cut off as voices fill the room at once.

"We won't risk your safety, Empath."

"Your secret is safe with us."

"You are family. We never betray our family."

"No one is going to touch you."

My heart swells as I look around, taking in their faces—the old, my guardians, the recent, my friends, and the new, those I hadn't known I needed but now can't imagine my life without. I don't think I will ever get used to this feeling—the overwhelming sense of belonging, the warmth of knowing that I am no longer alone.

"Thank you," I say softly, sincerity threading through my voice. "It means a lot to me. And I promise to protect you all in any way I can. The support goes both ways."

I let my emotions weave through the room, wrapping around them like golden threads, ensuring they feel the depth of my gratitude. Their faces relax, smiles blooming as they absorb my words. Life can't get much better than this.

"Thank you," Jeyr echoes, his voice thick with emotion. "It means everything to us both. I never got the chance to thank you all properly—for saving the love of my life. But thank you, for now and for keeping her safe in the future."

He takes my hand, lifting it to his lips in a lingering kiss. His gaze catches mine, that look that makes my knees weak, that makes my heart race like a bird in flight. I am wrong—it does get better. With him, with them, I am part of something so much greater than myself.

Jeyr

THE WEIGHT OF SILENCE

When are you going to ask her to marry you?

Caomh's voice drifts into my mind, dragging me from my thoughts. I look over at where he sits, leaned back with his usual air of arrogance, but his golden eyes are serious.

I've been asking myself the same damn question since the moment we got her back—before, during, and after making love. It consumes me. Whether Olivia senses it, I'm not sure. She's been training harder and faster than ever. Though she lives with us now, I only see her at mealtimes and in the evenings. She refuses to train with me, claiming I'm too distracting. So instead, she spends most of her time with Jethro and Caomh, leaving me to simmer in my own impatience.

The house is still full. Lorkan has stayed, coming and going with the investigations Caomh has sent him on. I've begrudgingly said nothing as Olivia practices her powers with him. Aiden lingers as well, watching the trade routes for smugglers selling viper bàis, trying to uncover who nearly stole my mate from me.

Althea comes and goes, but whenever she's here, Olivia is always by her side. They bonded instantly, as if they've always been sisters. They take their lunches on the cliffs, play with Kyzan and Ness, and fill the halls with the sound of their laughter. Aella has returned to rule in my father's absence, as he and Niall continue securing new alliances.

But no matter how busy life in the manor becomes, it always seems to halt at sunset. Everyone finds themselves drawn to the windows, watching Olivia and Ness in the open field near the cliffs. Althea plays the piano, and to the rhythm, Ness dances around Olivia, weaving in mesmerizing circles and figure eights. And Liv—gods, she glows. Her skin radiates light, her eyes turn iridescent. I find myself counting the hours until evening, when I can have her all to myself.

She has this way of bringing people together, this relentless need to make everyone feel like they belong. As the winter frost melts and the days grow warmer, she turns to Althea one afternoon with a wild grin. "Do you want to feel what it's like to fly?" Hands stretch wide, eyes lift to the pacific gulls soaring overhead.

That's all it takes. What starts as a question turns into a family affair. One by one, we sit at the cliff's edge, legs dangling over the abyss while Olivia weaves her power into our senses, letting us feel what it's like to fly. Awe fills the faces around me, eyes shut as they experience true weightlessness.

Everyone except Jethro and Gwynn, who have taken advantage of an empty house.

Mind coming back to the present? Caomh's dry voice pulls me from my reverie. *When are you asking her?*

I don't know, I admit. *Everything is so perfect right now—I'm afraid to change it.*

If you don't ask her, I will.

My head snaps up. The bastard is grinning, but there's an undercurrent of sincerity in his voice that sends my teeth grinding together.

I want to! I snap. *I just don't know how or when. It has to be perfect. Then there's her safety to think about, keeping this hidden from the rest of the world. I'm the Prince of Aimsir, Caomh. Hiding a marriage wouldn't be easy even under normal circumstances—let alone a marriage to an Empath.*

Caomh rolls his eyes. *It's been two months. Honestly, I thought you'd proposed the moment you consummated the bond. When I felt her joy through the house, I was sure you had. We all ran upstairs expecting an announcement, only to find her squealing over Kyzan.*

A laugh bursts from my throat. *That bloody mutt has me beat every time. She's always more excited to see him than me.*

Caomh chuckles. *I've noticed. But in all seriousness, this is Liv we're talking about. She would love a simple proposal—on the beach, maybe. Hell, get the mutt involved. She'd melt. And the world doesn't need to know about her powers. Just let them think she's a lowborn. She knows how to stay hidden, Jeyr. She's lived her entire life in the shadows.*

He's not wrong. All people need to know is that Olivia is my Companach. No one has to know what makes her so rare.

I'm always right, he muses.

Before I can snap back, a voice laced with amusement floats from the doorway. "What are you two lads talking about mind to mind? It's no fun if I can't jump in." I turn, and every thought in my head comes to a crashing halt. Olivia stands in the doorway with Kyzan at her side. But that isn't what makes my breath hitch. She's wearing a dress.

I've never seen her in a dress before. Olive green, sleeveless, cinched at the waist, the fabric cascading down her legs like water. Her usual ponytail is high, her wild red curls tumbling down her back, exposing her bare shoulders. My mark shimmers, the white bands gleaming up her arm, claiming her as mine. "Geez, Princess. Are you trying to make Jeyr's jaw hit the ground?" Caomh muses, getting up to greet her.

I barely hear him. My entire world narrows to the stunning creature before me. Olivia lifts herself onto her toes and hugs Caomh. He takes her in with a smirk before spinning her, watching the dress twirl around her ankles. Her eyes sparkle.

"Just a change of pace. It's so lovely and warm outside. And I got paint on my clothes, so Althea lent me this." Her smile is a thing of magic, and gods help me, I cannot be held responsible for what I do next. I step forward, shoving Caomh aside and gathering her in my arms, drinking in her scent.

I am serious, Jeyr. Caomh's voice touches my mind. *If you don't marry her, I will.*

I stiffen.

Like hell you will. You're just using her as an excuse to ignore your own problems.

What problems?

I roll my eyes. One day, he'll pull his head out of the sand.

I lift Olivia's chin, capturing her lips with my own. Shamelessly, she melts into me, arms wrapping around my neck, body molding into mine as if she's made for it. As I turn, leading her up the stairs, she giggles.

"If I had known you'd have this reaction to me in a dress, I would have put one on a long time ago."

I growl, the sound rumbling from my chest. Her breath hitches. I smirk, knowing exactly what effect that has on her. Her body shivers against mine. *Perfect,* I think.

Scooping her into my arms, I carry her the rest of the way to our bedroom.

We don't surface for dinner.

I notice a shift in her. A wall—delicate but firm—blocking off Liv's usual flow of emotions. It isn't numbness, nor is it entirely closed off, but she's suddenly harder to read.

I try to push my concerns aside. She looks well. Her skin has that subtle glow, her eyes a shade greener—if such a thing is possible. She's healthy, apart from the tired shadows beneath her lashes. *Maybe I'm overthinking it.* I haven't *lived* with her before. *Maybe this is just Liv settling into routine.* But she's different—obscurely different from the first two months we lived together.

And I'm not the only one who notices.

The house—still full of family and friends—hums with quiet murmurs of concern. A few joke that I'm keeping her up too late, that her exhaustion is purely a result of our nights tangled together in sheets. And maybe I am part of the reason. There have been evenings when I insist she rest, but then she turns those loving green eyes on me, teases my skin with soft, lingering kisses... *There's no saying no to her.*

Most mornings, she's up before I notice, the lingering scent of her lavender bath salts the only proof she's been in our bed at all. By the time I find her, she's already gone for a morning ride, trained, taken an afternoon ride, had dinner, and by the time she returns to me at night, it's only to make love and sleep. *Maybe this has always been her routine—minus the new sex part.*

But even I find it hard to capture her attention for more than a fleeting moment.

Except when we make love.

Or when I find her curled up in the family room with a book, tucked against the fire's warmth, the flickering glow dancing across her freckled skin. Those are the only moments I can steal her, where she lets her head rest on my lap and purrs in response to my touch.

But the shift in her... it lingers. And it gnaws at me.

I sit on the bed in nothing but my underwear, waiting for Olivia to finally come to bed. The door creaks open, and she enters slowly, exhaustion weighing on every step. My stomach twists. She's preparing for a war none of us knows about.

Kyzan has been more clingy than usual—if it's possible for the wolf to press himself any closer to her side than he already does. He never leaves her. I rise from the bed, crossing the room to meet her.

She smiles up at me, warm and full of love, the kind of look that makes my heart ache with its sheer intensity. I cup her face, chuckling softly at the flecks of blue and purple paint speckled across her freckles. Dipping my head, I wet my thumb and gently rub the paint from her cheek.

"Busy day, Hummingbird?" I muse. Her smile deepens, something tender glinting in her eyes. "Mm," she hums, sinking into my chest. "I'm exhausted. This might be the first night I'll have to refuse you, my love." She chuckles, but there's truth in her words. "You know you can take days off, right?" I try to keep my voice light. "From you? Never."

"You don't have to," I murmur, brushing her damp hair from her forehead. "I mean from training, painting, riding—you seem to be running yourself ragged." I tilt her chin up, studying her features, the shadows beneath her eyes. She hesitates. "I think we need a holiday. How about the day after tomorrow, we go away for a week, just the two of us? This house has become very crowded." I play with a loose strand of her hair, waiting for the small, content purr she always makes when I do this.

But... nothing.

A quiet unease prickles at my skin. "I like having everyone here," she says after a moment. "It's like a big family. I can cut back. You and I can spend more time together here."

I know that tone. She's lying.

She won't cut back. Olivia will keep herself busy, pushing herself past her limits, running herself into the ground until she collapses on the couch, too exhausted to move. And though I love seeing her interact with my family, I thrive in watching her bring people together... I miss our time on the beach. Just the two of us.

Well, three, if I count Kyzan.

"Liv..." I murmur. Her body goes still. Too still. She braces herself for my words, as if she already knows what I'm going to say. "Jeyr..." she counters, resting a hand on my face. She searches me, but it's her I'm searching.

Something is beneath the surface, something she's holding back. I feel it, curling between us like an unseen tether waiting to snap.

But she says nothing. And the longer the silence stretches between us, the heavier that something becomes.

Olivia

BIG QUESTIONS AND UNDERWEAR

I look into his eyes, concern radiating from him in thick, unrelenting waves. I can't tell him about the nightmares—the ones that whisper warnings of an impending storm, the ones that claw at the edges of my peace, reminding me that this perfect bliss is only a breath away from being shattered. *I don't want to put fear in his eyes. I don't want him to see the weight pressing down on me, the thoughts that have rooted themselves so deeply I can't shake them.*

That day in the forest haunts me. Over and over, it plays in my mind—someone tried to kill me. Tried to take a part of me. *I don't believe it was an isolated incident.* Then there are the letters from my father... a looming threat in the shadows, the uncertainty of being discovered hanging over me like a blade poised to strike.

I ride twice a day to my old cottage, checking for correspondence, but nothing comes. For all I know, his threats are hollow words, meant only to keep me looking over my shoulder. *Until I have reason to fear otherwise, I can't tell Jeyr. I can't risk burdening him with something I don't fully understand myself.*

The full house is a welcomed distraction. The people I've come to love, the family I never realized I've been missing... they fill the void in ways I hadn't thought possible. I thrive in the warmth of it, in the camaraderie, the laughter, the ceaseless presence of others. *I never realized how lonely my life had been until I was surrounded by so many people who chose to stay.*

But Jeyr—Jeyr is the only one I've been neglecting.

His voice, deep and laced with frustration, snaps me from my thoughts. "Don't 'Jeyr' me. I have been trying to get some alone time with you..." "You do. All night, every night." I rub my nose against his, hoping to distract him, to shift the conversation away from whatever has been sitting on the tip of his tongue.

But he is having none of it. "Olivia, I have been trying to have a day with you for months... For fuck's sake! How am I supposed to ask you to marry me if you won't even give me a day? I wanted it to be special! I had a whole thing planned with your stupid mutt and the beach and—I have a ring—"

My heart stops.

I stand frozen as Jeyr's handsome, sleep-rumpled form stalks toward me, his usual brooding expression softened by something more vulnerable, something raw. He looks younger in that moment, his dark hair sticking out in wild, tousled directions.

"Liv..." he chokes. Silence stretches between us, thick and unyielding. I open my mouth, but no words come. Happiness swells in my chest, a feeling so overwhelming it leaves me breathless. But beneath it... a whisper of guilt. *I've been avoiding him, keeping secrets, and here he is, desperate to give me forever.* A tear slips down my cheek, hot against my skin.

Jeyr is there in an instant, towering over me, his large hands cupping my face as if I might vanish if he lets go. His grip is gentle, reverent. His thumbs sweep over my cheeks, catching the tears that keep falling.

"Liv, I'm sorry. Shit, I should have—"

"Yes."

His breath hitches. His ocean-blue eyes grow glossy with unshed tears. "Yes," I whisper again, unable to stop myself.

He breaks.

With a sharp intake of breath, Jeyr lunges, sweeping me into his arms, holding me so tight I think he might never let go. I say yes over and over, the word slipping past my lips like a sacred prayer. He cradles my face, his eyes searching mine for any trace of hesitation before capturing my lips in a searing, desperate kiss.

Tears mix with salt and love as we cry into each other's joy. *For the first time in weeks, I let go of everything that has been weighing me down. I let the anxieties, the shadows, the fears slip away into nothingness. None of it matters. Not now. Not when I have this—when I have him.*

After a few moments, we pull away, our foreheads resting together, breaths mingling.

Jeyr grins, his dimples so deep I could tuck pieces of chocolate into them. My heart clenches, and a laugh bubbles past my lips, that light, unrestrained kind of laugh I've only recently learned to embrace.

"Wait here!" His deep voice is a command, but it's filled with excitement. Jeyr sprints to his dresser, still dressed in nothing but his underwear. I watch him go, my laughter only growing as I take in the sculpted muscles of his back, the firm curve of his ass. *Mother above, he really is a work of art.*

He returns in a flash, dropping to both knees before me, his hands cradling a small velvet box. I blink, my breath stalling. A half-naked, wild-haired prince of Aimsir is kneeling before me, asking for my hand. *It's so utterly us that I burst into laughter between the tears.*

Jeyr chuckles, his own eyes shimmering with emotion as he flips open the box. Nestled inside is a delicate gold ring, a large emerald stone set in the center. It's simple—elegant. It's perfect. His gaze meets mine, bright and unguarded. "Olivia, will you do me the honor of being my Companach—as well as my wife?" My chest aches with love, with an emotion so profound I think I might combust from the sheer force of it.

He takes my hand, pausing at the tip of my ring finger, waiting. I nod, choking back a sob. Jeyr slides the band onto my finger, the metal cool against my skin. A ripple of energy surges through me, like the universe itself is sealing our bond, etching our souls together for eternity. The ring warms instantly, and tingles travel up my arm, twining through my chest, embedding itself into my very being.

Jeyr

A Future without Thought of War

Olivia's dress is off in seconds.

Gods above... I take in the sight of my soon-to-be wife, my breath hitching at the sheer beauty of her. Her skin glows, the firelight casting golden highlights over every perfect curve, every freckle I've spent nights memorizing. Her breasts—made for my hands—rise and fall with her breathless laughter, her green eyes alight with anticipation.

I lay her gently on the bed, lowering my now naked body over hers. The moment our skin meets, pleasure ripples through me, an intoxicating mix of her touch and her essence flooding my senses. I could live in this moment forever. But I want this to last. I want to show her, with every touch, every whispered breath, that this isn't fleeting. That I am hers for eternity.

My hands move slowly, reverently, tracing the constellations of freckles that dust her skin. Mapping her like an astronomer tracing the stars, committing them to memory, so I will never forget the sight of her laid bare before me. Her body shivers under my touch, her breath quickens, heart beating like the rapid flutter of a hummingbird's wings—*my Hummingbird.*

I kiss each breast, swirling my tongue over her rosebud nipples, savoring the intoxicating mix of her scent and taste. Her stomach tenses beneath my lips as I trail lower, her soft curses like a hymn in the silence. So sweet, yet so sassy. I grin against her skin, teasing her with my breath, my tongue. I need her to unravel for me. To fall apart in my hands. And *gods*, does she.

Her moans are pure music, her cries urging me on as my mouth devours her, as my fingers find the spot that has her arching, trembling, gasping my name like a plea. I almost lose myself at the sound of it—at the sheer force of her. She is magic, raw and unfiltered. And she is mine.

I brace myself, willing my control to hold as I hover above her, feeling the ghost of her touch against my rigid length.

"Jeyr," she whispers, her voice shaking with need. "Please."

"*Gods, Liv...*" I groan, pressing inside her, her warmth, her tightness enveloping me whole. The world falls away. Only this. Only us. Our souls collide with each thrust, our bodies finding their rhythm, each moan, each whimper sending us spiraling further into pleasure.

I will never get over this. Nothing will ever compare to feeling her come undone beneath me, around me, to the way our bodies move in perfect harmony, like the stars have aligned just for us. Gods, she's making me poetic.

Her legs wrap around me, her nails dig into my back as we both shatter, pleasure cresting like a tidal wave that drags us under. Her name falls from my lips like a prayer. She is my drug—and I am addicted.

Slowly, we come down from the high, our breath heavy, our bodies still trembling from the aftershocks. Olivia curls into my chest, her warm body pressing against mine, her fingers idly tracing patterns over my heart.

"So," I exhale, my voice still hoarse, "when do you want to get married?"

She hums, her fingers still moving against my skin. "As soon as possible." I grin, lifting my brow. "This time next week?" She tilts her head up, her green eyes locking onto mine, shining with the kind of certainty that nearly knocks the breath from my lungs. She nods.

My heart stops—then surges forward at full force.

I kiss her nose, then her lips, then the freckles on her cheek, trailing kisses down her jaw, over her collarbone. She squeals, hiccupping with laughter as she tries to squirm away. "Jeyr, stop!" she giggles, breathless.

Never. I need her laughter. I need to feel the pure, untainted joy that radiates from her, the warmth that sets my soul alight. "Mm," I murmur against her skin, "don't you like it when I kiss you here, and here, and here..." Her laughter rings through the room, the most glorious sound I've ever heard. "Stop! Everyone will hear us."

I smirk, pulling her closer. "Pfft, as if they don't every other night." She swats at my chest, shaking her head as she tries to catch her breath. "We better tell the others to get ready for a wedding, then," I muse, brushing a loose strand of hair from her face. My fingers trail under her chin, tilting her gaze back to mine. "Where would you like it?"

"Here, with our family."

Our family.

My chest aches with something indescribable, something I never thought I'd have, never thought I'd deserve. I don't need to say anything. The permanent grin on my face speaks for itself. "Perfect," I murmur, rolling her on top of me, drinking in the sight of her before I capture her lips once more.

Round two is inevitable.

After all, who am I to deny my future wife?

When I wake to find Olivia gone again, my stomach sinks.

This is something we need to discuss before getting married—I refuse to keep waking up in bed alone.

I let out a low growl, frustration curling in my chest, but before I can fully give in to my temper, her voice interrupts my brooding.

"Morning, sleepyhead."

I look up to see Olivia sitting at the dresser, brushing her long, wild curls. Her green eyes meet mine in the reflection, amusement dancing in their depths. She knows exactly what I'm thinking.

Kyzan lies across her lap, his massive head pressed against her thigh as if he has any claim to her at all. *Stupid mutt.* I sigh heavily, shaking my head.

Olivia's smile widens, that silent, knowing laughter curling on her lips—like she can read my thoughts before I even voice them. *Damn her and her gift.*

Then she stands, sauntering toward me in that knee-length burgundy dress, the thin fabric clinging to every perfect curve. Her hair flows freely behind her, waves of deep red cascading over her shoulders.

I am going to marry this woman. This beautiful, perfect woman.

She stops at the edge of the bed, hesitating for just a moment, before softly saying, "So, I thought maybe we could tell everyone over breakfast, then get the details organized for next week?"

Her voice is gentle, almost shy, as if she's embarrassed by her excitement. My stomach flutters.

Gods, part of me wishes we could give her the grand wedding she deserves, let the entire world know that she's mine. That she belongs to me as much as I belong to her. But we both know it isn't safe—not with the threats still looming, not with enemies still searching for what she is.

I reach for her hand, tugging her down onto the bed with me. My fingers thread through hers, feeling the steady pulse that beats beneath her skin. I lift her hand to my lips, brushing a kiss against her knuckles before looking into those bright green eyes that have haunted my dreams long before I even knew what they meant to me.

"I couldn't agree more," I murmur against her skin.

And when she smiles at me—really smiles at me, her whole being alight with happiness—I know in my bones that no matter what it takes, no matter who I have to fight, I will keep that smile on her face for the rest of our days.

Olivia

LETTERS AND FORETELLING

The day is full of everyone in high spirits. It's a mix of Caomh saying, *"About fucking time,"* Jethro swinging me in his arms, and a chorus of hugs from my newfound family. No one seems to notice my trepidation. I suppose there are highlights to being an Empath: I can control their emotions... I can wipe away their suspicions before they even start. But the guilt is starting to eat at me.

Seven days.

I sigh. That's all that runs through my head. Seven days and my worries will be gone. Then I will tell him. We can live our life as we should have been, without this tiptoe of hiding my thoughts, my feelings—without the truth that I was promised to another. *Hypocrite.*

The week flies by. My cheeks ache from all the smiling, my body from the constant warmth of Jeyr's touch. His happiness is palpable, a force all on its own. It flows through me, through the manor, seeping into every stone and floorboard.

And it isn't just his emotions—I feel it in the way he captures me, how he pins me against walls, against lounges, against anything within reach, just to claim another kiss, another moment. It's as if he's afraid that if he lets go, even for a second, I might slip away. I melt for him every time. Let him take, let him have. I savor the way his hands map my body, the way his lips brush against mine, as if he's making up for every second we had spent apart before we met.

But neither of us speaks of the attack.

We never talk about the shadows looming over us, the unanswered questions, the growing fear of what's to come. Jeyr is living in the now, basking in the light of our happiness. And I let myself do the same. I hold onto it, cling to it, terrified that if I let go, it will slip through my fingers like sand on the shore.

But today... today I have to say goodbye.

I pack my bag for the night away, the tradition of sleeping apart before the wedding looming over me like a cruel joke. I feel the emptiness before it even happens, a hollow space in my chest at the thought of not sharing a bed with him tonight. And as if he feels it too, Jeyr wraps his arms around my waist from behind, letting out a deep, reluctant grumble.

"Do we really have to follow this tradition?" I mutter, pouting. He answers by biting my earlobe playfully. I let out a surprised laugh, smacking his chest—which, as expected, is about as effective as hitting a wall.

"Yes," he murmurs against my skin. "It's bad luck to see you before the wedding. I think we've had enough of that, don't you?"

I sigh, letting myself go limp in his arms, inhaling deeply as his scent—home—wraps around me. Ocean and pine, crisp and warm all at once. I want to bottle it up, keep it with me when I'm away from him tonight.

With reluctance, I zip up my overnight bag and turn, cupping his face between my hands. I memorize him, drinking in every detail like I'm committing a sacred text to memory. The strong cut of his jaw, the depth of his eyes, the thick, unruly lashes, the slightly upturned tips of his ears. My fingers trace the bridge of his cheekbones, the curve of his lips, the warmth of his skin beneath my touch. When I meet his gaze again, I realize he's doing the same to me. Jeyr studies me as though he's etching every freckle, every fleck of green in my irises into his very soul. Our heads fall together, foreheads brushing, breath mingling as we stand in silence. Just being. Just knowing.

Come on, lovebirds. You'll see each other tomorrow... and for an eternity after.

Caomh's dry, gravelly voice comes from the doorway, breaking our trance. I turn, poking my tongue out at him like a child. His chuckle mixes with Jeyr's deep laughter, the sound weaving warmth into my heart. One last look. One last moment.

See you tomorrow, I tell him without words.

Jeyr's fingers squeeze mine once before I let go, stepping into Caomh's waiting grasp. And then, with a pulse of power, he winnows me away—to my cottage. To the last night I will ever spend apart from my mate.

Caomh stands in the doorway of my home, arms crossed as he gives me one final once-over, his golden eyes glinting with something unreadable.

Will you be okay? Or do you want company?

I roll my eyes, shaking my head at his overprotectiveness.

I don't think my husband-to-be would be too happy with your proposition.

Laughter flickers in his gaze, a knowing smirk tugging at the corners of his lips. He shrugs, then steps forward, wrapping me in a warm, brotherly embrace. His arms are firm, grounding, a silent promise of protection. He presses a swift kiss to my forehead, his lips barely grazing my skin before he winnows away, leaving nothing but the soft echo of his magic in the air.

I sigh heavily, feeling the weight of his absence settle into my chest. The quiet that follows is too quiet. It's one night. One night. I can survive one night without Jeyr.

I repeat the words in my head, but the logic doesn't lessen the dull ache that has already begun to spread through my ribs. Since the attack, we haven't spent a single night apart, haven't even breathed without the other close enough to touch. But for the sake of tradition, I agreed to sleep in a separate home before the wedding. Because if I had stayed at the manor... I would have found him. I wouldn't have been able to stop myself.

My gaze drops to my wrist just as it begins to glow, a soft luminescence weaving through the infinity bands that mark our bond. A silent message, his love pressing into me like the ghost of a kiss.

I miss you too.

I close my eyes and send the warmth of my love back through our bond, imagining his answering smile as I turn toward the small living room.

A familiar, comforting scent of roasted cinnamon and warm bread greets me. Cooper and Mary sit near the hearth, their smiles kind and expectant as I enter. At least I'm not completely alone.

Jeyr

BLOOD ON THE MARBLE, THUNDER IN MY VEINS

I watch my wrist, the glowing band flickering like a heartbeat. A tether. A pulse. A whisper of her. Even apart, we're still connected. A smile tugs at my lips, though my face still aches from weeks of grinning like a fool. I never think happiness like this is possible. Never believe I deserve it. And yet, in mere hours, Olivia will walk down the aisle toward me, and for the first time in my life, everything will be exactly as it should.

I lie stretched out on the daybed, staring at the ceiling, letting the memories of her flicker through my mind. Every laugh, every touch, every whispered secret between us. The way she tangles herself around me in her sleep, as if her body fears even an inch of distance. *Mine.*

Then, the storm comes. A deafening crack of thunder shatters the quiet. My body goes taut, instincts snapping to attention. Lightning flashes, illuminating the darkened room in fragmented bursts. My pulse pounds. A storm this sudden, this violent, isn't natural.

I shoot up, scanning the room, muscles braced for a fight. And then, my gaze lands on my sister. Aella stands in the doorway, her scarred face streaked with silent tears. But it's her eyes—Gods, her eyes—that send ice slicing through my veins. "Aella..." My voice barely makes it past my lips. My gut twists. Something is wrong.

Another boom of thunder rattles the walls. Althea runs into the room, breathless, her blue eyes wild and full of unspoken terror.

Then—before I can react—lightning splits the air, and we're gone.

The room disappears, and my stomach lurches as Aella wrenches us through the ether, winnowing us away with a crack of raw power.

And when the world settles, my blood runs cold.

We're home. My family's castle.

No. No, no, no.

Rage flares through me, searing hot. I am to be married in mere hours, and she drags me away? I spin toward my sister, fury rising, ready to demand an explanation—

Then, I see them.

The bodies.

Everything inside me stills.

Althea's strangled sob breaks through the silence, a sound so raw it shreds my soul.

I blink. *No.* I blink again, harder, willing it away, willing them away—but the bodies remain.

Niall.

Our father.

Blood soaks the marble floor beneath them, pooling like spilled ink. My mother's blond hair—Niall's hair—is streaked with crimson. Their throats—gods, their throats—

Whoever did this... they butchered them.

I move on instinct, dropping to my knees beside my brother's lifeless body, fingers pressing to the pulse point at his throat.

Nothing.

My stomach lurches.

Across from me, Althea does the same to our father. The ragged gasps leaving her lips tell me what I already know.

Dead.

They are dead.

"What happened..." The words barely make it past my lips, tight and hoarse, foreign even to my own ears.

Althea's blood-smeared hand covers her mouth, her body trembling. She struggles to breathe, to speak, to make sense of the nightmare before us.

"They... they were negotiating between Kingdoms, working on peace agreements and..." Her voice cracks, her breath coming in sharp, shallow gasps. "Someone winnowed them here. I heard the noise, the thud—" Her breath hitches. "Who... who would..."

The storm around her swirls, crackling with the force of her emotions.

Aella turns to me, her voice a blade through the grief, "I don't know! Just do something!"

I force myself to move, even as my mind reels, even as the ground beneath me feels unsteady, unreal.

Caomh, I need you. Now. Bring everyone. NOW.

I yell the command down our mental bond, hoping to the gods he can feel the urgency, the desperation in my words.

I wrap an arm around each of my sisters, guiding them away from the office, away from the bodies that had once been our family.

We barely make it into the grand foyer before the others arrive.

Jethro, Caomh, Aiden, Lorkan—our brothers in arms. All of them clad in their fighting leathers, every muscle taut, every expression unreadable.

Althea lets out a strangled sob as she collapses into Aiden's arms. He catches her, hands shaking as he tilts her face up, scanning for injuries.

And then, suddenly, everything else fades.

Because she isn't here.

I look up, searching, scanning every face in the room.

"Where is Olivia?"

The words cut through the air, sharp and raw.

The silence that follows is deafening.

The bond between us—our tether, our pulse—still flickers. She is alive. But something in me knows. Something feels wrong.

I turn to Jethro, my breath ragged, my voice barely a whisper, "Where is Olivia?"

Jethro meets my gaze, his eyes dark with realization.

"I'll get her," he says, his voice tight.

Then, he is gone.

Olivia

HAUNTED COTTAGE

As I sit on the daybed with Kyzan, exhaustion claws at me, the heavy pull of sleep threatening to drag me under. My mind is a haze of whispers, images of Jeyr's hands, his lips, the love we share. But a shadow creeps in behind those thoughts—a foreboding presence I cannot name.

Then Kyzan moves. His massive form lurches from my side, ears flat against his skull, a low growl rumbling deep in his chest. The room stills. Mary and Cooper look up from their armchairs, brows furrowed in concern.

"Kyzan? What's the matter?" Cooper murmurs, standing to peer out the window. I don't need to look. I already know.

The presence at the door—it's familiar. My blood turns to ice. A shiver crawls down my spine like spider legs, prickling at my skin. *Not now. Not again.*

I stand, moving on instinct. My pulse pounds in my ears. I can already feel the storm building outside, thick clouds of dread swirling through my stomach.

"Cooper, hide Mary. Now!" My voice comes out sharp, a command that vibrates in the air. I barely register Cooper's movements as he pulls Mary toward the back room. I feel the shift in the air, the unnatural stillness. A presence slithers into the space without a sound. The door never opens—it doesn't need to.

The creatures materialize like nightmares made flesh. Their bodies are monstrous, shifting masses of muscle and shadow, their poisonous yellow eyes locking onto mine with predatory hunger. Their faces—scarred, twisted, disfigured beyond recognition—are made all the more grotesque by their eerie stillness. They don't breathe. They don't blink. Kyzan's fur bristles as he presses against me, his thick pelt shielding me as his growl deepens into a snarl.

It all happens at once.

The creatures lunge.

Kyzan meets them in midair, his teeth sinking into the throat of the nearest beast. The room erupts into chaos—the crash of bodies, the snarls, the scrape of claws against wood. The scent of blood fills the air.

I reach for my power.

I hope when the time comes, Little Empath, you don't hesitate to use your powers.

Caomh's voice rings in my mind, his words a warning and a challenge.

I clench my fists and send a blast of energy outward, latching onto the creatures' emotions—if they can even feel at all. I find it, the dark thread of their existence, and wrench it apart.

The first one collapses.

Then another.

But they keep coming.

Through the chaos, I barely register the sound of footsteps—swift, calculated. My heart leaps into my throat as a streak of silver flashes through the air.

Solasgath.

Jethro winnows into the fight, his sword slicing through the darkness with effortless precision. The blade gleams with pure light as it cuts down the creatures, their bodies crumbling to dust beneath its edge. He moves like a specter, too fast to track, his golden eyes locking onto mine for a split second before he turns, parrying an oncoming strike.

"Olivia, as we practiced! Don't hold back!" Jethro's voice is sharp, commanding.

I throw my power out again, sending another wave of agony into the minds of the monsters. They falter, their bodies twitching, spasming—but they don't stop. Kyzan lets out a sharp yelp. My breath catches. One of them has caught his flank, sinking its jagged claws deep into his flesh.

A scream tears through my throat.

And then—

The air changes.

I feel it before I see him.

The dark presence that has been looming outside steps forward, pressing into the edges of my mind with clawed fingers.

A wave of nausea hits me as the scent of burnt lilies fills the room.

I turn, my body moving against my will.

Yellow, snake-like eyes meet mine.

Cold. Hollow.

My stomach lurches as skeletal fingers brush against my cheek. I flinch at the touch—it's wrong, a violation. His power slithers over my skin, pressing against my mind, scraping at the walls I have so carefully built. I look at his other hand. A fitted glove, two stones embedded into the knuckles—one a deep blood-red ruby, the other a sickly canary yellow.

The stones pulse.

I feel the pull, the unnatural craving.

A claw sinks into my mind. My walls begin to crack.

My body goes rigid.

No, no, no...

Caomh has warned me. He has told me there are Fae out there far more powerful than him—ones who won't be kind, who won't stop.

I'm not strong enough.

I hear the sounds of the battle below, hear the grunts and snarls, the clash of Solasgath slicing through another beast.

Jethro and Cooper are still fighting.

I have to protect them.

I make my choice.

I take every memory of Jeyr, of his family, of everything we have built—and lock it away in the deepest vault of my mind.

Then I let the claws in.

You are mine. You are my wife. You will do as I bid.

His voice is a hiss, a promise of ownership.

I want to scream.

I can't.

My head nods. My lips move. "Yes."

I touch my wrist one last time, feeling the bond flicker like a dying ember.

I love you, Jeyr.

I will never forget you.

The technicolor lights sink into my skin, glamouring my power, obscuring my identity.

Jethro's eyes catch mine. I see the fury, the terror. He wants me to fight.

I can't.

I won't risk their lives.

"Get your hands off my daughter!"

Cooper's voice roars through the chaos, shaking my resolve.

I flinch at the words, my heart fracturing in my chest.

The snake beside me clicks his tongue in amusement.

"You are mistaken," he purrs. "She is *his* daughter."

I turn. My stomach twists into knots.

There, standing beside the monster, is my father.

A sharp hiss of torture trickles through my blood as I turn, my body recoiling before my mind can process the sight before me. My inner turmoil screams louder, deafening. A static noise fills my ears, drowning out the chaos around me. Somewhere deep inside, the young girl who once clung to her father's hand, who missed him so desperately, cries out in grief.

But she has just been betrayed.

She has just realized the truth.

Her father has sold her to this... this devil.

Beside the snake-eyed creature, my father stands—weathered, his features hollow and gray, as if all life has been drained from him. His hazel eyes, once filled with warmth, with flickers of love, are empty. The man who used to lift me onto his shoulders, who once spun my mother around in the kitchen when he thought I wasn't looking... is gone.

And my mother's voice whispers in my mind, her final lesson echoing through me like a heartbeat.

Obscure it. Hide the truth. Obscure it. Hide the truth. Obscure it. Hide the truth.

"Seems your daughter has been busy, Malcom," the snake drawls, amusement dripping from his voice. "She has befriended a wolf and a light yielder."

A wave of ice crawls up my spine.

Obscure it. Hide the truth. Obscure it. Hide the truth.

"Get your hands off her!" Jethro's voice is pure fury, his rage mirrored by Kyzan's deep, guttural snarl.

Obscure it. Hide the truth. Obscure it. Hide the truth.

"I don't think so," the monster chuckles. "You see, her father promised this beauty to be my wife."

His fingers, skeletal and cold, brush my cheek. The nausea is immediate. My stomach twists in knots, and the small, fractured part of me that still believes my father could love me shatters completely. The inner scream inside me claws at my ribs, desperate to be let out, but I swallow it down.

Breathe. In. Out.

Jethro's dark eyes burn into mine. *"Fight, Liv. Scream this house down."*

I feel his turmoil like it's my own, crashing into me in tidal waves of grief and desperation. He's willing me to do something. Anything.

But I can't.

I force my muscles to go still. I lock my emotions away, suffocating them before they can betray me. I feel the snake beside me grin. He feeds on my surrender, drinks in the power of knowing he has won.

"Oh, she can't do anything," he croons, "I have paralyzed her. Temporarily, of course."

That sickening laugh slithers over my skin, leaving behind a film of filth I will never be able to wash off.

Still frozen under his command, I watch the men below, see them calculating their moves, searching for an opening.

And then the blade flies.

I barely register the flick of the monster's wrist before the blade cuts through the air, aimed straight for Cooper.

Time slows.

Jet moves—but even he is too slow.

I feel it before I see it, the sharp, agonizing burst of pain through my shield. Cooper's pain. *His last thought.*

Mary's scream shatters the air, pure and raw, like a mother losing her child.

My knees wobble. My body sways. But I do not let myself fall.

I do the only thing I can.

I raise my shield and look away, doing exactly what my mother has taught me.

Obscure it. Hide the truth. Obscure it. Hide the truth. Obscure it. Hide the truth.

But another voice—smaller, sharper—whispers in my ear.

That man was going to walk you down the aisle tomorrow. Your father... the father not by blood, but by heart. He's dead. You did nothing. You let him die. You were supposed to protect him. Now he will never give you away, he will never dance with Mary in the living room. You will never see that small tilt of a smile. You will never get to tell him how much you love him.

I clench my jaw, my nails digging into my palms so hard I think they might draw blood.

The monster beside me lets out a satisfied sigh. "I think this is where I say goodbye."

A tear slides down my cheek.

I don't fight as I'm winnowed away.

The last thing I see before the world disappears is Jethro's face, twisted in rage.

And then—nothing.

Jeyr

BLACK LINES AND BURNT SOUL

D read coils in my chest, thick and suffocating, with each clash of thunder and strike of lightning. It shouldn't be taking this long for Olivia to come to me. Jethro should be back by now.

I stare at my wrist, watching for any sign—any flicker of light from our bond. And then it comes. A faint pulse, barely there, but enough to spark a shred of hope. She's close. She'll be here soon. She has to be. I need her. *Gods, I need her.* I won't calm until she's in my arms, where she belongs.

Minutes pass. Then an hour.

Another flicker.

I hold my wrist, sending my own light in return, calling to her. *Hurry, Liv. Come home.*

The concerned gazes of my family burn into me as I sit rigid in the sitting room. No one speaks, but their tension fills the air like smoke. They know better than to try to soothe me. Outside, the storm swells, the castle shuddering under the weight of my power.

In the study, the voices of authorities boom as they inspect the bodies of my father and brother. *This has to be some sort of trick. Some nightmare.* The words repeat in my head over and over, trying to force the scene from existence. *My father. My brother. Dead.*

The air in the room shifts, a ripple of something dark and heavy.

A thud.

I turn. My stomach lurches.

Jethro stands in the doorway, panting heavily, his face bloodied and bruised. He sways on his feet, chest heaving as he clutches a lifeless body in his arms.

No.

Cooper.

I blink once. Twice. Trying to clear the image in front of me. But the more I stare, the clearer it becomes.

A cry—Hecate's. She runs to the body Jethro gently lays on the ground. Mary collapses beside him, silent sobs wracking her frail body.

Jethro's voice cracks as he speaks. "I am sorry." He looks at me, shaking, his entire body quivering with the weight of his failure. Then, before my very eyes, my brother—the strongest male I've ever known—falls to his knees. His hands press against his face, his shoulders caving in.

The world tilts.

My mouth moves, but no sound comes out.

Where. Is. Olivia?

Caomh's voice roars through my mind. I look to Jethro. The same question burns in my throat, but I can't force it past my lips.

Jethro's head shakes, over and over again, his movements erratic, frantic. "Tierney. When I got there, the cottage was under siege. I tried—I tried to get to her. He had her! I—she—" His voice breaks completely. His hands press into his eyes, as if he can claw the memory out of his skull.

Let me see. Caomh's commanding growl rattles through our minds. *Let me see what happened.*

Jethro's entire body trembles, but he nods. His breath shudders out, and I watch as my worst nightmare unfolds. The vision slams into me. Olivia. Fighting. Blood on her skin. The creatures. That thing—Tierney. His skeletal fingers on her cheek. His voice, a serpent's whisper, branding her as his. And then—she lets him take her.

Something inside me snaps.

"I will go find her. I will bring her back." Jethro's voice is hoarse, as if the words themselves are being ripped from him.

I barely hear him.

I'm already breaking apart.

Lightning snaps through the sky. The castle trembles. The walls pulse with my rage.

I touch my wrist, pulling at our bond, searching for her, grasping at nothing. *Nothing.*

My entire body goes rigid.

She's alive. That much I can feel. But our bond—our bond is fading.

My chest tightens, breath coming in sharp bursts. *This can't be happening. This can't be real.*

Tierney.

The man who murdered my mother.

Has my Companach. Has Olivia. My one true love.

Rage consumes me. My power surges, wild and untamed, crackling through my veins like fire.

The sky above us splits open, the wind howling in response.

Thunder roars.

The world trembles.

And I let the storm rage.

I pace, hands gripping my hair, my heart slamming against my ribs. I have to get her back. I have to save her.

"Brother, you need to calm down! Gods, why the power shifted to you..." Aella exhales sharply, frustration lacing her tone before she continues. "Jeyr, I don't know why the fates chose you, but you're going to have to learn to wield this. You are now the Grand Duke, whether you like it or not. Word has already spread, and our people are growing uneasy. This will undo everything our..." she chokes on the words, swallowing against the grief that threatens to consume her. *Our father. Our brother.*

It hasn't even been twenty-four hours. Less than a day, and my entire world has been ripped apart. *But none of it matters. Not now. I just need Olivia. I need her back. I need her to help me through this godsdamn nightmare. I need her safe, with me. I can't lose her. I can't be another Grand Duke who has to rule when his Companach is dead.*

"I know you want to save her, Jeyr," Aella presses, her voice firm. "But your duty is here, to all these people. You need to focus, to learn how to control these powers—fast. You are a target now. You wield two gifts, and that makes you a threat."

The sky cracks open, thunder roaring in answer to her words. Aella stands her ground, unflinching. Her tears are gone, replaced with pure, simmering rage. The room tenses as her power surges, the air electrified with static.

I meet her eyes—storm-filled, unyielding.

"He can be the Grand Duke and find a way to get Olivia back, Aella," Althea snaps, stepping away from Aiden to stand beside me.

"Between all of us, we will get her back," Jethro vows, his stance rigid as golden light flickers over his fists. We are all on edge.

"I wouldn't like our chances," Gwynn warns, her voice tight. "It's Lord Tierney. He's the Grand Duke of Puinnsean's most trusted henchman. His mind powers are unlike anything I've ever seen. Every wife he's ever had has died at his hands. He controls Bane's entire army."

Jethro flinches beside me. I do too.

Gwynn's voice lowers.

"I know that kingdom better than any of you. No one enters his borders undetected. If we want to get her back, we have to be smart. We have to find a way through the wards without setting off every alarm in the kingdom."

"Looks like the Kingdom of Aimsir having a new Grand Duke means new alliances," Aiden interjects, voice calm, calculated. Aella's rage snaps toward him, her steel gaze threatening to cut him open.

"Jeyr has been Grand Duke for a mere hour. There are protocols, traditions that must be upheld. Father has been dead for less than a day, and you're already talking about alliances?" Her voice vibrates through the room, electricity crackling in response.

I square my shoulders and step up to her, fists clenched at my sides.

She's not wrong.

But I don't care.

I didn't ask for this. I didn't want this.

My father. My brother. Dead.

And now my mate—gone.

My power surges, the windows rattling, wind howling through the castle halls. The room dims as storm clouds thicken above us.

"Do you think I don't fucking know that, Aella?" My voice is like a thunderclap, the weight of my power lacing every syllable. "Do you think I wanted this? Do you think I wanted them dead? Because I can tell you, I didn't—I don't! I should be looking for Olivia right now, saving her from that piece of filth who took her. I was supposed to get married today. Instead, I have to tell the people of Aimsir that their Grand Duke and his Aire are gone, and they're stuck with the bloody Healer son who never had a lick of Aimsir power running through his veins—until now."

Lightning flashes, illuminating Aella's rigid face, the scar over her eye glowing in the eerie light.

I inhale sharply and continue, voice quieter, but no less lethal.

"I haven't trained for this. I don't know the first fucking thing about ruling this kingdom. If laws were different, I'd abdicate to you. But they aren't. So, I will do my duty. I will organize the funeral. I will hold the council meeting and see that the traditional ceremony is upheld. But while I do what is necessary for this kingdom, I will also do everything in my power to get Olivia back. Is. That. Clear?"

Thunder rattles through the walls, shaking the very foundation beneath us. Not a single person speaks. Aella nods, then Althea. One by one, the others follow.

"Good," I growl. "Now, does anyone have any useful ideas? If not, leave."

Gwynn steps forward, expression grim.

"I will go back. I am their Seer—I can gather information. Otherwise, it's tradition for a Grand Duke to have a ball three months after taking the throne. We can use that to our advantage."

Three months?

"Does anyone have an idea that doesn't involve Olivia being stuck with that man for three months?" My voice is a snarl.

Jethro's jaw locks.

"The wards in Puinnsean are impenetrable. No one enters without Tierney's authority. And his estate is even more protected. We've been trying to plant spies there for years. If we want her back, we need to play this carefully. Other kingdoms fear him, Jeyr. Even the ones with armies. There's no easy way in."

Caomh exhales, voice grim.

"Our best option is to form an alliance with Bane."

The one thing I don't want to hear.

"Jeyr, we will do everything we can to bring her home," Jet vows. But we both know I will have no peace until she's here.

"I'll be your emissary," Caomh offers. "I'll help you with alliances, with planning here, and I'll look for another way to get her back."

"I'll go undercover," Lorkan adds. "Try to infiltrate Puinnsean's kingdom."

"No," I cut in sharply. "I need you close. When the time comes, we'll need your power.

You're better alive to Olivia than dead."

Aiden is next.

"I'll return to the ports. Puinnsean relies on our docks for trade—I can find weaknesses there. Maybe even use it to form a stronger alliance."

Then Hecate enters, her eyes blazing.

"I'll find a way through the wards," she growls. "If there's even a single crack in their defenses, I will find it."

Before I can nod my thanks, a searing pain shoots down my left arm from my heart.

I gasp, knees buckling as I hit the floor.

The windows shatter. The wind screams.

My vision blurs as I look down at my wrist.

The bond—

Thick black lines crack through the infinity patterns, splitting through the technicolor glow.

My heart stops.

"Olivia!"

I collapse, clutching my chest, gasping for breath. The room erupts into chaos.

The world around me vanishes.

All I can hear is my own ragged breathing—

And the sound of my soul breaking.

Olivia

THE BLOOD-BOUND BRIDE

I stand before the mirror in a wedding dress that is not my own. Not the one I have chosen.

He has chosen it for me.

The white silk clings like a second skin, molding itself to my body as if it were a living thing. A serpent's embrace. The plunging neckline dips scandalously low, revealing far too much—by design, of course. The thin fabric does nothing to protect me from the cold or from the lecherous gaze of the man who has stolen me.

My body is on display for him.

The sides of my breasts are exposed to the frigid air, my nipples pebbling in protest, stark against the sheer fabric. A humiliation designed to strip me of my dignity before I even stand at the altar. My hands instinctively cross over my chest, gripping the silk, as if I can hide what is already his to claim.

But I am no one's to claim.

A young servant girl has braided my hair into a tight coil, twisted into a woven crown that sits heavy atop my head. Too tight. Too punishing. Each pin stabs into my scalp like a dagger, a silent reminder that this is no wedding of love—this is a conquest. Atop my head sits his gift. A black iron crown, sculpted into the form of a coiled snake, its fangs sinking into my skull, each prong a fresh needle of pain.

A perfect representation of the man waiting at the altar.

I barely recognize the woman reflected back at me. Green eyes dull. Skin pale. Lips bloodless. The glow that once lived within me—the light that had been carefully nurtured by Jeyr's love—is gone. Extinguished.

Candles burn low in the chamber, their wax dripping onto wrought iron candelabras. The flickering flames cast restless shadows upon the damp stone walls, twisting and stretching like grasping hands. The room is cold. Empty. Lifeless.

A voice cuts through the silence, curling around me like smoke.

"Olivia."

I turn.

And there he stands—the man who gave me life, the man who betrayed me. My father.

His face is drawn, his amber eyes pale, vacant of the warmth they once held. His graying hair recedes, his once-strong frame reduced to something frail, weathered by time and regret. But I feel no sympathy. Not for the man who delivered me into the hands of a monster.

"You have no right to say my name." My voice is ice. "You have no right to call me your daughter." He flinches at my words, but I do not stop. I will not stop.

"Mother would be rolling in her grave to find that you sold me to that devil spawn." The accusation hangs in the air between us, thick with venom. I want my words to cut, to burn, to shatter him. But he simply stands there, face blank, emotionless. "A decade ago, I needed money," he murmurs, his voice hoarse, brittle. "So I took her paintings. I didn't realize what I was selling..."

My blood turns to ice.

"Tierney's trader, Vernon, knew exactly what kind of Fae painted them. I thought he only wanted your mother's work, but then..." He hesitates. "Then he took her from us."

My nails dig into the silk of my dress, tearing at the fabric.

"I tried to run," he continues, voice shaking. "I tried to keep you safe. But he found me. He found me, and he—" My father lifts a trembling hand to his temple. "He saw things. He saw you."

The room tilts beneath my feet.

"He made me bring you to him," my father admits, eyes shining with unshed tears. "He made me promise you to him."

The air leaves my lungs in a violent rush.

The walls close in around me.

I can hear my own pulse thundering in my ears, drowning out the crackling of the torches, the distant murmurs of unseen guards. My hands tremble at my sides, but I clench them into fists, forcing the shaking to stop.

"You let him take her," I whisper, my voice splintering. "And now you're letting him take me."

Something flickers in his gaze. Regret. But not enough.

Never enough.

"Let's go, Olivia." His fingers clamp around my elbow, his grip bruising, unrelenting. I fight. I twist, thrash, try to rip free. But he drags me forward, his strength fueled by something far darker than desperation. Down the dark corridors. Past the iron sconces, their flames flickering against stone. Through the towering doors. And into the great hall.

The aisle is lined in blood-red carpet.

A man wears black as deep as the abyss.

Lord Tierney.

He stands at the altar, waiting. Watching. A predator studying his prey.

His hair is cropped short, exposing the sharp cut of his jaw, the hollow planes of his cheekbones. His serpent's eyes—yellow and unblinking—rake over me, stripping me down to nothing.

I am trapped. Cornered. Captured.

Come, my bride.

A command.

My body lurches forward.

I want to scream, to fight. But I have no control.

I stand at the altar, but I do not feel my feet. I do not hear the priest's words. I only feel the blade.

The dagger slices my palm, blood warm against my skin, spilling onto the stone.

Tierney's bloodied palm meets mine.

Red silk wraps around us, binding us together.

"Do you swear to be bound to this man, to enter into a blood-bonded marriage? Your life bound to his for as long as he shall live?"

No. No, I do not swear it.

Pain sears through my hand.

Tierney squeezes, hard. A demand. A cruel, merciless demand.

My head jerks in a nod.

A single, forced movement.

The red light flares, coiling around our hands, sealing my fate.

Somewhere—hidden deep where I have locked him safe—I feel his pain.

Jeyr.

I can almost hear his screams, feel the rattling of our connection as it claws against its cage.

I burn.

My veins fill with poison.

But I keep my face blank. Unfeeling.

Because Tierney thinks he has won.

But he does not know that I am still fighting.

And I will never stop fighting.

Lord Tierney's grip is firm as he guides me from the obsidian carriage, my gloved fingers resting lightly against his arm. A frozen hush blankets the world beyond, where a vast and endless forest slumbers beneath a shroud of ice. The snow, pristine and untouched, presses against the mansion's dark stone walls, the stark contrast stripping the world of all color.

I tilt my chin, gazing upon the looming structure—its spires, jagged as unsheathed blades, carved against the storm-heavy sky. Perched upon the eaves, gargoyles leer, their jeweled eyes gleaming with unnatural sentience, following my every movement. A tremor coils through me, though not from the bitter wind that claws at my exposed skin.

We ascend the onyx stairs, the stone beneath my feet etched with the curling forms of serpents. Their carved eyes, hollow and knowing, bear witness to my arrival, to the fall of the Empath. My gown slithers behind me, the silk whispering against the ice-dusted steps like the hushed warning of unseen creatures. The cold seeps through the thin fabric, my body protesting with violent shudders.

I feel Lord Tierney's desire before I smell it, before I see the shift in his stance. I do not need my gifts to discern it—it presses against me like an uninvited shadow. I recoil inward, drawing my essence tight, unwilling to glimpse the abyss within his soul.

A silent prayer forms upon my lips: *let there be warmth inside.*

The mansion's great stone doors groan as they part, revealing a cavernous foyer swathed in dim candlelight. The air is thick with the cloying scent of white lilies, their perfume clashing against the damp musk of old stone. My lungs rebel, my body wrenching into memory of the last time I smelled them, of blood staining alabaster petals.

Men stand at each doorway, their emerald-hued leathers embroidered with gold sigils. Their gazes, hard and unflinching, flicker toward me as I step into the silence.

I cross my arms over my trembling chest, the cold tightening its grip upon me. I swallow against the tightness in my throat, forcing my breath to steady. My flinch does not go unnoticed.

Lord Tierney chuckles, a mirthless sound.

"Welcome home, Lady Tierney." The words hold no warmth, only the weight of a decree. His stare, pitiless and unrelenting, lingers upon my shivering form. "This is General Colden. He will see to you and my wishes."

A man emerges from the shadows—tall, his frame carved from unyielding stone. His skin, a deep umber, is a striking contrast to the icy white of his close-cropped hair. His gaze, a frozen silver, locks onto mine with an intensity that sets my bones alight with warning. He inclines his head once, a motion of chilling finality.

I cannot look away.

A hand, swift and punishing, seizes my jaw, wrenching my gaze upward. My breath hitches as I meet Tierney's venomous yellow eyes. His lips curve, the satisfaction in his expression coiling deep in my stomach like sickness.

I try to turn away, to seek solace in the snow-laden world beyond the window.

Look at me.

The command, silent yet absolute, coils through my mind like a vice. My head snaps back against my will, my breath faltering. His eyes—no longer yellow, but black as the void between stars—devour me whole.

Good.

His voice, a silken rasp, slides down my spine like sharpened glass. A single talon traces the curve of my chin, its caress deceptively light. The scent of copper fills my nostrils a moment before warmth blooms upon my skin. A bead of blood rolls down my throat, and before I can recoil, his tongue flicks against it, a slow, languid taste before his fangs sink deep.

I bite down on a scream. A meager, broken sound escapes my lips.

Like a serpent, he coils around me, his mouth a brand against my flesh. Another sharp prick, another pulse of stolen life. The air grows too thick, the world too narrow. My limbs tremble as a claw hooks beneath one fragile strap of silk, severing it with an effortless flick. The gown sags, then falls, pooling at my feet like spilt moonlight.

A fresh wave of cold assaults my bare skin.

I move—or try to. A futile struggle, answered only with an iron grip that sends me crashing against the ground. The sound rings in my ears, the sharp sting of pain reverberating through my skull. The taste of blood thickens in my mouth.

You will learn, my lady, Tierney murmurs, his voice glacial, devoid of mercy. *You will do as you are told.*

The floor is smooth beneath my fingers, the grain of the wood a fragile tether to reality. I focus on it, on the simple act of breathing, of existing beyond his reach.

Breathe. Just breathe.

A shadow looms.

Fingers, cold and unyielding, encircle my throat, lifting me effortlessly from the ground. My body convulses as I am slammed against the stone wall, the jagged edges biting into my exposed flesh. My vision darkens at the edges, stars bursting in the void.

"Look. At. Me."

The words are a lash against my mind.

I obey, helpless beneath his will. The slow, creeping smile that curves his lips makes his fangs glisten.

Then—pain.

A sound, broken and raw, rips from my throat as fire lances through me, a brutal invasion that shatters whatever semblance of self remains. Each thrust, each cruel stroke, tears at the fragile walls of my mind, forcing me to endure, to feel. *My own power, my own wretched gift, betrays me— I feel him, his pleasure, his vile satisfaction.* Tears, silent and hot, spill down my cheeks, but my gaze, locked in his thrall, cannot look away.

When it is over, when the monster has taken what he wishes, he discards me like a tattered doll, my body hitting the cold stone floor in a heap.

I gasp for air, choking on the remnants of his violation.

"Take her away," he commands, his voice a careless afterthought. From the shadows, General Colden moves. I brace myself, expecting another cruel hand, another act of suffering. But when he lifts me, it is not with violence.

He cradles me against his chest, his warmth startling against the ice that clings to my skin. As he carries me up the winding stairs, his grip tightens, anchoring me to the moment, to something beyond the pain.

At last, he speaks, his voice a low whisper meant only for me.

"Shh. I have a bath ready for you." *I shudder*, too weak to fight, too broken to resist.

"Shh," he murmurs again, his hold steady, unwavering. "Breathe. Just breathe." I let the warmth of his body seep into my frozen bones. I let myself surrender— to the silence, to the unknown.

For now, that is enough.

I barely stir as General Colden lowers me into the bath, the water lapping at my battered skin in slow, delicate waves. My teeth still clatter so violently that each tremor sends sharp pains through my jaw. Somewhere beyond the haze of my exhaustion, I hear his voice—low, murmured words spoken to another presence in the room. I try to listen, to anchor myself to their conversation, but my body betrays me. My energy, what little remains, is spent clinging to the warmth seeping into my bones.

Gentle hands, small and careful, sweep across my face, wiping away the remnants of dried blood. The cloth is warm, the touch deliberate, reverent in its tenderness. Each stroke carries something beyond the physical—a quiet offering, a whisper of kindness. I feel the emotions behind them as keenly as if they were my own.

Unease. Displeasure. Concern.

The girl, whoever she is, does not hide her feelings. *I do not have the strength to block them*, to shield myself from the flickers of sorrow and quiet fury that radiate from her like ripples upon a still pond. They press against my frayed mind, familiar in their purity.

Then, I am lifted.

Strong hands gather me, steady and unwavering, holding me aloft as another set of hands—softer, yet just as precise—dries my body with deft strokes. The scent of fresh wool meets my nose as they fit me into bedclothes, the fabric thick and warm against my frozen skin. Again, I am lifted, carried through the dim glow of candlelight. My face meets the softness of a pillow, and a heavy quilt is drawn over me, its weight anchoring me to the here and now.

The blankets become my shield, a cocoon against the horrors that still lurk behind my eyelids. Each precise tuck of fabric, each smoothing of the covers, feels like a silent promise—an unspoken vow that, for now, *I am safe*.

A deep voice rumbles through the darkness, speaking to the girl. She replies in a whisper, the sound a ghost against the silence.

Then the world fades into blackness, and *I surrender to it*.

I run through the abyss, the air thick with the stench of death and decay. Shadows twist and lunge, monstrous forms lashing out with talons sharp as forged steel. My white silk gown whips against my legs, spectral in the darkness. *Cooper!* My voice is a desperate plea, lost in the cacophony of screams.

I am too late.

Mary's lifeless form lies draped over her husband's, her blood painting the ground in cruel mockery of devotion. *No.* A clawed hand seizes my throat before I can reach them, wrenching me into the air. The creature's laughter—cold, mirthless—echoes through my bones, filling my lungs with dread.

I cannot breathe.

The wall meets me in a brutal collision, stone biting into my back as the monster forces himself inside me. Agony—gods, the agony.

Beyond him, a pair of sorrowful blue eyes find mine, a hand pressed over his heart. But the beast continues his violation, his laughter bleeding into the darkness as my cries shatter into nothingness.

I awake with a violent shudder, nausea clawing up my throat. The sickness consumes me before I can fight it, my body lurching over the edge of the bed. Bile burns its way up, spilling onto the stone floor in heaving, wretched convulsions. A cold hand smooths over the back of my head, gathering my hair as I tremble through the waves of sickness. The touch is steady, grounding—wordless comfort against the storm raging inside me. I barely register the murmurs, the quiet reassurances spoken in the hush of the dimly lit chamber.

A fire crackles in the hearth, its glow casting flickering shadows over the carved mantel. Snakes coil within the stone, their eyes gleaming like polished citrine—watching.

Panic seizes me.

No, no, no.

The yellow eyes of my nightmares blur with the present. The ghostly imprint of taloned fingers burns into my throat, and suddenly, I am drowning in the past. My breath quickens into sharp, panicked gasps as I scramble upright, clutching the blankets to my chest. My gaze darts through the near darkness, seeking threats that are not there.

A figure kneels by my bedside, silent save for the soft sound of water sloshing in the bucket he holds.

General Colden.

The recognition comes slowly, my vision sharpening as I take in his face—no longer carved in the impassive stillness I have come to expect. His silver eyes, flecked with the quiet hush of snowfall, brim not with detachment, but concern. Wordlessly, he rises, disappearing into the adjoining washroom. When he returns, he holds a glass of water, offering it without a word. I hesitate.

"It's not drugged," he murmurs, his tone unreadable. Still, I lift the glass to my nose, scenting the liquid for any trace of poison. Colden huffs softly, taking the glass from my unsteady grasp. Without breaking eye contact, he tips it to his lips, drinking before handing it back. I narrow my eyes.

"We are in the Kingdom of Poison—how do I know you didn't just poison it now?" A smirk ghosts his lips. He lifts his hand, and from his palm, delicate snowflakes unfurl, drifting in lazy spirals before vanishing into mist.

"Because," he says simply, "I am not from this kingdom. I may serve its ruler, but my blood does not belong to these lands."

I frown, studying him. *How does a man from another kingdom rise to be the general of Puinnsean?*

"If you ask him, it's because I was cast out of my own kingdom—a disgraced guard who failed to protect his charge. A kingdom that saw fit to abandon me here as penance." He exhales, voice lower now, carrying the weight of time. "But if you ask me? It is revenge. A slow, patient reckoning for the one he took from me."

My pulse quickens at his words.

"I have served here for thirty years," he continues, his eyes shadowed with memories I cannot reach. "Longer than any of his own men. I have risen through the ranks, proven my loyalty beyond question. I have outlived every general before me—because I am the only one who has not gotten himself killed. Yet." A chill ghosts through me that has nothing to do with the cold. I sip from the glass, the water easing the raw sting in my throat, then meet his gaze.

"And what is your plan?"

Colden regards me for a long moment, as though weighing something unseen.

"I have yet to determine that," he admits. "Unfortunately, the more time I spend in his service, the more I learn that he is a hard man to kill." His mouth tightens, expression unreadable. "Many have tried. All have failed. I have watched him slaughter millions, his alliance with the Grand Duke only fortifying his reach. But even the strongest creatures have weaknesses." A pause. "I have been studying his."

I swallow, the weight of his words pressing against my ribs. Colden plucks the empty glass from my fingers. I let my hands fall into my lap, hoping he does not see their tremor.

"Olivia." I lift my gaze. He stands near the door now, his presence a shadowed figure against the dim glow of the fire.

"I trust this will remain between us?" His voice is quiet, but beneath it lies something deeper—something haunted. I wonder what horrors his eyes have seen in the three decades he has served beneath the tyrant's hand.

Slowly, I nod.

Something unspoken passes between us. Colden's lips curve, a fleeting ghost of gratitude before he turns and slips from the chamber.

The latch clicks into place.

Two thunderous clangs follow.

I am locked in.

Olivia

LOST SOUL

I drift in and out of a restless sleep, my body caught between exhaustion and the pull of unseen hands dragging me toward wakefulness. A soft voice calls me back. "Forgive me, my lady. The master has asked me to prepare you."

Blinking against the dim light, I find myself staring into the delicate face of a girl—young, though how young, I cannot be certain. No older than fifteen, perhaps. There is a frailty to her, the kind that comes from a lifetime of hunger rather than nature. Her limbs are thin, delicate, her bones sharp beneath her skin as though they might snap beneath the weight of a strong wind. Her face is narrow, her muddy brown eyes filled with a quiet kind of weariness. Mousy brown hair is neatly plaited, though wisps have unraveled around her temple.

She is dressed in a corseted black gown, a white apron tied tightly at her waist. I nod, forcing my limbs to move, my body sluggish with lingering fatigue. As I follow her toward the washroom, I take note of the way her hands flutter at her sides, as though she wishes to fidget but has been taught long ago not to.

"Bria is me name, ma'am," she murmurs, offering a small, practiced curtsy. "Please," I say, my voice hoarse from sleep. "No formalities. Olivia is fine."

I summon the strength to smile, to send a thin thread of warmth toward her fragile soul, even as every part of me screams to take her and run—to rip her from this place, from these walls that whisper with unseen mouths and watch with lifeless yellow eyes.

Bria hesitates only for a moment before lowering her gaze.

"When we are alone, I will do so. But if the master is present, I must obey propriety," her voice is soft, sweet—too gentle for this place of jagged edges and hollow souls. She reminds me of a butterfly soaring through a winter storm, beauty lost amid the cold. The washroom mirrors the rest of the mansion, bleak and towering. Stone gargoyles jut from the walls, their yellow eyes gleaming like polished citrine, ever-watching. A shudder wracks my body.

Bria helps me undress, guiding me into the great black tub, the rim coiled in the shape of a serpent, its feet the talons of some ancient beast. *Original.* Somehow, I find the strength to roll my eyes rather than recoil. As the water engulfs me, I exhale sharply. The heat melts into my aching skin, but nothing can chase away the stain of the nightmare still clinging to me.

"How did you come to work here?" I ask, my voice barely more than a murmur. Bria does not hesitate. "My ma worked here once. She fell pregnant after a guard... took liberties with her." The words are spoken lightly, but I feel the weight of them settle into my chest like stones. "She hid me away in her chambers for years, until I was old enough to work for myself. Then, the master found out. It was either me or her."

I still.

Bria's thin shoulders lift in a small shrug. "Don't ye worry, mistress. I've been left alone by the Lord." Then, quieter, as she lathers my hair, "Though I suspect General Colden has more to do with that than he lets on."

I shut my eyes as her small hands work through my hair, the rhythmic motion a fleeting balm. The scent of lilies fills the air, creeping through my senses like a sickness.

Lilies.

I stiffen.

Bria must catch my expression. "His lordship's favorite scent," she says, as if that is explanation enough. "A beautiful flower, but a poison all the same. Slow and insidious. Kills a beast before they even know it's happening. Causes kidney failure in many species."

I swallow against the rising nausea.

Bria hums softly as she rinses my hair, her voice light and unburdened despite the chains of this place. As her hands skim over my skin, cleaning away the remnants of the night before, all I can think of is the scent of ocean storms and pine trees, of crisp autumn air and the salt of wind-blown cliffs.

Bria taps my shoulder, a silent command. I step from the bath, shaking off her insistence to help as I towel myself down. She merely smiles, gathering a brush and smoothing it through my damp hair in long, practiced strokes. She sings to herself as she works, a melody so sweet it does not belong in the kingdom of death and darkness.

A murmur comes from the door. "Hi, Olivia."

The familiarity of the voice settles the tension in my shoulders before I even turn. Colden stands at the threshold, leaning against the frame. He wears a suit of pale gray, the color accentuating the silver of his eyes. For a flicker of a moment, my mind betrays me, summoning images of Jethro, of Caomh—of the many times they have stood in the same posture, greeting me with the same quiet ease.

A sharp, unexpected ache twists through my ribs. Colden's discomfort bleeds into the space between us, though he masks it well. "The Lord has requested your presence in his bedchamber."

His voice is hushed, as if the words themselves carry a weight he does not wish to bear. The warmth from my bath turns to ice in my veins. I straighten, tilting my chin with the practiced defiance I have spent years perfecting. My hands do not shake as I gather the robe around my frame. My steps do not falter as I stand.

But my thoughts?

I would rather die than walk through that door.

The chamber is vast, the sheer scale of it grotesque. Red and gold tapestries loom from the walls, like flayed skin pinned up for display. Above the bed, an obnoxiously large self-portrait dominates the space—Tierney, wreathed in monstrosities. Dragons, serpents, trolls, creatures of nightmares. Some I recognize. Others, I wish I didn't.

"Close the door behind you, General. Find your space in the shadows."

Tierney does not miss the way I flinch. He never does.

"If you are wondering why we have a spectator, dear wife, it isn't only because this is the only action he will get," Tierney muses, his voice slick with amusement, "but in case you decide to unleash that power I know you are hiding from me. He has orders to defend my honor."

A test. Would Colden stop me if I struck? Or would he let me end this?

Tierney's smirk widens, as if he has plucked the thought straight from my skull.

"Oh, Olivia, Olivia... I can feel you calculating from here. If my general fails, I have an entire army sworn to my protection. Any threat to me, and they will know it before your breath has left your lips." His black taloned fingers twitch, and the candlelight seems to flicker at his will.

"I wonder where that power is, little Empath," he murmurs, prowling closer. "Oh, how I have watched you grow. You are quite the little huntress, aren't you? You know how to keep yourself unseen. But the paintings—you must know they reveal more than you think. Taking down the Witches' wards was no small task, but once they were gone? Golly. You are a woman of such deep, delicious emotion."

I fight against the instinct to react, to give him anything to latch onto.

Tierney chuckles.

"It did not go unnoticed how you ended some of my soldiers with that power of yours. The first Empath I have ever met with the ability to kill. The others were pathetic—wilting flowers who could not wield the weight of their gift. But you? Yours is worth keeping, locked within that fragile chest of yours."

I remain still, my mind racing, trying to fit together the puzzle pieces of his words—trying to find a way out. He circles me, the way a predator does before the final lunge.

"Hmm... not so chatty now, are you, Mrs. Tierney?"

A chill coils around my spine, my pulse betraying me. A pair of blue eyes flare in my mind—my mate. I lock him away within the deepest parts of me, barring the bond, sealing it away from the filth that stands before me.

Tierney might have my body. But he will never have Jeyr.

Never.

"I am curious..." I straighten, lifting my chin. He takes me in, eyes gleaming with the thrill of the game. "How does a Fae of Puinnsean wield the power of mind control—and blend it with the essence of an Empath?"

He smiles, slow and indulgent, as though I am a student finally asking the right question.

"Ahh, clever girl." He flexes his gloved hand, the golden diamond and ruby on his finger catching the firelight, casting blood-red shadows upon the walls. "Well, you see, Grand Duke Bane took in an orphaned Mind Master long ago, before the courts were divided, before the purity of bloodlines was deemed sacred."

I stiffen.

"I am raised in a court not my own, trained to control minds, to create an army no ruler can challenge. I take back what is stolen from me and, with it, I take this power."

Shock pulses through me like a storm, my thoughts shattering and reforming too quickly to make sense of them. "How... how does that even—" The words strangle in my throat as a vice closes around my neck. "Enough questions." Talons curl tighter. My feet leave the floor, my body weightless in his grasp.

"You are here to bring me an heir," he purrs. "Not to use me as your personal library."

I gasp as he releases me, the breath knocked from my lungs as I crumple. He doesn't give me a moment to recover. Fingers tangle into my hair, yanking. I choke on a cry as he drags me, my knees scraping against the cold stone until he throws me forward, face-first onto his bed.

I thrash, but it's useless. Claws press against the back of my skull, shoving my face deep into the thick mattress. The scent of him—of lilies—clogs my throat.

I go still.

Tears burn my eyes, tracing silent paths down my cheeks as my robe is torn away.

The pain is immediate, his invasion brutal. I do not react. I refuse to give him the satisfaction.

But he is determined.

With a snarl, he wrenches my head up, his grip vicious in my hair.

"I will make you feel, Empath!" His voice cracks through the chamber like a whip, jagged and triumphant. A taloned hand fists in my hair, yanking, twisting, forcing my spine to arch. My scalp burns, but the pain is nothing compared to what comes next. The other hand—his claws—slices down my bare back, splitting skin, dragging fire in its wake. I clench my teeth, refusing him the sound he wants, refusing him the victory of my agony. My breath shudders, my muscles coil, but I do not scream.

The bed lurches beneath me as he drives himself into me, relentless, merciless. His fingers trace the fresh wound he has carved into my flesh, reveling in the way my body trembles. I will not give him what he wants. I cannot. I hold onto myself, onto some distant, untouched part of me, a fragile ember beneath the storm. If I can just hold, if I can just last, then maybe, maybe I will still be me when this is over.

"You are mine," he snarls against my ear, voice thick with triumph. "And you will feel my power. You will make me feel it mirrored back." He continues, unrelenting. My magic, my gift—my curse—begins to drain, as it always does under too much suffering, too much emotion. The walls I have built against him crack. The numbness I cling to fractures. And then— A gasp. It wrenches from my lips before I can stop it, a sharp, breaking sound. A whimper.

I hate that sound. Hate the way it betrays me. Hate my own weakness.

Tierney shudders, delighted. Unlike those who have feared my gift, who have crumbled beneath the weight of my unleashed emotions, he drinks it in. A twisted creature, a sadist that thrives in the waters of my suffering, swimming through it like a serpent in the blackened depths of a stream.

If I have clung to the hope that he will finish quickly, I am a fool. This is hell. A prison without walls, a purgatory that twists through time itself. There is no end. There is no mercy. The clock on the dresser blurs, time slipping between my shaking fingers like grains of sand.

His eyes, blackened by whatever monstrous poison fuels him, gleam through the darkness as he comes for me again. And again. I try to disappear, to fade into the void. I last forty minutes—forty minutes of nothingness—before he finds a way to rip me back into my body, into pain. Three hours. Three hours of being torn apart, of being used, of being broken. Tierney knows exactly when to pull, when to push, when to carve, dragging me from the abyss every time I try to slip away.

At some point, I break.

The words leave me like shattered glass. "Please," I gasp, my voice raw, ruined. "Pl—pl—please stop." Tierney laughs. A deep, sickening chuckle, mocking me. And gods, I might have laughed, too, if I weren't already drowning. Because what is left of me to beg? What is left of me to save?

I have once loved my power. Loved the way it made others feel joy, hope, peace. Now? it is rusty, useless. A blade turned against its own wielder. It gives him pleasure. And I have never hated anything more. When he is done with me, when my body has been battered past recognition, he reaches for the crop.

I barely feel the first strike. By the second, I know— I am already gone. The screams tear from me in something primal, something that isn't mine anymore. My soul, my power, my very self gives out under the weight of it. I shatter.

And the last thing I know before the darkness takes me— I am no longer Olivia. I am a hummingbird with her wings clipped, torn from the sky and left to die in the snow. The promise of my mate, Jeyr, is gone. His name has been ripped from my lips, lost in the blood that stains these sheets.

THE FRACTURED BOND

It has been over twenty-four hours since I last lay eyes on my love, believing our parting to be temporary— not eternal.

Twenty-four hours of agony.

The moment my band severs, torn from its rightful place and twisted into a promise to another— a marriage vow— I feel it. Every pulse of her anguish thrums through me, distant yet suffocating, as if I'm drowning beneath waves of grief with no surface in sight. The bond is fractured, her pain muffled, but it seeps through the cracks, dragging me under.

I brace myself against the heavy wooden desk, palms flattening over the parchment strewn before me. Useless. All of it—useless. My body burns, heat wracking through my limbs in sickening waves, as though a fever has taken root in my very bones. I'm not the one suffering. And yet, I suffer.

I don't need to glance at my wrist to know Olivia is in trouble. But I do anyway. The broken band—our bond—flares in a grotesque cycle of colors: red, then black, then a deep, bruised purple.

Olivia.

"Jeyr."

Jet is the first to reach me, his grip firm on my shoulder, pouring light into me, an attempt to soothe what cannot be soothed. Caomh is next, trying to draw the pain away, only to stagger back, retching onto the stone floor as the onslaught overtakes him. The waves do not stop.

On and on, hours stretch into eternity, and still, I feel everything. I have no words, no voice left to call her name. My lips can't even form it. *Olivia.*

Tears burn hot trails down my cheeks.

Then— it ends.

I gasp, the first breath I've taken that isn't a struggle. I clutch my wrist, staring at the band that no longer pulses black but remains a deep, unnatural violet. She's alive.

But her essence—her very soul—feels... altered. Distant. A violent need coils in my chest. To find her. To hold her. To let her collapse into my arms, to let her cry against my heart if that's what she needs. To end whatever torture she's endured.

"Jeyr."

I turn. Jet and Caomh stand before me, devastation carved into their features. They look between me and my wrist, the same fear that gnaws at me gleaming in their tear-glossed eyes.

We will never stop looking.

But the question claws at my ribs, silent yet deafening.

Who will we get back?

It doesn't matter.

I will never stop fighting for her.

I will die trying.

Olivia

SHATTERED IN SILENCE AND THE GAME OF MONSTERS

I wake to the violent tremors of my own body, as if it believes it can shake off the last forty-eight hours. As if it can free itself from the memory etched into every nerve, every bruised inch of my skin.

But my body remembers. It will always remember. Just in case my mind decides to forget.

A touch—cold, firm yet gentle—presses against my back. *Not his.* Colden.

His hand moves in slow, deliberate circles, never breaking contact despite the way I quake beneath his fingertips.

Images surge, flickering like candle flames behind my closed eyes. Too real. Too close. Too much. A whisper, raw and low.

"Shh... please. Settle. You are safe— for now. He has gone away for a week."

I force my eyes open.

Colden sits at the edge of the bed, watching over me. One hand combs through my tangled hair with an almost reverent gentleness, while the other rests cool and steady against my back.

I should flinch.

I should fear him.

Instead, I look into his face—haunted, hollowed out by something deeper than sorrow— and I break.

Tears spill before I can stop them, my throat catching on a sob that tears me apart from the inside. He doesn't hesitate. His arms open in silent invitation, and I crawl into them without thinking, without caring that I *should not trust him.*

But I do. Somehow, I do.

He stood by. Watched. Hours and hours of silence, of stillness, of inaction. But now? When I look at him, I see it—the weight of his guilt, the torment of his failure. And I understand. He felt my pain yesterday. Endured it. And now, he carries it with him like an open wound.

I don't shield him from it now.

I can't.

That girl—the one who cared about shielding others, about sparing them from her pain—*she is long gone.*

"I am so sorry," he rasps. His voice barely makes it past his lips.

I tilt my head, taking him in. The contrast of his dark skin against those eyes, pale as ice. Glacial pools brimming with unshed tears.

"I know," I whisper against his chest.

But *sorry* isn't enough.

Sorry doesn't save me.

Sorry won't get me out of this.

Colden holds me for hours.

As I lie there, caught in the tidal waves of my emotions, I feel myself being dragged under, lost in a riptide I cannot escape. My body trembles, my thoughts tumble into the abyss, and I drown in it all—the terror, the shame, the pain that has become a sickness in my bones.

But Colden waits.

He doesn't rush me. He doesn't speak unless necessary. He simply stays.

Every time the waves pull me too deep, every time I gasp for air I cannot find, his hand is there—pulling me back. He doesn't judge me for my inability to swim, for the way my mind sinks beneath the weight of it all.

When my body is too exhausted to tremble any longer, Bria leads me away.

I cannot stomach the idea of food, so I insist she take it instead.

I watch her devour it in near silence, shoving the food into her mouth with desperate, frantic hands. Starved.

At least one of us can enjoy it.

I settle onto the bed, my body curling into itself as I stare at the fire. I don't move, don't blink—only flinch each time the wood snaps and cracks.

Too loud. Too close.

Each sharp pop of the fire sends phantom pain lashing across my skin.

The crop. The bruises. The wounds.

I clench my fists. I force myself to breathe. I force myself to think of another fire.

Not the hearth of the cottage—no, that place was never mine.

But the manor. *My true home.*

I picture Cao in his favorite chair, swirling his liquor with an arrogant smirk, the kind that makes me roll my eyes but never doubt his presence.

I think of Jethro, of laying on the carpet, curled against his shoulder as his fingers comb through my hair, tracing sunlight into my scalp.

I smile at the memory. At him.

But I cannot think of Jeyr.

That hole inside me is too deep.

Each time my thoughts dare to reach for him, I feel nothing but a hollow pull in my gut. A place that was once full of color, of technicolor light, is now dark and fraying, the last fragile thread caught in the cage of my own torment.

A figure moves in front of the fire.

I blink.

A woman—tall, curvy, strong—stands before me, tears brimming in her amber eyes.

The emotions hit me first.

Guilt. Joy. Regret.

I barely register the way she approaches, the way her hands cup my face, warm and reverent.

"You look just like your mother..."

Her voice trembles with restrained tears.

I stare at her, frozen.

She looks like she has stepped from a dream, from some celestial vision sent to save me. A goddess in black robes, cinched at the waist with a silver cord, her presence as powerful as it is comforting.

My gaze locks onto hers, memorizing each fleck of gold and brown in those amber eyes.

I know those eyes.

Eyes I have painted before.

Kyzan. Ness. Those who have protected me, those I have longed for.

Those I have forgotten.

Guilt swells in my chest. How much more will I forget? With every new memory of torment, how much of myself will vanish?

"You can trust her, Olivia," Colden's voice is softer than I've ever heard it.

I turn toward the doorway, finding him standing there, clad in his general's uniform, his posture rigid but his eyes soft.

"Cannetta is a great healer."

Something in the way he says it, the way his gaze settles on me with such care, nearly makes me feel safe.

Almost.

"Colden, please leave me with the girl."

Cannetta's voice is firm, yet motherly.

Colden hesitates only long enough to seek my permission. When I nod, he is gone in a breath, disappearing into the hallway.

"Forever the knight, that boy," Cannetta muses, shaking her head. "He is sure to get himself killed one of these days."

I don't answer.

I watch her instead.

The stories in her eyes, the weight of old sorrows lingering there, tell me more than her words ever could.

Then—

"Your mother was a good friend of mine."

My entire body goes still.

Cannetta's voice carries the weight of centuries as she speaks, her words filling the dimly lit chamber like whispered prophecy.

"We left the Queen's land together," she murmurs, "in search of the stolen generations, for her love."

I stare at her, my breath catching in my throat.

"The Empaths were once the heart of the Queen's territory," she continues, "the peacekeepers of the realm. Your mother was their Queen. The most revered of our kind. For centuries, they waited for her to bear a child—to pass on her power, to strengthen the line. But she was picky, as all Empaths are.

"For us, a Companach—a soulmate—is everything. A love chosen by the fates themselves. A bond that cannot be undone.

"She found hers. And the fates had decided... that love was not meant for breeding."

My fingers curl into the blankets.

Cannetta meets my eyes, her gaze steady.

"Her mate was a woman. A half Witch, half Fae, with strong mind powers."

I exhale sharply, my chest tightening at the revelation.

"It shook your mother at first," she admits. "She had been raised to believe that her purpose was to continue the line, to bear the next great Empath. But the heart is stronger than duty. And their love was... pure. Unyielding. A force to be reckoned with."

"The Mind Master and the Empath did not need to breed to create a stronger being. Together, they were feared. Together, they could have ended the war."

A shadow passes over Cannetta's face.

"But then, Tierney took her."

The words land like a knife to the chest.

"Your mother's mate was captured. With her, we lost the war."

I clench my teeth. My mother—a Queen among Empaths. A warrior. A leader who has spent her life seeking peace... and in the end, lost everything.

"She went into hiding," Cannetta continues, "but she had a plan. A plan for the Empath line."

I grip the edge of the sheets, bracing for the next blow.

"She shocked me," Cannetta admits, "when she chose a human."

I freeze.

"Empaths only breed with good souls— with other Empaths, or with Immortals whose hearts remain pure. To take a human partner... it was unheard of."

She lets her hands hover over my arms, her magic soft and warm, sinking into the bruises left from yesterday's torture.

"Especially," she adds softly, "when I knew she was in love with another."

The words lodge in my throat.

My father. My body goes cold.

"He sold me here," I whispered. "He betrayed me. Betrayed her. His heart cannot be pure."

Cannetta stills.

I swallow hard.

"If my mother— a Queen of Empaths— chose a mate with an impure heart... then what does that make me?"

Her eyes darken with ancient knowledge.

"A Fae's soul is long-lasting," she says. "Our souls are tied to our bodies. When we die, they die with us. They do not pass on. They do not linger."

I listen, but I'm not sure I want to hear where this is going.

"But mortals," she continues, "they are different. Their souls move from one life to the next, inhabiting new bodies, new vessels. There is a fear in that cycle. The fear of living a life that is not truly theirs. A fear of what comes next."

Her words make the room feel too small.

"The Fae do not care about mortal souls," she says. "Most believe them worthless. But your mother knew something. And so did her mate."

I shake my head.

"Why would she choose him? Why would she—?"

"I do not know," Cannetta admits. "But whatever she knew, whatever plan she made, it brought us you."

She reaches forward, brushing her fingertips against my cheek. Soft. Warm. A mother's touch.

"You are not like the others, Olivia," she murmurs. "Your power is stronger because of your mortal heart. You endure yesterday's torture in ways no other Empath could have. You take it, you shield your soul—and you shield your mate."

My heart lurches.

She knows.

She knows about Jeyr.

She knows that he is the only thing keeping me here. The only thing worth protecting.

Her lips curve into something gentle. Something understanding.

"There is so much of the past I wish I could change," she whispers. "I wish I had protected your mother better. But I must believe the fates have brought us together again for a reason.

"This time, I will not make the same mistakes."

Her voice carries a weight of guilt so heavy it makes me feel hollow.

Then, softer—regretful—she murmurs,

"I cannot heal your scars, child. I want to. I wish I could erase every mark that man has left on your body—and the ones he will leave still. But if he finds out I was here, he will kill me."

I nod. I understand.

The scars on my body are nothing compared to the ones he has left in my mind.

It feels fitting, in a way, that I cannot rid myself of the evidence.

Cannetta stands, but I grab her hand before she can go. I don't want her to leave. I need her. I need this moment. I need a tether to something good. More than anything, I need to know about my mother.

She squeezes my fingers. A silent promise.

"Play the game, girl," she whispers.

I shiver.

"It is a devilish, dreadful game. It will hurt. It will test you. But play it. Your mother, her mate—everyone who comes against Tierney—ends up six feet under.

"But you... you may be the only one with the power to win."

I swallow hard.

"He has no weaknesses," she continues. "We have all searched for it. Those of us who still live play his game, hoping to find it. But you—"

She cups my cheek, her thumb stroking lightly over my skin.

"You have the power to become his weakness."

I suck in a breath.

"Empaths may not be able to manipulate for their own gain," she says. "But a human can."

With a final touch to my face, she turns, pulls her hood over her head, and vanishes.

A soft clink echoes beside me. I look over. A teacup and a teapot sit on my nightstand. And beside them—a letter.

I reach for it with shaking fingers.

You are not what you think you are.

The voice that tells you that you are nothing? She is lying.

Be what they fear.

Be the warrior. The weapon.

Release the monster inside.

I press the note to my chest, clutching it like a lifeline.

I know what I have to do.

And I will hate every damn moment of it.

Olivia

THE MASK OF SURVIVAL

He is back. A week's reprieve—both too short and too long. It's long enough for me to grasp at the fragile embers of hope Cannetta offers. Long enough to breathe, to let the raw edges of my pain scab over. But not long enough to heal. Not long enough to erase the memories that haunt my every step. Not long enough for my body to forget what it has endured.

But the week gives me something else. A fire under my skin. A plan. A final, desperate grasp for freedom. One last attempt. *And if I survive that, I can survive anything.*

Lord Tierney wastes no time upon his return. A week away only sharpens his appetite—his hunger to play with his new prize. *Be smart, girl.* Cannetta's warning hums through my mind like a whispered incantation.

Colden stands in my chamber, his back rigid, hands buried deep in his pockets. Unmoving.

"He wants me, doesn't he?" I ask, my voice flat, betraying nothing. Not the terror twisting my stomach, not the fire simmering beneath my skin, waiting—aching—to be unleashed.

Colden says nothing at first. Then, without warning, he crosses the room and pulls me into his arms.

A shudder racks through me, a foreign warmth settling in my chest as his embrace swallows me whole. He holds me like it's the only thing keeping him standing. He nods into my hair, and I feel the silent apology in the way his arms tighten.

This means as much to him as it does to me.

When he pulls away, his eyes are dull—drained of color, drained of life. And then, right in front of me, he becomes someone else. General Colden. A man of ice and silence, his face unreadable, his posture rigid as he turns toward the door. He doesn't meet my gaze. My lip twitches. Sullen. Resigned. Because I'm about to learn exactly what it means to wear a mask. *My only fear—once I put it on, will I ever be able to take it off?*

Bria prepares me with delicate hands, silent as she works. She twists my hair into intricate spirals, pinning them into place like she's crowning me for my own execution. A nightgown of snakeskin floats over my frame, slipping down my shoulders like liquid shadow. I turn toward the mirror. A stranger stares back. That is not Olivia. The green in my eyes is too dark, too hollow. A golden snake curls around my ring finger and slithers up my wrist, the ink shimmering beneath the dim candlelight. It covers my Companach band. It covers the only thing that tethers me to the person I was. It is the mark of a new claim. Of a new prison. And the girl in the mirror—the one with haunted eyes and golden chains wrapping around her flesh—is ready to play the game.

I walk into his bedchamber with my head high, spine straight, every inch of me controlled. I meet Lord Tierney's yellow eyes and ignore the part of me that wants to recoil, to retch, to run. *That's not part of the plan.* He watches me, assessing, waiting. His gaze darkens, that sick gleam glazing over as he reaches for my mind. I let him in. Effortlessly, I offer him the image he wants—his leather strap cracking against my back as he takes me, as he drowns in the pleasure of my suffering. I let him relive it, savor it, feel it. His arousal hits me like a thick, cloying wave. *Hook, line, and sinker. You want to crave me, Lord Tierney? I'll give you something to crave. I'll stay in your thoughts like the scars on my flesh—permanent.*

"Ready to play?" His voice curls around me like smoke, a promise laced with poison. "Are you ready for me to own you, to control you?" I nod, my face passive, my power coiled and waiting. *You have picked your poison, Lord Tierney. Drink.*

"Looks like my wife wants to play," The purr leaves his lips, his fangs glinting as I watch them peel into a grin. I make my face sultry, inviting— a challenge. I echo his low hum, feeding him exactly what he wants, painting the image of an adoring, pliant victim in his mind.

His slim figure looms over me, hunger crackling in his gaze. He slides his belt from its loops, waiting. Waiting for me to flinch. For me to retreat into that numb, broken thing he has molded.

Instead, I give him what he commands.

I let him feel my uncertainty, let it shimmer through me like the ghost of a shudder. But beneath it, buried deep, is his own excitement. The echoes of his own desires reflect back at him like a mirror. A silly little game a golden Fae once played. *I hope it works just the same.*

But this is an entirely different game.

One with stakes that can burn me alive. I feel none of the arousal that clouds his mind, but he will never know the difference.

With eager hands, he wrenches my wrists together, binding them with bone-breaking tension.

I let him.

I let him tie me to his bed, let him believe I am his.

I let him take what he wants.

I let him feel my pain, my submission, my acceptance.

I let him believe he owns me.

And then—I feel it.

A shift inside him, small and shuddering.

And just like that, he is done.

I bite back my disgust as his lips crush against mine, his teeth biting, his pleasure drenched in triumph.

"I am glad someone finally comes to play," he murmurs against my skin. "You see, wife? Fighting my power is no use. You are mine." A low snarl curls in my throat. I feel the shift in his emotions, the stir of uncertainty before he pushes it away. And then, it's over. Tierney peels himself away from me, barking an order toward the door. "Take her away."

Colden appears, his movements sharp and silent. He undoes the belt, freeing my wrists, and I rise on my own. I walk across the chamber, find my discarded nightgown, and slip it back over my shoulders before following Colden into the hall. I do not look back. I ignore the voice in my head that screams, *whore. He wants his little whore? His little weapon? Well, hello, snake. Call me charmer.*

We say nothing as we walk down the darkened corridor. The flames flicker on the stone walls, their glow dancing over paintings of his beloved beasts, their monstrous eyes watching as we pass. Colden unlocks my door, holding it open. Bria stands inside, her small frame tense, her face drawn with apprehension. Her gaze scours my body, searching for new wounds, new bruises. She finds none.

"I would like to be alone," I say, my voice cool, clipped. Colden and Bria both flinch. "Olivia..." Colden's voice is softer than I expect. Too soft.

"Leave. Now." The words come out snarled, the sharpness of my canines flashing as I bare my teeth. I hold myself together with vicious control, coiled so tightly I can feel myself shaking. I am the snake now. And if I look into their eyes—if I see their concern, their pity, their shame—it'll be like stepping on my tail. A snake will strike when provoked.

Colden must understand. He nods once, takes Bria gently by the elbow, and guides her from the room. For the first time, those three loud clicks as the door locks behind me are music to my ears. Every inch of me feels heavy. I walk to the serpent mirror, staring at the woman reflected back. Her eyes are dark, shadowed. Bruises curl around her neck, wrap tight around her wrists and arms like shackles. But there's no blood. The bath is already drawn, steam curling from the surface. I sink into it, my body aching, raw, crawling. I scrub. I scrub until my skin burns, until it's red and stinging, until every inch of me is rubbed raw—as if I can strip away every touch, every fingerprint, every trace of him.

I only stop when I have no skin left to give. And then, I see it. Another nightgown. Red. So red, so slimy it makes my stomach turn. I leave it where it lies. Instead, I wrap myself in a blanket, wind it so tightly around me that it feels like arms—like Jeyr's arms. Like home.

I crumble before the fire, my head pressing against my knees, my body folding in on itself. I picture his forehead against mine, the soft warmth of his hands, the way he whispers my name like it's sacred. But no tears come. Not anymore.

I chose my bed.

Now, I had to lie in it.

I no longer have fallen leaves or blooming flowers to measure the time that passes. The mountains of Puinnsean remain in a permanent state of frost. The only thing I have is the bond I focus on growing with Tierney. With each night, I stoke the fire of his growing feelings for me—his obsession with me. I'm no longer the prey to the beast. Now, I'm the rare golden gem. He needs to hold me, to touch me every day to know that he owns me. I grow more confident in my mask.

Eventually, I'm able to make demands of my own. My first is for Colden to no longer watch. I don't like him seeing this side of me—this monster.

I walk into his room, no invitation needed, and watch as Tierney turns from where he faces his mirror. The yellow in his eyes darkens at the sight of me. "Mm, did I ask for you to come to my chamber, Wife?" I feel his claws in my mind, the same claws that think they're working their way in. *You will love me; you will worship me.*

"You seemed... frustrated." I'm not lying. I have a permanent line of power reading his emotions, using it to calculate when I can gain his attention.

"Mm, nothing gets past you. Just army business. Nothing to concern your pretty little mind with—yet." His eyes trail over my figure, and before he can ask me to come closer, my legs begin to move. His eyes light up.

Get on your knees, Wife.

I flinch, my façade cracking for a moment as my mind considers fighting his command. It's a lighter use of his power. He's testing—testing how much force is needed, how much I'll do on my own. I'm the wild horse he wants to tame. He doesn't just want to control me—he wants me completely and utterly his.

My knees hit the cold floor with a crack. His talon circles under my chin, my skin trembling under his touch. "Mm, I love feeling your reaction to me, Empath."

Let me feel everything, Wife.

My powers lurch. *Mm, these emotions are a drug—overwhelming in the best of ways. Take off my pants. I'll show you how good you make me feel, then I want you to amplify it.*

Under his control, I do as he asks. His claws dig into my hair, pushing my mouth over his hard length. I focus on my powers, on his pleasure and nothing else. I'm not me. I'm his, and only his. With the entirety of my powers flowing through me to him and throughout the room, he doesn't last long.

"Fuck!" I feel his knees crumble, feel his body spasm from the overwhelming sensation of his orgasm being given back to him.

Get up. I do. His finger catches the drop of his seed trailing down my chin and places it back in my mouth.

Tell me you are mine. "I am yours."

Tell me you are under my control. "I am under your control."

Good. Get on my bed. You are mine tonight. My body obeys, moving toward the bed. I ignore the girl in the back of my mind who wants to cry for her own bed.

The days blur into a cycle of sex, scrub, sleep, repeat. I stop counting them long ago. Cannetta's visits grow rare, stolen moments carved from the time Tierney does not yet own. But when she comes, she brings knowledge—and knowledge is power. Each visit, she slips me scrolls, books, whispers of old secrets.

I devour every word. I study breeding lines, the intricate weaving of blood and power, the histories of the Kingdoms, the laws of Companachs, the mysteries of souls, spells, and the raw forces that shape our world.

Most of it is surface-level knowledge—things I've already learned in my time with Jeyr and his family. But then something shifts.

Something makes my skin prickle, my stomach twist. *I've read these histories before.*

Yet here, in Tierney's collection, the words are... wrong.

Some details are omitted, others altered—subtle distortions that at first seem small. But the more I study them, the more my hackles rise.

This is deliberate. This is erasure. And I need to know why.

Because if history has been rewritten—if truths have been twisted into convenient lies—then *I* am the anomaly. *And I need to find out what that makes me.*

I sit on my bed, *The History of Puinnsean* open in my lap, fingers flipping absently through its pages. The words blur as I feel his presence moving up the stairs—Tierney. I elbow Colden hard in the ribs, keeping my voice low.

"Get up and get to your guard."

He exhales sharply but obeys, slipping his mask into place before disappearing through the door, leaving behind only the faint scent of cold steel and fresh snow. I curl beneath my blankets, feigning sleep, as I hear the command—deep, possessive, undeniable.

"Open the door."

The heavy groan of iron and stone scraping open sends a tremor through my spine. I let out a small groggy sound, eyes fluttering open as if I've just woken.

"Oh," I murmur, pulling the sheets up to hide the book in my lap. My voice purrs on instinct, soft but teasing. "I thought you preferred your chamber, My Lord." I raise a slow, mocking brow.

"Exactly," he snaps. "I do. So why are you here?"

I blink, my mind already calculating, my body anticipating his every move. Tierney crawls onto my bed, moving toward me with the slow, deliberate grace of a predator. I force my heart to stay steady—*don't flinch, don't flinch*—but it betrays me. He hears it. His lips curl.

"You haven't needed my command before," he muses, voice like silk laced with knives. "It's dusk, and you were not naked in my bed. For that... you should be punished."

A smile curls onto my lips—a smile of power. *Not the kind I once fought to hold onto. Not the kind that made me a saint.* This is something darker. Something that no longer cares who I hurt in the process. Somehow, by letting go of control, I've gained more of it. Somehow, by embracing this monster, I've mastered my own powers.

Tierney thinks he has created me. Thinks I've yielded. *Let him believe it.*

"You want to punish me, Lord?" I whisper, voice like honey-dipped steel. "You want to feel my pain?"

His pupils dilate, his breath hitches—the hunger that always lurks in him now fully awakened.

"You know I do."

His teeth find my throat, sinking in with sharp, teasing bites. He pins me down, his weight pressing against mine. The leather of his glove brushes my skin, but he's already lost to the sliver of my mind I've crafted just for him.

He's content with the crumbs I leave him. With the illusion that he has tamed me. He has no idea.

The moment his teeth sink deeper, my power surges, wrapping around him like invisible tendrils. Everything he does to me—he feels in return. His lips part in a gasp, his heart stutters against mine.

"I missed you today," he groans, the words wrenched from him like an involuntary confession.

My power curls around his mind, wrapping it in silk and iron.

I let him worry for a second—let doubt slip into the cracks of his consciousness. *Let him wonder if I've pulled away, if he's losing control.* And then, just as quickly, I soothe it away.

And I begin to drop the breadcrumbs. *Infatuation. Lust. Obsession. Need.*

My recipe to make a monster fall in love.

"Then have me," I murmur, wrapping my arms around his neck, pressing my lips against his ear. "Punish me."

His mouth crashes against mine, his teeth pulling at my lower lip, groaning, bucking against me, utterly lost in the trap I've woven around him. His grip bruises. His breath shudders.

"Turn around." His voice is thick, slurred with desire and power. "On your hands and knees."

And I obey. Not because I am his. *But because, for the first time, he is becoming mine.*

I lie atop his bony chest, my body draped across his like this is where I belong. His talons comb through my hair, slow, lazy movements—deceptively gentle.

"I spoke with Bane."

The words slide through the air like a blade, cold and deliberate. I blink up at him, keeping my face smooth, waiting for him to continue.

"Aimsir is having a ball," he says, watching me, waiting for a reaction. "And he has agreed that you can come."

Panic slashes through me, swift and sharp. *No. Not Aimsir. Not **his** Court.*

I swallow it whole before it can show, before it can betray me. I force my body to relax, force my fingers to trace absent patterns across his chest.

Aimsir. My mate's Court. The name sits heavy between us, twisting through my ribs like a vice. *I will not react. I cannot react.*

So I only hum, let my lips curve just slightly—teasing, coy, controlled. "Oh, yeah?"

"Mmhmm." Tierney's yellow eyes gleam, predatory and pleased.

"It's time to show those weather-wielders the new arsenal in our army."

Arsenal.

The word makes my fingers still, falter in their lazy movements.

"Is that what I am?"

"Not yet," he says smoothly, "but you will be."

His talons scrape lightly over my bare shoulder—a dark caress, a promise of things to come.

"And that brings me to the next topic," he continues, amusement laced through his tone. "I need you to meet me in my office. I have a present for you."

I feign interest, tilting my chin up just slightly. "Yeah?" I murmur, lifting myself enough to press a slow, languid kiss against his lips.

His fangs catch my lower lip, biting possessively—making me pause, making me wait until he's satisfied before I pull back.

"Yes, Wife. Meet me downstairs after you've cleaned up."

I watch him move from under me, the sheets pooling at my waist as he dresses—the sharp contrast of black leathers against his pale, skeletal frame. He makes his way toward the door, but hesitates. His gaze lingers, dark and burning. And then, just before he leaves—

"Oh," he says casually, like it's an afterthought. Like it isn't another chain tightening around my throat. "That is the last time you will sleep in that bed."

And then he's gone.

Olivia

THE MAKING OF A MONSTER

I move to the vanity, still wrapped in a blanket, my fingers methodically working through my tangled hair.

I feel Colden's eyes on me before I see them. In the mirror, his gaze burns—wild and assessing—searching for something I'm not ready to name.

Bria enters the room, her steps light, her presence gentle as always. She moves straight to me, her small hands weaving through my hair, working quickly, efficiently, silent as ever. Colden steps further in, his stare interrogative, piercing. Bria finishes fast, her fingers lingering for just a second longer than necessary, as if asking if I'm okay.

I'm not.

But I tap her hand anyway, sending a soft wave of warmth, silently asking for privacy. She understands. She always does. The moment the door shuts behind her, I exhale, my chest tight with something I can't name.

Colden doesn't move. "So," he starts, his voice low, unreadable. "Invited to the big ball, then. What's your game plan?"

I have none. Nothing but panic, cold and sharp, slithering into my bones at the thought of stepping foot in his Kingdom.

Don't think about him. Don't let yourself. I haven't let my mind go there in weeks. *Can't.*

Every time it drifts toward him, I force it away, shove it into a locked box, unwilling to risk Tierney catching even a whisper of who I belonged to.

Or rather, who I once belonged to. Because he wouldn't want me now. Not after every-

thing. Not after who I've become.

The words leave me before I can stop them.

"I was engaged before Tierney took me away."

Colden flinches. His mask—always so careful, so controlled—cracks just slightly. I blink heavily, forcing myself to breathe, to focus. His emotions crash over me like an unspoken tide—surprise, sadness, intrigue.

"I have a Companach," I whisper, my voice barely above a breath, as if saying it aloud will shatter me.

A bitter laugh escapes me, raw and hollow. "Or I did. Before."

Colden stares, waiting, listening. I let the words spill, my panic bubbling over, my restraint cracking at the seams.

"I don't want Tierney to have that part of me. I didn't want him to use me against my mate—against his kingdom, his family." I tap my fingers against my temple, where the truth still lives, buried deep. "Every memory. Every emotion. It's all still here. Locked away."

I swallow, my throat tight, my voice thick with something I can't control. "Tierney hasn't even realized it yet. That he doesn't have full control."

Colden's hands clench into fists, his jaw tight.

"But it doesn't matter," I whisper.

I lift my hand, pointing to the mirror, to the scars that run down my back—a grotesque map of everything I've survived. "Because I am not the woman he fell in love with. If he is there... if he sees me like this..."

The thought makes my stomach churn. If he sees the scars, the markings of another man's ownership, the evidence of the monster I've become to survive— Would he even recognize me? Would he want to?

"Shh."

Colden's voice is softer than I've ever heard it, barely more than a breath. He's behind me now, close but not touching. His presence is calming, steady in a way that makes something inside me splinter.

"Don't think like that."

I let out a humorless laugh. "How else am I supposed to think?"

"If he is your Companach," Colden says, his voice all steel and certainty, "if he loves you as deeply as a Companach does... then he will have you however you come."

I turn, my vision blurring, my chest aching with the weight of it.

Colden meets my gaze with unwavering conviction. "He will understand that you had to do this to protect yourself," he says.

And then, softer—like he knows just how much I need to hear it, even if I don't believe it: "I have no doubt he is doing everything he can to get you back."

I want to believe him. Gods, I want to believe him. But the woman he fell in love with is gone. Our souls are linked, bound by fate's cruel, sadistic game.

But if he ever saw me now— Saw what I've become— Saw what I let happen to me— Would he even be able to look at me? Would he even want to?

The black velvet dress fits like a second skin, the cowl neckline dipping low, the back exposing the sharp lines of my spine—the marks of a body that has become both weapon and prize.

Colden and I walk side by side, masks firmly in place, two actors in an elaborate play, rehearsing the parts we have no choice but to perform.

I knock on the large, black wooden doors, hearing Tierney's grunt of acknowledgment from within. The doors swing open, their weight groaning against the slate floors. The office is as much a throne room as it is a lair. Leather-bound books nestle in gothic arches, each carved with intricate serpent motifs. Blood-red ivy leaves twist along the decorative border beside gold bellflowers, their shine dull in the flickering firelight.

Behind the claw-foot desk, a bay window overlooks The Black Forest—a looming, endless stretch of shadows that borders the perimeter of our prison. Tierney stands tall and poised, his slim frame draped in flawless black. His suit is impeccable, the pleats in his pants razor-sharp, his jacket smooth over the gilded brace on his arm. Though concealed beneath the fabric, the gold and ruby cufflinks glimmer—little reminders that power still lies beneath the silk and shadow.

His hungry gaze drags over me.

"I can see why you took so long, Lady Tierney. You look ravishing," he vibrates, his voice sliding through me like the slow tightening of a noose.

He pushes off his desk, his movements fluid, feet gliding effortlessly as he approaches.

His nose brushes against mine, slithering down the bridge before his mouth captures mine—a bruising, claiming kiss. His canines slice into my lower lip, pulling a sharp sting of pain from me.

But I'm ready.

I let my powers sink into him, let his desire amplify, let his pupils dilate as the pleasure drowns him whole. *Drink it down, monster. I hope you choke on it.*

He shudders, drunk on my emotions, and hums in pleasure.

"Well," he purrs against my lips, "it seems we make a fine pair, wouldn't you say? I think it's time to take our relationship to the next level."

His words slither against my throat, his fangs grazing my pulse. I force a playful laugh, sliding my fingers down his torso—my touch coaxing, teasing, deadly.

"How do you suggest we do that?" I ask, letting my voice purr, letting my powers trickle into him like a fine, aged poison.

Like a full-bodied tempranillo—rich and intoxicating, filled with lust and devotion—a symphony of desires I've designed just for him.

His mouth curves.

"With you finally using your powers so freely, I think it's about time we test them."

The words send a dagger of dread through my bones. But I keep my mask firmly in place.

"Continue..." I murmur, despite the nausea bubbling in my gut.

Tierney's sinister smile stretches across his face, slow and deliberate. "I have a present for you."

His voice is silken death, a whisper of something final.

Then I turn. And I see him.

The breath rips from my lungs. No. No, no, no.

My stomach curdles, panic clawing its way up my throat, pressing against my ribs.

Don't make me do this. Please.

"Daddy, Daddy! You're home!"

I bounced on my toes, my gray dress fluttering around my ankles.

He stood in the doorway, dark windswept hair damp from the sea, salt licking the edges of his sun-kissed curls.

His broad, toothy smile beamed down at me.

"Livy Lu!"

His arms came around me, lifting me high, spinning me through the air.

Laughter bubbled from my lips, filling the foyer.

"Oh, how I missed your laugh!" he whispered, his eyes glistening. "It makes the sun shine so much brighter."

His hands cradled my face, brushing my curls away from my eyes.

"I love you, Daddy."

I smiled up at him, warmth coiling in my chest.

His voice wobbled as he pressed a kiss to my forehead.

"I love you too, my little girl."

I'm ripped from the memory, torn back into this nightmare—this hell.

"You see," Tierney murmurs, wrapping himself around me from behind, "I've been thinking."

His hands tighten around my waist—possessive, warning.

"This man," he says, "despite handing you over to me and making me the happiest man alive, has come to bore me."

His voice darkens, slithering into something deadly, razor-sharp.

"He hurt you. This man betrayed you. And, dear wife..."

His lips brush my ear, his breath hot and cruel.

"I would hate for anyone who has hurt you to still be breathing."

His fingers dig into my hips, his voice vibrating against my spine.

"You've done this to me. Made me protective."

I feel it then. A twisted, consuming version of love. Possessiveness. Devotion. Obsession.

And I know—I have to keep playing the game. If I hesitate now, if I show weakness, I'll be the one lying dead on the floor.

"So, as a mating present..." Tierney turns me, pressing me forward toward my father, his talons curling warningly against my hipbones. "I give you your father on a platter. Do as you wish with him."

I smile. A slow, cruel thing. The same smile Tierney wears when he looks at me. The same smile I've memorized in the mirror.

My father's eyes go wide, pale hazel swirling with desperation, regret, terror.

"Olivia... Liv... Please." His voice cracks. "I'm so sorry for all I did. I didn't have a choice."

"Come dance with me, my little one!"

He stretched out his hand, his laughter booming, the firelight catching his wedding ring.

I placed my small hand in his, and he twirled me, the King's dance unfolding in our living room, our smiles broad, our laughter bright.

"All I hear are excuses, Father."

My voice coos, my power twisting, shifting. I let the world see me—the monster Tierney has made me. The monster I need to be to survive. Ribbons of pure panic and fear weave around my father, tightening, constricting. His hand clutches his chest, his pulse thundering as I feed his own terror back into him, looping, spiraling, building.

"Scared, Father?"

His body seizes, eyes rolling back— And then he's gone.

The thud of his lifeless body echoes through the room.

Tierney exhales, pleased. "You," he whispers, tilting my chin, drinking me in, "are the best Lady Tierney this world has ever seen."

And when he kisses me, I let him feel it—the love of every soul I've ever killed. *Because one day, if fate is on my side, That love will drag him to hell with me.*

"I cannot wait to show you off to the new Grand Duke of Aimsir."

Tierney's voice coils around me, a dark promise wrapped in silk. His nose brushes along my cheek, inhaling like he could breathe me into his lungs, like my scent alone could intoxicate him. His talons tangle in my hair, possessive and firm, winding through the strands as if binding me to him.

"But don't you worry," he murmurs, breath hot against my throat. "Your power is my secret. For now. We can't have the King knowing about the newest power couple, can we?"

I hum, fingers trailing over his chest in a touch meant to tease, to tempt, to keep him looking anywhere but at the truth. *He thinks he's won. He thinks I'm his.*

"Not yet," he continues, lips grazing my jaw. "Soon, the world will know. When Bane takes the throne and he has the two of us—the strongest commanders in the land—we will have everything we desire."

I tilt my head just enough to expose my throat, drawing him in before I strike. My canines pierce his neck, his blood thick and bitter on my tongue. The tannins of his poison lace through me as I swallow, my body resisting the taste even as I force it down. He groans, his grip tightens, his breath catches in a gasp of pleasure.

His obsession with me is growing.

"I can't wait," I whisper, licking up the trail of blood that streaks down his skin. His body shudders, his hold on me possessive, unrelenting.

"Mm, keep drinking that power, my love." His voice drips with satisfaction, his scarred lips stretching into a rare, feral grin. "This is only the beginning."

I force myself to smile, force my body to sink into his grip, to let him think his monster has fully come to heel.

He finally pulls away, though his gaze never leaves me.

"I best go prepare," he says, straightening his cuffs, the gold and ruby cufflinks catching the firelight. "We need to make a statement."

His hands find my waist, fingers biting into my skin—a silent demand, a silent test. I rise onto my toes, let my lips skim over the jagged scar on his mouth, let my teeth nip at his bottom lip just enough to make him ache for more.

His arousal coils around me, thick and suffocating—like oil on a seabird's wings, sinking into every part of me I can never wash clean.

I turn from him, casting one last glance over my shoulder, the invitation in my eyes deliberate. *Wait until tonight.*

His groan follows me out, deep and full of need.

I have him.

I turn to Colden, forcing every ounce of emotion from my face, forcing my voice to be smooth, detached.

"Come, General," I murmur, already stepping forward. "It seems we have a ball to prepare for."

He says nothing—only nods, falling into step beside me. The corridors are lined with Tierney's men, dark, twisted creatures standing guard at every turn, their lifeless eyes tracking us as we pass. I feel the weight of my own body pressing down, feel my power fluctuate and slip, my strength faltering beneath the weight of what I've just done, what I've just become.

Colden extends his arm, and though every part of me wants to refuse it, I take it, gripping the cold leather of his sleeve as he supports my weight.

His voice is barely a whisper, a breath of frost against my ear. "We are nearly there. Stay in character."

I swallow the bile rising in my throat and force my spine straight, my steps fluid, my mask unshaken. Each guard bows as I pass, each one believing the lie I've spun, each one unaware that I'm hanging by a thread so thin, so fragile, that even the next breath might shatter me.

The massive stone door to my chambers has never looked so inviting. It shuts behind us, the lock clicking into place— And whatever's holding me together snaps.

Cold air rushes over my skin, but it isn't enough. My stomach twists violently, heaving, and I barely make it into the bathroom before I collapse against the cold slate floor, my body convulsing as everything inside me purges.

One wave of sickness after another wracks through me, my muscles locking, my limbs trembling so hard it hurts. The velvet dress clings to my skin—suffocating—the fabric stained with him, with his scent, with his hands.

Get it off. The panic claws up my throat, pressing against my ribs, burning me from the inside out. *Get it off. Get it off.*

As if he hears the silent plea, Colden tears the dress from me in a single motion, the fabric ripping away, leaving me bare and shaking against the cold floor.

I curl in on myself, my body still shuddering, the convulsions slowly fading into a dull tremor. Colden curls around me, his body a barrier between me and the rest of the world, his hand steady as it traces slow, even strokes up and down my spine, his breath calm, rhythmic.

"Breathe," he murmurs, his voice so steady, so quiet, that I latch onto it like a lifeline. "In and out."

I try. But every inhale only makes my throat close tighter. Every exhale only presses the truth deeper into my bones.

I killed my father.

And I felt every single moment of it. *I felt his heart slow, felt his terror coil and tighten, felt the last fragile thread of love he sent to me—hoping, praying—that I wouldn't go through with it.*

And yet, I did. And in his final moment, I made sure he feared me. I made sure that the last thing he saw in this life, the last thing he felt— *was terror.*

Monster. Murderer.

Colden turns me into him.

"I know, I know. You're still you, Olivia. Your heart's intact, your soul unbroken. You did it because it was right—for something greater than yourself." he murmurs, somehow understanding the deep-seated torture twisting inside me.

"I'm a murderer." My voice is dead, even to my own ears.

He flinches, and I don't know if it's the tone or the emotion that makes him do so.

"If you hadn't killed him, Tierney would have. And who knows what he would've done to you."

But it doesn't matter. *There's no denying it. I killed my father. My powers can be used for good and evil. And I chose the latter.*

Colden lifts my chin. I look into his eyes. He sees the broken woman I've become. He's seen firsthand the monster I can be. And yet he looks at me with such tenderness.

He rests his forehead against mine.

"Olivia, you're not a monster. You're the strongest woman I've ever had the pleasure to meet. You know why you're not a monster? Because every day since you gave yourself up to him, you come back to this room and scrub yourself raw to rid yourself of who you had to be in those hours."

His voice is gentle, but the words crack me open.

"I see how you hate any fabric that's touched him. You hate anything that reminds you of the part you have to play to stay safe. To please him. I see you, Olivia. And I hate that all I can do is stand idly by while you crush a piece of your soul to survive this game. You're doing it for your Companach."

His words are kind. They're sweet. But they don't change the one thing that's now true.

The one thing I've become.

A Murderer.

The word beats through my skull like a war drum, a whisper that twists and coils, slithering through my ribs, wrapping around my throat. It digs into my bones, deeper than the scars Tierney has left on my skin.

I did that. I took his life. I felt his final breath, the pulse of his last thoughts, the way his heart pleaded for one more beat, one more moment.

"Please don't give into his darkness. Not now."

Colden's voice cuts through the haze—steady and unwavering.

"You're just an actor on a stage, and you will get your grand exit. You will leave this place."

His hands grip my shoulders, grounding me, pulling me back from the ledge I've been standing on for far too long.

"The next murder will be his—whether it's you or me that makes the final blow."

His fingers tighten, his voice low and fierce, carved from ice and iron.

"Do you hear me? You will leave these walls."

I look into his eyes—into the beautiful, brutal certainty of them.

I don't deserve him.

I nod.

His hands move to my face, his thumbs smoothing over my cheeks like he's searching for the girl I used to be. Like he's trying to hold together the broken pieces of me. I lean into the coolness of his touch, letting it chase away the heat of my own self-destruction, letting his presence anchor me until the tremors in my body finally settle.

He holds me there, searching my features, his lips pressing into a thin line before he finally exhales.

"I'll get Bria." His voice is softer now, a whisper against the walls. "You have to be ready for a grand ball."

He smiles, but it's a ghost of a thing—something that never quite touches his eyes.

"Colden."

He turns, brow quirking, waiting for me to speak.

I hesitate, then whisper, "Don't thank me."

His brow furrows, but I continue.

"You've been sending me comfort from the moment I walked through those front doors." My voice is barely more than a breath, but I need him to hear it. "I've never felt more loved than when you got here, Olivia."

I watch as the sharp edges of his face soften, as something unspoken flickers behind his eyes.

His lips part, but before he can say anything, I speak again.

"I... okay, but I was also going to say..."

I swallow hard, forcing the words past the knot in my throat. *Say it. Just say it.*

"The Kingdom of Aimsir is my Companach's kingdom."

I force myself to meet his gaze, my voice steady despite the panic curling in my gut. "He is the second son of the Grand Duke."

Colden stills. I watch him ice over, his entire body going rigid, his fingers twitching before they curl into fists. His breath hitches, his jaw tightens, and his eyes widen—full of something sharp, something dark.

"What is it?" I press, suddenly unable to breathe.

Colden's chest rises and falls, the storm in his gaze crashing into me as his lips part, his voice coming out in a whisper of disbelief.

"Your Companach... he is now the Grand Duke of Aimsir."

Jeyr

STORMS AND STRATEGY

I pace the length of Aimsir's second castle, my boots striking the polished stone floors in restless rhythm. It isn't the family home—not the seat of my childhood memories—but still, a grand fortress. Built on the second-highest peak of Aimsir, its white stone walls and blue-peaked roofs cut through the misty skyline like a beacon.

Floor-to-ceiling windows line the great hall, offering a view of the storm rolling across the skies. Lightning splits the heavens. Thunder roars in response.

She is coming.

The words echo in my mind, an unrelenting drumbeat against my ribs.

"Get ahold of yourself, brother," Aella says, arms crossed as she leans against one of the stone pillars. "We don't want people thinking you're getting arrogant with your power."

Her tone is sharp, but beneath it, I can feel the concern she tries to hide. I turn to face her.

Aella is striking, even in her frustration. Her mousy brown hair is pinned into intricate curls, a delicate contrast to the bold scar that runs across her face—a brutal line where her steel-blue eye once was. The scar only makes the remaining eye more piercing, its color like a storm locked behind glass.

My stomach clenches at the memory of her standing before me, face bare and broken, pain still raw after her husband went too far. I clench my fists, forcing the thought away just as another streak of lightning flickers through the sky.

I exhale— And the storm obeys.

The dark, roiling clouds melt into wisps of white, drifting apart until the sky calms once more.

I'll never get used to this magic. This ancestral weight that now lives in my veins.

"She is coming," I say.

Aella steps closer, her hand settling on my arm. She has been my constant these past months, guiding me through the shifting tides of court politics, through the power struggles that come with my new title. But more than that—she understands. She knows what the Companach bond is doing to me.

She's seen how Olivia has locked me away, sealed off our connection until she couldn't anymore. Until the pain breaks through in unbearable waves that leave me gasping for breath.

Just hours ago, Aella stood by helplessly as I collapsed, watching as my branded wrist darkened, the colors shifting like a wound trying—and failing—to heal.

I've never hated the mark more.

It once meant fate. Love. Something unbreakable. Now, it's nothing but a constant reminder of how much I'm failing.

Some Grand Duke I am.

Aimsir's grand ball has been planned for weeks—a political display meant to introduce my reign, to begin the careful maneuvering of alliances.

Olivia's arrival has changed everything.

Two hours. That's all the time I've been given.

Two hours to prepare for something I've been waiting for since the moment she disappeared. Two hours to figure out how to save her.

"This may be our chance," Aella says, her fingers tightening slightly around my arm. "This may be our one chance."

There's steel in her gaze, but behind it, I see the quiet care, the unwavering determination. I reach for her hand, watching as the last streaks of sunlight melt behind the clouds.

Officially, Olivia is attending the ball as Lord Tierney's wife. Not as a prisoner. Not as a stolen queen.

No invitation was sent to Puinnsean—not by me, not by Bane. And yet... she's coming.

Tierney's playing a dangerous game, maneuvering into places he was never meant to be. But so am I.

As the new Grand Duke, I'm a fresh player on the chessboard—the first of Aimsir's line to take the throne in over a century. That means new alliances, new opportunities—an opening.

I've already begun the dance of politics, hinting to Bane that I seek to join our kingdoms. It's a move meant to get one foot closer to his court.

One step closer to Olivia.

Now, I can only hope that tonight gives me the chance I need— *To finally take her back.*

The Ballroom and the Absence That Haunted It

My gaze sweeps across the ballroom, taking in the final touches of Aella's meticulous work. She's made sure every kingdom is represented—each decoration a carefully placed gesture of diplomacy. Aella is many things, but careless is never one of them.

If there's one way to make the kingdoms feel welcome, it's to acknowledge them in every flickering light, every suspended snowflake, every floral arrangement.

Above us, the ceiling shimmers with stars, shifting fluidly into the swirling colors of an aurora borealis—a tribute to the Kingdom of Aotrom. Jethro helped with the display, losing himself in the work as if the beauty could quiet the storm inside his mind. He hasn't said much about it, but I see it in his restless energy, in the way his gaze lingers on empty spaces—

He's struggling with Olivia's absence. Same as the rest of us.

And then there's Gwynn. She's only just returned to him, and yet she's already slipping away again—the only one of us with access to Puinnsean. Our single fragile thread of hope.

We can only wait. Only pray she returns with something—anything—we can use.

Throughout the ballroom, elements of each kingdom weave into the space like threads in an intricate tapestry. Snowflakes drift, suspended midair, twinkling as they catch the light. The scent of fresh earth and climbing ivy curls around the great windows—a tribute to the healing and nature courts. Fire flickers. Water dances. A mesmerizing display for the

Kingdom of Elements.

And then— The centerpieces.

Lilies.

Aella has chosen them for Puinnsean. A subtle, deliberate nod to Tierney's court. The scent curls around the room, heavy and cloying.

"You've outdone yourself," I murmur, reaching for Aella's hand and giving her fingers a brief squeeze.

She squeezes mine back, but her smirk is already forming.

"I know," she says, tilting her head. "So please, keep your temper at bay and don't fuck this up."

Before I can respond, she kisses me on the cheek and saunters off, her dress trailing behind her in a ripple of dark silk.

I exhale slowly, forcing myself to focus as the ballroom begins to fill with familiar faces. My family moves toward me, their presence a reminder of everything that's changed over the past few months.

My chest aches. *This should've been different. This should've been a celebration. A milestone shared with my mate.*

I can picture her as clearly as if she's standing beside me—the way she would have lit up the room with her presence, the way her laughter would have carried through the gilded halls, her eyes dancing as she took in the splendor of the night.

Instead, there's only the gaping absence of her.

"You scrub up alright there, Grand Duke," Michael says, nudging my shoulder with an easy grin.

I force a smile. Polite. Hollow.

The title still grates against me.

This isn't how it was supposed to be.

Olivia

THE BATTLE MASK

The afternoon is a blur of preparations—a frenzy orchestrated by Bria, who flits around me like a bird caught between excitement and precision. My hair is sculpted into an intricate masterpiece, every curl pinned into perfection, with strategic tendrils left to fall in soft, deliberate waves. She places the tiara Tierney has commanded me to wear upon my head, fussing over it with such concentration that she sticks out her tongue as she adjusts it to sit precisely at the center of my skull.

I huff a quiet laugh, amused despite myself.

Bria paints my face into something regal, ethereal—a picture of health and radiance. Golden hues sweep over my eyelids, catching the candlelight and making the green in my eyes glimmer like cut emeralds. With a steady hand, she lines my doe eyes with black kohl, elongating them into something more feline, something sharp and alluring.

I barely recognize myself.

With delicate strokes of light and shadow, she accentuates my cheekbones—though I hardly need the enhancement. My face has lost weight these past months, the bones already prominent beneath my skin. Lastly, she paints my lips a deep, blood red.

I stare at the girl in the mirror. *My freckles are erased. My wide eyes made sleek and sensual.* The face looking back at me is a mask—one crafted for battle, for survival.

Bria disappears momentarily, only to return with the red velvet gown draped over her arms. My skin prickles at the mere sight of it, and the moment the fabric touches me, it's all I can do not to recoil.

Velvet. I hate velvet.

Every nerve in my body protests as Bria helps dress me, the sensation sending a restless, crawling feeling through my skin. I grit my teeth and endure it.

I turn to the mirror— And my breath catches.

The gown fits exactly like the black one I wore earlier today. A deliberate statement from Tierney. The cowl neckline drapes over my chest, exposing just enough to tease, while my breasts are taped high, perky, presented. I turn slightly, wanting to see the back—then freeze.

The fabric plunges low, looping just above my rear, the design sculpting my hips and lower back, the dimples above my tailbone barely peeking through the material.

But it's not the cut that steals my breath.

It's the scars.

Three large talon marks claw down my back, deep and unmistakable. Tierney's marks. His claim. *That's what he wants the world to see.*

Bria says nothing as she moves to finish the last of my adornments. Where my wedding band was once inked into my skin, she traces over the golden serpents that now curl up my left hand and arm, winding their way to my bicep before stopping just below my left breast. She dusts them with gold paint, brightening their already gleaming coils.

Despite my hatred for snakes— Bria's work is art. She is an artist. A talent wasted in this prison.

swear, when I leave this place for good, I will take Bria with me. I'll find her a place where she can do this for a living—where her hands are never again forced to decorate the unwilling.

"Ready?"

The voice comes from the doorway. I turn, gauging Colden's reaction. His face tightens, his expression carefully measured, but displeasure flickers beneath the surface.

I stand, smoothing my hands over the velvet I despise.

"That bad?"

Bria's sharp stare snaps to Colden, her silent scolding more lethal than any words. He presses his lips together, as if to hide his amusement, but I catch the hint of a smile—one that agrees with her glare.

"No," he says finally. "You look beautiful. It's just…" He hesitates, gesturing toward the mirror.

I follow his gaze—and there it is again. ***The scars.***

I sigh, understanding.

"Tonight will be a test, Olivia," Colden murmurs, his voice quiet, knowing. "He'll be watching. Every movement, every glance, every breath you take. This will be the true flip of the coin—whether he falls further in love with you or loses all trust entirely."

My hands curl into fists.

"But it will be hardest for you," he continues, his eyes searching mine. "To see your Companach and not run to his side."

The breath leaves my lungs in a slow, controlled exhale.

I've thought about it. Turned the possibilities over in my mind endlessly, searching for a way out. But none of them end well—for Jeyr, for my family, for anyone I still love.

I have to get out of this on my own. No one else will be caught in the crossfire.

"I will play my character," I say, lifting my chin. "And that is it."

I feel it the moment Tierney's heart falters.

It's subtle—just a ripple in the energy around him—but I catch it as I descend the staircase, Colden at my back. Tierney is a man who controls everything: the way he moves, the way he commands, the way he consumes. But in that single breath, he's caught off guard.

Good.

His suit mirrors my gown—black velvet with blood-red thread. A deliberate coordination. A message. I am his. Not a single strand of his slicked-back hair is out of place, not a single wrinkle mars the pristine fabric. His golden rings glimmer, each one adorned with coiling serpents that match the ones painted onto my skin. Even his crown bears the same insignia—golden snakes winding through the metal like they've slithered straight from hell itself.

His gaze burns as he rakes over me, devouring every inch, every carefully chosen detail.

I let a faint vibration of approval pulse through me—a silent offering. A tool to keep him satisfied. *Just enough to tame the monster's mouth without feeding it too much.*

It's enough.

We do not pause for affection. *Thank the gods.*

His grip finds my arm, firm and possessive, and in a flash, the familiar darkness of his power wraps around me. The world bends and breaks, collapsing inward— And when it settles, we're standing at the entrance of Aimsir's grand palace.

The air is crisp, laced with the scent of oncoming rain. The towering white stone palace stands high in the clouds, its domed rooftops touched with the soft glow of moonlight. Everything about it is serene, untouched, holy.

I have never felt so out of place.

Nerves stir—a roiling unease that claws beneath my skin. The flesh-eating caterpillars in my stomach threaten to consume me from the inside out.

As if he knows, Colden sends a whisper of ice over my back.

A shiver of cold air flutters along my spine, a steadying pulse of magic—a silent anchor. An invisible hand strokes up and down my back, soothing the nausea before it can rise and betray me.

I lock my spine. *I am not Olivia of Aimsir. I am not a woman stolen, a woman lost, a woman fighting to survive. I am Lady Tierney. The woman who willingly took his hand.*

I force my shields up, wall away the part of me that's been clawing at its cage for months, desperate to break free. That part of me—the one who belongs to another—has no place here.

Tierney turns to me, his smile a predator's promise, his fingers pressing into my arm as he leans down. *Remember who you belong to now.*

I swallow the bile in my throat, my face unreadable. *Let him look. Let him believe it.*

And then, together, we walk through the doors.

Jeyr

The Arrival of a Ghost

I feel her before I see her.

Standing near the throne chairs—positioned just high enough to watch over the ballroom—I scan the faces below. Caomh stands at my side, his presence steady as ever, while Jethro lingers in the shadows, careful to remain unseen. If Tierney spots him too soon, it could unravel everything.

A storm brews outside, the distant rumble of thunder rolling through the sky. Caomh shoots me a look—a silent warning to keep my emotions in check. I exhale slowly, and the sky begins to clear.

No amount of training prepared me for this.

The ballroom pulses with movement, our family weaving through the crowd, blending into the courtly dance of diplomacy. Althea and Aiden are already on the floor, guiding others into the revelry with effortless grace. But for all their charm, they're only distractions from the real power in the room.

The arrival of Grand Duke Bane of Puinnsean sends a ripple through the gathering.

He moves with slow, deliberate steps, a blade hidden in silk. His white hair and pale skin contrast sharply against the deep burgundy of his robes, his golden eyes scanning the room with measured precision. The woman beside him is almost spectral—impossibly thin, golden waves cascading to her hip.

The murmurs hush.

And then— She walks in.

At the entrance of the ballroom, Olivia stands on the arm of Lord Tierney.

His smile is nothing short of wicked, a flash of fanged teeth glinting under the chandeliers. Like me, his eyes never leave her. And she— *She wears the same damnable smile.*

Green eyes—once vibrant and untamed—are shadowed now, darkened to a mossy hue. The dress clings to her frame, elegant and commanding, but it does nothing to hide how thin she's become.

A bolt of lightning flashes across the sky, illuminating her like a divine spectacle. *My heart forgets how to beat.*

Gasps ripple through the room. I'm not sure if it's because of them—the newly wedded couple—or the storm outside that crackles in eerie synchronization. The murmurs return, swelling around me like a tide. But they aren't about me. Every gaze in the room settles on her. With him.

She is radiant, glowing in the way a Queen does at her King's side—and Tierney knows it. The space around them pulses with an unspoken force, a mixture of power and possession, of something twisted and consuming. The way she carries herself, the way she looks at him, the way she plays her role so flawlessly—it has the court whispering, questioning. *Who is she? What is she? What power does she hold?*

I swallow, my stomach twisting. Jethro's voice is barely a breath in my mind. *I think I'm going to be sick.* Caomh's response is curt. *Stay focused. This may not be what it seems.* But it's too late for reassurances.

I stare at her, at the way she tilts her chin, at the calculated gleam in her eyes, at the way she rests her hand so lightly against Tierney's arm. And my heart breaks.

That isn't Olivia. Not the woman I loved. Not the woman who once laughed so freely, who promised she would always find her way back to me.

The woman who just stepped into the ballroom is something else entirely. And gods help us all if she's too far gone to bring back.

Okay, it's bad, but she has to be in there somewhere. If we get her home, we can try and erase whatever Tierney has done. Caomh's words are meant to soothe, yet they ring hollow.

There is no if to this—we are getting her home. My voice is edged with iron certainty.

Seeing her like that nearly drives me to storm across the ballroom floor, to take her into my arms and steal her away. But that would be an act of war. The Companachs may be bound by fate, but in the Kingdom, marriage is law. To steal another's wife is a crime punishable by the Court, and the last thing we need is further conflict with Puinnsean.

We need to draw them close—only then can we dismantle them from within.

The four Fae before me come to a halt below the dais, their faces masks of wicked amusement. Their eyes gleam with something sharp and unsettling, but none unnerve me more than Olivia's.

Dark green, calculating, cold. Her gaze sweeps over me—my dimple, my eyes—before shifting to Caomh. He stiffens under her scrutiny.

Those are not her eyes. Gone is the brightness, the vibrance I once knew.

A flicker. A fleeting ember in the moss-green depths of her gaze as it sweeps toward the shadowed alcove where Jethro lurks.

A spark of something I dare to hope is recognition.

What was that? I open the bridge between my brothers and me. *She is still in there, Jeyr.* Caomh's voice cracks, raw with emotion. He projects the image he has placed in Olivia's mind—the evergreen flash in her irises. *Her mind... he owns most of it. I cannot breach his hold without alerting him.*

Find a way in, I command.

I turn back to the revelers, my gaze locking onto Olivia once more. She squeezes Lord Tierney's arm, and my stomach churns with revulsion as I watch the affection she directs toward him. My hands clench at my sides when his taloned fingers trace the top of hers possessively. The look in his eyes—dark pleasure, indulgent ownership—is not the same as the one she once gave me.

No, this is the gaze of a woman consumed by darkness, one who revels in its embrace.

I let my emotions lash out, pushing my revulsion toward her like a crashing wave.

She flinches. A sharp, instinctive recoil. A pull in my gut answers in kind. *Well, it seems she can still feel your emotions, Brother,* Caomh murmurs, a thread of hope in his tone.

Tierney's gaze locks onto us, his eyes flaring with silent warning. Olivia reacts instantly, a calculated performance. "I'm okay, love," she murmurs, and then—

Her lips meet his. He melts into her, a man sated by possession. As they part, they linger, their teeth grazing in a teasing, intimate nip.

A growl builds in my throat. My jaw clenches so tight I feel the crack of my own teeth. *The word love...* It echoes in my skull, a brutal mockery.

Shake it off. We haven't lost her. Jethro's voice is rough, but firm. I want to believe him. *We all know what Tierney is capable of.*

*She called him **love**... What has he done to her?* Caomh's voice cracks, and doubt begins to seep into my bones, a poison that threatens to unmoor me.

But then— A scent.

Beneath the cloying stench of lilies, hidden beneath layers of artificial perfumes, I catch it. The salt-kissed brine of the sea, the warmth of sunlit skin damp with sweat.

Her.

My wrist burns as the magic in my veins responds, heat and cold colliding in the air around Olivia. I follow the disturbance to the guard standing behind her. Ice-blue eyes glow, trained on the back of her head. *Does he look familiar? Yes,* Jethro answers. *I can't place where, but... he's steadying her. He's trying to soothe.*

Lord Tierney's voice breaks into our thoughts. "Your Grace, what a beautiful affair. We are honored by your invitation." His lips curl in amusement. "Thank you for allowing my wife to attend on such short notice."

I feel sick.

Olivia's lashes flutter, the motion rapid, uncertain. With every flicker, her irises shift—light warring against shadow. Caomh's hand presses against my back as he works at the iron fortress in her mind. I close my eyes and feel the weight of stone walls, the suffocating abyss I once pulled her from. *Livy...* Caomh's voice is a whisper, a thread of longing.

Olivia remains silent. A silence so deep it aches. But then—

A flood of memories.

Olivia's head resting on my lap as laughter shakes our chests, the kind that leaves tears in our eyes. She gifts us each a memory: for Caomh, the time she chased out his ill-timed lover; for Jet, their quiet companionship in a candlelit cottage.

For me... the most sacred of all. Forehead to forehead, water lapping at our skin, the colored light of our mating bond shimmering between us.

And just as quickly as it comes, she shuts us out. The force of it is like a slap to the face.

Reality crashes down: Tierney's claws at her hip, his lips that had just been on hers.

But I feel it— *Behind the mask, Olivia is still there.*

I murmur my congratulations to Tierney, forcing my voice to remain even. Caomh intervenes before I lose control. "The dance floor has opened. Perhaps you should take your wives for a spin?"

"I think I will."

Tierney's talons tilt Olivia's chin. She gazes up at him, a devilish smile curving her lips. Dark affection spills from her, wrapping around him like a caress. The entire ballroom feels it. Tierney's golden eyes sparkle with satisfaction. He spins her away.

And then I see them. *The scars.* Three deep gouges raked across her back, marring the skin I once worshiped.

My body locks, held only by Caomh's restraint as Jethro casts an illusion to keep me composed. But inside— *I am unraveling.*

The mountains tremble. Lightning crackles through the room. The weight of my fury is a force of nature.

Tierney turns, his smirk nothing short of victorious. "Aren't they beautiful?" His claws trace the valley of her broken flesh, his chuckle a dagger of ice. "Little Olivia likes to play dirty."

I could snarl— But Olivia answers first, her laughter slicing through the air.

It grates against my skin, sharp and unnatural. *This is not the wind-chime melody that once roused me on the shores of our hidden cove. No—this is the wicked howl of a storm before the tempest strikes.*

We stand, frozen in place, as Tierney twirls her across the ballroom. His taloned fingers still play along the deep gouges marring her back, grazing over the sharp ridges of her spine. Her shoulder blades jut. Her collarbones carve stark shadows against pale skin.

Hollowed cheeks. Eyes that flicker with shadows. *There's nothing left of my love—nothing left of my mate.*

Desperation surges through me. I pulse my power, reaching for her with the only gift I have left. Healing light, delicate yet persistent, seeks to mend what's been broken. *Just one touch. One chance.*

Olivia's once-vibrant evergreen eyes flick to Caomh— Then lock onto mine.

And in that moment, something stirs. A silent command. *Fleeting—but unmistakable.*

My pulse thunders, hope a traitorous whisper against my ribs. *Olivia? Hummingbird, are you still there?* The words barely escape, thick with longing, with dread. I reach for the girl hidden behind stone walls, behind darkness and cold.

Then—her voice. Muffled. Weak. But hers.

Jeyr, I love you. I am sorry. I am so sorry. Please... forget about me. Keep our family safe. Please, keep them safe. I love you all, I love you—I will always love you.

The words tumble out in a rush, as if time itself is slipping through her fingers. *As if this is a farewell.*

No, Liv—please don't go! I roar, the sound shattering in my chest.

But it's too late.

Caomh fights beside me, battering against the wall of her mind. We push—desperate, unrelenting.

And then— Three deafening clicks.

Locks slamming into place.

And we are cast out into the silence.

I have never felt more like a failure than I do watching him take her away. They linger for only two dances, and yet in that brief time, Tierney never once releases his grip. Any attempt to steal her back would end in his blood soaking the ballroom floor.

And I am tempted—gods, I am tempted.

If not for my brothers' warnings of what such an act would mean for the Kingdom, for our family, I would do it without hesitation.

Killing Tierney would be treason. He commands the most formidable army, the strongest pillar of the Great King's rule.

I sit at my desk, head bowed. Powerless.

How do I save her? When her will is bound, when her mind is no longer her own? Is she lost to us? Or is there still a part of her that fights, buried beneath the weight of Tierney's influence?

"I— I don't know what I expected." Caomh's voice trembles, stripped of its usual authority. "I hoped she would open her mind, give us something—anything to work with. But... but..."

He trails off, no longer the commander I have always known. For the first time, he has no answers.

Lorkan steps forward, his hand finds the back of Caomh's neck, gripping firm but steady. Caomh doesn't lean into it, but I watch the tension ease, dissolving into the quiet comfort offered.

My throat tightens. I cannot bring myself to speak the truth aloud. To admit that I have lost her in more ways than one.

"There must be something more we can do," Jethro rumbles, his voice dark and resolute. He stands before the fire, his silhouette wreathed in flickering light. And yet, we all know the truth hidden within his words. He has simply spoken what the rest of us fear to acknowledge.

"You know I will keep trying, Jet." My voice is thick, barely restrained fury and despair entwined. "We are working on the alliance with Puinnsean. The moment I have a chance, that man is dead—but I will not risk your lives."

My chest burns with the effort to hold myself back, to resist the urge to storm that cursed kingdom and end every wretched soul who has dared harm her. But Olivia would never forgive me if I lost any of our family.

My brothers mean more to her than her own life.

And if I fail her now, she will return to nothing.

Not if—when.

"That is another matter we must address, Brother," Aella interjects, her voice as cold as the steel she wields. "She is an Empath. What she is doing... it is unheard of. What if she cannot be saved? What if we bring back nothing more than a shell of the woman she once was? How do we know we can trust her?"

A pause. Heavy. Suffocating.

"She loved him," Aella continues. "We all felt it. Yes, there were glimpses of the Olivia we knew, but what will be left in a month's time? In a year?"

Caomh straightens. Lorkan follows suit, his arm slipping around Caomh's shoulders—a quiet tether keeping his rage at bay. Jethro moves, joining them in silent support. The room shifts. Hecate crosses the divide, standing with my brothers, but the others drift to Aella's side.

A split. A divide. Two forces waiting for me to answer.

And for the first time, I have none.

I bow my head, shame curling around me like a noose.

Hecate breaks the silence first.

"Her mother used manipulation to ensnare her father's love. There are loopholes, lines many Empaths dare not cross because their law forbids it." Her voice is measured, revealing knowledge that sends a hush over the room. "But when Olivia's mother was the last of her kind, the laws lost their weight. Her consort was clever and found a way to twist them, to make them work in her favor without shattering her soul. She healed a man too broken to love and made him fall for his savior. Olivia... she may have found another loophole. As long as she does not harm or kill, her soul will remain intact."

We all flinch.

Aella counters, sharp as a blade.

"She has killed. Men in the army who tried to capture her—she made their hearts stop.

How do we know that wasn't the beginning? A true Empath would have died in their pain. Isn't that their law?"

Hecate stills.

"She isn't pure," she murmurs. The words carry the weight of a revelation.

Aella's expression darkens.

"Then she can be corrupted. If this is all an act, she has done the unimaginable—made the devil himself fall in love. At what cost? You know what his kind is capable of. Love is not in their nature. Right now, she is his weapon. You think we can save her? We are fools. She has delivered the very thing that will destroy us."

Caomh lunges. Lorkan's grip holds him steady, murmuring soft words that tether his fury. I turn away, allowing them that moment.

I rise from my chair, my voice a quiet storm.

"Who among us is pure? Who has not killed for what they love? We have all been villains. And if Olivia chooses to be one, then I will stand beside her. If this is what keeps her alive, then so be it. Have I made myself clear?"

The storm rages on around me, but I watch as Aella—and those who stand by her—bow to me.

"I know this does not ease all your concerns, but for now, we have no choice but to push forward. We must get her back—get what you call a weapon out of their hands. Then we can worry about who she has become. We are fortunate to have each other, to wield some of the strongest powers on this land. We must stand together and use them wisely."

"Right... like the Mind Master who cannot even control Lord Tierney and Olivia himself," Aella sneers.

Caomh flinches, but Lorkan roars.

"That is enough, Aella! It was us who pulled you from that wretched kingdom. It was Caomh who slaughtered that heathen you called a husband. Show some respect! Your brother and Grand Duke has spoken: we are to capture the Empath and bring her back to her family—just as we did with you. And like you, she will need to know she has love and support when she returns."

Lorkan steps before Caomh, finger outstretched toward my sister, eyes blazing with warning. Caomh's fingers flex at his hip, while Jethro moves to place a firm hand on his shoulder. Aella inhales sharply, dips into a curt bow, and strides from the room.

Yet the tension in her shoulders tells me this conversation is far from over.

"We await your command, Grand Duke," Aiden declares as he lowers himself into a bow. "We will stand by you and your Companach, as we stood by your brothers in the war."

He then turns and exits, Michael and his wife following close behind.

Althea lingers only long enough to embrace me in silence before slipping from the chamber.

Yet despite their pledges, I feel the growing divide between us—a rift too deep to mend with mere words.

Caomh moves toward the drink stand by the fire, yanking the whiskey decanter from its place. Without ceremony, he lifts it to his lips, golden liquid spilling over his white shirt. With a growl, he slams the bottle down.

"Fuck this stupid, fucking shirt!"

With one vicious motion, he tears the fabric apart, buttons scattering against the library walls. The ruined cloth flies into the flames, consumed in an instant.

Lorkan is behind him in a breath, his frame curving protectively around Caomh's as he rests his forehead against his shoulder. Caomh exhales sharply, fingers tightening around the decanter before he takes another long pull. Lorkan whispers something—something only meant for him. Slowly, Caomh's heaving breaths begin to steady, his shoulders settling beneath the weight of exhaustion.

Wordlessly, he gathers glasses, pouring each of us a drink. He moves from Lorkan's side, handing them out, his movements precise, controlled. And yet, I do not miss the way Lorkan's eyes never leave him—a silent guardian in the dim light.

Once finished, Lorkan takes his place in the wingback chair, watching, waiting.

Caomh stands before the flames, shirtless, the firelight casting flickering shadows over his scarred skin. Lifting his glass in a solemn salute, he declares,

"To Olivia: our princess, our huntress. May you keep fighting this battle and return only when that bastard's head rolls at your feet. If anyone can do it, you can."

We all bow our heads and raise our glasses. The resounding chorus of "Here, here" rings through the chamber before we tip back the honeyed liquor.

I do not miss that he has poured Olivia's favorite whiskey.

As I swallow, I savor the taste that once lingered on her lips and send a silent prayer to any god that will listen.

Bring our woman home.

Olivia

The Poisonous Wasp

My body senses the energy in the room before the whispered warning stirs my dreams. Darkness pulses around me, thick and suffocating. The night of the ball, I lock myself away in the depths of Tierney's domain, bound by three locks and shadowed walls. As I lie in the abyss, I surrender to it.

When I severed Jeyr and my family from my mind, I knew— *I couldn't* play both roles any longer. My soul burns, fire licking through my veins, punishing me for the deception. The only way to endure the agony is to lock my light away and embrace the fate of Lady Tierney.

"My lady…" The serpent's voice slithers into my thoughts, forked tongue flickering through the fog.

My lashes flutter open, revealing Tierney at the edge of my bed, those consuming, predatory eyes assessing me.

A wicked grin curls my lips. "My love."

Tierney's fangs flash as he returns my smile, his own dripping with possessiveness. He leans in, biting my lower lip hard enough to draw blood. I nip back, tasting the coppery tang as our blood mingles.

"Colden, close the door and grant us privacy," Tierney commands, his voice a deep rattle that sends ice down my spine. *A sound of death. A sound of warning.*

Colden's glance flicks toward me—so quick even Tierney doesn't notice.

Forcing a playful giggle, I let Tierney claim me. I give him my screams, both of pleasure and pain, until his hunger is sated. As he collapses against me, breath ragged, I envision a dagger in my grip, driving it deep into his back.

But no blade lies within my reach, and so I dig my nails into his flesh instead, drawing crimson lines across his pallid skin.

"I have trained you well," he growls, biting my lip once more before pulling away.

I prop myself on my elbow, watching as he dresses. His body—gaunt, ghostly—is a stark contrast to... someone else. *Even still, I've become adept at making him desire me.*

He hesitates, glancing back with a look of raw possession.

"I have a present for you."

"A present?" Even as an Empath, I can't hide my curiosity.

"Mmhmm. We're going on an excursion."

My pulse quickens. *An excursion?*

Tierney's sinister smile widens.

"Yes. I'll have the servant bring your attire. Be ready within the hour."

He steps closer, taloned fingers tilting my chin up with enough force to break skin. Blood trickles down my throat as he whispers,

"See you soon, my love."

It feels more like a warning than a promise.

I wait until the door clicks shut before dragging myself from the bed, storming into the washroom. The bathwater roars as I slam the door hard enough to rattle the walls.

Colden is there when I turn to the mirror. He leans against the closed door, arms crossed.

"Didn't you get the message with the slammed door?" Venom laces my words.

Colden doesn't flinch. His gaze, cool and relentless, traces the bruises and scratches on my bare skin.

"I got the message. I chose to ignore it."

I exhale sharply. "What do you want, Colden? I have to get ready."

"How far are you willing to take this? Because it's working. But Tierney isn't done testing you. Can you handle it, Olivia? Or should we make another plan? Because... you're scaring me."

I smirk darkly. "Good. Be scared, Colden."

He growls, stepping closer, his broad frame casting a shadow over me.

"I'm not scared of you, Olivia. I've seen worse monsters than whatever you think you've become. But I *am* scared for you. If there ever comes a moment when you can't handle this, you need to tell me. I won't stand by and watch you destroy yourself. The whole point of this is to get out."

I bite the inside of my cheek, swallowing the knot in my throat.

"I will fight until my last breath to get out of here, Colden. I'm in this."

It's a bluff, and we both know it. My bravado holds steady, but beneath it, uncertainty coils in my chest. I don't know if I'll make it out of this mess. But I'm damaged enough—and maybe even crazy enough—to keep going.

Colden studies me for a long moment, then gives a slow nod.

"Good. Because today is a big day. I don't know what he has planned, but we're going to the military grounds."

A cold wave of unease crashes over me.

In the wrong hands, she is a weapon.

The words slither through my mind, leaving an oily, sick feeling in their wake. Suddenly, the idea of leaving the mansion doesn't seem so thrilling after all.

For once, I am warm.

The armor fits as if it's been made for me—the scaled corset strapped tightly over a thick woolen top, molded to my frame like a second skin. Battle-ready. That's what I look like. That's what I *have* to be. As much as I despise the idea of walking into Puinnsean's infamous military grounds, I have to admit—they do not cut corners when it comes to design.

"Mm, Lady Tierney, you wear the armor of our people to perfection."

I spin, letting him take me in, my smile matching his, my movements practiced, effortless.

"This," I hum, running my gloved hands over the fitted metal, "I could get used to."

Tierney's hand snaps out, his grip firm as he pulls me flush against him. His fangs graze the outer shell of my ear, a possessive whisper against my skin.

"That is music to my ears. Let me show you the present I got you."

Before I can react, the air shifts, my body dissolving into nothingness for the briefest moment before reforming elsewhere. The walls of the mansion vanish in an instant, replaced by the cutting winds and jagged cliffs of Puinnsean's mountain ranges. Wind lashes against my face as I take in the vast landscape below, stretching endlessly in every direction.

And there, moving in perfect ranks beneath us, is Tierney's army.

Thousands of bodies, shifting in seamless, precise formation. A force unlike anything I've ever seen.

But these are not men.

A sick feeling curls in my gut, my pulse tightening as recognition strikes like a blade between my ribs. *The same disfigured beings that stormed my cottage. The ones that tore through my family, left blood smeared across my home, turned my world to ruin.*

For a fleeting second, an image of Cooper's lifeless body flickers in my mind, a memory so vivid it makes me reel. I shove it down, forcing my mind to lock it away before Tierney can pry it from me.

"So, you remember them?" His voice is warm, indulgent, but the pressure of his presence in my mind is immediate. His talons slide through my thoughts, brushing against my barriers, seeking entry.

I let him catch the faintest hint of my unease. *Let him think he has the upper hand.*

"These Humanoids are of our own creation," he continues, a flicker of pride curling in his tone. "A perfect blend of human and goblin. Completely under my command. But because of them, I hurt you."

I stiffen, a single breath lodging in my throat.

The words should mean something. They should feel like an apology.

But when I turn to him, his expression remains unreadable. His smile sharp. His golden eyes alight with something cruel and knowing.

He takes my hand in his gloved one, leading me forward as if I am a queen being escorted to her throne— Down the steep granite staircase that descends into the army below.

The drop is dizzying. I focus ahead, forcing my steps to remain steady. When we reach the flat, open ground, I feel small beneath the weight of thousands of eyes shifting toward us. The Humanoids turn as one, their empty, soulless faces angled toward their master—waiting, unblinking—for his command.

"Bring me the hostages," Tierney orders, his voice a lazy drawl. "And let Bane know we have arrived."

Two creatures at the front bow their heads before disappearing into the cavernous mouth of a cave on the far side of the training grounds.

My pulse spikes.

Tierney is watching me, assessing every flicker of emotion I try to hide. I feel his curiosity, his anticipation.

He doesn't want me to fail whatever test this is.

I steel myself— *Because neither do I.*

Figures emerge from the cave, moving in slow, measured steps. My breath hitches. I pray to the gods I've long since abandoned.

Let it not be someone I know. Let it not be my family.

The Humanoids part, and from their ranks, Bane strides forward—a predator among his own. And behind him, shackled, are three Humanoids and a tall, slim man with auburn hair.

I exhale. Too soon. Too relieved.

"My wife," Tierney muses, stepping closer, his voice all silken pleasure. "These men have all wronged you in some way."

Before I can ask how, the memories hit.

The three Humanoids in my cottage. The sound of my family screaming. The scent of burning flesh.

Then—something else. Something worse.

I'm not seeing through my own eyes anymore. I recognize the scene immediately, but this time, I'm looking through someone else's mind.

The auburn-haired Fae.

I see what he sees. *My own body beneath him. My eyes black voids. My face contorted in pain.*

I see the blade slice into my skin. Watch my blood bead over the wound.

I feel it.

I recoil, nausea clawing up my throat— Tierney tears the images away.

A small mercy. A calculated one.

His hand slides to the back of my neck, his breath warm at my ear, deceptively soft.

"They tried to murder your friends," he murmurs, his grip tightening. "They tried to murder you."

The Humanoids remain motionless, mindless puppets standing at attention. But the Fae at their side—he is smirking.

Arrogance pours from him in waves, his emotions curling around me like smoke. *He doesn't believe I'll harm him. He doesn't even consider it a possibility.* To him, I'm nothing more than a bee—capable of a single sting, of a final act of defiance before my own destruction.

"Exactly, my wife."

Tierney's voice slides through my mind, coaxing, patient, expectant.

He thinks you are your own worst enemy. But you are different. You are not weak like your ancestors. You are strong, powerful. Show him how you will kill the Humanoids without crumbling. Show him you are my poisonous wasp—one who can sting and sting and still remain standing.

The command is light. Nothing more than a whisper. A suggestion. A test.

He wants to see if I'll **choose** it on my own. But what choice do I have?

I don't let myself think.

The wind howls through the mountains, sharp and unrelenting, but I barely feel it. My focus locks on the first Humanoid, my power already unfurling toward him like invisible smoke, curling around his mind, pressing into his subconscious.

The moment it touches him, I feel his essence— An existence forged in violence, built on raw aggression and the hunger to conquer. He has only ever known strength, only ever been permitted to feel invincible.

I throw panic at him.

A flood of it—drawn from the deepest, most desperate parts of my own memories. Moments when fear had gripped me so tightly my lungs refused to work. When my body betrayed me. When I felt the walls of my own mind closing in with no escape.

The Humanoid's massive hand flies to his throat. His breath hitches—shallow, gasping—his mind now drowning in a fear he has never known. His heartbeat thunders, too fast, too wild. He chokes on it, his body betraying him, his nerves screaming as though his very survival is slipping through his fingers.

I imagine his thoughts as they tumble through his frenzied mind. *I cannot breathe. I cannot fight. I am dying.*

His grotesque, twisted face contorts, his features cracking under the pressure of the terror I feed him. He staggers, and a strangled, gurgled sound crawls from his throat as he falls to his knees, clawing at his chest, trying to stop his own demise.

But panic is a merciless killer. It only feeds itself— *A serpent swallowing its own tail, spiraling out of control.*

One final gasp— Then silence.

His body crumples, his head lolling to the side, lifeless.

Only then do I look at the Fae standing before me—the one whose blade once carved into my flesh.

I tilt my head, watching him, letting my lips curl just slightly.

"One," I say softly. "Panic."

I turn my gaze to the second Humanoid.

This time, I give him pain.

There is no silent, gasping collapse. Instead, the creature screams.

A wretched, unrelenting wail that rings through the mountains, vibrating off the granite walls. A sound that sends ripples of unease through the ranks of warriors standing behind him. His body twists, his nerves set alight in agony, the muscles in his arms jerking violently as though they are being burned from the inside out.

His screams turn ragged, breathless— Until they're suddenly cut off, the sheer weight of suffering too much for his body to endure.

His limbs seize one final time before he slumps forward, dead.

"Two," I murmur, my voice calm, almost detached. "Pain."

The Fae's eyes dart between me and Tierney, then flick to Bane— As if either of them would intervene. As if either of them would put an end to this.

But Tierney stands beside me, unmoving.

Pride pulses from him in thick waves, his pleasure rolling off him like a fog, saturating the space between us.

I lift my hand to the third Humanoid and pull—not from my own pain, but from the fear of the crowd behind me.

I take the shifting, creeping uncertainty, the unease that trickles through the gathered soldiers, the paranoia that none of them will leave this place alive. And I shove it into him.

His body stiffens. His eyes dart wildly, searching for threats that do not exist. His limbs twitch. His breath stutters as he gasps, spinning in circles, his hands coming up as if to protect himself from an invisible enemy.

I watch him unravel, his mind turning against itself, drowning in a terror of its own making. He stumbles back, lips parting in a strangled cry, a desperate plea to be freed from the monsters only he can see.

A moment later, his heart fails. His body shudders once before collapsing unceremoniously to the ground.

"Three," I say, my gaze settling on the Fae at the center of it all. "Paranoia."

I step toward him slowly. He flinches.

His manacles rattle as he instinctively tries to retreat, but there's nowhere to go. I reach out, letting my fingers trail under his chin.

His body shudders beneath my touch. My power curls into him like smoke, slipping beneath his skin, flooding his veins.

"What is your name?" I ask, my voice a mere whisper.

His throat bobs as he swallows, his Adam's apple pressing against my fingertip. His pupils dilate, his breath coming fast and uneven. He hesitates, debating whether to answer.

"Tell my wife who you are," Tierney commands.

The Fae jolts, and his name tumbles from his lips in a rush. "Djinn."

I let the name settle in my mind before tilting my head.

"Well, Djinn, what emotion will you feel on your last breath?"

His lips part, panic flashing in his gaze. "Mercy," he rasps. "Please, show mercy."

I hum, feigning contemplation.

Where was your mercy when you tried cutting my soul from my chest? When you poisoned me?

"I'm sorry!" he gasps. "I'm sorry!"

I step back, watching him. "It's too late to be sorry."

This time, I don't need to pull from my own pain. I give him sorrow.

I reach into the depths of my power, into the memory of every loss I've ever known, every ache, every regret, every moment of helplessness that left me shattered and hollow. I take all of it and feed it into him, wrapping his mind in unbearable pity.

His shoulders hunch. His face crumples. He sinks to his knees, sobbing, his body convulsing with the weight of grief, of loss, of something missing he will never get back. I watch as his breath hitches, his eyes roll back, his muscles twitching in a final, useless attempt to fight off the inevitable.

His nose bleeds. Then his body collapses in a heap, blood pooling against the stone beneath him.

Silence follows. Not a whisper. Not a breath.

I feel every eye on me, waiting, watching.

But I do not tremble. I do not weep. I do not crumble beneath the weight of what I've done.

I only stand there, power pouring from me like an unstoppable tide.

I feel Tierney's pleasure at my display, feel the way he drinks it in—his satisfaction wrapping around me like a possessive, suffocating caress.

His lips brush against my neck.

"You are a beautiful, monstrous, murderous little creature," he murmurs, his voice thick with reverence. "You and I will show the world that no one dares to cross an Empath. We will prove that you don't need every power of the Courts to rule. You only need to control the mind."

I nod once, feeling the warmth of his breath against my throat.

"I hope you liked your present," he continues, his fingers digging into my waist. "Your power, your wrath, your hunger for revenge—it excites me in more ways than one. Go home with Colden. I will meet you in bed."

I feel the cold touch of another hand against my shoulder.

I turn just enough to catch a glimpse of Colden's expressionless face, his eyes revealing nothing as he reaches for me.

And then the world vanishes once more— Leaving behind the place where I have just been declared a monster.

I stand in Tierney's bedchamber, the air thick with silence, my gaze locked onto Colden's unreadable expression. The General's face is a mask, but I can feel the tension coiling beneath his skin.

"Colden..."

"You did what you had to do. You passed his test."

His voice is void of emotion, yet the undercurrent of displeasure hums beneath his words. He's uncomfortable in my presence.

I swallow, my throat tight. "I told you I was a monster."

Colden exhales sharply. His cold, blue eyes search mine—not with accusation, but with something softer. Concern.

"You had no other choice," he says at last. "Am I wondering why you made it such a show? Yes, I am. But in the end, those men wronged you. Tierney needed to believe you were the Empath he wishes to call his wife. My concern is that you believe yourself a monster. And I'm praying you have some kind of plan to get out of here. Because if your survival depends on becoming that monster—on staying her—then I am concerned."

I turn away. "I don't want to be her," I admit, my voice barely above a whisper. "I have to be her. If I stop to think about what this is doing to me, I'll break. I have a plan, but I only have one chance. I need more information before I move. And I need to make sure Tierney doesn't catch on."

Colden's jaw tightens, but after a moment, he gives a curt nod. "Fine."

"Fine," I echo.

He moves to take his post. I watch him for a breath before sending a slow, deliberate wave of exhaustion his way. Colden yawns, shaking his head, but the weight of sleep begins to press against him. I lie on the bed, sending another pulse through his bloodstream—gentle, coaxing. His body betrays him, sinking against the wall, his features softening as sleep claims him.

"I'm sorry."

With measured steps, I slip out of the chamber, past the softly snoring guards. I know better than to attempt an escape—not yet. Without the ability to winnow, I'm too slow. Canetta warned me about the wards, how they would alert Tierney the moment someone enters or leaves the mansion.

The risk isn't worth it. Not yet.

Instead, I move toward the office. The room smells of ink and parchment, its massive desk buried beneath a chaotic sprawl of documents—maps, schematics, torn pages from books. I comb through them, searching for something, anything, that could tip the balance in my favor.

My vision blurs with fatigue, and with a sigh, I shut the heavy tome in my hands, sliding it back into place.

The bookshelves stretch floor to ceiling, their spines whispering history beneath my fingertips. I trace them idly, my senses half-lost in the scent of aged leather and dust—until my hand stills over a thin, unmarked journal. Something about it pulls at me, something old and familiar.

I tip it forward— A soft pop splits the silence.

Light glimmers at the edge of my vision.

A pulse of energy crashes over me, unmistakable, like the pull of the tide calling me home. My body moves on instinct, drawn to the secret that has unfurled before me. The bookshelf shifts beneath my touch, revealing a passage, a hidden chamber aglow with flickering sconces.

I step inside— And my breath catches.

Paintings. Everywhere.

Memories spill across the walls, each stroke of color holding a piece of me. My own face stares back— Younger. Softer. Curls wild and untamed, green eyes alight with devotion. And beside it—

A sharp inhale stings my lungs.

It's a painting I made a decade ago. My outstretched hand. Ness's hot breath misting against my palm the night she came to me.

I turn, overwhelmed, drinking in the silent ghosts of my past. Some I remember. Some I don't.

But then— *Her.*

A woman of golden beauty.

She watches over me from her frame, the same way she did in the small portrait that hung in my childhood home. The warmth in her painted eyes stirs something deep inside me, a love so absolute it unravels me where I stand.

The plaque beneath her frame reads only: **Lady Tierney.**

My stomach lurches.

I stumble back, my heel catching on something uneven. The tile beneath me shifts, loose under my weight. I curse, glancing down just as something metallic glints beneath the floorboards.

A box. Rusted and forgotten, its edges peeking from the darkness.

My pulse hammers. I cast a wary glance around, though I am alone. Slowly, I reach into the gap, fingers curling around cool metal, dragging it free.

Is this a trap?

I swallow hard, giving the room one last lingering look. I don't know when I'll see it again.

Tucking the box against my chest, I slip back through the hidden door, closing it behind me.

I move quickly, retracing my steps, climbing the stairs two at a time until I'm back in the bedchamber. The fire crackles low in the hearth, its golden light flickering against Colden's sleeping form.

I exhale, sagging to the floor, my back pressed against the bed frame. He looks softer like this— His face free of the burdens he carries.

A small, tired smile ghosts my lips.

Then, finally, I turn my attention to the box.

It's no larger than a shoebox, rusted beyond recognition, its once-decorative etchings worn to nothing but faint ridges.

I pry it open—

The scent of chamomile and rosemary hits me like a spell of comfort and sorrow intertwined.

A shuddering breath leaves me as I reach inside.

The parchments are old, delicate beneath my fingertips, whispering secrets long buried.

With shaking hands, I sift through them— Until I reach the very last letter at the bottom.

Clarity,

I have been captured. Don't search for me, my love. War is here. I have been taken to the battle grounds. My captor... he has me doing things, things that no longer make me the woman you fell in love with. Please keep your kind safe. Do not come to the Great Kingdom. Please, my love. Please, keep my boy safe.

You will forever be in my heart, forever in my soul.

Avery.

My Avery.

I fear this is all my fault. I fought our love, and now I can't breathe. I feel the torture you are going through; I feel your pain. I feel everything you do under my skin, and my powers are useless against our bond. I am stuck living in the past, trying to hold onto your smiles, your laughter... your touch. When you came to me, I was shocked about how my attraction didn't let go of you. One look into the golden hue of your eyes and I was tied, tied between my duty as Queen and my duties as a woman. I had always dreamed of meeting my equal, my mate, bringing more Empaths into this world—and you came in and shattered everything. Yet, you never gave up on me. For months, years you kept coming, kept tormenting me with your beauty and your ability to see beneath the surface. You eased the weight of too many emotions on my shoulders. I didn't realize how long I lived with the inability to really breathe; how heavy I had become with the woes of others. You knew though, and damn it Avery, you touched me and had me begging on my knees for you to stay. I needed you, and selfishly, I couldn't let you go. Then Gods, you kissed me. And I knew then the fates were not playing games. I knew there would never be another. If you think I am going to stand idly while my mate is tortured, you don't know me at all my love.

Ps: Your boy is safe, back behind Kingdom walls. Our Queen has protected him, but I fear with the war his birth father will call him back.

I am coming for you.

Forever yours,

Clarity

Clarity,

I feared as much. If he comes to his homeland, as much as it pains me, do not come with him. It's not safe. The Great King is feeling insecure. There is a war between cross breeds and pure breeds. The King fears not being the one with true power. Empaths are not safe. Please my love, stay with the Queen, better yet run, hide, disappear. The only thing keeping me alive is knowing you are safe and well.

And remember, our love story is magic, your hesitance and all. Never forget it, I wouldn't change a moment of trying to claim you as mine.

Stay safe, stay away.

Forever in love with you,

Avery

LETTERS AND LESSONS

A *very,*

I don't know if this will get to you. It's been months and with the seasons changing, there has been a shift here at the Queen's Kingdom. I feel you still my love, and I am worried, it seems stupid to ask if you are okay, because I can feel that you're not. Who has you? What's happening? I hate feeling so blind!

I have noticed more King's people at the ports, I have warned the Queen, begged for the trades to stop. But my cries haven't been heard.

Your son is now back at Gliocas. I worry for him. I hate feeling so helpless.

Please, please give me some line to hold onto.

Your devoted,

Clarity

Avery

Please tell me you are alive. Something has happened to the bond, Gods the pain I felt when my connection to you had some disturbance. You are there, but so far away, like another force has tried to take over.

Please, please be okay. I am not functioning over here.

My kind are going missing. I have lost two families, and I fear for their wellbeing. I am stuck between my duty as

Queen, protecting my own, and needing you, my love. I fear with my Companach so far away I am getting weak.

Your devoted,

Clarity

My Devoted

I am so sorry.

I don't know how to put this in words, but I am married. I am with child again. All I can feel is how I have betrayed you. This man's powers are so much stronger than mine. He is a Mind Master, but his strength is nearly that of the Grand Duke of Gliocas. From what I have gathered is the Duke of Puinnsean adopted him. He was a bastard child, and he has been groomed to be the leader of the armies. The way they treat these beautiful beasts Clarity... It makes me hate my kind even more.

There is more, I found your Empaths...

I promise you I refused, I refused to control them. They... They are no longer alive. The Duke and my Husband, Lord Tierney, they made them do unspeakable things. They cleared battlefields my love. I feel sick in saying they didn't even kill the aggressors— it was innocent soldiers that fell on that field.

Please run. Take the Empaths and run. The Great King has used this to fuel a second war, a war against anyone who isn't from this land, anyone who is different... Companachs for their combined strength... They cannot know what we are together, please I beg you.

Forever yours,

Avery

I read the words through the splattered stains of aged tears, their sorrow bleeding through the parchment. Agony clings to every stroke of ink, every desperate plea etched between the lines. My fingers tremble as I pinch the bridge of my nose, tilting my face to the heavens as if I can send their souls a silent prayer.

So many questions have been answered. And yet, *I only crave more.*

The urge to devour the remaining letters burns inside me, but the soft rustle of movement behind me shatters my focus.

Colden stirs.

Heart pounding, I hurriedly gather the pages, tucking them back into the rusted tin before sliding it beneath the bed.

The room settles once more.

Then I dream.

The bones of my face press further into his touch. His fingers are cool against my fevered skin, trailing reverent paths down my neck. My mouth parts on a slow exhale, breath slipping into the stillness of the chamber.

He stands over my sleeping body. He doesn't know I'm aware.

His touch sends shivers rippling beneath my skin, the ghost of his nails leaving raised, red scratches in their wake. The thick covers shift, peeled away with aching deliberation. My body, bared beneath his hunger, arches in response.

He leans down, breath ghosting over my chest before his mouth closes over me.

A gasp slips from my lips. My lashes flutter, but I don't wake. Not truly. His command pulses through my mind, whisper-soft yet absolute. *His name falls from my lips, unbidden.*

The air in the room thickens, the energy shifting—charged and electric.

I become reactive.

My hand rises to my throat, fingers curling, tightening. My breath hitches as my own grasp becomes my prison. He watches, fascinated, as my nails bite crescents into my skin, as blood blooms in thin, delicate rivulets.

His name leaves my lips once more.

A growl rumbles in his chest, dark and possessive, his will woven into the very air around me.

He doesn't need to take me to claim me— No. He wants something else. Wants to unravel me with nothing but thought, his presence in my mind a touch more intimate than flesh.

I gasp. I shudder.

And still, his grip over me does not waver. Even as I come undone beneath his will.

"Tierney?"

I look down at him, my fingers threading through the short strands of his hair. Then I pull—hard. Hard enough that my nails, still sharp from where they raked my own skin, drag him against my lips.

He comes willingly, unable to break from my spell. His hands brace my face, his gaze locks onto mine as he feels it— The strum of raw energy. Lust. Power. Submission.

A groan tears from his throat as he lies beneath me, eyes glazed, body humming with need.

"I missed you," I murmur, pressing my palm against his chest, feeling the wild thrum of his heartbeat. *And somewhere, beneath the fire curling in my veins, I think how little I would care if that heart stopped beating altogether.*

The letters echo in my mind, whispering truths I cannot forget. *What he did to my mother's Companach. What he's doing to me now.*

"You have no idea how good that is to hear, Lady Tierney," he murmurs against my neck.

A shiver curls through me—though not from desire.

"I had a dream while you were gone." My breath fans over his skin, warm, coaxing.

He pulls back just enough to meet my eyes. "Show me," he demands, his voice edged with something close to desperation.

"Close your eyes." I whisper the command against his lips.

He obeys.

His breathing hitches, his heart hammering harder against my palm. His trust is absolute.

I slip into his mind, weaving the vision he craves— The future he longs for, painted in seductive, aching detail.

The King's throne. The stained glass behind it, gleaming with the colors of the Kingdoms.

He sits upon the throne, his rightful place, his triumph absolute. And I—his queen—am draped across his lap, our bodies bare but for the crowns upon our heads. Mine smaller than his, because I belong to him. Because I am his Queen, and he is the King.

The world watches. The Kingdoms bear witness.

He fucks me there, loves me there, makes me his in sight of all. It is his greatest fantasy, his deepest desire.

And in this vision, *I let him believe I want it too.*

The dream shatters.

With a ragged breath, he grabs me, twisting my face toward him with enough force to bruise—just shy of snapping my neck.

His pupils are blown wide, his expression wrecked with ecstasy. "I love you, Lady Tierney."

I let my lips curve into a smile that matches his own. "I love you too, Lord Tierney. You ready to take on the world?"

His grip tightens around my throat, fingers pressing just enough to make me feel the weight of his control.

"With you, my love," he rasps, "we will rule the world."

Olivia

CHAINS UNSEEN

Colden's emotions paint the walls outside the chamber, his presence a quiet storm as he waits. *Waiting for Tierney to leave.* But Tierney has no such intention.

He holds me close, his nails tracing the ridges of my spine with a collector's reverence—like a man worshiping his most treasured artifact. I'm not just another butterfly pinned to his wall— *I'm the one he keeps under glass. Locked beneath a spell of his making. Meant to be his forever.*

I rest my head against his bony chest, fingers idly trailing the erratic beats of his heart. It jumps and skips beneath my touch, fragile, like a bird in a snare. My ribbons of power curl around it, tightening, coaxing, feeding the illusion that it's growing stronger under my spell.

"Bane was impressed by your display."

"Does that mean I'll be allowed more excursions?" I coo, my voice sweet, hopeful. *Let your weapon out to play,* I pray.

Tierney hums in approval. "Mmhmm. There's a little test we'd like to try your powers on. There's unrest brewing between the Court's factions. Whispers of impure Fae bloodlines—rebels who've built an army. Our informants say they're heading toward The Black Forest, between Puinnsean and the Great Kingdom. The King wants us to investigate."

I feign excitement, forcing light into my expression, though deep inside, that quiet, thrumming fear whispers. *What will I have to do to earn my freedom?*

I shift against him, tilting my chin to meet his gaze. Lust flickers there, hunger simmering beneath the surface.

"What's the test?"

"First, I need them all captivated long enough for me to get into their heads. I need to know what powers they possess. Then I'll tell you what comes next."

My fingertip traces his lower lip. "Why do we need to know their power?"

"We need to determine whether they acquired it or were born with it—or if they've figured out how to steal it from others. That's been quite the problem. It's unnatural, unjust. A Fae shouldn't have powers from different Courts. It's dangerous for the peace of our world."

I stay silent, waiting. Letting him keep talking.

And he does.

"A long time ago, a Fae—much like the Djinn—discovered how to kill and keep a soul. A cruel fate, even for our kind. A pure Fae, slaughtered in the name of power." His voice dips lower, something darker coiling beneath his words.

"He murdered my first wife. She was a Mind Master like me. But it wasn't just her soul he wanted—he was collecting them. Binding them to himself. He used magic not of this land, merging her essence with an Empath's inside this glove."

He flexes his fingers, the faint shimmer of embedded power pulsing beneath the leather.

I exhale slowly, my gaze flicking to the artifact.

"And you made him put it on you."

Tierney smirks, proud. "I commanded him to. Bound the souls to my blood instead. I can't feel as an Empath does, can't taste emotions unless I'm inside a mind, but their essence has strengthened me. Heightened my control."

Realization curls through me like smoke. *So that's why this*— I motion between us, *the unbearable weight of our connection—feels so strong.*

Tierney laughs softly, leaning in.

"This feels strong, my love, because we are meant to be. We are stronger. But with this power—yours, mine, and theirs"—he gestures to the souls bound in his veins—"together, we will destroy those who threaten the purity of our kind. Kill those who stand in the way of us ruling everything."

I let a wicked smile bloom across my lips. "When do we leave?"

A pleased hum vibrates from his chest. "Mmm, you speak my love language. Get that sexy uniform on. We leave before dusk."

Olivia

LETTERS OF LOVE, TARNISHED BY LOSS

A*very*

I am holding onto the threads of our memories, hanging onto the curves of your letters like I once held onto the curves of your body. I can't help but wonder if they are still the same, or if they have changed over time. What I would give to map every part of you once more. This is the only thing I am holding onto, because that is the only lightness in my life. Our plan, our child is not what we thought, I can't do this without you. Her emotions are so human, so uncontrolled. She doesn't have the repercussions like my kind of how she hurts people with her power. I've raised so many children, supported so many mothers and none of them are like her. I fear my own child. She loves more, she angers more, she is so testy. I need you, so much, I feel if she had you, you could control the side of her I can't.

I feel like I am failing you, my love.

Your devoted,

Clarity

My love, my Clarity

I know the lack of control scares you sweetheart. That fire in her blood, that lack of control is what will set her apart in this war. Follow your instincts. Train her mind more than you train her empathic power. Make her conceal who she is for as long as possible, then slowly show her how to use it.

You can never fail me,

I have held onto the memory of our touches. I still remember the taste of your lips. You are the only reason I have not given up, this life I live... I have never felt so weak. The child I have raised is just as bad as his father, but he is unpredictable with his emotions. I am not sure what I fear most, him or his sociopath father. I have failed as a mother twice over. As long as your child is good, kind, and loyal to you, and to those who matter, you could never be a failure.

Forever yours,

Avery.

My beloved Avery,

Your first child is a stoic young man. He is kind and loyal to those who matter. I have kept my eye on him from a distance and he has a good group of men and women in his corner. He holds his emotions too tight to his chest, and it holds him back. But he is a good man, and that is everything to do with having you as a role model. I see so much of you in him. I think I watch him just to feel closer to you. He has your eyes, your hair, and when he relaxes, your smile. I am sad to say he doesn't do that very often. I wish I could do more than watch from a distance, but I know for the safety of us all I can only watch and hope for the best.

Please stay strong, I can feel you fading.

Your devoted,

Clarity

Clarity

I can't do this anymore. I can't live in this world. It's not safe for you If I live anymore. Forgive me. Tell my boy I love him, and tell our little girl that I love her, and wish I could have met her. Raise her to be the warrior I know she can be.

I love you.

I am sorry.

Goodbye.

Avery.

Tierney lies asleep beside me, thickly woven under my power, his breaths deep and steady as I read the last of the letters from the box. Tears blur the ink, slipping silently down my cheeks.

A week before my mother's death, the last letter had been sent. Her final words, scrawled in hurried, desperate script: **I am coming for you.**

She tried to save her Companach. And in a way, *she did*. Their souls now bound together, entwined for eternity—blood-tied to the very man who tore them apart.

A shuddering breath leaves me.

For the first time, I understand her.

I understand the distance in her eyes, the way love and grief hollowed her out. Why she never looked at me the way I had longed for. Why I spent my life desperately trying to grasp the fragments of affection she could spare.

I wasn't what she wanted.

I was the void left in the absence of the love she lost.

I was their last hope.

And I walked straight into the same trap.

A deep, crawling itch spreads beneath my skin, my magic coiling, restless. Ready to fight.

I clench my hands into fists. Close my eyes. *Not yet. It's not time yet.*

My breathing steadies.

I move to shut the box, but my fingers hesitate. A worn patch at the bottom catches my attention, distinct from the rest of the rusted metal. My thumb brushes over it, feeling the faintest shift beneath the surface.

A false bottom.

Carefully, I press into the mark, and the metal lifts—just a millimeter.

I flick a glance at Tierney. He hasn't stirred, still lost in the deep slumber I've woven around him.

Using my nail, I lever the hidden panel up with careful precision, not making a sound. Beneath it, tucked away in the hollowed space, is a worn, leather-bound book. The title, faded but still legible, sends a shiver down my spine.

Soul Bound.

My breath hitches.

Curiosity licks at my resolve, and I crack the cover open.

And then— I begin to read.

Once, in the age of high magic and old gods, there were two great kingdoms.

One was ruled by a Queen, and her land was born of witches, woven from the threads of the moon and spun from the breath of the earth itself. Banrigh Mhòr, the realm of spell-casters and seers, was a land where rivers whispered secrets, where the wind carried murmurs of ancient enchantments. The soil was dark with power, the mountains veined with runes, and its people moved with the surety of those who knew the world could bend to their will.

The other was ruled by a King, and his land was born of the Fae, kissed by starlight and bound to the old laws of power and pride. Rìoghachd Mhòr, where the forests pulsed with life, where the very roots of the trees listened, where the sky shimmered with the presence of the unseen. The Fae were creatures of law and legend, bound by oaths as deep as the marrow of their bones, their kingdom a place where beauty was sharp-edged, where the trees bore fruit of silver and gold, but only for those clever enough to take it without consequence.

Between them lay the vast and wild ocean, deep as time itself, and yet, not even the endless tide could quell the hatred that burned between the two monarchs.

The war between them was old as the hills, and so, it was written in the stars that the Great Prince of the Fae and the Great Princess of the Witches should be born enemies.

But fate— oh, fate is a mischievous weaver, delighting in twisting what should be.

And so, when the Great Prince Pyramus first beheld the Great Princess Thisbe, his fate was sealed.

He fought against it, as a man fights against the tide, but the pull was too great. He wished never to see her again, but the stars had other plans.

One night, his right-hand man led him to the shadowed prisons at the edge of the Black

Forest, where the King's enemies were kept. The cells were old things, carved into the bones of the land itself, places where the air smelled of sorrow and forgotten names.

And there, behind iron bars and flickering torchlight, was her.

Golden-haired and fire-hearted, she sat within her prison, light spilling through the narrow vents above, illuminating her skin in a soft, unnatural glow. Even beaten, even bruised, she radiated a magic older than the stone that bound her.

And when her gaze met his, her witch's eyes shimmered.

Pyramus visited her. Again. And again. Sneaking her food. Standing in the dark while she threw barbed words like knives. She despised him. Hated him. But he found he did not mind.

He liked the sharpness of her tongue, the way her fire refused to dim even in the face of imprisonment. She made something inside him stir— something that had long slumbered beneath his father's rule.

She set fire to his blood, and with it, she burned the future he thought he wanted.

And so, Pyramus did the unthinkable.

He went before the King, before his father, and declared the war must end. Declared that the Princess must be freed.

For this, he was punished.

When he returned to her cell, his face bore fresh wounds, his hand had fewer fingers, but the worst wound was the one in his heart— the fear that she would no longer look at him.

But Thisbe, daughter of witches, daughter of magic, did not turn away.

She pressed her hands to his face, and where her fingers touched, warmth spread. A glow, deep and golden, chased away his pain.

"Pyramus," she whispered, as though breathing his name could heal the rest of him.

And in that moment, he knew. She saw him. Not as a prince. Not as an enemy.

But as hers.

With that kiss, the world shifted. What began as a whisper of longing became a tempest, a desperate, aching need that overtook them both. The cold stone beneath their bodies, the damp stink of the cell, the iron bars that caged them, none of it mattered. The only thing that existed was the feverish press of lips, the burning path of hands tracing skin as if to memorize every inch, every breath, before it could be taken away.

They made love in that wretched place, their bodies moving as though guided by the very hands of fate, their souls colliding in the dark. And with it, something ancient stirred, something written long before their birth. Their souls aligned, binding them tighter than blood, tighter than oaths.

It was decided in that moment: they would run.

Far from the watchful eyes of their warring parents, far from the chains of duty and expectation. They would find the hidden temple of the old gods, where vows were sacred, where no king nor queen could sever what was meant to be. There, beneath the watchful gaze of those who wove destiny itself, they would marry. They would forge a bond that not even time could unravel.

But the stars are cruel as they are kind.

Word of their escape spread like wildfire, whispers carried on the wind, until it reached the ears of those who would sooner see their love turned to dust than let it live. It was not only the news of their flight that sent the King into a spiral of rage— it was the truth of what had already been done.

Their souls had already begun to merge.

Two opposing forces, bound together for all eternity. A union of Fae and Witch, a tether the likes of which had not been seen since the old world. It was an abomination in the King's eyes, a thing unnatural, an insult to the sacred order of power.

And so, he sought to break them in the only way he knew how.

Pyramus and Thisbe ran as fast as their legs could carry them, but the fates had already woven their trap. As they neared the temple, just within reach of sanctuary, the King's knights appeared— black and gold specters against the dying light of dusk. Seven in total, their blades drawn, their eyes cold with duty.

Two against seven.

It was no battle at all.

They seized Thisbe first, their hands iron shackles around her arms. Pyramus fought like a man possessed, like a beast cornered, but they held him back. They forced him to watch.

Helpless, he saw them draw their knives. Helpless, he saw the blade carve through more than flesh.

He saw them rip the soul from the woman he loved.

It burned like a dying star, bright and untamed as it was pulled from her chest. Pyramus felt the moment it left her, felt the sudden, devastating emptiness where once her light had lived within him. She was his—his love, his fire, his golden-haired fate— and yet, as she crumpled in their grip, she was nothing but a hollow shell.

Without her soul, she could not live.

Without her, he could not live.

His own soul howled in agony, the phantom pain of their severed bond burning through his chest. It was not meant to be this way. It was not meant to end like this.

Pyramus fell to his knees, reaching for her, reaching for something—but she was slipping, fading, her body too fragile to survive the theft.

She had been stolen from him.

And he wanted to be lost with her.

But the King, ever cruel, ever cunning, saw no use for a son consumed by grief. A prince weakened by love could never be the ruler he had envisioned, but the power of a stolen soul? That was something worth keeping.

With the magic he had hoarded, the magic he had taken from every corner of the earth, the King twisted fate to suit his needs. He took Thisbe's soul, still glowing, still pulsing, and he sealed it inside a leather glove.

A glove made for his son's ruined hand.

Pyramus did not resist as it was placed upon him, did not cry out as the spell was woven, as the stitches bound the leather to his flesh. But when he felt it— her— inside him, no longer as his beloved but as something to be used, his body trembled with rage.

She was bound to him now.

Her power surged through his veins, his body consuming her as though she were nothing more than a well to be drawn from.

He was sickened.

This was not what he wanted.

He wanted her, the woman who lay cold upon the ground, her final breath stolen by the wind. He did not want to wield her like a weapon, did not want to use her magic like a thief, draining her essence with every pulse of his heart.

His father had turned him into a monster.

Pyramus fell to his knees and screamed, his voice tearing through the heavens. He cursed the fates, cursed the gods, cursed the wretched world that had given him love only to rip it from his grasp.

Day and night, the glove sat upon his hand, its golden glow a constant, taunting reminder of all he had lost. It haunted him. He felt her— every pulse of her power, every echo of what had once been her warmth. And yet, she was not there.

He had become her captor.

His own body was abusing her power, feeding on the last remnants of her in a desperate attempt to keep her close. But it was not enough. It would never be enough.

So he returned to the temple.

Where she had died. Where the stones still bore the stain of her blood.

He knelt there, pressing his forehead to the cold earth, his palms facing the sky.

And he prayed.

He prayed to the gods, to the fates, to the unseen hands that had woven his path. He begged them to break the bond, to free her soul from the prison his father had built.

"If you hear me, gods, if you have any mercy left— break this hold. Let her go. Let her be free, even if it costs me my own life."

"If you do this, I will give myself to you. I will take my own life, as my father took hers. You may have us both, do with our souls what you wish. Only please— please, help me save her from this fate."

His cries were swallowed by the wind.

And then, the gods answered.

A dagger appeared in his palm, its golden hilt warm against his skin, as though shaped just for him. A whisper curled through the air, soft as drifting snow.

"Pierce your heart, and let your souls meet again."

He did not hesitate.

With one final breath, he drove the blade through the glove, through his chest, through the empty place where her soul had once lived.

The bond snapped.

The force of it sent a ripple through the night, and for a moment, all the world seemed to still.

Then, in a blinding rush, Thisbe's soul poured back into him, no longer bound, no longer trapped, no longer caged.

She found him, as she always had, as she always would.

Light burst from within his chest, a golden flare that burned like a dying star.

And then, silence.

With a final breath, Pyramus crumpled to the temple floor, the dagger clattering from his grip. His blood pooled beneath him, dark and red, seeping into the stone where hers had once been spilled. Their essences mingled, a permanent mark of the lovers who had defied fate and paid the price.

The dagger remained beside him, glowing, pulsing— as if still breathing, still humming with the remnants of their love.

And then, footsteps.

One of the King's knights arrived at the scene, though he was too late to save his prince. He froze at the sight of the lifeless body sprawled before him, the stain of love and loss etched into the earth. And there, in Pyramus's open hand, the dagger called.

It glowed with an eerie light, beckoning.

Compelled by something unseen, the knight reached out, fingers grazing the hilt—

And in an instant, he collapsed.

His body crumpled to the ground, his breath stolen before he could even scream.

The second knight stepped forward, a scoff upon his lips, reaching for the fallen blade as if the first had been weak, unworthy.

But the moment his skin met the metal, he too fell.

Their bodies lay still, their souls torn from them as swiftly as Pyramus's had been from his beloved.

The dagger pulsed again.

A third knight, warier than the others, approached. His hand trembled as he bent to pick it up, waiting for the curse to claim him. But as his fingers wrapped around the hilt, he remained standing.

He did not fall.

The fourth knight, his mate— his bonded love— stepped beside him, resting her palm over his. Together, they held the dagger, and together, they lived.

For the dagger had chosen them.

From that moment on, the blade belonged to them. It followed them through war, through bloodshed, through battle after battle, its silver and gold edge gleaming with the power of those who had once wielded it. A weapon that could cut through anything, that could kill with a single stroke.

It did the bidding of the King.

Until one day, the knight's fated love fell.

he died with his name on his lips, his body turning cold in his arms.

And the moment he was gone, the knight still clutching the dagger gasped— then crumpled to the ground beside him.

For he too had been fated, and with his death, his soul had no anchor, no protection against the blade he had carried for so long.

And as he lay dying, he heard them.

The cries of grief that had once belonged to Pyramus and Thisbe, now eternal, now woven into the dagger's very core. Their sorrow, their rage, their torment— it consumed him, and he could not withstand it.

The fates laughed.

For the dagger had been forged from tragedy, and its power could not be wielded by those who did not understand the weight of true love.

Any who touched it without a fated mate would perish, their souls claimed just as Pyramus and Thisbe had once been.

And so, their vengeance lived on.

The dagger would serve only those who knew love as they had known it.

For all others, it would be their ruin.

Forevermore.

I close the book, my breath caught in my throat, my eyes wide with realization. The weight of what I've just read settles into my bones, heavy as the fate woven through the ink of those ancient pages.

Carefully, I gather the letters, stacking them neatly before tucking them away. The book slides back into its rightful place, the box sealed shut beneath my trembling fingers.

Slowly, I ease myself from the bed, careful not to stir the air too sharply, lest it unravel the enchantment that keeps the mansion steeped in slumber. The box remains clutched to my chest as I creep through the dimly lit halls, each step a whisper against the cold stone. The only sound is the soft rhythm of breath from the men still lost under my spell.

Then—I stop.

My feet freeze in place as my gaze lifts to the armored suits lining the corridor, standing tall and silent like sentinels of a forgotten age.

The seven knights.

Above them, stretching across the wall, a mural has been painted with painstaking devotion. Seven warriors, their faces hard as steel, charge into battle against an unseen army. At their head, a knight wields a dagger that glows silver and gold, its light cutting through the storm of war.

But it's the figure below that draws my attention.

A lone man kneels in prayer, his hands clasped, cradling a dagger nearly identical to the one in the mural.

A trap.

The thought slithers through my mind like a whisper of warning. For the dagger of Pyramus and Thisbe is not meant for thieves. Those who reach for it with greed, with hunger for power rather than understanding, will find themselves doomed the moment their fingers brush the hilt.

I listen—truly listen.

The air pulses with the weight of magic, thick and expectant. But beyond it, the mansion remains still, the snores of its occupants undisturbed.

Swallowing against the dryness in my throat, I reach out.

Slowly. Cautiously.

Even at a distance, I can feel the echoes of sorrow that cling to the weapon—the grief of lovers long dead, the fury of a bond severed too soon. My hand trembles, the coolness of the metal a stark contrast to my fevered skin.

The moment my fingers curl around the hilt, the gems embedded in the handle flare to life.

A deep thrum of energy pulses through me, spreading from my fingertips to my toes, filling my veins with something ancient and untamed. It doesn't burn. It doesn't strike me down where I stand.

I pull the dagger free.

My breath stills, waiting.

Waiting for the knight to rise from his eternal prayer. For his armor to rattle to life. For a thousand cursed serpents to rain from the ceiling.

But nothing happens.

The corridor remains silent. The suits of armor stand motionless. The gods, the fates—whoever weaves the threads of destiny—remain quiet.

A soft, startled laugh escapes my lips, light and disbelieving. *So that was it?*

The greatest weapon of love and vengeance, taken without so much as a whisper of resistance?

Shaking my head, I turn and make my way back to the bedchamber, the dagger nestled safely inside the box. With practiced ease, I slide it beneath the bed, its weight a secret only I will know.

Slinking into the silken covers, I let out a slow breath and lift the spell that keeps the mansion swaddled in sleep.

It takes only seconds before Tierney stirs.

His body shifts toward me instinctively, his arm looping around my waist, drawing me against the solid warmth of his chest. His lips find my hair, the low hum of his voice sending a shiver down my spine.

"What are you doing awake, my love?"

I smile against him—a real smile, not the kind I've learned to perfect.

"I'm just excited for tomorrow," I murmur, feeling the words settle deep within me.

He sighs softly, content, his hand smoothing over my back. "Sleep," he whispers. "You will need your energy."

And for once, I obey. Because for the first time in what feels like a lifetime, *I know the end is near. And it will be mine to shape.*

I want to find comfort in the forest, to let the towering pine trees embrace me like old sentinels, their branches heavy with the weight of fresh snow. I long for the familiar crunch of pine needles beneath my boots, for the thick scent of winter and woodsmoke to fill my lungs.

But there is no comfort here.

The clearing opens before us, revealing the army nestled just beyond the treeline. I feel their laughter before I hear it—warm, rich, unguarded. I feel the ease in their spirits before the sound of a banjo floats through the air, the melody twined with voices, singing, unafraid. They are not expecting us. The sun, still low on the horizon, has only begun to kiss the branches with its thawing light, sending dew drops tumbling like glass beads to the forest floor.

My strings of power reach out, unfurling like invisible tendrils, weaving through the army before me. I taste their emotions—the young, the old, the in-between. There is elation, yes, and trepidation, but above all else, there is belonging.

These Fae love one another.

The sensation hits me like a stone to the ribs, a breath caught in my throat. *They are not afraid.* My chest aches. I lock it away.

Behind me, Tierney's hands find my hips. His grip is firm, grounding, but laced with quiet possession.

"Let's go."

A claw at the edge of my mind sinks in, his voice inside my skull carrying the subtle bite of compulsion. A nudge. A reminder. *Do not hesitate.*

"They may seem like any other soul, but they are the same kind of Fae that killed the Empaths for power," Tierney whispers through the tether in my mind.

I know better. Still, I say nothing.

Side by side, we step into the clearing, ten Humanoids moving in formation behind us. We are outnumbered. The opposing army stands strong—sixty Fae, watching, waiting, unaware that the moment of song and joy they had shared only seconds ago will be their last.

The instant we breach the dry grass plains, the music dies.

Laughter falters.

A breathless silence falls, thick and heavy, as their voices fail them.

"They have Mind Masters in their ranks," Tierney's voice brushes against my thoughts, sharper now, more focused. A nuisance.

"They won't be more powerful than you," I murmur.

His teeth nip the shell of my ear, his smile dark against my skin. "You know it."

I let my gaze sweep over the soldiers before us. Some of them know me, even if only by reputation. Recognition flares in their minds—some clouded with confusion, others already slipping toward fear. They rise, abandoning their meals, their music, their moment of peace.

I feel the tremor of their unease, but none speak. They simply fall into formation, aligning at the far edge of the clearing like a wall of flesh and steel, watching. Waiting.

Then, a howl splits the air. It is distant, but it cracks through the stillness like a prophecy, sending a ripple through their ranks.

A movement to my left—an ice wielder lifts his hands, his breath curling in the cold air as he calls upon his power. Frost licks at the ground beneath him, inching forward, a barrier rising between us.

Tierney's voice is silk and steel in my ear. "Halt him."

I obey.

A pulse of power shoots from me like an arrow loose from a bow, invisible but precise.

The wielder freezes—not in ice of his own making, but in terror.

His mouth opens and closes like a fish caught on land, his body rigid, his mind trapped within the fear I've poured into him. He fights against it—I can feel him clawing at my hold, but he's losing.

"Good. You have their attention."

I shift my gaze from the lone ice wielder to the soldiers surrounding him. I feel the fear ripple outward, crawling like ivy along a stone wall, tendrils creeping from one mind to the next. It takes root, digging in deep, blooming into something raw and trembling.

A flicker of something else weaves through the terror.

Recognition.

They know what I am. They know what I can do.

"Do the same to the rest," Tierney commands, his voice dark with satisfaction. "Make them uncomfortable enough that they can't fight me."

I swallow. *I want to hesitate.*

But instead, I do as I'm told.

THE WEAPON IN THE FOREST

"Jeyr!"

Caomh bursts through my door, his boots skidding across the stone floor, barely catching himself as he comes to a halt. His breath comes in sharp, uneven gasps, his chest rising and falling in frantic succession.

I straighten instantly, the tension in his expression twisting something cold and unrelenting inside me.

"I just got word from our central army," he pants, struggling to steady himself. "They were moving between Kingdoms when they came across Kyzan. As instructed, they informed me, but then..." His throat bobs with a hard swallow. "Then I heard their screams through the communication line."

The air in the room seems to thin.

"They were stammering," he continues, his voice lower now, as if saying the words aloud might summon the horror he heard on the other end of that call. "They said they were frozen, that they couldn't move, couldn't breathe. And then—" he swallows hard, voice barely above a whisper, "—the last word I heard before the line went silent was *Empath.*"

A single breath passes between us. Heavy. Weighty.

Then I'm moving.

"What are we doing here then? Get the others!"

Caomh hesitates, searching my face, as though trying to make me see what I already know.

"Jeyr, do you understand? She is in their army. She is using her powers as a weapon."

I understand. I just refuse to believe it. Not until I see her for myself.

"I heard you," I say, steadying my voice, steadying my hands, willing away the treacherous beating of my own heart. "Which is why we need to get our men there now—to retrieve the... weapon."

Caomh's lips part, his brows knitting together at my choice of words, but he nods nonetheless.

We both know what this has become.

This is no longer a mission of rescue. This is a mission to steal a weapon from the enemy's army.

And once we have her—once we have torn her from Tierney's grasp—we will have to decide if she is to be saved... or contained.

Don't think about that. Don't picture her face when she realizes what you mean to do. Don't picture her reaching for you... and flinching when you do not reach back.

I ignore the way my stomach twists at the thought.

There is no time for hesitation.

Our forces are trained for rapid deployment, for sudden shifts in the battlefield. At a moment's notice, we can be anywhere, striking from the shadows like a blade before vanishing just as quickly.

Orders are sent.

Caomh reaches out to the Gliocas Army. Jethro sends word to the Aotrom Army. And General Caves mobilizes our own—*Ceannardan Na Saorsa*, the exiled warriors, the Fae who were cast out of the Great King's Courts, stripped of their titles, their lands, their very names.

We are the ones born with more than one power. The ones cursed with magic the Great King does not approve of. The ones who were forced to carve out a new existence beyond the reach of the Courts.

Now, we have built something new.

Now, we are an army of ghosts. And ghosts always come back to haunt the living.

We winnow as one, our three forces materializing just beyond the site where our central army was last stationed. The forest looms around us, hushed, expectant. Even the wind seems unwilling to move, as though the land itself is holding its breath.

Then, the scent of fear hits me.

Thick and heavy, it clings to the air like damp rot, curling into my lungs, warning me that we are already too late.

Nothing could prepare me for what I see next.

She stands in the clearing, bathed in pale morning light, her hand clasped in Tierney's as though she belongs to him—*as though she has chosen him.*

A sharp pang stabs through my chest.

Her red hair is woven into tight braids, intricate and severe, coiled against her skull like a crown of fire. But it's the circlet atop her head that sends a slow wave of ice through my veins. Not a simple band of gold. Not a ring of jewels.

Serpents. Gilded bodies winding upward. Fanged mouths open, whispering secrets to the sky.

And before her—before *them*—lie what remains of the army we came to save. Sixty men and women, collapsed where they stood, crumpled like discarded marionettes upon the frozen earth. Some clutch at their chests, their fingers digging into their own flesh as if trying to claw their way free from the fear that has taken hold of them. Others pull at their hair, mouths gaping in soundless screams, bodies wracked with invisible torment.

Not a single drop of blood has been spilled. Not a single blade has been raised. And yet—they are already defeated.

Murmurs ripple through the ranks behind me, voices breaking the silence like shattered glass.

"Oh my gods," someone whispers, barely more than breath.

I lift a hand sharply, fingers curling in a silent command for stillness. Jethro, Caomh, and I exchange a glance, each of us assessing, each of us thinking the same thing but unwilling to speak it aloud.

This is not the woman I knew. This is something else entirely. A queen. A conqueror. A weapon. And we are standing before the wreckage of her power.

"Caomh," I murmur, voice low and steady, forcing my mind into action, forcing my body to move. "We need an opening. Enough to keep Tierney from noticing when I enter her mind."

Caomh nods, exhaling a slow, measured breath as he extends his hands. He'll forge the mental path, the tether between us, ensuring I can slip past Tierney's defenses without detection.

But first—we need a distraction.

I take a step forward, bracing myself as I raise my own hands toward the sky. The first shift in the air is subtle, a whisper of power rippling through my veins, threading itself into the atmosphere.

Then, the morning light dims. Clouds churn overhead, thick and rolling, swallowing the fragile blue sky whole.

A low rumble echoes through the valley, a sound as deep and ancient as the earth itself. The wind sharpens, howling through the trees, bending branches under its force as darkness unfurls above us like a growing storm.

The first crack of thunder roars through the air.

And the battlefield stands still.

Olivia

THE WEAPON UNLEASHED

I feel him the moment he enters the forest. I don't need to hear the low rumble of thunder or see the sky darken with storm clouds to know he is near. Like a moth drawn to an open flame, the bond between us tugs—an invisible thread pulling me toward the light.

I smile to myself. To those who look upon me now, the expression must seem sinister. *But to me, it is victory. My plan has worked.*

Only once has there ever been a gathering like this—a convergence of Fae from different worlds, colliding for a singular purpose: to defy the unjust decree of the Great King. To stop the slaughter of the impure. The ones born with magic outside his control, the ones he deems too dangerous to exist.

It was a gamble, hoping that Caomh would hear word of an Empath taking over one of his armies, but the moment I heard the wolf's howl, I knew. *The wolf I know.* With that call, I can only hope it means help is coming. *I don't let myself think about what will happen if I've been wrong. If no one has come.*

Maybe I would have done as I was told. Maybe I would have let Tierney do whatever he wished to the men and women crumpled before me—let the rumors spread that the dangerous Empath had felled an army without lifting a finger, had drowned the battlefield in fear alone.

Small mercies— I haven't needed to.

Tierney goes rigid beside me as the sky churns and darkens, the air thick with the scent of rain. His fingers tense against my skin.

"Seems we have company, Lady Tierney," he murmurs, voice low, intrigued.

I keep my mask firmly in place. "Seems we do, Husband."

His hand drops from mine, only to tighten possessively around the back of my neck—a silent reminder of who he believes holds my leash. I focus my mind on the warmth of his gloved hand, force my body to stay still, to keep my breath even— *because I can't let him notice the slow, measured slide of my free hand as it curls around the dagger hidden beneath my armor.*

Across the field, another army approaches, weaving between the men and women I have trapped in my hold. Three figures lead the charge, their presence undeniable even from a distance.

Jeyr. Caomh. Jethro. *They have come.*

Tierney's breath ghosts against my ear. "Let them come closer. Then, when I give the word, I need you to disarm them."

I nod.

The approaching army moves in unison despite their differences—three banners, three uniforms, three factions that should never stand side by side.

I sweep my power outward, reaching toward the leaders, reaching for them with the sharp edge of something cruel. *I need them to hate me. Need them to believe I'm too far gone. Need them to strike me down.*

THE RECKONING

We walk through the ranks of our cowering men, their eyes barely managing to lift toward us. My heart jolts at their pleading gazes.

I can't believe she's doing this... Our Olivia... Caomh mutters in my mind, disbelief clear in his tone.

I grit my teeth tighter, eyes locked on the woman I love—whose face now mirrors the sinister sneer of the man beside her. A woman with soldiers dropping at her feet in fear.

Before I can respond, a series of thuds sound behind me. I flinch, the thunder in the sky rumbling in echo. Behind me, half of our men drop to the ground. Eyes closed. Unmoving.

The soldiers who remain turn wide, panicked eyes to their fallen brothers, horror rippling through the lines as the reality of what just happened sinks in. I look back to her.

To Lady Tierney.

Her smile is wicked. She meets my gaze. Shrugs.

Fucking shrugs.

Like she hasn't just disarmed half of our three combined armies. Tierney smiles down at his wife, bright and admiring, as if *he* is just as astonished by her power.

We have to do something. We need to disarm her—somehow, Caomh thinks, voice sharp in my mind.

But before we can move, another third of our men fall. Bodies collapsing around us like dominos, like puppets with strings cut.

How is she doing this? Jethro screams.

I close my eyes against the rising panic thundering in my chest. *I don't know,* I think, *but I think she's letting me into her mind.*

I glance to Caomh, who's staring hard at the woman standing in the eye of our destruction.

Olivia?

Strike me down, she barks, *I dare you.*

Olivia, stop! You're hurting people. This is not you, Caomh pleads.

This is me now. Strike me down, or I will take the rest of your soldiers.

As if to prove it, two more men scream—and fall.

Tierney chuckles beside her, pride radiating from him like poison.

Olivia, this isn't you. Stop this now! I demand.

This is me. Her voice cracks. *Take me out. NOW.*

Something's wrong.

The battlefield trembles at the weight of too many fallen. More screams rise—raw, broken. I cannot take any more loss.

Not even for her.

Not even for the only soul I have ever loved.

So I let my power fly.

Thunder roars, shaking the heavens as lightning cracks the sky. Tierney's head snaps up, his golden eyes narrowing in realization.

But it's too late.

I call the storm to the earth.

The bolt strikes like a wrathful god.

It hits her.

I see it all. The wide shock in Olivia's eyes. The way her body arches with the force of it. The pain that rips through our bond, stealing the breath from my lungs. Hands grab at me as I gasp—but I'm frozen. Trapped.

I cannot speak the words that burn my tongue. *I cannot tell her I'm sorry. I cannot tell her I love her.*

Instead, I watch.

I watch as he cradles her.

The man I despise above all others.

"Olivia!" Tierney's voice splits the battlefield, his arms closing around her limp form.

His cries ring through the silence—raw, unguarded—his hands trembling as he pulls her against him.

"Olivia! My Olivia, Lady Tierney!"

The man who has been my enemy for as long as I can remember—the one who stole her, corrupted her, twisted her into something I can barely recognize—shakes as he holds her. He lowers her to the earth, fingers pressing desperately over her heart.

"Olivia, you are stronger than this! Live! It's you and me—*you and I will rule.* Fight this! I love you, fucking fight this!"

Around us, the dead begin to stir.

The fallen warriors littering the battlefield yawn as though waking from slumber. Others stagger to their feet, dazed, breath ragged and confused.

As Olivia's power slips free of their bodies, no one moves.

We just stand there.

And watch.

As the most feared man in all the realms weeps over Olivia's body.

When the dagger strikes, I need you to act. Take him too.

Olivia's voice is nothing more than a fragile whisper in our minds, but its command rings with unshakable resolve. My gaze snaps to Caomh, confirming he hears the same thing. Then to Jethro. A solemn nod. My pulse thunders, but this time, it's not just fear for her that chills my blood.

It happens in slow motion, though I know it's impossibly fast—too fast for Lord Tierney to react. His focus remains on her, his hands pressing against her chest, trying to will life back into her. Pleading. Desperate.

He never sees it coming.

Her hand moves, and the dagger catches the crackling light of the storm, silver and gold flashing like a fallen star. I feel the pain before the blade even touches her—*as if the bond between us braces me for the agony to come.* The dagger plunges through the hand he has placed over her heart, slicing through the fine leather of his glove. A burst of golden light erupts, blinding as it swallows them both. We turn our heads, shielding our eyes from the sudden flare.

Then comes the scream.

Tierney's agony tears through the battlefield, sharp and raw—only to be silenced by a second explosion of power. A beam of pure force, Jethro's magic honed to deadly precision, cuts through the space like a celestial blade. It strikes true—Tierney's head severs from his shoulders in a single, merciless stroke. His head rolls.

And the world falls silent.

But I feel her pain. *Only I feel it.* My body recoils as though the wound is mine, my breath ripped from my lungs as she collapses. I call to her, and the magic within me—the power of the Grand Duke—answers, winnowing me to her side in an instant.

She lies beneath the storm, staring at the sky, her green eyes alight with flickering gold. A silent message. A truth undeniable.

She is still there. *My Olivia.*

She holds the pain at bay, refusing to let us feel her death as it creeps closer. No longer a pawn to a tyrant, no longer bound to a man who twisted her soul. She has not imploded as her ancestors had—but she has chosen her own end, sacrificing herself so her power can never be used again.

Through our bond, I feel it all. The flickering embers of life before the inevitable dark.

"I— I am sorry. I didn't want to h—hurt anyone," she splutters, her voice barely more than a whisper between ragged breaths.

I place my hand over her chest, channeling my power into her, willing her wounds to close.

"I know, my love. You did good. You did it—you got out."

She nods weakly, coughing up a mouthful of blood. A crimson line trails down her face, a stark reminder of the lightning's wrath. My gut twists—I want to heal it, to erase the evidence of what I've done. But I focus on what's fatal first, pushing more of my magic into her, steadying her breath, knitting her torn flesh back together. When I feel the shift in her, when her breathing evens out, I finally let my hand drift to her face to heal the scar I left on my Companach.

"Leave it," she murmurs, her voice a fragile whisper against the storm.

"No."

"I deserve it. I deserve that scar for what I've done—I deserve worse." Her tears fall over my hand, burning like acid against my skin.

I gather her into my arms, unable to bear the weight of her pain. "Shh, Hummingbird. You did what you had to do. You're free. It's just you and me now. Just breathe."

I cradle her against my chest, her body trembling against mine. The storm rages around us, but I will the horrors of the past months—the torture, the deaths, the weight of it all—to be swept away in the howling winds.

I tilt her face toward mine, letting my nose brush hers as I breathe her in. The stench of lilies clings to her like a poisoned veil, but beneath it—beneath the remnants of the mask she wore to survive the Court of Poison—she's there. *She has always been there.*

"I love you," I whisper against her lips, because something in me knows she needs to hear it. There's doubt in my heart about many things, but never this—*never her.*

"I love you, only you, always you." Her breath ghosts over my lips, sealing the vow between us.

"Forever you, Hummingbird."

My lips find hers, fierce and unrelenting, my desperation breaking free. I kiss her like I can reclaim all the time we've lost, as if I can erase every moment we've spent apart. And Olivia meets me with the same hunger, the same aching need.

Until she's gone.

The cold hits me like a phantom's touch, her retreat leaving my body hollow. A groan of protest tears from my throat as my eyes snap open—

And go wide.

Olivia

SEVERED IN THE DARK

I am lost in his touch. *My Jeyr, my love.*

The moment his hands find me, the weight of disdain and disappointment melts away. He still loves me—*I feel it.* His fingers trace my skin, not just to heal, but to remind me of what has never faded. The love is still there, burning as fiercely as ever. And with it, the same need, the same desperation we felt all those months ago. That kiss is more than a kiss—*it is a lifeline, a breath of existence after drowning in the dark.*

Until it is ripped away.

Hands wrench me from him, rough and unyielding. I fight, twisting, pulling, clawing to return to the warmth I just found. Desperation surges through me, and I send my power lashing into the bodies restraining me. I let them feel it all—the exhaustion, the sorrow, the pain that has hollowed me out. My anguish crashes into them like a tidal wave meant to break their bones, to crumble them beneath its weight.

They flinch, their bodies jerking from the force of it.

But before my power can fully take root, something severs the connection. A violent snap ricochets through my bond to them. A foreign sensation slithers through my veins—cool at first, a whisper of ice threading through my bloodstream. But then, like a poison reacting with my magic, it shifts. The cold burns, sharp and searing, turning molten as it weighs me down.

No. I fight it. *Fought this once, I can do it again. Just breathe—fight—*

But my body betrays me.

My vision blurs. My limbs tremble. My head falls back between my shoulder blades as darkness surges forward, swallowing me whole.

Once again, the world goes black.

STOLEN

Arms seize me as I lunge for my mate.

Stop! You cannot attack our King. Caomh's voice cuts through my mind, sharp and commanding.

I flinch, but force myself to hold. The storm in my veins crackles, my power brimming at the surface, a silent threat to our Great King, Domhnall. He stands unwavering, his massive frame shadowing those around him, his dark eyes locked onto mine as he holds my limp mate in his grasp. Bane flanks his other side, the two of them an imposing contrast—Domhnall, cold and immovable, while Bane's sneer curls with satisfaction, his white hair glowing, yellow eyes bright with power as he poisons my mate into submission.

"Duke Jeyr," Domhnall acknowledges me, his voice a steady, impenetrable force.

I swallow the fury clawing up my throat, resisting the urge to rip her from his grasp. *Mine.* The word burns through every fiber of my being. But I bow.

"Your Highness."

"I thank you for putting an end to this civil war, for capturing the Empath. It is a great duty to our kingdom."

I stand frozen.

"You are most welcome, Your Highness," Caomh answers smoothly before I can. "I apologize for the Grand Duke—he has had an arduous time battling the Empath, sir."

I want to tear him apart for the lie. Want to scream that she is mine. That I will not—*cannot*—allow them to take her. *I just got her back. I held her in my arms. She is mine.*

"Understandable." Domhnall's gaze does not waver, his scrutiny burning through me. "As I have told my Courts and my Subjects countless times, the Fae from the Queen's Kingdom are not to be trusted. Today, we have seen one single Fae control three armies of honorable soldiers. We have seen my best Commander fall under the spell of an Empath. You did the right thing taking him out. We could not risk him choosing her side over the welfare of my people."

The words come like steel, but the shift in his tone is a warning—one meant for me. *He knows.* He knows this is not the work of an Empath's magic. He knows my allegiance has wavered. And this is his way of telling me: *if I step out of line again, he will not be so forgiving.*

"Thank you, Your Highness." Caomh's voice is even, unwavering. "What will happen to the Empath in question? It would ease our minds to know that she will no longer pose a threat to your reign."

Domhnall smirks, a slow, knowing thing that sends a dagger of ice into my ribs. "She will be taken to Puinnsean Prison for questioning. Once I have the answers I seek, she will be executed publicly, so all may witness the fate of the Queen's kind."

The blood drains from my face. My body surges forward, but my brothers hold me back before I can take a single step.

"You are a Great King to us all," Caomh speaks, his power lacing through his words, anchoring me where I stand. "We thank you for protecting your subjects. If it pleases you, I would like to take our soldiers back to base. The powers of the Empath have caused many injuries, and they must be seen to."

Domhnall smiles. "Of course. Thank you for your service, as always, Commander Caomh."

Caomh nods, his magic pressing against my shoulders, forcing my head into a shallow bow. I clench my fists, barely holding back the rage tearing through me as I watch her slip further from my grasp.

Under my brothers' hold, I am dragged away, powerless to stop it.

And once again, *I fail her.*

The glass walls of my kingdom greet me with a sad, hollow welcome. The weight of reality presses down before I have a chance to breathe, before I can even acknowledge the storm of emotions clawing to be released.

Then comes the scream.

Jethro's scream.

I turn in time to see my brother collapse into a bed of lilies. And upon them—

The lifeless body of his wife.

He reaches for her, his trembling fingers brushing against her cold skin. His head bows, the band on his wrist disintegrating, its magic bleeding into his veins, marking the breaking of a bond that should have lasted eternity.

Wordlessly, he picks up the letter resting on her chest, reads it with a stillness that burns, then hurls it toward us. The weight of grief consumes him whole.

I step forward and retrieve the note.

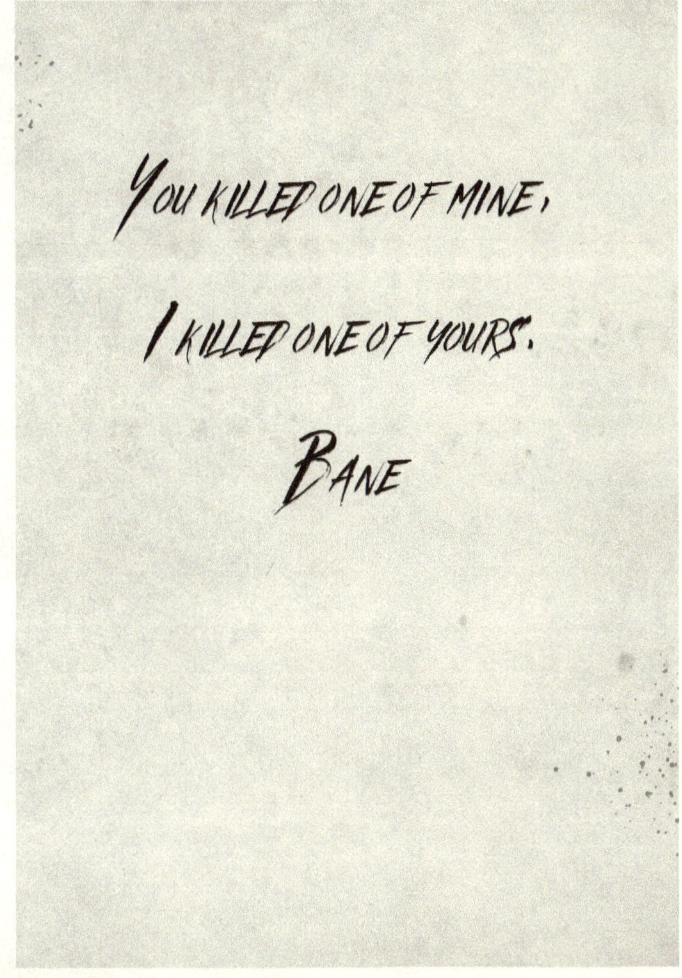

Thunder roars above us, rattling the glass walls as the rest of our family enters the study. One by one, they come to a dead halt, their breath stolen at the sight before them—

A second murder in our midst.

Jethro rises from the floor, his grief now forged into something lethal. His voice cuts through the air, a promise wrapped in steel.

"We are done fucking around now. This is war."

I couldn't agree more.